WHEN
WARS
WERE
WON

Also by Hugh Aaron

BUSINESS NOT AS USUAL

WHEN WARS WERE WON

by

Hugh Aaron

STONES POINT PRESS
P.O. Box 384
Belfast, ME 04915

COVER by Mary Reed, Imageset Design
EDITED by Barbara Feller-Roth

FIRST EDITION

Aaron, Hugh
WHEN WARS WERE WON
Library of Congress Catalog Card Number: 95-69538
ISBN 1-882521-02-1

$16.00 Softcover
Printed in the United States of America

To Alexis Silkin,
a warm friend, and delightful sailing partner
who departed this world too soon.

Who is the happy warrior? Who is he
That every man in arms should wish to be?
It is the generous spirit, who, when brought,
Among the tasks of real life, hath wrought
Upon the plan that pleased his childish thought:
Whose high endeavors are an inward light
That makes the path before him always bright.

Wordsworth

TABLE OF CONTENTS

FOREWORD

Young Hal Arnold doesn't know much about war or life or anything else. He certainly doesn't fit the Hollywood image of "The Fighting Seabees," battling the Japanese while driving his growling bulldozer into a hail of gunfire like John Wayne. In fact, Hal Arnold isn't really much of a war hero at all, except he did his duty like so many other millions of men in World War II and, unlike so many others, Arnold survived.

Hugh Aaron's novel is about the wartime experience as seen through Hal Arnold's naive and idealistic eyes. So many World War II books today focus on grand strategy, operational campaigns, giant horrific battles and tales of heroism, complex and weighty stories of fiction and non-fiction, especially as we celebrate the 50th anniversary of the end of the war. Hugh Aaron dares to depart from the common model of a war novel. Instead, Aaron devotes himself to the men and women who endured World War II in the Pacific. Their everyday lives, fears, joy, love and loss combine to make war "a felt experience" as Henry Steele Commager would say.

And Aaron succeeds all too well. Remember, this is a novel; it is fiction. Keep telling yourself that as you read, because from its first page to its last, this book is too real, too believable to be fiction. Aaron's young Seabee is just a kid, thrown in with older men, sent to the Pacific to fight and hopefully come out alive. The young Seabee thinks he knows what he's getting into, but he really doesn't have a clue. His adventures are humorous and poignant, filled with life's lessons, simple pleasures and unnerving disappointments. But for young Hal Arnold, the war dissolves his innocence and turns him into a man, with all his uncertainty and hesitation.

Nations may wage war, but it is men and women who fight and die, suffer and survive, endure and rise to meet the challenge of mankind's folly. No one portrays the "little guy" in a big war better than Hugh Aaron. And this novel proves it. When you finish reading it, you tell me this isn't a true story.

WILLIAM D. BUSHNELL
Colonel, U.S. Marine Corps (Retired)

PREFACE

This novel is partly about being an American. During World War II patriotism was in fashion and we had never been more united. Everyone pitched in and did his or her part to win the war. Raised in and molded by the Depression, we were charitable, optimistic, certain of our correctness in the use of power, and proud of who we were. But the seeds of our future errors and moral deterioration were already sprouting. They were clearly visible during our sojourn in the Philippines and were as destructive to those we saved from the occupying enemy as they were to us a generation or two later.

The protagonist in this novel is nineteen years old. Disillusioned by the contradictions between reality and his country's democratic ideals, exposed to the ways of men more experienced than he is, he comes to see his own people, their surface stripped away, for who they are. Some achieve nobility, and some are destroyers. Some are natural leaders; most, including the leaders, are not. Eventually he learns who he is, and is not always proud.

The novel is mostly about how best to confront life, life that in wartime is temporary and often dangerous. Should one live simply and apart from it all, or in the thick of civilization? With the world about to emerge from war, the protagonist must choose between his own culture and the more emotionally rich culture he found overseas where love and friendship thrive.

When Wars Were Won was written in the early eighties when the pain of the Vietnam War still lingered in our national psyche, and a senseless violence and coarseness in our relations with each other had eroded the unity and civility prevalent during World War II and the early postwar period. This novel stands in stark contrast to the Vietnam experience. It portrays a world where violence was rational and men had a sense of mission. It recaptures how life used to be.

The Naval Construction Battalions (dubbed the Seabees) during World War II were unique, consisting of highly skilled tradesmen, mostly mature family men, some in their fifties, who under the severest conditions dedicated their outstanding talents to winning the war. I doubt whether such an experience will ever be duplicated in the same way again. If this humble memoir serves in any way to enhance the lore of that organization, albeit from the limited point of view of a young man who reached no rank higher than a third class machinist's mate, then I would be gratified.

PROLOGUE

"I shall return," said General MacArthur in 1942 when the Japanese attacked Luzon and forced him to leave.

"I'll be back," said I, Hal Arnold, departing the very same island of my own free will when the war was over almost four years later.

MacArthur returned as conqueror. I returned to be conquered.

When the jet from LA landed on the tarmac in Manila that sultry afternoon, I was thankful for the solid feel of land beneath its wheels. Air travel frightens me. I was reassured by the earthbound sight of palm trees in the flat distance and of the terminal building and maintenance hangars. I had not been back for forty years, not since our troopship put into Noumea harbor after a lonely Pacific crossing during World War II. As I walked across the tarmac from the plane, I recalled the Filipino patriot Benigno Aquino, who was assassinated on this very spot, walking as I walked, only a few months before. Many believed that the president of the Philippines had him killed.

By prearrangement I expected my old friend Barry Fortune to greet me at the gate. Instead a young man appeared from among the crowd.

"Mr. Hal Arnold?" he inquired, reaching to take the carry-on suitcase from my hand.

"Yes," I replied, surprised, "but how did you recognize me?"

"You are exactly as Mr. Fortune described," he said with that clipped Filipino way of pronouncing English words, an accent I had almost forgotten.

Being practically bald now and my face resembling a dried peach wearing rimless glasses, I had to be unrecognizable from the smooth-faced, gangly lad whom Barry had known. "I don't believe you," I said.

The bright young man, smoothly brown, wearing an open-necked white shirt and white trousers, broke into a smile. "Mr. Fortune said to look for a man who resembled a giraffe."

1

"That's more like it," I nodded and followed him to the luggage retrieval area.

"Mr. Fortune wishes to apologize for not being here," the young man said as he led me to a cream-colored Mercedes limousine.

Barry must be getting soft, I thought. I never knew him to apologize for anything.

We traveled along a highway bordered by thatched shacks, probably the same ones I had seen there in 1945, testimony to the unchanged poverty with no war to blame it on. Entering the city I saw the Intramuros, the walled old section now restored, whose perimeter had been largely blasted to rubble when I last climbed it. We passed the gleaming white buildings of the university campus, which remained untouched during the war, an oasis of order then.

Soon we were circling the imposing granite post office with its magnificent row of Doric columns. Once reduced to a silent shell resembling an ancient Greek ruin, the building was now returned to its original grandeur. Manila before the war was called the Pearl of the Orient. It had become a pearl again, so why hadn't the appellation stuck? Would I find out?

Pulling up to an opulent new high-rise hotel with a canopy and doorman out front, New York style, the chauffeur accompanied me through revolving doors to the desk.

"This is Mr. Arnold," he said, introducing me to the impeccably attired, graying manager, who shook my hand warmly.

"Welcome, sir. May you have a delightful stay with us. The presidential suite is ready and waiting."

"Oh, I don't need anything so elaborate," I said nervously. "Any simple room would do."

"Ah, but you are Mr. Fortune's guest and we must follow his instructions."

"Mr. Fortune has made a mistake," I said, showing annoyance. "I'd prefer an ordinary room." Observing the manager's increasing distress, I went on. "I don't have to be impressed." As I've aged, I suppose I've become stubborn, perhaps irascible, less inclined to compromise.

The chauffeur cut in. "Mr. Arnold, do you realize that Mr. Fortune owns this hotel?"

"Well, no, I see, no, I didn't realize."

2

Grinning, the chauffeur continued. "Then you can understand his wish."

This was more than a chauffeur, I surmised. Perhaps Fortune's chief adviser? One could never tell about Fortune's associates.

My good friend Barry Fortune was a successful business magnate, crony to the president of the Philippines, and renowned internationally throughout the business world—a world as distant as possible from mine in academe. Barry refused to allow our old friendship to wane. He maintained casual but continual contact through an occasional Christmas card or an invitation to a family event, such as a daughter's wedding, or by sending a newspaper clipping of one of his exploits. During those early years of establishing himself in the Philippines, he "gifted" me with a few shares in one of his enterprises, a brewery. At the time, contrary to a prior resolution, I lightly accepted them since they were of little value then. The shares have since multiplied substantially, yielding considerable and steadily increasing income.

The presidential suite was elaborately appointed although it was wasted on me, a confirmed Spartan. First off I tried to reach Barry by phone, succeeding only after penetrating several layers of protective staff.

"Hal, it's absolutely wonderful hearing your voice. You sound exactly the same," he said excitedly.

"And so do you, Barry. So do you. Is it possible neither of us has aged over the past forty years?"

"Well, I certainly haven't," he chuckled.

"But I have," I said. "I must learn your secret."

"Don't give an inch, that's all," he said. Although in his early seventies, his vigor and drive showed no sign of abating.

"Ah, my friend, I can't wait to lay my eyes on you again," I said. We had not seen each other since I left the islands at the age of twenty-two when we were Seabees. During the long interim we had rarely corresponded, for Barry disliked writing letters, especially personal letters. I last saw him waving from the dock at Subic Bay while I stood in the throng of sailors high on an aircraft carrier deck. He had shouted above the din, "Everything I have is yours, but don't expect me to write."

"I'll be back," I hollered in return.

3

Barry's voice in the phone interrupted my reminiscing. "My chauffeur will pick you up at seven."

"That will be fine," I replied.

"We'll have dinner, just the three of us. She's dying to see you," he said, she being his one and only wife of many years.

"Same here," I said. "Is she as beautiful as ever?"

"Hal, more so, positively more so. She won't give an inch either."

"Yes, I remember, that's how she was," I responded cheerily.

"Tell you what," he said. "If you want to take a peek at me in advance, turn on your TV at three. They're broadcasting the ribbon-cutting ceremony for my newest office building downtown in Makati." Makati was the city's high-rise commercial district.

"Wouldn't miss it for the world," I said.

They were the last words I ever spoke to my good friend Barry Fortune.

At three o'clock I sat in my suite watching the gathering of celebrities on TV. In English, a commentator identified the more prominent members who stood on a raised platform just beside the entrance to the shining bronze skyscraper. Present were several ambassadors, including the U.S. ambassador; a famous Filipino actress; an American rock star; the city mayor; the chief justice; the army chief of staff, formerly the president's chauffeur; many prominent businessmen; the president, not looking well; his wife, appearing ravishing; and, of course, Barry, whom I recognized immediately despite his white hair, jowly face, and a portliness he never had as a younger man. But his bearing — confident yet relaxed — was unmistakable. How quickly one adjusts from the mind's obsolete image of a friend to the new reality.

The camera panned the large crowd, mostly young office workers and shoppers, who filled an entire block of the commercial district. Speaking into a microphone, the president recited the benefits of the free enterprise system and extolled Barry's entrepreneurial contribution to the economic vitality of the country, which, although unacknowledged, happened to be declining at the time.

4

Summoned by the president, Barry rose from his seat and stood facing him to receive an award. A shot was heard. Others followed, *crack, crack, crack*, and Barry, wrapping his arms around himself, staggered and fell forward off the platform onto the pavement.

Stunned momentarily, some of the dignitaries dropped to the platform, others to the street. Men in business suits lay beside stylishly dressed women. They were motionless so that one couldn't tell the dead or wounded from the unscathed. The commentator was incoherent amid the commotion and confusion. Meanwhile the teeming, screeching mob panicked and dispersed like a disturbed colony of ants. When I think about the scene now, several weeks later, I tremble and my heart beats rapidly. Somehow it is still too shocking and unbelievable to grasp.

It was reported in the press that the assassination attempt on the life of the president resulted in the deaths of two ambassadors and an American businessman, which was inaccurate because Barry Fortune had renounced his U.S. citizenship long ago. His death has been particularly hard for me to take. How happily I had looked forward to our reunion, and to a summer with the Fortunes in the islands. It would have been the medicine I needed to mitigate my loneliness over the death of my wife the previous winter. And it would have been a much-needed sabbatical from teaching English at UCLA. Yet I had come to the Philippines for something more — to recapture somehow in this poverty-stricken land the simplicities of a warm and spiritual past. I knew I would run the risk, once in the islands, of never emotionally returning to the States.

Fortune's funeral was no less impressive than that of a national leader. In attendance were representatives from the major western nations, and a few Communist countries, including the USSR. The vice president of the United States was there, as were the president of Brazil, the Japanese prime minister, and a score of corporate chairmen from the world's most prestigious companies. Yet so well had my friend shunned publicity, to most people around the world the name Barry Fortune held no special significance.

As we stood surrounding the grave that gray torrid morning, I watched the faces of the high and the mighty and searched for a clue to their true feelings. Perhaps I was unjust to Barry, expecting to find insincerity, but I recalled well his method of operating. Had all these luminaries owed him something, submitted to his subtle intrusions and demands? The scale may have been grander and perhaps the style more polished than in the old days, but the net result would be the same. He must have used them all to achieve his selfish ends.

It is time his story was told, the true man revealed as very few had known him. This account spans a period of barely thirty months during the war while I changed from boy to man, and viewed from both vantage points. It draws on my crystal memory of certain events as well as sources that have been passed on to me, such as a poorly kept diary of those years and hundreds of letters to my parents and to Lucia, Barry's one-time love but not his wife. I hope that this memoir will help alleviate my sorrow at losing him, for from the beginning of our friendship and through the years of silence, my caring for him never ceased.

I

The Crossing

"**I** know you'd like to learn our destination, men. So would I." Silver-haired Comdr. Jeremiah Rutledge spoke to the entire battalion, all 1,080 of us, assembled in the vast drill hall before we boarded the trucks that took us to the big troopship in San Pedro Harbor.

"Frankly, I can't tell you. Not yet, not until I open this." He held up a manila envelope. "Our orders, men. I'll read 'em when we're in midocean. But I assure you our mission is important. The Command has given us a big assignment. And I know this: I can count on you, can't I, men?" We roared. He surveyed our eyes until we were silent. "Remember, we're Seabees. We're a can-do outfit." He raised his fist. "For us the impossible only takes a little longer, right, men?"

Wild with eagerness, again we roared. His brief, simple exhortation was stirring and I joined the frenzy.

We were on A deck, in the heaving bow. The reek was unbearable — unwashed sweating human bodies crammed onto cots four layers high. The stagnant air was thick with humidity; the sole compartment porthole had to be closed at night to avoid revealing our position. A pinprick of light in the ocean darkness was as telling as a stark beacon to the Jap sub that was allegedly pursuing us.

I slithered onto my second-tier cot, having barely six inches between my nose and the bloated, swaying canvas above me. Inhaling in small gasps, I hoped to avoid the stench; it was no use. But thinking of Barry Fortune helped, thinking of the incident that had occurred a few hours earlier. Fortune was a new man to our outfit, and in trying to break the ice he got off to a bad start.

"You're full of shit, Fortune. Nobody knows where we're goin'," said Bull Dunham. "Not even the commander. You

7

heard him." The tone was derisive. The men within earshot, almost the entire compartment, laughed mockingly.

Fortune was a medium-sized man, an ordinary-looking guy, the sort one might listen to from politeness and then forget, except that his complexion was unusually pasty and smooth, quite unlike ours, and his eyes were cool and unregistering, void of any sign of emotion.

From his jeans pocket he pulled a fat packet of bills held together by a metal clip, peeled off several, and flung them on the gray painted deck. "There's fifty bucks says I'm right."

Instantly every one of us dropped our petty concerns—I even put down the Tolstoy novel perched on my chest—and waited in suspense for the challenge to be met. No one made a move to match the fifty.

"How'n hell you so sure?" demanded Bull.

"The code number," said Fortune calmly. "It's stenciled on every crate, every piece of equipment, and it tells where we're going." He paused to let his words sink in. "Our code number means Finschafen."

"Where in hell is Finschafen?" someone piped up. I could feel a change, suddenly a tentative readiness to believe our seer.

"In New Guinea," replied Fortune.

"Where in hell's New Guinea?"

"It's a goddamn hole," someone else said.

"I used to pass it on the Staten Island ferry," Bull quipped.

Others blustered: "Bet that's where the fighting is, right?" "Sonofabitch, 'bout time we got some action."

"I'll show you where it is. Anybody got a piece of paper?" responded Fortune, now heady with confidence.

A sheet of letter paper was passed down. As we knelt on the compartment deck and crowded around him, Fortune drew a crude map showing Australia and the large island of New Guinea above it, and to the right a string of dots representing the Solomon Islands and bloody Guadalcanal, a name that carried a special terror for us.

"Finschafen's about there," Fortune said, pointing to the tip of a large cape. "It's above Milne Bay, north of Buna and

8

Lae." His finger moved from one point to the next, locating places that were familiar to us from fairly recent newspaper headlines, places infamous for their fierce battles and enormous carnage and the fearful tenacity of the Japanese soldiers who seemed to place no value on life, least of all their own. For them to die in battle was the noblest end possible, a terrifying and baffling ethic.

"How come you know so much, Fortune?" Bull persisted, still suspicious and resentful.

"I was there before the war, okay?" said Fortune, staring the questioner down. But his confident answer served only to further distance him from the rest of us. He was too unbelievable, an oddball. Furthermore, despite his otherwise ordinary appearance, he was too clean.

When morning came the porthole was opened and I caught a narrow glimpse of the brisk blue sea. The compartment emptied quickly as we departed for our saltwater ablution under the misguided belief that it would clean and refresh us. In fact it only strengthened our odor and made our skin feel stickier; it was a deception, a mere facsimile of the real thing.

During good weather days I remained above deck daydreaming of a landfall on the horizon, a mountain with a silver streak, presumably a waterfall plunging down its side from the summit. I had a premonition that whether it was imaginary or not, someday it would be real. Hour after hour I watched the flying fish leaping before our bow as it furrowed through the astonishingly inky sea; hour after hour I watched the roiling green wake streaming like a snake into the distance behind us. It was as if time were concretized, transformed into visible form.

Being only nineteen then, life had immediacy; the fresh past was worthless history — once over, quickly forgotten — and the future, offering hardly more than a chance of an early death in battle, was threatening. But worse — the here and now being no picnic — what was there to celebrate? On rainy days I stayed below buried in *War and Peace*, a pure escape, a longed-for world, under control and ordered and inevitable.

9

After watching Fortune, I soon realized that he was an anomaly. His shirt and jeans were always freshly ironed and clean, his face was smoothly shaven and powdered, his eyes were clear, not like ours—bloodshot from chronic lack of sleep. But most of us were too engrossed in our individual miseries to care about or even notice his uniqueness: What the hell, he was cut from different cloth anyway. But to me, that was exactly his fascination.

As for solace I had Billiard Ball, a former professor of Romance languages at Columbia, brainier, more intellectual, more polished than anyone in the battalion. A good friend, he too was a misfit, immediately obvious when he spoke in his clearly enunciated English. But he aroused no resentment; rather he was respected, perhaps because of his powerful physique: He was six foot five. No one would dare tangle with him.

Making friends with Fortune was a slow process. Even when we were thrown together fortuitously in a pinochle game, I was unable to draw him into conversation, particularly small talk. "Ever play poker?" I asked.

"Yup," he quipped.

"How about a game sometime?" Silence. "Huh?" I pursued.

"Forget it," he said. He dealt a hand.

"Why not?" I pressed.

"I never lose," he said, ending it. No doubt I was attracted to geniuses.

In calm weather dusk at sea was especially serene and beautiful, even mystical. It was my favorite time of day. The ship, barreling through the still air, created a light breeze that felt like warm velvet. Delicately the ocean billows darkened to lavender; behind us when the moon rose, our wake became a twisting channel of glittering tinsel. We were drawn from our hole below decks and talked only in hushed tones as we were caressed by the air.

Fortune sat on the deck against a crate. When the dark was deep enough to show the stars, he pointed to the sky. "Southern Cross," he said to no one in particular.

"Where?" I asked, seizing the chance to make contact.

10

"Follow my arm," he said, thrusting it into space. "Goddamned long time since I've see it." His voice was nostalgic, as if he had just run into an old friend.

"How long?" I asked.

"Five years, maybe more," he replied. The air was pungent with the smell of sea brine mingled with creosote from the thick hemp lines wound around the capstans. Fortune studied the full sweep of the sky now dense with stars. "Terrific place, the tropics," he commented. "Ever been in a rain forest? It's wild, raw—know what I mean? Except for the Poles, it's the last frontier. Y'know the teak and mahogany on a single acre are worth millions."

"Tropical rain forests—yes," I said. "I know what they're like from Tarzan movies."

Fortune chuckled, "Hell, those movies were made on Catalina Island."

"Really?" I said, crestfallen. "The forest wasn't genuine?"

"Don't worry, you'll get your chance to see the real thing," he assured me, amused at my consternation. "I've lived in the forests of three continents—the Congo, Brazil, and Burma—and I have news for you: There's really no Tarzan."

We laughed, warming up to each other.

"What on earth were you doing in those places?" I asked. My impressionability was obvious.

"Very little on the ground; I used to run a flying service."

"You were a pilot?"

"Sort of, until I cracked up."

"You cracked up?"

"Yes, but not in the head."

"In a plane, you mean?"

"That's right, in the jungle."

"Where?"

"It doesn't matter."

"Are you putting me on?"

"Some natives found me—little bastards, pigmy types, amazing people; they carried me for days. I was smashed all over, delirious; they dropped me at a missionary hospital."

"Not Schweitzer's?"

"Who?"

11

"Albert Schweitzer. He had a hospital in Africa and played Bach."

"Never heard of him. Anyway, this was Burma."

Fortune was like an old man reminiscing about some trial of his youth, yet he was only in his early thirties. His face was now smooth and slightly rounded, bearing no sign of the tough ordeal. "In a few months I recovered," he continued.

"And then you returned home?"

"Had to," he said. Becoming wistful he studied the Southern Cross again. "Goddamn, it'll be good to see orchids growing wild. I had malaria, and well, kind of heart trouble."

"My God, you certainly had your share, didn't you?" I wondered how he qualified for the Seabees with a heart problem. Could I believe him? It was all too fantastic.

Although this conversation established our rapport, the thaw had really begun during a chance meeting a few days earlier as we stood at my usual spot by the bow rail staring at the flying fish. I asked him how he managed to keep so clean. He told me that he had access to a private stateroom with a head and shower. So absurdity answered audacity, but at least he answered.

"Name's Hal Arnold," I said, extending my hand. When he took it, his felt like a soaked rag. He smiled wanly, saying nothing, seeming preoccupied. "You truly amaze me," I said.

"How's that?" he replied, looking amused but curious.

"That you know our destination—I mean, especially since the commander doesn't know." A flying fish caught his eye and he followed its graceful trajectory. "It's really fantastic," I continued. "How did you know?"

"Easy," he said.

"You have my word it won't go any further," I reassured him.

"I don't care. Tell anyone you want," he replied. He paused awhile, seeming to delight in toying with me, keeping me on tenterhooks. "I was the one who typed up our orders," he said finally.

"You what?" His simple answer was startling.

"Before joining the battalion I worked at the vice admiral's headquarters."

"And that's all there is to it?" I responded.

12

"Actually I'm an OSS operator," he said sarcastically, pulling my leg. (OSS — Office of Strategic Services is now the CIA.) And that was that.

Our friendship began in earnest with that conversation under the stars. Until then Fortune had judged me of little use. After all, what could an unsophisticated kid like me, still wet behind the ears, possibly know? Yet, after exhausting more promising possibilities, I was all he really had. I certainly showed an interest in him; apparently I belonged to no clique.

Then Billiard Ball warned me: "Watch out. When he's done needing you, he'll toss you away with the garbage. Can't you see he's a conniving opportunist?"

"How can you say that? You hardly know him," I protested.

"Gut feeling, intuition. I've run into his kind before."

I ignored Billiard Ball because I knew that he was inherently distrustful and often bitter, and that the "truth" he spouted was frequently colored. Yet he was basically gentle. He had a sturdy, severe face, wide cheekbones, a heavy straight nose, and a solid chin with a hint of a cleft. When a youth he lifted weights, giving him thick shoulders and a bull neck. He appreciated his nickname, referring to his shiny bald pate with a fringe of blond hair above his ears, and his given name, Roger Billiard.

Early in our friendship Billiard Ball notified me that he was a first-rate genius, a fact I should constantly bear in mind. From anyone else I'd have taken such a declaration for arrogance; with Billiard Ball it was merely setting the facts straight. Yet for all his brilliance, he dwelled on his cynicism and professed no way to improve his lot. I still had faith in man back then; institutions awed me and I was trusting. My gut feeling about Fortune was that he was harmless, undoubtedly worth cultivating as a friend.

"God, what I'd give for a freshwater shower," I announced as Fortune and I stood at the bow rail. Fortune dropped his gaze from the sublime Southern Cross to my

13

ridiculous, grubby, stubbly face and my wrinkled, sweat-splotched blue chambray shirt. At best, I appeared naturally unkempt because of an awkward gangliness. With shameless frankness I confess bearing a resemblance to a giraffe: tall, slender, small head, long neck. Yes, it's true that I have much to compensate for, but it rarely gets to me.

I believe that at that moment Barry Fortune discovered Hal Arnold, suddenly realizing that I needed him, maybe even more than he needed me.

"Stay behind in the compartment tomorrow morning, okay?" stated Fortune. "Don't go to breakfast."

"What do you mean? We get only two meals a day," I said.

"D'you want a shower or not?"

No question it would be worth even starvation if necessary. "Sure, okay," I said.

"You'll eat, but later," he then explained. "Forget the chow line, okay?"

"Okay, okay," I sang in a joyous refrain. My God, I thought, it was all this and heaven too.

That night I slept happily below deck, for the morning held exquisite promise, a sort of rebirth. After the electric lights went on, signaling the arrival of the invisible dawn, and the morning trumpet snapped us awake with reveille, the compartment began to bustle. Groaning, we dragged ourselves to the gurgling sluice and waited in line to urinate. We looked as bad as we felt. Our mouths tasted foul. Some of us doused our faces and torsos with seawater, only to feel worse. The optimists among us took saltwater showers. Then with an aluminum mess kit and cup clanking from his belt, each man joined the circuitous chow line that snaked into the ship's depths. Staying behind as instructed, I waited with Fortune for the last sailor to leave the compartment.

When we were finally alone Fortune motioned me to follow. "Say nothing," he said. "I'll do all the talking from now on."

He wasn't furtive in the least as he led me on a confusing course through a maze of companionways. Indeed his manner was nonchalant, as if we were on a sight-seeing stroll of the ship's interior. I marveled at his mastery of the vessel's layout in spite of the interminable route we were taking.

Eventually we reached a grand salon resembling a posh hotel lobby, with ornate red-tapestried walls, a high art deco ceiling, and huge overstuffed sofas and chairs arranged in random groupings across a polished parquet floor. The room teemed with army and navy officers lounging about in dress uniform. Some were women, then new to the services as nurses or Wacs, making up the first contingent headed for the Pacific war zone. A gaiety pervaded the room, promoted by the highballs (so early in the day?), which most held in their hands. Save for the uniforms I'd have assumed that this was a luxury cruise to a tropical resort island.

At first I was awed by the scene, then as it sank in I was outraged. On the very same vessel, in one section barely a few hundred feet away, were my comrades stacked together in a miserable, stinking compartment, and here in luxurious surroundings was a pampered elite acting like members of a royal court. Was this democracy? The American way? Hell no! From then on I became a silent rebel resentful of the service caste system.

Later when my ideals were again offended, my rebellion burst its bounds. How naive I was; yet even in hindsight, after a lifetime of maturing, I prefer the world of my innocence to the real one. That scene in the salon, forgotten only a few days later but remembered always in a deeper sense, was a momentous event in my personal development. It marked the beginning of a struggle of conscience that still simmers as I write.

"When we cross the lounge, act natural," Fortune advised. Feigning easiness, we strolled side by side bubbling and gesticulating like French politicians. No one paid us any attention.

"How did you learn your way around the ship so well?" I asked.

"Not so long ago I was a paying passenger," Fortune explained matter-of-factly. "She was the *Columbia* then, biggest U.S. liner afloat. Eleanor Roosevelt christened her." Pausing in the middle of the room, he gazed about. "Crossed the Atlantic on her twice."

Catching the eye of an officer in a small group playing cards, Fortune nodded slightly.

"Is he your friend?" I asked.

Passing over my question, he continued. "She was a beauty, a truly great ship. She could carry a couple thousand people in style, but not the fifteen thousand they've crammed aboard her now." His voice quavered. I remember the incident so well because rarely during our friendship had he shown strong feelings. "They've raped her and made her into a shell," he said. "This very room—I used to have dinner here every night when it was filled with glamorous women in gowns and men wearing black ties. An orchestra played over there and everyone danced."

Just as we were leaving the grand room, he turned and momentarily took in its sweep. "It's still beautiful, isn't it? It's all that's left. Everything else has changed." He took off in a rush. "Let's go," he called over his shoulder. "You wanted a shower." I was breathless trying to keep up.

Our journey ended in a long, remote, carpeted companionway lined with stateroom doors. Fortune inserted a key into the lock of one and motioned me to follow. We stepped into a neat, comfortably appointed cabin with a curtained porthole and a bunk made up with a smooth white blanket with wide, horizontal blue stripes and a freshly ironed white pillowcase at its head. Soft navy blue wall-to-wall carpeting covered the floor. The room was marvelously quiet—an enclosed retreat, a rare peaceful haven, pleasurable and refreshing, not unlike a secluded corner of a cool woods on a hot summer afternoon. I was elated, and saddened too. Would I live long enough to ever know again, however briefly, such privacy and luxury?

Unaware of how forcefully the room was affecting me, Fortune immediately made himself at home and began removing his clothes, inviting me to do the same. "Go ahead, take your shower first," he said, pointing to a doorway at one end of the cabin. I held back still skeptical, fearful of intruding. Did we have permission? "Don't be ridiculous," he said. "There's a razor in the medicine cabinet." It was too glorious. But whose room was this? He grew irritated. "Do you want a shower or don't you?" Of course I did. "Then take it, damnit. I'm giving you special dispensation."

Never was a shave and hot shower more purifying. My spirit was restored. Fortune took his, routinely of course, looking the same afterward as before, since he was forever clean. Then, changing into fresh clothes that he retrieved from a dresser drawer, he acted dismayed as I put my old soiled ones back on. "I'll have clean clothes for you next time," he promised, apologizing. "What's your size?"

Next time. Next time. Those words were sweet music.

A score of "next times" followed. As the trip became a habit, I soon led the way, eagerly working my way through the now familiar maze like a trained mouse seeking a reward, finding at the end that cabin monastery where I immersed myself in its holy waters to cleanse my body and soul.

Fortune never explained his apparent free use of the cabin. Was his connection the officer in the salon? Was it the ship's captain himself? Who could say how high or low or convoluted his connections might be?

After that first shower in the oasis, Fortune led me through a complex series of corridors deep into the ship. We emerged in an enormous kitchen where dozens of sweating men wearing white aprons and white bandannas tied around their foreheads labored over massive steaming cauldrons of brew and giant pans of hash. One of the men, sporting a tall chef's hat, swaggered with fierce authority between the vessels, pausing here and there for a taste from a long ladle. Spying Fortune, the chef raised a forefinger, which Fortune acknowledged with a victory sign.

"How do you like your eggs?" Fortune asked.

"My eggs?" I replied, bewildered.

"Yes, your eggs."

"Over lightly," I said hastily.

Fortune made a sign, a finger of one hand up, and a finger of the other down. "With bacon and corn muffins, I suppose?" My eyes aglitter, I nodded, yes. "And you have a choice—orange or tomato juice or melon." This was too much; I was unable to decide. "Hell, take all three," he said, annoyed with my indecisiveness. "We'll have some coffee, okay?" I agreed. "Freshly ground, y'know, nothing less," he assured me.

I just knew it had to be. "Of course," I said.

"We'll top it all off with apple pie," he said.

"Pie for breakfast?"

"They're for the officers' dinner tonight," he explained, pointing to a tall rack at the opposite end of the kitchen where the pies were stacked for cooling, "but we can have some while they're still hot—with a slice of cheddar on top if you'd like."

Hell, sure I'd have the pie. Where is it written that pie is prohibited for breakfast? It also occurred to me that it might be my last piece of pie ever. I was completely caught up in the gluttony. "Absolutely," I said.

Sitting at a small metal-clad table in a corner of the kitchen, we were served on plates of bone china, the standard officers' club service, and given neatly folded, ironed napkins. I ate ravenously, partly from hunger due to the two meal a day rations, insufficient for a still-growing lad, and partly from fear that this feast would be an unrepeatable event.

"It's not your last meal, y'know," Fortune remarked. "We'll be doing it again." But it was so incredible that I wasn't about to take a chance.

After our plates were clean, twice so for me, Fortune thanked the chef. As they shook hands I thought I saw something pass between them. The chef said something about nothing being too good for old customers. "Nothing like LA, eh, my friend?" Fortune replied.

That day was the start of an entirely new and sustained life-style. The voyage was no longer an agonizing, unendurable experience. It took on some aspects of a vacation cruise, such that my indignation over the contrasting standards of living aboard soon evaporated. But an uneasy conscience took its place as I watched my friend Billiard Ball grow progressively depressed and disheveled. If only I could invite him to visit the monastary with us, or if that was too risky, then to go in my place. When I suggested it to Fortune, he adamantly refused.

"Tell a soul," he said, "and that'll be the end of it for you."

In a few days we entered a tropical zone where storms were rare, enabling me to sleep undisturbed in the gunwhale on deck. The night patrols became lax in enforcing the rules as the voyage lengthened, and in fact an easy informality crept into our relations with one another, and with the officers as well.

Now I too, like Fortune, was a spic and span anomaly; now I too was confident and felt special. And the price couldn't have been more right. Fortune, it seemed, exacted nothing but my friendship. Indeed he was generous, even touchingly so. Take the wristwatch incident. My watch had come loose while I was leaning over the rail and fell off my wrist into the sea. Observing this, Fortune unstrapped his, insisting I have it. Although at first I was swept up in the material benefits of our relationship, in time the warm rapport that developed between us counted for more. A void in my life was filled as he substituted for the older brother I longed for but never had. If there was a catch, it escaped me.

But Billiard Ball's warning persisted. I was also haunted by the admonitions of my father derived from his long experience in business and its lessons in human nature. He used to say, "Remember, nothing comes for nothing. No human motive is pure and selfless." Was it coincidence that he, with hardly a grammar school education, and the highly sophisticated Billiard Ball had arrived at a similar view of their fellow man? Still it was at odds with mine, which was based on trust. I rejected the voices of doubt and gave Fortune my unflagging loyalty.

During the following days and weeks I listened to more of my new friend's story. He had requested a transfer to our particular outfit while at the vice admiral's office after he had learned that we were headed for an advanced base. He also liked what he had heard about our commander, a highly regarded civil engineer noted for his boldness and courage in taking on tough assignments. Fortune was seeking a surefire opportunity to encounter frontline hostility. "Action! I thrive on it," he said.

Before enlisting in the navy, he, with a partner, owned and operated a successful business in Los Angeles designing and installing sound systems in theaters, nightclubs, and movie studios. At the vanguard of a new technology, the business prospered, and Fortune—the entrepreneurial talent—and the partner—the technical genius—grew wealthy in a short time. As Fortune put it, "We became muchomillionaires."

Fortune hadn't married. There was no time for commitment except to the business. Anyway, it wasn't necessary, he said, with so many beautiful and exciting women around; the Hollywood scene was wallowing in sex.

"And how about having children someday?" I asked.

"Only if they could be born adults," he replied.

There was a commotion and shouting on deck; our first landfall, a low rise, appeared faintly on the horizon. We rushed to the rail and stood patiently for hours as gradually the bluish hills of New Caledonia came into sharper relief and turned a rich, deep green. The ship entered a glittering bay brightly specked with whitecaps. We saw white-walled, orange-roofed houses scattered among the lush, gentle hills rimming the bay. The land, the hills, and the dense green vegetation were visual poetry. I had no idea how much I had missed the sight of land and how bound to it I really was.

A dozen launches appeared, and all afternoon until well past sundown they plied back and forth between our ship and a distant dock, unloading most of the thousands of soldiers, nurses, and Wacs. The rest of us watched and waved from the rail, shouting good wishes and envying them their nearby Noumea paradise.

When the morning sun broke above the horizon, the ship lumbered silently out of the harbor to the open sea with only a fraction of the original complement left aboard. In less than two days we steamed into another bay, a long, glassy inlet with sheer, forested hills rising steeply along its sides. For half a day the vessel moved gradually deeper into its embrace to its very end. This was Milne Bay, the easternmost extremity of New Guinea, a primitive, wild, seemingly threatening place, exhibiting a rawness that frightened me.

Throughout the night our entire battalion, equipment and all, transferred on pontoon barges under searchlights to a small rusting freighter moored nearby. Despite an oncoming squall, the freighter lifted anchor as soon as the gangway was pulled. As we passed by the towering ship that had been home for a month, I felt a pang of sadness. I knew I'd miss the well-appointed cabin and the amenities that went with it, but nothing else.

As the freighter traveled northward, the coast was constantly visible in the hazy, humid distance off our port side. When we passed Buna and Lae, they were no longer just places on a map; now they were real, right there frightfully in sight. In two days we entered the harbor at Finschafen, a quaint and homey refuge surrounded by a flat, palm-forested plain extending as far inland as we could see. Fortune had called it right after all.

The ship tied up to a dock, the gangplank was dropped, and we marched down single file, each with a steel helmet on his head, a duffel bag under one arm, and a pack on his back. Waiting on the dock in loose platoon formation for the last man to debark, we sweated in the heavy, sultry morning air and speculated anxiously about our future. The word was passed: The battalion before us had just been wiped out in combat. The rumor spread among us like a terrifying firestorm. We were the doomed battalion's replacement. Fortune grinned, hardly able to contain his elation. No question, he had joined the right outfit.

II
Finschafen

Adjusting

"By the way, you've been assigned to my unit," Fortune said while we stood awaiting the signal to march into the palm forest.

"Baloney," I responded. "Don't you know I'm on permanent KP, consigned to it for the rest of my life?"

"You'll see," he said.

In this instance, doubting Fortune's magic was well founded. Most of the men in the battalion were mature (our average age was thirty-five). They were skilled tradesmen: carpenters, mechanics, heavy-equipment operators, welders. Name the skill and we had the man. The younger men, such as myself—unskilled, taken fresh from high school, deprived by the draft of any opportunity for further education—were selected for duty in the construction battalions specifically to do the menial jobs. We performed the kitchen work, the ditch digging, the camp housekeeping, and any minor routine maintenance tasks that might come up. This is not how I had imagined fighting a war would be. Not that I expected or wanted a high-risk assignment; I wanted to do something visibly constructive, driving a bulldozer perhaps.

"You'll see," Fortune repeated, "no more KP. I won't say that getting you transferred was easy. That chief of yours is one sonofabitch. Problem is they need all the dummies they got to do the shit work. So I promised him—well, I persuaded him—and he agreed to let you go. He's running scared, y'know."

Paroled! I wasn't confident that they wouldn't slap me back into KP if I transgressed somehow, or if I crossed Fortune. My debt to him was growing substantially. I wasn't as relieved and overjoyed as I expected either. I had pangs of

22

guilt over leaving behind KP coworker friends who were in the same fix but weren't fortunate enough to have a sponsor to rescue them.

The specialty of Fortune's unit, communications, was entirely alien to me, and I was unsure how I could make a contribution. His crew was experienced, consisting of telephone linemen and radio maintenance men from civilian life. "Stick with me. I'll teach you," Fortune had assured me. In the back of my mind, I intended to make sure that I would never be called on for KP again. The more skilled I could become, the less chance that could happen. "Don't worry, I'll make you a pro, an indispensable member of my team, so you can forget KP forever." My benefactor had read my mind.

No doubt Fortune had clout. Obviously his rank was no factor, being only a first class petty officer, designated by three chevrons on the upper sleeve. From my vantage point, that of a lowly seaman second class, a first class petty officer was no mean rating. It commanded respect, earned as a result of superior technical expertise in one's field. But it carried little weight beyond the circle of the platoon or the specialty unit. Fortune said that it gave him less visibility; by that he meant, I discovered, room for maneuvering and manipulating. After all, how powerful could a middling first class petty officer possibly become? Not that he sought obscurity. No, he simply wanted to be taken for less than he was. He could easily have secured a commission, since he had a degree in electrical engineering from Western Reserve. An enlisted man's rank, he felt, would also bring him closer to where the action was, closer to the gut work, where he would know firsthand what was going on.

Furthermore, as he put it, "Shoulder bars don't mean shit. A man's a leader or he isn't. No one can make him one." Of course he included himself among that select group who were natural leaders, who didn't need to be appointed. I could hardly disagree with his observation; except for Rutledge, not an officer among us qualified for their leadership roles, but many of our enlisted men deserved the highest respect.

Commander Rutledge was a noncareer three striper. His handsome, craggy face broke into a smile easily and often.

However, when he blew off steam, which was frequently, he was sure to get results. The man's wrath could attain volcanic proportions. Since he spent most of his time in the field rather than in his detestable office, his face had a dark tan, which contrasted strikingly with his deep-set blue eyes and silver hair. He was a model father figure. He reminded me of Lewis Stone, the distinguished actor, a taller, younger version perhaps.

Offhandedly, Fortune made a stunning prediction: "Commander Rutledge will never make it through."

For a moment I imagined he said: Nice day today, isn't it? The way he said things didn't necessarily fit their sense; he practiced understatement. Astonished by his remark, I waited in suspense for further clarification.

"Rutledge is a civilian at heart. He's too goddamned democratic, and it won't work. The navy regulars will chew him up."

After we moved off the dock, platoon by platoon, in orderly fashion, we set about erecting our square canvas tents in a checkerboard pattern in the shade of the canopy of palms. I flung myself on the soft earth and lay there absorbing its damp fragrance. I was fed up with hard, hot, lifeless steel decks. The fertile earth! I longed for it.

The land was part of a coconut plantation that belonged to an American soap company. At night, often when the air was still, coconuts crashed down onto our tents. Being untested in battle, unsure of how close the Japs might be, our imagination keen, we were terrified by the racket the coconuts made. Peeking out between the flaps, we hallucinated an enemy invasion. Our guns had no ammunition, thank heaven, so we lay frozen in our cots awaiting the worst, until morning when the light saved us. This scene was repeated for several nights. Had the Japs actually come, no doubt we would have ignored them from disbelief and let them butcher us.

Often when the camp was secured for the night and all was quiet, a hair-raising scream would split the silence. Lo, a friendly python had found a bunk-mate, a warm body to nestle alongside. Most of us thought this was hilarious.

24

Indeed there was a suspicion that some of the reptiles might have been planted. None of them ever really caused harm; contrary to reputation, none had ever crushed our bones or strangled us. But they themselves suffered many casualties, either by being shot or hacked to death with a machete.

Eventually we accepted real and imagined dangers with aplomb, but a new situation soon wore us down. Our oceanside retreat showed a vicious side during the monsoon season, which brought a relentless torrent week after endless week. All pathways became a slippery, viscous mire. Our boots doubled their weight with mud, which was carried into the mess hall, into the commander's office, into our jeeps, onto our cots. Somehow it even got into our food. Our heavy equipment bogged down in it and gave up. Even when at last the blessed sun appeared, the mud lingered under the palms for weeks; the coastal road dried out to a powder so fine that every passing vehicle spewed up a contrail of choking dust. There was no happy medium.

Meanwhile, Fortune seemed unmoved by any of nature's extremes. From prior experience he certainly knew what it was like to live in the tropics. But his equanimity may have been less heroic than I at first assumed. He managed to make life more bearable simply by living better than the rest of us. Except for the commander of our battalion and the commanders of the companies, only Fortune lived in his own private tent. Among the petty officers, and even among the junior officers, there were mutterings of resentment against his "fancy" lifestyle. I complained that he was inconsistent. Hadn't he turned down a commission so he could be alongside us in the thick of the action? Didn't he say he felt uncomfortable with the elite establishment? Yet he chose to live apart from us, like a kind of holy man. After all was said and done, didn't he really believe he was better, in a class by himself? "Not better," he replied, "but definitely in a class by myself."

Thus I failed to recognize that I too was an object in the edifice of power and influence that he was building. He was serving many others as well who were more interested in their small private gain than in any obligation they had

25

incurred. Fortune dealt at first in mostly small favors, loss leaders so to speak, which he performed out of the goodness of his heart. One such opportunity arose during a morning muster, while a junior lieutenant was inspecting us as we stood at attention, a boring process designed to give the officer a sense of purpose. A leather key ring hanging from his belt suddenly broke and the keys fell to the ground and scattered. He reacted with a mixture of embarrassment and annoyance, the latter principally because he knew there were no consumer-type items to be had in Finschafen, least of all key rings. After he had dismissed us, Fortune approached him and offered to replace the item. The lieutenant was skeptical but, having nothing to lose, agreed to accept the offer.

Wasting no time, Fortune visited the navy supply ship that had just docked and requisitioned a half-dozen American flags. When he returned to his tent he removed their hardware, part of which consisted of spring clips that made ideal key rings. The lieutenant got his, Fortune took one for himself, and the rest were put away in safekeeping for future use. What happened to the flags? Fortune burned them in a steel drum behind his tent without giving it a thought. I was troubled by what he had done; it was a dishonorable and sacrilegious act. When the officer to whom he donated the key ring asked where he got it, Fortune explained, "From the U.S. flag, sir."

The officer was puzzled. "Who?"

"Lieutenant Ulysses Simpson Flag, sir, on the supply ship." Fortune spoke with a straight face, but his eyes twinkled and I barely suppressed a giggle.

"Oh," the young officer said, and dropped the matter.

Student, shadow, son figure, alter ego—all these aptly describe my connection with Fortune. I rarely left his side from early morning until retiring for the night. I joined him in every task he was doing, regardless of my ineptness and inexperience.

What patience he had! He gave me a crash course in state of the art electronics, which involved tubes and heavy wiring.

I learned how to repair radios and transceivers and telephones. At some assignments I became expert, in particular the stringing of telephone lines along poles. No one could match my agility as I clambered up the poles like a squirrel. My mates used to kid me. "You sure you don't have Papuan blood in you?" they'd say. But I was younger than the rest of them then, in my physical prime, and they weren't yet old enough to admit to themselves that they were past theirs. Once again I was someone, a specialist possessing a prized skill, a person to be held in esteem for his expertise. And I owed it to my friend Barry Fortune.

In about six weeks, having mastered the basics of electronics, I was able to tackle projects on my own. The major ones were winding down, however. Only repair and maintenance jobs were available; the zest and novelty of starting from scratch were over. Like the humidity, the days hung heavy again, dragging on week after monotonous week. Fighting a war was dull business, consisting of infrequent brief spurts of furious activity, sometimes violent and deadly, as I would learn soon enough; but mostly it was waiting, rushing, and waiting.

Fortune, however, never sat waiting; his pot was always boiling. Indeed, he was anxious to have the major installations completed so that he could be free to pursue his private interests and unleash his entrepreneurial talent. He took for granted that I would be a participant in his wheelings and dealings. I consented reluctantly, tentatively, fascinated as an observer at first, then ultimately revolted. From the expert I learned how one corrupts, cheats, and manipulates, buys influence and uses it for selfish ends. The lessons, I must say, relieved the monotony.

The first lesson began at the movies. Fortune had invited me to drive with him to an open-air theater on an army base about ten miles from our camp down the narrow, dusty coastal highway. The only real escape from our predicament, movies were an addiction, awakening a surprising sentimentality and an unabashed patriotism in us. But Fortune was immune to all this. He always said that he didn't like movies: His idea of escape was playing cards all evening.

27

He seemed bored and he fidgeted during the movie that night, frequently turning away from the screen to stare in the direction of the parking lot behind the theater which was simply a jungle clearing jammed with hundreds of jeeps.

At a crucial scene in the movie, when Carole Lombard slapped Clark Gable and he slapped back, Fortune nudged me. "Let's go," he said. I have been known to shush noisy culprits in a movie theater with profanity and threats of violence. Interrupting my attention to a movie brings out my worst side, unlike any other circumstance. "Not yet, goddamnit!" I said, keeping my eyes fastened on the screen.

"Now!" he said. "I'm leaving."

"Not 'til it's over. Are you out of your mind?" I exploded.

Standing up, he pulled me by the arm. Still watching the screen, I administered a hard chop to his forearm. "It'll be too late when it's over," he whispered.

By then the audience around us was growing impatient; there were shouts of "shut up" and "down in front." I knew that a serious ruckus would start if I continued to resist; besides, Fortune's phrase "too late" aroused my worst fear. Too late for what? It had to be business, monkey business. I gave in. "Fuck you, Fortune," I said, uncharacteristically.

Walking up the aisle fuming, I stared enviously at the rapt faces in the audience. When we reached the parking lot, which was lit intermittently by the reflection of the screen, we located our jeep after several mistaken indentities.

"You drive our jeep back to the base. I'll be right behind," Fortune said.

"How?" I asked.

"Whadya mean," he retorted.

"How do you intend to follow? In what? We arrived together, I believe."

He sighed. "Look, do what I tell ya. Drive it and don't ask questions."

"What in hell's going on?" I demanded.

Without answering he disappeared into the blackness amid the maze of vehicles. In only a few minutes I heard a motor start and saw headlights blink on. I did the same and wended my way out of the jumble. Once I was on the coastal road Fortune's headlights appeared in my rearview mirror. Then I understood what he was up to. The movie was a pretext, a clever way to suck me in as his accomplice in a jeep-stealing scheme. And the jeep I was driving, wouldn't that be illegitimate too? Why hadn't that occurred to me before? Having become familiar with Fortune's distorted code of ethics, I could anticipate his rationale: C'mon, sailor. How can you call it stealing? Stealing from whom? From the army? Hey, we're on the same side, y'know. From the U.S. government? C'mon now. Y'know what I call it? It's an unscheduled transfer, that's all.

I tried to work off my anger as I sped back to camp much too fast. Fortune clung to my tail. I parked in our abandoned transportation storage area, which was lit up from pole lights overhead. Fortune pulled up beside me in a brand-new, still-clean army jeep.

"You're a sonofabitch, Fortune," I screamed. He laughed, and my fury escalated. "Don't ever try to trick me again," I said with acid in my voice.

"Trick you? You drove my jeep back, that's all," he said derisively.

"Shit, Fortune," I fumed, "I resent being used. I won't be a part of your schemes."

"Y'know the trouble with you? You're too goddamn pure. You act like a judge." His face bore a fixed grin, which, I suspected, masked a genuine contempt.

"Do it one more time, Barry, and I'll request transfer to KP." Nothing I could have said would have driven home my resolve more. Fortune knew well how I detested KP. I was prepared to return to "prison."

His grin dissipated and his eyes dropped from mine. He was momentarily at a loss, silenced and motionless. He climbed out of his jeep and walked to mine. "Remember, this is a war," he said, sitting beside me. "Anything goes. All's fair. Understand? I'm not expecting you to do anything you don't want to. But I hope you'll toughen up, because if you don't you'll be dead. Understand?" He hugged me to him. "Understand? I don't want to lose you, friend."

His explanation softened me. I could not help but be moved. He was what he was, wheeling and stealing and

29

manipulating because of some inner compulsion, much as a drunk drinks. Under Fortune's special morality he saw nothing wrong in what he did; in fact it gave him a thrill, a sense of achievement. He had created his own private anarchy. But how far would it go? Where would it stop? I was afraid for him just as he was afraid for me, with my more sensitive, circumscribed morality.

"The saying goes, 'All's fair in love' too," I said.

"Yeah, sure, but there's no place for love out here," Fortune responded.

Was there ever a time when we needed love more? I thought. And wasn't he wrong, really? We loved our wives and our girlfriends back home with an idealized passion that far exceeded actual experience. What about our man-to-man friendships? Wasn't there a kind of love between some of us? What would one call our friendship, our mutual concern for each other? A convenient acquaintanceship?

Heeding my warning, Fortune excluded me from his more daring escapades, although from time to time I was involved in some minor foraging. Instead he found a role for me, one that began innocently enough but that eventually caused me much inner agony and conflict. He asked if I would be his surrogate in a love affair. Quite literally he meant it when he said that there was no place for love in New Guinea, for him, that is.

On the hood of his new jeep, Fortune had a garish head of a fox painted. It looked rather like a coat of arms — brightly colored red, green, and yellow — and it covered the entire hood surface. It was rendered by our battalion sign painter for a fifth of whisky. The emblem was a celebration of Fortune's love for Lucia Fox, his girl back home. I thought it was a crass display, cheapening the meaning of his love for her. But only I among Fortune's friends and contacts knew the true significance of this flamboyant decoration. Everyone else assumed that it was some sort of trademark, quite apt actually. The symbol suited his style. He acted like a clever fox, and soon everyone called him that — Fortune the Fox.

30

Would I be good enough to do him a favor, he asked, and write Lucia Fox a letter? Did he mean type one, to his dictation? No, no, he meant compose one to save him from having to do it himself. I balked. How could he expect me to do that? She was his girl. What could I possibly say? But he was lousy at letter writing, he said, and he knew that I was always writing somebody. Furthermore he heard from the censors I was good at it. From the censors! Was there no goddamned privacy in this outfit? Did Fortune have to pry into everything I did?

His love for Lucia was unlimited, he explained. It was she that nursed him in that remote jungle hospital after his airplane accident. She was his healing angel as he lay helpless for weeks, mending slowly. She was the "heart trouble" he had referred to back on the ship. (It was a scene right out of Hemingway.) How could he not have fallen in love with her? And she with him, a brave soul dropped from heaven, temporarily bereft of his manliness, someone to dote on, someone to rejuvenate, someone to receive her love.

Lucia Fox also liked to write. In fact she wrote him every day and he couldn't possibly keep up. He felt terribly guilty about that. But worse, by his not writing she was beginning to worry that he wasn't well, that he was wounded, or worse. If only I'd write to assure her that he was all right. She would believe me. In one of his rare letters he had written about me, had told her of our friendship, of my good character and loyalty. So how about it? Would I do him a favor? Just write once in awhile, explaining that all was well?

What if it wasn't true? I asked. What if he was ill or wounded or—I cut myself short, refusing to consider the worst scenario. What would I do then? Well, in that event I should lie, he said. It was the least I could do for a friend. Nothing wrong with a little white lie to keep everyone happy, he said. Then he must do the same for me should something happen. He agreed, and I gave him my parents' address.

My first letter to Lucia Fox was noteworthy for its self-consciousness and brevity.

Barry has asked me to keep you informed from time to time of how he is. As I believe you know, he and I are close friends. I'm attached to his platoon, I work in his communications unit, and I'm indebted to him for teaching me his trade.

Being very young, only a kid really, and quite shy, I don't have a girl, so Barry offered to lend me you, which, although mighty generous of him, is, I think, most presumptuous. He made me agree to one condition: When the war's over he wants you back all to himself. I'm agreeable, except the decision is yours as much as his, maybe more so.

He asked me to tell you he misses you terribly and in the not-too-distant future he promises to write. Were you to insist on receiving only his letters and not mine, I would understand.

Barry's good friend,
Hal

The first sentence of my closing paragraph was pure fiction, and I wrote it with mixed feelings. It expressed what I thought Fortune should have told me to say. As he himself said, what harm is there in a little white lie?

III
Finschafen

Lessons in Chutzpah

Fortune was beseiged with distractions, strictly of his own making, of course. His trading and bargaining and manipulating were nothing short of an obsession. As the pace of his activities quickened, his personality acquired a breathless ebullience. His daring fed upon itself. He became the quintessential Seabee; he believed he could do the impossible. Through his largesse he acquired power, the kind possessed by politicians in big cities.

From all ranks the men sought out Fortune for favors and they were soon indebted to him. Thanks to Fortune, the lower echelon officers, who normally had to borrow jeeps from the transportation pool, soon had their own vehicles. After a time so did the CPOs (the chief petty officers, highest of the noncoms). The jeeps were not "stolen," hell no, and not "procured," the euphemism applied to other types of contraband acquired through unofficial channels. Fortune coined the phrase "liberated vehicles," reflecting his special arrogance.

Fortune was frequently offered tidy sums for his favors. "What'll it cost me?" the men would ask in response to his generosity. "Forget it," Fortune would say. Money bored him, understandably; he had millions stashed away back in the States, which no one in the battalion realized except myself. "Maybe someday you can do me a favor," he would tell them. Such vagueness made the men feel strangely uneasy, for the debt was a nagging burden, and each debtor knew that eventually Fortune was bound to call it in. "Profligate generosity is bound to be suspect," Billiard Ball warned me, "and your friend will soon be the most despised man in the outfit."

33

Despite disliking Fortune, and with grudging admiration, Lt. Comdr. Reinhardt Gluck, our obtuse executive officer, had frequently used him and obtained satisfaction. In desperation Gluck had come seeking a gift to present to the commander for his birthday. It was to be a small get-together that was about to take place in officers' country. Not that Gluck was particularly fond of the commander, nor were any of the officers for that matter. But what a marvelous excuse to get in some heavy drinking. If someone got soused, how could the commander, who was normally a stickler about the moderate use of alcohol, and was abstemious himself, possibly object?

Fortune's special skill at procurement earned him certain privileges: the freedom to leave the base at will without notifying his lieutenant, and the right to have a tent all to himself, with a plywood floor, no less. (When the next supply ship arrived with a load of lumber, all tents had plywood floors.)

Fortune was regarded as the only dependable conduit for obtaining any item unavailable through normal channels. The range of goods in demand was unlimited. (Fortune and I were baffled when someone placed an order for condoms. There were no women in Finschafen, only the outlandishly primitive natives, but they were out of the question. Or were they?) To keep apace of the demand, Fortune formed an organization of entrepreneurial clones. In it were a dozen enlisted men, consisting mostly of members of the communications group and a few volunteers from outside who, having a natural aptitude for monkey business, were attracted to him.

Lieutenant Commander Gluck, Rutledge's right-hand man, number two in command, was among those who resented Fortune's "highfalutin' living," which Gluck said should be reserved only for officers. It was obvious to everyone that Gluck had ambitions to be number one. More than once he implied that he was the better man for the job. Unlike our lean, trim commander, Gluck was jowly and paunchy from gluttony and drinking too much beer. He exercised his rank like a Chinese mandarin, sitting back ordering others to do his bidding, never moving a whisker. He tended to make boisterous announcements, typically conversing louder than necessary, as if everyone within earshot should miss nothing he said.

When Gluck entered the communications tent looking for Fortune, I was leaning over a workbench assembling a recently appropriated transceiver of mysterious origin. The plywood floor shook under Gluck's clumsy weight, disturbing the delicate work I was doing. Annoyed I looked up, taking in his flat brush of a graying crew cut. It was a hazy, sticky afternoon, and Gluck's moon-shaped face was shiny with sweat. There was a hint of panic in his squinting eyes, and his jaw was tight.

"Where's Fortune?" he demanded.

"I'll get him for you, sir," I said.

"Make it pronto," he announced.

Only a lieutenant commander, a rank below Rutledge, Gluck nevertheless insisted that everyone address him as commander. Although before the war he was a field civil engineer supervising highway construction, he claimed that he was not truly an engineer, but rather an architect. Perhaps so, except that he pronounced the *cb* in architect as one would in the word *Chicago*.

Upon enlisting in the Construction Battalions, Gluck qualified only as a reserve officer. This rankled him, since he wished to be regular navy, but he realized that his aspirations were unrealistic. Deprived, in his view, of meaningful status, he suffered a certain sense of inferiority. No matter that his colleagues, the commander included, were reservists as well. Of all our officers, Gluck was the only one who sported a sidearm. It hung in a black leather holster from a wide leather belt that girded his bulging middle.

After returning to the communications tent with Fortune, I found Gluck examining, but not daring to touch, the partially assembled transceiver.

"What's this?" he asked.

"It's a two way radio for Bull Dunham," Fortune replied.

"Part of our complement?" Gluck asked.

"No, sir. Not this one. Just procured it."

Gluck leered knowingly. "Tell me, who's Bull gonna talk to? Who else's got one besides you?"

"We're working on that, sir. We figured it would be a good idea for every senior officer to have the ability to communicate with Bull's transportation shed in the event of a breakdown in the field."

"Wal, I'm all for that, but where in hell you gonna get the radios?" His pronunciation of radio rhymed with patio.

"There are more transceivers where this came from," said Fortune.

"Y'know you're a fuckin' genius," Gluck said, and he slapped the genius's back in admiration.

"Now I got a tough one for ya," said Gluck. "I need a box of Havana cigars, pronto."

Clearly his request was absurd; he may as well have asked for baked alaskas. But Fortune, even more incredibly, said evenly: "Just a box, sir?"

Gluck, having expected some objection, replied haltingly, "I...I said a box. That's what I said. Fifty."

"I see," said Fortune, "and when did you say you needed them?"

Perplexed by Fortune's coolness, Gluck shifted from one foot to the other. "Tonight! I need 'em tonight for the commander's birthday party. You tellin' me you know where there's a box of Havanas? Hell, I've scoured the whole damn island of New Guinea. If you're shittin' me — "

"Commander, I can't give you a guarantee, but I've got a pretty good hunch where to find some."

"Where?" Gluck immediately rejoined. Staring into Gluck's eyes, Fortune remained mute. "Wal," Gluck continued, "if you find 'em, I'll not be likely to forget a favor, y'unnerstand."

"Yes, sir, I do," said Fortune.

The timing of Gluck's request was poor, with scarce commodities virtually unobtainable. The chain of islands to the north was aflame with intense action, preventing the scheduled replenishment of essential supplies. It was common scuttlebutt that for weeks Gluck had been on a frantic search. He had stuck his neck out too far when promising the commander Havanas for his birthday.

Sensing this, Fortune decided to use his advantage. "You know, sir, a persuader of some sort would help."

Without hesitation Gluck pulled from his hip pocket a thick wallet stuffed with bills. I wondered why anyone would carry a wad of money around in uncivilized Finschafen. "Okay, that's unnerstanable," Gluck replied. "How much you talkin'? It's gotta be within reason, mind ya."

Fortune barely suppressed a laugh. "That stuff won't work, Commander Gluck. I need something of value to trade with. Money's worthless."

A flash of comprehension suddenly struck Gluck. "Well, I'll be a sonfabitch," he exclaimed. "So that's why I couldn't find any goddamned stogeys around here."

Fortune swooped in. "But a case of good Canadian whisky would do it."

"A what?" Gluck screeched.

"It would clinch it, sir."

"A whole goddamned case of hooch, you say?"

"Yes. Canadian, sir. That would do it."

"Y'know, I oughta simply order you."

Fortune's neck grew taut. With an icy voice he replied, "Yes, you could do that, but without the whisky I'd be sure to come back empty-handed."

It was a clash of personalities: the brutish hound versus the crafty fox. The more Gluck screamed, the more Fortune was determined to concede nothing.

"When I procure the Havanas, sir, I'll need a sidearm."

"A what? You gonna hold someone up?"

"No, sir, I'm going to pose as an officer, and a sidearm will make it more convincing."

Gluck protectively covered his holster with his hand. "Forget it. I dunno where'n hell I could lay my hands on one."

"There's yours, sir," Fortune said.

"You mean use mine?" Gluck retorted.

"I'd like to keep it," Fortune said.

Dumbfounded, outraged, Gluck whooped, "You want my balls, too?"

"I know you won't have a problem replacing a pistol, sir. After all, they get lost or stolen."

37

"Forget it, Fortune, forget it."

"Yes, sir," Fortune replied, seeming contrite, but then quickly adding in a fit of ultra-chutzpah, "including the Havanas, too, of course."

"You're a goddam sonofabitch, y'know. You want flesh," Gluck seethed. But he unbuckled his holster belt and tossed it on the worktable, where it bounced, undoing the fine adjustments I had just made in the transceiver. "You damn well better produce," he said as he stormed from the tent. A moment later he shouted back, "Pick up the fuckin' hooch at the officers' club, pronto."

In less than half an hour, Fortune and I were barreling down the dusty, two-lane shore road in his garish jeep. A case of whisky jounced precariously in the rear seat. Our outfit always had a copious supply of booze, for no doubt the Command considered libation as essential to ultimate victory as food and ammunition. Drinking was rooted in navy tradition. Billiard Ball reasoned that John Paul Jones must have been an alcoholic. The army units around us had no whisky at all, prompting Billard Ball to comment: "Thank heaven. If we expect to win the war, at least one of the services has to stay sober." The army boys, therefore, placed whisky on a par with women, a scarce commodity, valued far above most things.

Still, the army had certain goods either better suited to the tasks at hand than ours or oddly missing from our complement: radio equipment and medical supplies, for instance. And they seemed to have a well-balanced inventory of spare parts for their equipment, a proficiency we lacked. Since the Seabees was a land support force, a new and alien entity, perhaps the regular navy failed to comprehend us, which would account not only for our supply problem with critical items and the excess of so-called luxuries, but also for the clashes in policy that were to surface later on. The army's materiel was lighter and designed to keep the service mobile; ours was more cumbersome, requiring that we stay put. We were like ranchers; they were like frontiersmen.

Our destination was the rear echelon of an army hospital unit whose main body had moved to a forward base up the coast. "Medical units have everything," said Fortune. "It's just like in civilian life. Did you ever meet a doctor who was hard up?"

Judging by what we saw as we pulled into a remote clearing about twenty miles from the docks, the medical profession, at least in the army, was faring badly. Standing doubtfully in the high grass, its roof sagging and side flaps torn, was a long ramshackle tent. The crude sign dangling askew above its entrance at one end read: 1056 Medical Supply Unit, U.S. Army Medical Corps, Lt. R. A. Jenkins, O.C. Directly below the sign, sloppily painted on the olive canvas, appeared the slogan, "The Price Is Always Right." The initials O.C. meant officer in charge. Had Fortune made a mistake? "It's like the slums, only in the jungle," I said.

Upon entering the tent from the outdoor glare, I smelled the unmistakable aroma of cigar smoke. Fortune grinned, pleased that his hunch concerning this source was on the mark. But the question remained: Was it Havana smoke? Nothing less would do.

As my eyes became accustomed to the dimness, I could make out through floating streaks of blue haze a small unshaven man wearing a green undershirt and baggy GI trousers. A soggy cigar jutted from his stained lips. He was sitting behind a battered wooden desk, his booted feet resting on the desktop as he balanced himself precariously on the rear legs of a creaky oak office chair. A worn girlie magazine lay open on his lap. He seemed startled at our entrance

"Yeah?" he barked. Appearing to be in his mid-thirties, Fortune's contemporary, he wore no symbol of rank.

"Where can I find Lieutenant Jenkins?" asked Fortune.

"Who's askin'?" the man retorted without removing his stogey.

"I'm Lieutenant Fortune, Naval Construction Battalions. It's important that I see Lieutenant Jenkins; it's very urgent."

"I dunno if he's here. What's it about?"

"I'll tell him when I see him," said Fortune testily.

"We're gettin' ready to move out, y'know, an' we're busy as hell."

"We won't take much of his time; just mention 'whisky' to him. Will you do that?"

39

"Chris', you're dreamin', sailor, if you think we got whisky. I don't know why the hell every chickenshit outfit in Papua thinks we're some kind of PX." Disgusted, he slapped his thigh with the girlie magazine. "Jeez, now it's the fuckin' navy."

Fortune sat on a corner of the desk and thumped his knuckle on the top. "Wait a minute. You got it wrong, soldier. Tell your OC that we got the whisky."

"You got the hooch?" he screamed, unscrambling his feet from the desktop with such haste that he lost his balance. His chair fell backward against a tall stack of cartons which crashed down around him. As he struggled to disentangle himself, Fortune and I rushed to remove the boxes, which were so light as to seem empty. "Chris', you mean...you're not pullin' my leg now...you got the real stuff?"

"You bet, soldier," said Fortune, offering his hand. "Get your OC. Will you do that?"

"You got him, friend, comin' up from bein' on his ass, every goddamned miserable bone of him," said the man, grasping Fortune's hand and bounding to his feet. "Lieutenant Jenkins, that's me, always ready to do business. Pull up a crate and make yourself at home — your assistant too — and let's talk about this. Now what ya got?"

"The best...the finest Canadian," said Fortune.

"A case, ten cases, how much of it?"

"All depends, Lieutenant."

"Okay, okay, what're ya after?"

"Havana cigars, Lieutenant."

Jenkins removed the soggy stogey from the corner of his brownish lips. Holding it high between his thumb and forefinger, he studied the sad remnant momentarily. "It's a possibility, sailor, a definite possibility."

"I'm talking about Havanas, Lieutenant...only Havanas, not any old stogeys," Fortune emphasized.

Jenkins blinked as if hurt. "We ain't a chickenshit outfit, Lieutenant."

"I'm sure you're not...a trade with the best for the best, that's it, right?" said Fortune, satisfied that he had latched onto the real thing. "What do you say we drink to that?"

I ran out and retrieved a case of whisky from the jeep. Uncapping a bottle, Fortune poured neat portions into three paper cups that Jenkins had mined from one of his boxes. I sipped, making a wry face, while Fortune took his slowly. Jenkins swigged his down in a gulp and extended his cup for seconds. "It's the very best. I can see that you're not shittin' me, friend," Jenkins said exultantly.

Enhanced by the whisky, the two men warmed up to each other in anticipation of the terrific deal they were sure to make. A coincidence came to light: Both were born and raised in Detroit, and although they lived in different neighborhoods and attended different schools, they had indeed both played football, so they must have competed at some time or other. Need it be added that both were ardent Tiger fans? They lapsed into a lengthy and, for me, boring nostalgic excursion of their childhood during the prosperous twenties, when their town was burgeoning into the automobile capital of the world.

Soon the conversation turned to the present, and Jenkins, having a willing ear in Fortune, unloaded all his gripes, especially his bitterness at having been relegated to command an insignificant and practically forgotten remnant of his unit. He took it personally: Wasn't he good enough to be up there in the action with the rest of them? As he poured out his soul, Fortune poured more and more whisky, with a view to softening him up for the haggling.

I wondered at the coincidence of Fortune running into a fellow Detroiter. Or was it a coincidence? So often did situations just fall into Fortune's lap the way he wanted them, was it possible that he had planned them in advance? But if meeting Jenkins was a coincidence, how did Fortune learn of the medical unit, of its whereabouts, and its inventory of cigars?

My musings were interrupted by Jenkins' thick and robustious words: "Chris', I musht'uv tackled ya a tousand times." Fortune now had the lieutenant exactly where he intended to have him, inebriated and malleable.

When we departed Jenkins's private hellspot, our jeep was laden with a surfeit of loot, things we didn't really need for which we had no imaginable use. But so well did the bargaining go that Fortune couldn't resist overreaching himself and acquiring not only what he sought, but also whatever he considered might someday come in handy. His rationale was, "You can never tell what we'll run out of. At some time or other out here, everything is bound to become scarce."

"But not hundreds of hypodermic syringes. No way, not those," I argued, turning to look back at a half-dozen cases bouncing in our rear seat while we scurried from the clearing. Fortune smiled condescendingly. Had I missed something? Did I lack vision? We had no shot-in-the-arm drug culture back in 1944, at least not in the Seabees and not among the youth of our generation. We preferred alcohol. "Wait 'til the women come," Fortune said, "and we all get the clap, and they have to shoot stuff into us. They'll need a lot more than the few lousy syringes we got here."

Our treasure consisted of many more items than I can recall. But some stand out, among them the urine flasks, chosen because they would make excellent wine decanters; not only one but two cedar boxes of Havanas; and, best of all, a secretarial-sized office typewriter. It was Fortune's gift to me, which literally sent me into raptures of boundless appreciation. "Now you'll have more reason to write the Fox," he said. I was too excited to care about the small condition he had attached to his generosity.

After reaching the winding and pocked coastal dirt highway, Fortune accelerated the jeep, barely holding course on the curves as we swerved and rocked. High on his success, he was celebrating by speeding. Even under normal circumstances he seemed always in a hurry to get to his destination, as if time spent traveling was a waste, although once there he was remarkably patient, calm, deliberate and calculating.

"Slow down, Barry. Please. What's your hurry?" I pleaded, but to no effect, indeed quite the opposite; he seemed amused at my rising panic. Did I hear a siren? Out here? Had the idea not been absurd, I would have prayed for a cop. That wail, a city sound, was simply too incompatible with our surroundings to be real. But when I turned to look behind us, I saw a plume of dust in the distance stretching back along the highway. "Do you hear it?" I shouted. Extending his neck like a fleeing goose, tightening his lips and his grip on the steering wheel, Fortune floored the accelerator. "It's gaining on us," I said. "Maybe it's the shore patrol. Better stop, Barry."

"No Shore Patrol out here," he said, maintaining his concentration. I had to admire his skillful handling of the vehicle, and above all his professional coolness. "Betcha they've got a souped-up job," he said.

But our pursuers continued to close the gap, so that I could eventually make out a white MP insignia on the hood of their jeep. There were two men aboard waving their arms wildly and mouthing words, obscenities no doubt, which were impossible to hear above the screeching siren. Soon they were upon us, catching our dust. "They're MPs," I shouted, tugging at Fortune. "They're right behind. For God's sake, give up."

Then in a sudden surge, they drew alongside. Staring at us, their faces red with anger, they pressed ever closer, attempting to force our jeep off the road. Without warning, Fortune pulled away into a shallow ditch and slammed to a stop. Our pursuers, caught off guard, swept beyond, disappearing into a billow of yellow dust. But then we saw them turn around. "You're a dead duck, now," I said, disheartened. "Maybe both of us are."

"Just let me do the talking," Fortune said as the two MPs approached. The hefty one with two bars painted on his helmet, a captain's designation, hovered over us without speaking, no doubt needing time to bring his fury under control. Suddenly he reached for Fortune, clutched him by the shirt front, dragged him from his seat, and flung him to the ground, where he fell to his knees.

"Who in fucking hell do you think you are?" roared the MP captain. Unlike an ordinary man, who should have been cowed by such rage, Fortune remained impassive, offering no resistance, allowing the officer to do whatever he wished. The captain was a large, brutish man in his forties with an authoritarian manner, obviously accustomed to being heeded. Tearing into his silent, limp victim, he unraveled his blistering wrath, shaking Fortune from time to time and making him flounce in the dusty ditch like a rag doll. It was a scene of such utter humiliation for Fortune that in empathy I had to hold back tears.

In time the captain's anger was expended, after which there was a long silence while he recovered his equanimity. Fortune tried to speak, but no sooner would he begin than the captain would shut him off, saying, "Nothing, do you hear me, nothing can ever justify your goddamned audacity." He enunciated clearly.

"Sir," said Fortune, still on his knees, "I don't blame you for being sore as hell. Just hear me out."

"What's your outfit? Speak up, goddamn you. Who's your commanding officer? Speak up. You hear?" demanded the captain.

"Seventh Fleet, Seventy-sixth Naval Medical Unit, sir, and if you'll allow me, sir, I can explain why I couldn't stop."

The captain turned to me. "Drive the vehicle back to your unit, you hear, and report to your commanding officer. Tell him the army's incarcerating this man." I nodded in acknowledgment and slipped behind the wheel of our jeep.

"Our outfit isn't in the vicinity, sir," explained Fortune. "It's up the line, in action, sir, supporting the new MacArthur offensive. Unfortunately the marines are taking on a pile of casualties. You see, sir, we're a medical unit and I've been sent back down here to secure some badly needed medical supplies and—"

The captain cut in: "You say you're part of a medical unit?"

"Precisely, sir." Fortune asked that I break open a box of syringes. Calm now, the captain took note of them and of certain other items that were especially ambiguous, particularly the highly visible typwriter. "That," Fortune explained, anticipating the captain's skepticism, "will replace the one we lost in a direct hit on our headquarters. It's hell up there, sir. Right now a plane's waiting for us at the airstrip to take us back up. If you'll accept my apology, I'd appreciate it, sir, but I hope you can see why I didn't want to stop, being on such an urgent mission."

Mollified, motioning to his partner to aid Fortune, the captain ordered, "Get up, sailor. Get up off your knees."

Rising, Fortune massaged his legs. "Thank-you, sir."

Almost courteously, the captain added, "You should have told me you were on a special mission right off and we could have avoided this misunderstanding."

"I'm sorry, sir. Yes, I should have." As Fortune began dusting himself off, the captain helped, brushing his shoulders, and seemed relieved that our newly established hero showed no ill effects from his ordeal. It was an astonishing reversal of circumstances, taxing my capacity to fully grasp how it happened. Fortune had concocted a scenario so unquestionably credible that I, too, hadn't I known better, would have believed it.

But he hadn't fully extricated himself yet. The captain climbed into his jeep, while his driver leapt behind the wheel, and he waved his arm forward as if leading a cavalry charge. "We'll get you to the airstrip, sailor," he said. "Follow us." Then he shouted to his driver, "Let's move, damnit, the sailor's in a hurry."

One would think we had a pregnant woman aboard ready to give birth. With siren blaring, they rocketed down the road as we followed, choking in their funnel of dust, hardly able to see the tail end of their jeep. I confess having felt a thrill in being led by an escort, especially one that blatantly advertised our "importance." And there was a certain pleasure in pondering the twist of circumstances, in having our adversary transformed into benefactor.

But I knew also that we were being led into the unknown; the moment of reckoning was yet to come. For how long could Fortune continue the fiction he had created? How did he propose delivering us out of it?

"I'm working on it," he cackled, beaming over the prospect of another contest. "It all depends on what we find when we get there. But you can bet we'll find a way." There was no doubt that Fortune's earlier grandeur had returned.

As soon as we approached the dirt airstrip, a mere slash in the jungle, Fortune appraised the scene, observing the

45

array of aircraft parked in revetments: the sleek fighters, the bulbous bombers, and the cargo planes, and in particular a DC-3 parked on the edge of the strip itself, its side hatch door wide open and inviting, as if ready for loading and subsequent takeoff. We headed directly for it. "After I board her," Fortune explained, "hand up the cartons, and do it fast."

"Then what?" I asked, seeing in Fortune's tactics only delay and not a solution.

"Let me worry about that," he said brusquely.

The MP captain and his partner stood by, watching us as we carried on our charade. Then satisfied that their mission was complete, they took off with a wave, hollering, "Give those damn Japs hell up there."

Fortune hollered back, "See you in Manila."

After they had disappeared, we lay back on the floor of the fuselage, laughing, slapping each other, and congratulating ourselves. "Barry," I said, overwhelmed with admiration, "you can work miracles."

As I drove us back to our base, Fortune, feeling triumphant, relaxed and smoked a Havana. He had indeed given an unforgettable performance, a prelude perhaps to greater ones yet to come. After all, life's excitement lies in its surprises, in the suspense of not knowing what's going to happen next. Fortune had the knack of honing events into high drama. Suddenly, the future held promise, and my nagging premonition of inescapable doom at a tender age quietly disappeared.

IV
Finschafen

Settled In

Lucia Fox's reply arrived less than a month after I had written her. Apparently my letter passed the censors intact; after all, what could have warranted deletion? But one never knew what would or would not get through. I resented the censorship, the invasion of my privacy, especially as my correspondence with Lucia developed into a personal drama, laden with the complexities of powerful and ambivalent feelings. It was troubling to suspect censors acting, in my view, as nothing more than voyeurs watching the progression of our relationship. I knew who they were, and some were among the battalion's intellectual elite; Billiard Ball was one of them, although he said he never examined his closest friends' letters. I avoided befriending them.

(Many years later after the war during a battalion reunion, when I would have welcomed that someone remembered my letters to Lucia, I learned that my suspicions about the censors were unfounded. No one had really known or cared. Such is the self-consciousness of youth.)

"My dearest Hal," Lucia's reply began with a warmth that made me blush. I was unaccustomed to terms of endearment. "I can't thank you enough for writing and for offering to keep me informed of my beloved Barry. I do so worry about him. He always works too hard, giving little thought to his own well-being. I hope you will join me in trying to slow him down. And please encourage him to be careful. So often I have seen him do foolhardy and dangerous things."

Her words, like those of a concerned mother, were uniquely appealing, reminding me of my own mother, whose love I cherished. I found irresistible Lucia's plea for a partnership in so noble a mission as caring for a friend. How

47

well she knew her Barry! I was hooked by the end of the first paragraph.

The letter continued: "I should confess that I expected to receive your letter. In one of his all too short and infrequent notes, Barry told me of your friendship, and of how sensible you are. I know you will be a good influence on him. Please, please write again. I miss him so very much. I cannot tell you how much your letters will help." She signed her letter, "Most gratefully yours, Lucia."

Persuaded now that I should stay on as Fortune's surrogate correspondent, I nevertheless felt unsure of where the role would lead. Could I really be effective in moderating Fortune's excesses? Wasn't it the other way around, he usually coaxing me into participating in his escapades despite my feeble protests? But who could blame me for trying to save myself from all that deadening monotony, that unutterable boredom in that vaporous palm forest?

The very correspondence itself was bound to brighten my day. How intriguing it would be, I thought, to remain uninvolved yet the sustaining link in their relationship. Perhaps it would give me some hold over Fortune in the event things ever got out of hand and he called in my debt to him. That was my father's voice, I suppose, warning me to protect myself. And there was another consideration that I dared not admit to myself. It was Lucia herself, whose letter had so impressed me with its lovingness and apparent good sense and honest realism. I wanted to learn about her and become her friend.

Once the early surge of demand slackened for goods that Fortune could procure, his business began to run out of steam. Becoming restless, he embarked on exploratory forays into the hinterland and I accompanied him. As if obsessed he ceaselessly searched for native villages, the more primitive the better. When he found one, he mingled with the natives, trying to communicate in sign language, thoroughly enjoying himself and they him. I had never seen him so happy and uninhibited, so unguarded, so free and open. When long ago the natives nursed him and carried him to the jungle hospital in Burma, he had neglected to thank them for saving his life. Perhaps he was doing it now over and over again.

On one such occasion, we traveled by jeep for miles along a rough and deteriorating corduroy road deep into the hilly hinterland, then for several miles more by foot to a primitive village of pygmies who practiced, Fortune advised me as we entered their compound, ceremonial cannibalism. But he hastened to assure me that they were reputedly unwarlike and ate only their own kind. Even so I was suspicious, seeing them as somehow soiled and repulsive, and I begged him not to linger. Ignoring me, he plunged into their midst.

Most of them had bloated stomachs and black smiles; what few teeth they had left were darkened from chewing on betel nuts. Although they seemed happy and good-natured, I remained wary as several emerged from their conical grass huts and surrounded me, all the while jabbering, no doubt sizing me up as a potential morsel. Many had dabs of white in varied patterns decorating their faces and bodies; others were dressed in flashy regalia. They were surely ready for a party—a feast of human flesh.

I did a double take when I saw a white man and woman wearing British tans and pith helmets, sally forth from one of the thatched huts. Ignoring us, encircled by a swarm of prancing pygmies, they ambled to a small thatch-roofed gazebo raised high on stilts in the middle of the village clearing. The natives nearby immediately lost interest in Fortune and myself and joined the throng. Led by the white man and woman, they burst into a pidgin English chorus of the British national anthem followed by "Rule Brittania." So stirring and powerful were the lady's high soprano and the gentleman's tenor voices that I too joined in, nudging a reluctant Fortune to do likewise.

So much for Fortune's search for excitement and danger. He didn't seem to appreciate my jibes on the trip back. "Since when have the pygmies converted the British to cannibalism?" I asked. "I suppose they always sing 'Rule Brittania' before carving up their victim."

◄ When Wars Were Won ►

During this phase of our unit's operation, settling in and then waiting for the big assignment, make-work projects were devised to keep us busy: policing the grounds for cigarette butts, having daily bunk inspection, and from time to time, when our leaders ran out of ideas, doing close order drill. The enthusiasm so prevalent on our arrival was waning; a laxity was insinuating itself into our daily lives. The boredom was perverse. We yearned for some action even if it offered the possibility of dying.

I finished *War and Peace*, saddened that it was over. Few of us were readers except Billard Ball, one of my three tent-mates. He read mostly books in French, but there were also heavy Chinese tomes in his footlocker that he occasionally pored over. His English reading consisted only of poetry: Eliot, Pound, and Auden.

On Sunday afternoons Billiard Ball and I often ambled along the beach discussing our books and life in general. "I don't self-indulge by reading novels," he volunteered. When I asked if he had read *War and Peace* and been impressed by its sweep and magnificence, he stopped to stare at the ocean and smile at my seriousness. "Tolstoy depicted a world of innocence. It doesn't apply to us."

"How can you say that?" I argued, placing myself before him with my back to the sea. "He showed the horror and confusion of war. And strategy hasn't changed, nor has the Russian winter. It's defeated the Nazis too."

Sighing, Billiard Ball scowled and lowered his eyes to mine. "The scale of things is different now," he explained. "The whole world is in flames and nothing is untouched. Look out there." He motioned toward the sea. "Cook and Gaugin found a paradise; now it's a bloody hell." He fell into a brooding silence, then announced, "Keep your dreams. We all need them, so ignore me." When I asked him what his dreams were, he replied, "I don't dream anymore."

Though Billiard Ball wasn't happy with his lot as a lowly member of a Seabee battalion, he accepted it. His pessimism was based more on a cosmic view of things. Yet we were unaware of the Holocaust in progress then, nor could we have imagined the capability for obliterating humanity that would be revealed to us in little more than a year hence. We were a generation of comparative innocents living in a time when wars could still be won. But I'm not sure that Billiard Ball, a man before his time, believed so.

In the heat of the afternoon, we resumed our walk along the shimmering beach, glancing now and then at the rumbling turquoise sea. "Home's out there," I said sadly, scooping up some sand and sifting it through my fingers. "I wonder if we'll ever see it again."

"Oh yes," Billiard Ball said, briefly hugging me to him, "you and I will always manage. We're survivors."

V
Finschafen

A Good Man for the Battalion

Commander Jeremiah "Jerry" Rutledge's patience was drawing increasingly thin as we sat tight and the war progressed implacably northward. Finschafen had become little more than a recuperation area for the troops needing a brief respite from the strain of battle. Rutledge yearned for an opportunity to show our mettle, to meet a crisis that would require a superhuman effort, never doubting that the outcome would be anything but victorious. He prized his command, dedicating himself to its cause every waking and sleeping moment. Constantly functioning at a steady high, his presence ubiquitous, he never displayed weariness. Impatient for that special mission, that big action, that strategic assignment, for which our battalion was cast from its first day in the Camp Peary drill hall, he envisioned a major construction project, a sub base or a harbor for at least cruiser-class vessels. He knew it would be, it had to be, something fundamental to the advance of the armed forces.

The battalion was hardly a formidable military organization; our combat training was too superficial. Still we were psychologically prepared to defend ourselves. As the commander said, "Our job is to build, not destroy." He took special satisfaction in that feature of our role, but he added, "If we must, we'll fight and then, by God, the Japs had better watch out because we're unbeatable. Right, men?" He took his own exhortations very seriously, and although his officers seemed bored, the rest of us were genuinely stirred.

My first personal contact with Commander Rutledge occurred during our month-long stay at a training camp in Gulfport, Mississippi. "Sir, I wish to put in a request for transfer," I said meekly, my lips gone dry, while standing at attention before his desk. Along with a stream of others, I was taking him at his word. "Remember, men," he had said time and again, "my door is always open to anyone with a grievance." Understandably this was an unpopular policy with the officers, who grumbled at what they interpreted as an undermining of their authority. However, since he had little faith in either the navy's or his officers' high-handed methods, that was precisely what the commander intended. No matter how petty his men's grievances, he always listened attentively and nodded sympathetically. And his answer was forever the same, a laudatory refrain: "You're a good man for the battalion."

In desperation, having become distraught over weeks of demeaning KP duty, and after repeated vain appeals for relief up the chain of command, I sought an interview with Rutledge. My morale had broken after being assigned to a daily detail whose task consisted of emptying and cutting off tops and bottoms of reeking, maggot-ridden cans of rotting creamed corn.

"So you want to do something important, eh?" the commander said, making a tent with his hands as he sat behind his desk. "Well, I hope you can see it would be a mistake to transfer to some two-bit outfit where you'd be worse off, especially with all the opportunity we have to offer right here. Of course every job's important, mind you, even KP." Rising he walked to my side of the desk and placed an arm over my shoulder. "But I understand your predicament, son. Doing those menial jobs is hell, eh?" He shook his head, emphasizing his compassion. "At ease, son, at ease. Be assured it's only temporary. I can see you're a bright young man, and at the proper time we'll fit you into a slot that will suit your abilities."

To control my elation I stared at a framed photo of Franklin Roosevelt, which stood on a corner of his desk. "Our battalion, my boy," he continued in a seductively confidential manner, "has a great destiny, and you would do well to be a part of it. Y'know, son, I wouldn't swap a single man here, and that includes you. Your chief tells me you're a hard worker, a fine man for the battalion. So have patience. Return to your regular duty and we'll call you soon enough to do something more to your liking."

Before I realized that the interview was over, he gently led me by the elbow to the door and saluted. "Thank-you for coming to see me, son. I need more men like you. You're a good man for the battalion."

Suddenly lighthearted, no less affected than if I had communed with FDR himself, I departed with a lilt in my stride. Even after learning much later that my encounter with the commander scarcely differed from that of many others who requested transfers, my admiration never waned. I would always be "his" man.

The commander's enthusiasm and sense of mission were compelling and electric, and his patrician appearance, his self-assured demeanor, inspired confidence and hope. In his mid-fifties, tall, lithe, and forever smiling, his angular face bronzed and weathered, his hair always groomed in sculptured silver wavelets, he would have passed for a maturing movie star. Perhaps the enlisted men's adulation was excessive, but it was understandable. Rejecting navy tradition, Rutledge favored these men, providing for their comfort and well being, often at the expense of his officers. As a result, tensions between himself and his staff were rife, giving him occasion to erupt into uncontrollable fits of temper. Added to this was his frustration at marking time and accomplishing nothing.

Despite Fortune's early favorable impression of the commander, he soon adopted an ambivalent and somewhat tentative view of him. On the one hand he approved of Rutledge's disdain for his officers' creature comforts, and he was especially delighted with reports of his friction with the Command. And those temper tantrums were downright enchanting. On the other hand Fortune was repelled by "that goddamn pap the commander spouted, that can-do, superbattalion, great destiny shit." Fortune admitted being puzzled. Did the commander actually believe his own line, or was it a manipulative technique to motivate us? And if both were true, then our leader had to be functioning on the fine edge of madness. His fanatic dedication to a goal, his idealistic behavior and patriotic zeal incited Fortune to a frenzy of disgust. Despite this, midway through our stay at Finschafen, the commander and Fortune discovered each other and formed a symbiotic relationship.

It began in the commander's private office tent which contained a blond wooden desk and chair at one side facing the entrance steps and a bare, little used cot at the opposite side. Due to the arrival of the monsoon season a thick coating of mud had been tracked onto the plywood floor.

The commander's jeep was laid up in the transportation shed awaiting the replacement of its worn-out rotor that was expected to arrive on the next supply ship at some indefinite time in the future. After a few days, the commander's patience exhausted, he commandeered a rotor from one of the junior officer's jeeps, thus restoring his own to service. But most of the rotors in most of the jeeps seemed to be especially vulnerable and similarly worn, so that in only a few weeks, as the commander claimed one rotor after another up through the ranks, right to Gluck himself, every jeep in the battalion, including, finally, the commander's very own, was disabled; Every jeep, that is, save one. It was seen zipping about here and there, bearing a distinctive fox emblem on its proud hood.

It was a sad and dismal sight to see the battalion's jeeps, stored neatly arrayed in silent rows, deteriorating under the moist palms beside Chief "Bull" Dunham's transportation shed. Tempers flared easily among the officers as they resentfully slogged through the mud on foot.

"By heaven, Gluck," the commander fumed, "I say to hell with the goddamned Command." He pounded his desk so hard his blotter jumped and the photo of FDR fell over. "If it doesn't float, they're not interested. They're sinking us on land, Gluck."

"They're SOBs, Jerry," Gluck commiserated. "They'll never understand us. Maybe you and I made a mistake. We should'a joined the Army Corps of Engineers instead."

Ignoring Gluck's uneasy remark which smacked of battalion disloyalty, the commander said, "It's a simple matter of educating the navy to the realistic needs of a land force. That's all it is."

"Wal," said Gluck, "I say it's a heluva way to run a campaign. First they don't give us any ammunition and now it's rotors." Exactly how bullets would be used in peaceful Finschafen was a question that never occurred to Gluck. Once again he sported a sidearm at the hip, a new, pearl-handled affair. Swaggering about, his ego reconditioned, he was in top form, ready to attack any obstacle that stood in his way. He awaited Rutledge's assent.

"Get Chief Dunham in here," Commander Rutledge suddenly thundered at Lieutenant Commander Gluck, who frequently suffered the brunt of Rutledge's frustration. "I want to get to the bottom of this goddamned rotor situation once and for all."

Fearing a violent outburst of the commander's roiling impatience, Gluck immediately sent a messenger after Dunham. In only moments Dunham appeared and stood breathless at attention before the commander.

"You mean to tell me you can't find a solitary goddamned rotor in the entire area?" the commander demanded.

"That's right, sir," Bull replied in hoarse, blunt New Yorkese. "I'm afraid there's none nowhere." Indeed Bull was more disgusted than the commander over the rotor shortage. In civilian life, having operated an automotive repair garage for taxis in midtown Manhattan, he was accustomed to frequent emergencies and being under pressure. But he made sure he always had a sufficient supply of spare parts.

"Well, maybe you ought to try the Japs up the line in Wewak," the commander said sarcastically.

"Yes, sir. Uh, no, sir," Bull answered, blinking from the commander's sting.

"Damn," Gluck piped in, "gimme a platoon and ammo and if those SOBs got some, I'll get 'em."

"Be at ease, Dunham," the commander said, noting Bull's stiffening stance and ignoring Gluck's absurd offer. "The fact is there have to be rotors on this goddamned island, right, Dunham?" At each word he thumped his fist on his green desk blotter. "And you damn well know where they are."

Baffled, Bull scratched his stubbly cheeks with a crevassed, grease impregnated hand. In his early fifties, he was one of the "old" men of the outfit. "I'm not sure I getcha, Commander," he said.

"Well, just look around, Chief. Just look out there." The commander pointed to the entrance through which the sultriness of a grey afternoon seeped in. "There's one in every jeep that passes on the coast road."

"Wal, I'll be," Gluck exclaimed. "That's a capital idea, Jerry, downright capital. Why'n hell didn't I think of that?"

Chief Dunham, usually alert and unflappable, felt the need to confirm the commander's point. "You mean...?"

"Exactly," the commander interrupted, his face becoming red. "I don't give a damn if you have to steal them. Is that clear, Chief?"

Considering himself unjustly put upon, Bull boiled within. His job was to order what was needed, not procure it. If, despite having run out of replacement parts, he had kept many a ten-wheel truck or bulldozer or diesel generator going, he did so by calling on Fortune. The commander and Gluck were unappreciative bastards. They took his past efforts for granted.

"Y'know, Jerry, speakin' of those army jeeps runnin' around out there, we still got one operating in the battalion. Isn't that keerect, Chief?" Gluck demanded of Dunham. Agitated Bull shifted his eyes back and forth from Gluck to the commander, and nodded. "Fortune's chariot, keerect, Chief?" Gluck pressed on. The air within the tent was thick and still. Wet blotches appeared in the armpits of Gluck's rumpled tan shirt. Bull rubbed away pearls of sweat forming on his forehead with the back of his hairy hand. "So it's a simple matter of just taking the rotor from his jeep, keerect, Chief? And, by the way, that brings me to the real big question: What keeps Fortune's jeep goin'? You know the answer to that, Chief? He got a special rotor or somethin'?"

"Good question, Gluck," chimed in the commander. "What's your explanation, Dunham?"

Torn between saving his own skin and Fortune's, Bull abandoned his usual coolness and blurted, "Somehow he keeps finding new rotors for himself."

57

"Y'mean you've replaced more than one of his?" the commander pursued.

"I just put in his thoid, sir."

"Goddamned Fortune," Gluck whined.

As the war of the islands stretched further away to the east and north, and the sea battles intensified, the frequency of supply ships slowed to the point that often even food had to be rationed. Fortune had begun accumulating critical items, especially things that wore out. His sources, always unorthodox, were, of course, secret, and the location of his cache even more so. "The stuff is out there among the damned cannibals," he would say cryptically. "They'll eat anyone who gets near it."

Bull Dunham had a special arrangement with Fortune, providing automotive services in exchange for needed parts. As part of the deal, Bull promised to give top priority to any maintenance and repair work on Fortune's jeep, such as tune-ups, lube jobs, washes, and waxing. Bull even installed super-shocks and a fresh canvas roof supplied by Fortune. But it galled the chief to be so beholden to Fortune, a mere first class petty officer, and to be at his beck and call. One of these days he would tell him to shove it.

"Bull's my man," I heard Fortune crow. "I've got him right here under my thumb." Fearing that he would be blamed if he let the Transportation Department collapse, Bull felt he had no choice but to accept Fortune's behind the scenes support. And after seeing Gluck's and the commander's panic over the rotor situation, his fear was confirmed. Still, he was troubled at risking the Fortune connection to save himself.

"Christ, Fortune runs rings around the whole lot of you," the commander exclaimed, sitting back in his chair, and shaking his head in admiration. "Let's get him in here and see what else he's got up his sleeve."

Standing at ramrod attention before the commander's desk, Fortune feigned his most pliable demeanor. Contritely beside him stood Bull whom he assumed had spilled the beans about their deal. "They tell me you have your own jeep," the commander said, his eyes piercing and accusatory. "Not bad, not bad at all for a petty officer."

Since this was old news, indeed common knowledge for some time, Fortune awaited a clue as to what the commander was getting at. "Yes, sir, I find it very useful in doing my job at communications."

"And they also say you have a corner on distributor rotors," said the commander. "Is that right?" He glanced at Gluck, expecting his approbation.

Dunham shifted his feet.

"You could say I had access to some, sir," Fortune replied.

"Access to some, eh?"

"That's right, sir."

"And you're aware you have the only jeep in the battalion currently operating?"

"No, sir. I didn't know that."

"Now cut the shit," Gluck interjected. "This is the commander you're talking to."

"Of course he knows he's got the only functional jeep, Gluck," the commander said with a short laugh, "and I'll bet he knows I know he knows. Don't you, Fortune?"

"Yes, sir," Fortune said, unable to stifle a grin.

"Well, let's start at the beginning, eh?" said the commander. "Tell me how it's done—the jeep for instance."

"Very simple, sir. I traded a case of Scotch for it."

"You mean to say—you mean that's all? Nothing more?" The commander seemed to need a moment to recover from his astonishment. "At ease, Fortune, be at ease."

Loosened and unworried, Fortune explained. "Commander, the army will trade anything for hard stuff. They're nothing but a bunch of deprived alcoholics." Although his exaggeration was intended to be facetious, his fresh memory of Lieutenant Jenkins gave it some credence.

"On that, I'll agree, Jerry," Gluck said. "Maybe we got our problems with the Command and all that, but the army's a second-rate outfit, can't compare with us." For a moment Gluck had overlooked the fact that a wet navy is often a drunken navy.

"Come, come, Gluck, didn't I just hear you praising the Corps of Engineers? MacArthur is doing an outstanding job, wouldn't you say?"

59

"Wal, MacArthur, sure, sure," said Gluck, hastening to explain. "I'm not including him, y'unnerstand."

"Now tell me about the rotors, Fortune," the commander said, his mood relaxed and conciliatory. "The chief tells me there aren't any spares to be found on the island."

"Because you got 'em all stashed away someplace, right, Fortune?" said Gluck.

"I never said Fortune was hoarding them, sir," Bull quickly interrupted.

"I know that Chief Dunham has his hands full keeping the equipment running," Fortune explained calmly, "so I help him out once in a while."

"Cut out the pussyfooting, Fortune," Gluck snapped, placing his hand on his holster as if he were about to retrieve his gun. "Come clean. How many you got?"

"Forty-seven, last time I counted, sir," Fortune replied proudly and without hesitation.

"What did I tell ya, Jerry. I know this man," Gluck said.

"Just a minute," the commander said in amazement. "You mean to say you have almost four dozen rotors?"

"Yes, sir."

"How did you manage to come by this treasure trove?" Keeping his eyes glued to Fortune's, the commander rose from his chair, walked from behind his desk, and stood facing him.

"They come from the army junkyard," Fortune said casually.

"What junkyard?" Bull shrieked, forgetting that his superiors were the interrogators.

"About twenty miles south of here. I got the rotors off forty-seven wrecks for forty-eight cans of beer."

Of course had he realized the battalion's desperate plight, Fortune assured the commander, he would certainly have given Bull the parts. This was unadulterated falsehood. Bull had pleaded with Fortune for help, but because he had nothing more to offer in return beyond what he was already giving, Fortune refused him. Still, Bull chose not to contradict Fortune's phony excuse. When he needed spark plugs, or brake shoes and linings, or fan belts, they were his for the asking.

Commander Rutledge seemed to see in Fortune a young Ford or Rockefeller, a true entrepreneurial spirit, a man living by his wits who thrived on getting things done. He placed his hand on Fortune's shoulder. "You're a mighty good man for the battalion, son." Fortune beamed, elated by his redemption.

From that day on, Bull Dunham's Transportation Department prospered, with every jeep and piece of idle equipment reactivated. Rutledge declared Fortune a hero; Gluck declared him no better than a sleazy Arab wheeler-dealer straight from the bazaars. Fortune, thinking he had the commander's blessing in every undertaking, became more and more daring. Gluck had been right about Fortune's fatal flaw, which I had only just discovered: He had no sense of where his limits lay, of where to draw the line beyond which the risk becomes overwhelming. I had to admit that the line for Fortune lay far beyond the perimeter of most mortals; indeed there were moments when I thought it had disappeared beyond the horizon.

VI
Finschafen

Springtime in New Guinea

"**P**assover is approaching," said Billiard Ball, my esteemed gentile friend, as I lay on my cot reading. "I hear a Jewish chaplain at an army unit up the coast is giving a seder for anyone who wishes to attend."

"Really?" I said evasively, preferring to concentrate on re-reading the final pages of *War and Peace*.

"Perhaps you could find some time in your busy schedule to join me in commemorating the historic flight of the Jews from Egyptian bondage," Billiard Ball said acidly. "You're Jewish, aren't you?"

Religion, God, ritual—they held no meaning for me. I had been rebelling most of my youthful life against American Jewish practitioners who, expecting me to conform, took it for granted that I believed as they did. Thus alienated from my ethnic group, I found comfort instead in my identity as an American.

"I'm not really interested," I said.

"That's shameful," he said. I squirmed, distracted, unable to resume my reading. "With Jews like you, how do you expect your co-religionists to preserve their ethnicity? In a few centuries your people will become as extinct as dodo birds."

"What's it to you, a lousy gentile," I countered.

"Because it's essential that our country retain its ethnic diversity. As our originality declines the more we become the same," he replied in a professorial tone. "Of course it's a losing battle, but why hasten it?" I was unmoved, and unresponsive. "Then what the hell am I worrying about? I'm a fool concerning myself with future generations when the whole damn world's heading backwards."

He pricked my guilt feelings. True, I never succeeded in actually denying my heritage, rooted in a Russian past only a generation away. Yes, I was an American, but I was more than that. Billiard Ball understood: I belonged without belonging; I was a Jew, a nonpracticing one perhaps, yet one because the world said I was.

"I've been to seders before," I said defensively.

"Oh, I'm not surprised," he said. "You can't be all non-Jew."

"Actually it's rather heartwarming. It's being together that does it," I said.

"Not the ritual? Not its meaning?" he asked.

"No, it does nothing for me."

"You read from the Torah, don't you?" In fact he knew the ritual cold as well as the story behind it.

"Yes, we take turns reading from the Torah."

"Then you'll change your mind and join me?" he asked. I agreed and informed him that it was in English for those who couldn't read Hebrew.

"I'm quite able to handle the Hebrew," he said dogmatically.

"Damn right. I forgot," I said.

Actually it would do me good to commemorate Passover. After all, what other proof was there that spring had truly arrived? April was upon us, but one could never tell in that musty, unchanging climate of worn green vegetation. I missed those tiny precious signs of renewal: a crocus tip pressing up through the earth, the tree buds bulging, seeming to become alert. I missed the northern spring burst of freshness, of lengthening days. My inner rhythm, it seemed, demanded it and felt deprived.

"Good," Billiard Ball said. "We'll go to the seder together, I as your gentile guest and..."

"No, no," I interrupted, "you've got it wrong. I'm your gentile guest." He laughed enjoying my too-obvious attempt at being witty. "Would you mind if I asked someone else to join us?"

"Of course not," he rejoined.

"Fortune. He's Jewish, too, y'know."

After remaining silent for a moment while coping with his surprise, he said, "Don't you think he has much more in common with the Egyptian Pharoahs than his own people?"

Fortune and I never made reference to our common religious and ethnic background, yet somehow we assumed a kinship, an unspoken understanding. Perhaps we knew from casual expressions or references to relatives whose names were typically Jewish. No doubt it was a powerful factor in establishing a bond between us. Furthermore he seemed to be no more spiritually inclined than I, nor less alienated. Here was a man who would let me be a heathen, if that's what I was, a man who would not judge me.

By contrast Jewish society in my hometown of Newton, Massachusetts, was judgemental and narrowly ethnocentric. I preferred to mingle in the melting pot and become assimilated. To be anything else was suffocating. My parents expected me to attend Friday night services, which I found meaningless. They expected me to join Jewish youth organizations whose members consisted mostly of rich, self-centered, crude young men whose interests centered on comparing notes about the nice Jewish girls they had screwed in succession during previous weekends. Then, of course, I was expected to marry my own kind, a stricture virtually handed down from Moses himself. Why was it that the only girls in high school whom I found attractive, whom I admired and in some instances loved from afar, were always gentiles? And why was it that none of them seemed able to abide me? Was it because I was Jewish or simply because I looked like an awkward young giraffe? Better neither, but if it had to be, better the latter.

Being in the service certainly satisfied my need to be incorporated into the national fabric, yet Billiard Ball somehow plucked a deeper chord within me—the need to affirm the sources of my being. "You don't seem to realize who you are," Billiard Ball had said. "You're nothing more than a small part of a continuum, but that in itself is a responsibility. Where's your perspective?" Always seeing things on a cosmic scale, he gradually influenced my thinking, both bringing me out of myself and providing a glimpse of the confusing depths within.

He was the definitively educated man; of course, the navy didn't know what to do with him. Of what use was his academic brilliance, of having acquired the highest learning our civilization offers, of having the capacity to see far beyond our petty circumstances, of having the ability to teach and inspire? What could he possibly offer toward building airstrips, roads, docks? So he joined that repository of useless souls, the KP gang, of which he was undoubtedly its most illustrious member.

Awed by his encyclopedic sophistication in virtually any subject, I held Billiard Ball in the highest regard. Only later did I discover his flaws and, later still, forgive him for having them. There were also others in the KP gang with college degrees and impressive civilian credentials, one of whom was an oil geologist named Blackall, a frequent visitor to our tent. The two would enter into discussions far beyond my ken on such subjects as relativity, the uncertainty principle, painters of the Italian renaissance, transcendental meditation, the Bhagavad-Gita, ancient Hebraic literature, and the significance of the Confucian era. Once I overheard them discussing the geology of the Venice, California oil drilling channel, on which Blackall was an expert. Yet Billard Ball was able to hold his own, using technical terms that demonstrated suprisingly comprehensive knowledge of the field. If there was anything Billiard Ball didn't know, I hadn't discovered it.

He also predicted Fortune's reaction to my invitation to a seder: "If he agrees to go, there has to be something in it for him," he snorted.

True to prediction, Fortune's reply in response to my invitation was, "Don't waste my time. I've got more important things to do."

Using Billard Ball's argument I said, "If we're Jews we should act like Jews. Don't you realize there are fewer and fewer of us left?"

"Well I'm not denying what I am," Fortune protested.

Seeing I had struck a sensitive spot, I said, "Yes, but you're not exactly declaring it either."

"Who else will be there?"

"How in hell do I know. A lot of Jews. Some army nurses too, I suppose."

My reference to nurses seemed to clinch it. "Okay, we'll drive up in my jeep," he said.

"That isn't what I had in mind," I told him. The commander had arranged for a ten-wheel truck to transport the ten or so of us wishing to attend the seder. Since our unit had only a Protestant chaplain, a highly moral and dedicated man who sincerely tried to minister to us all, the commander was nevertheless sympathetic to the minorities who were "left out." Here was an opportunity to make it up to us, and Gluck concurred: "I got nothin' against helpin' out our Jew boys."

"We're all going up together in a truck," I explained to Fortune. I rather looked forward to the event with some excitement. Unexpectedly I found myself wanting to be among my own people, even to travel together. It really wasn't enough to be an American and a Seabee, not out there. I longed for a more warmly human association—my family. And this was the nearest thing to it.

"Don't be ridiculous," Fortune said, meaning that riding in the back of a truck was beneath him. "You'll drive up with me—in style." We argued, and the more he insisted the more adamantly I refused, until it became a contest, expanding completely out of proportion to the apparently minor issue involved. "After all I've done for you," he finally said, "you owe me something."

"Yes, you're right," I replied, overwhelmed with indignation and outrage, "but no longer. I mean it this time. I'm requesting a transfer to KP." The argument was over. Silenced, realizing he had gone too far, he watched me storm off in blind anger.

When I got back to my tent, where I found Billiard Ball engrossed in reading his Chinese tome, I felt oddly lighthearted and free, as if I had just cast off a heavy burden. "We can forget Fortune," I said bitterly. "He's not interested." Detecting my agitation, Billiard Ball lowered his book and waited for me to reveal more. "I'm going to be your KP buddy again," I said, and after a moment's thought added, "Y'know, for once, I don't think I'll mind."

"It's really not so bad. There are compensations," he reassured me. "Look at it this way: Maybe we can't do a thing with our hands, but remember, we're the brainy ones, the intellectual elite of the outfit. I see it as a golden opportunity."

"For what?" I demanded.

"Well, to resume your education."

"My what?"

"We've got a historian, a philosopher, a mathematician, an astronomer, a geologist, and myself. What do you say? Maybe we could start you with some Plato and take you right up through Bergson. How would you like that?"

"You're humoring me," I groaned.

"Absolutely not. I'm dead serious." And so began my college education more than two years before I had a chance to formally enroll.

Despite KP, the segment of my Seabee career upon which I was about to embark turned out to be surprisingly happy. The camaraderie among the KPs was spirited and gratifying; never complaining, always laid back, with nothing to gain or lose, they were a good-natured, brilliantly witty group of intelligent human beings, quite unlike the fast operators of Fortune's scheming outfit who were so intensely competitive and serious. In place of the adventurous escapades with Fortune, I found another kind of excitement as a witness to scintillating, mind-boggling conversations and as a student of those smothered intellects who ached to teach and become again what they once were. They infected me with an enthusiasm for the learning disciplines and a sense of wonder that has lasted to this day. I can never be idle, never for a minute be without a book or involved in an experience that doesn't enlighten. Never letting up on me, they made learning a veritable way of life, a durable compulsion.

Billiard Ball was the most assiduous teacher of them all. Even as we stood next to each other behind the counter serving dinner, he would have me conjugate a French verb, or quiz me on a tract from St. Thomas Aquinas. But he gave me much more: a part of himself, and an enriching, caring friendship upon which I came to depend and return in kind. Not until much later did I realize in an instant of shattering revelation how deep it had gone.

At the time, the saddest consequence of my rift with Fortune lay in the likely conclusion of my correspondence with Lucia Fox. Since Fortune was its raison d'etre, how could

I or she justify its continuation? I would miss her cheery words and kind expressions and, most of all, her growing dependence on me. That ineffably trusting nature and selfless caring for Fortune were so refreshing and such a contrast to the ways of warriors. And now that my letters were a significant factor in nurturing their love, I was concerned that it might wane and that she would be hurt. What could I tell her? I wrote: "It seems that Barry and I aren't getting along lately; we're not seeing eye to eye on a lot of things, but I want you to know that I wish him only well, and if he needed me in a crisis you can be sure I'd be there."

I may have been less than honest. Those soft words belied my hard feelings, my growing disillusionment with a man who was my benefactor, and whom I knew I still cared about. My short note continued: "Barry is a most fortunate man to have your love. I wish you both happiness after the war, when I know you will be together. Thank-you from the bottom of my heart for your friendship. Please understand why it is better that I no longer write." Perhaps the real question was, did I understand why.

"How can you read that trash?" Billiard Ball asked in exasperation, pointing to *Gone with the Wind* lying on our tent table. "Don't you see that sort of material won't last? Ten years from now it'll be forgotten."

In between my more scholarly reading assignments, I managed to find time for pleasure reading, but in that I also had a higher purpose. It was a quest for perspective, for a keener understanding of what war does to us, what it was doing to me. I thought I would learn more from fiction than history.

Contrary to Billiard Ball's claim, I was struck with the uncanny similarity of the world of *War and Peace* and my own world. There was the same playing out of vast heroic dreams and overweening ambition, the same strategic blunders and the same chaos despite fanatical attempts to control it. When I picked up *Gone with the Wind* I saw the scenario repeated.

68

Yet though both books dealt with the passing of an era, I failed to perceive in them any similarity with the transiency of my own, that I too was actually living through the passing of another era. If I survived the war, I imagined that I would return to what I had left. How could I have known then that I was participating in the last war to be won, that soon no corner of the world would escape the possibility of obliteration? How could I have known then that American society would never again be as unified, that in a few years it would tear at itself in a torment of shame over the blind use of massive military power? Our goal then was so marvelously simple: the preservation of our threatened nation. Who would have dreamed that the goal would become even simpler: world survival. Those who died never doubted that the world would go on forever, but the rest of us lived to doubt. It was an era of innocence, no less obsolete and irrelevant to today's dangers than the Southern Confederacy and the Napoleonic campaigns.

"Here, read this instead," said Billiard Ball, handing me a book he had just retrieved from his footlocker. "Do you know it?" It was Thomas Mann's *The Magic Mountain*.

"No," I said. I reminded him that he had given up on fiction.

"With exceptions, always with exceptions, my friend. This is one of my favorites, the story of a consumptive young man in a remote sanitarium. The hero considers the question of involvement, of whether or not to participate in the active world."

"What choice is there?" I asked.

"We have none really," he said and then he sighed. "Damn, what I'd give to find such a mountaintop. They'd never get me down."

VII
Finschafen

In a Class by Himself

Life without Fortune was as quiet and peaceful as a lily pond. Not that I was bored — I was intellectually stimulated — but to my surprise I missed the excitement and riskiness of our adventures together. Each night after cleaning up the chow hall, I returned to the tent, lay down on my cot, and began reading the day's assignment in my teachers' books. Each night I could hear music drifting across the quiet darkness. Some melodies were familiar. One night the music overwhelmed my reading and I put down my book and simply listened until I fell asleep. The next night, unable to concentrate, I listened again, enchanted, while my tent-mates, except Billiard Ball, slept. He lay on his cot absorbed in a book. "Isn't it beautiful?" I said. Shrugging his shoulders, he went on reading as if the music hardly existed.

On such a night one of Fortune's men from communications entered the tent. "Fortune wants to see you," he said, perspiring and distraught. I told the man I wasn't interested. "He's very sick and may be dying," the man said solemnly.

Alarmed, I jumped up from my cot and followed him among the rows of palms across the camp to Fortune's tent. On the way we passed by a shelter with flaps raised, from which the music originated. Inside I saw a half dozen of our boys sitting on cots and homemade wooden stools listening to a phonograph on a plywood table. The exquisite theme of the first movement of Tchaikovsky's Sixth Symphony, the mournful "Pathetique," was playing. It was a background for tragedy, evoking my worst fears over what may have befallen Fortune.

Dying? Had he shot himself by accident with his wretched sidearm? Was he ill with jaundice, a not uncommon

70

ailment transmitted through our rat contaminated bread flour? Could it be dysentery, debilitating but never fatal, which struck everyone sooner or later? Perhaps he had contracted dengue fever, a short-term sickness with malaria-type symptoms, which was ravaging our camp and for which there was no known effective treatment. Sick bay was overflowing; new fever victims were left to heal themselves in their own tents. As we walked, my heart pounding anxiously, I learned that Fortune had been incapacitated for about a week, confined to his cot. The doctor had said nothing could be done; it was a matter of waiting until the fever passed. Try to make him as comfortable as possible, that was all.

But after a week, Fortune failed to improve, and instead seemed to worsen, lapsing at intervals into a state of raving delirium during which he would blabber about a fox. "He'd just go off his rocker," said the messenger. "Then when he'd come out of it, he'd ask about you, how you were, y'know, and I'd tell him okay because I had seen you around. I'd ask him if he wanted to see you, and he'd say no—until the last time."

When I entered Fortune's tent the air within was heavy and smelled acrid with sweat. Fortune was lying on his cot, his sunken eyes staring unseeing at the hot olive green roof. A week's growth of beard failed to hide how thin and wan his face had become. He was only a feeble shadow now and I was frightened for him. His tan shirt was sweat soaked and clung to him. Without warning an uncontrollable shivering wracked his body. I covered him with a blanket and sat by him for the remainder of the night.

At 4:30 in the morning I reported directly to KP, then at 9:30 I visited sick bay. Doctor Cunningham, a quiet mousy man with a small black mustache, had a blasé bedside manner. "I'm worried about Fortune, sir, and I wonder whether you'd take another look at him." Assessing my request, the doctor sat behind his desk impassively. I tried to orient him. "Barry Fortune, sir, one of the dengue victims."

"Oh, yes, Fortune, the sailor with the jeep. Now you needn't worry, young man," the doctor said calmly. "The fever is short-lived and has to take its course."

"Yes, sir, I realize that, but it's been a week and he..."

"A week?"

"Yes, sir, and no letup in his fever. I'm worried it might not be dengue."

"As I say," the doctor stated with increasing firmness, "he'll improve. People typically recover from dengue."

"Right, sir, but Fortune has had malaria, and isn't it possible that..."

"Young man, I'm extremely busy with an epidemic of fever on my hands and I haven't time to argue. I suggest you trust my diagnosis and try to make him comfortable."

"Maybe some quinine would help him, sir. I hear it's better than the atabrine we're taking."

The doctor got up from behind his desk and walked to the door. "Next," he said. A new patient, yellow and sickly with jaundice, walked in, signalling the end of our interview, and possibly Fortune.

During the next several days and nights I stayed with my friend. Our plump commissary chief, a kindhearted, jovial soul, excused me from duty. "Hell," he said, "half the battalion has lost its appetite anyway." Due to the high incidence of illness, the demands on the kitchen and KP hands had lightened considerably.

Trying to assuage Fortune's frantic chills, I wrapped him in a blanket and applied a towel soaked in ice water (with ice secured from the commissary reefer, another gift from the chief) to his burning brow. During his calmer and more lucid moments I managed to get him to take some grapefruit and pineapple juice, procured by trading some of Fortune's own liquor in a manner that would have won his admiration.

Each night I listened to the music nearby, a soothing, entertaining companion as I sat and dozed by the side of my restless patient. By the third day of my nursing Fortune passed a crisis, after which the alternating episodes of chills and burning fever became milder and less frequent. Soon I felt safe to leave his side for brief periods.

At the first opportunity I visited the music tent, finding there only one acquaintance, the oil geologist, and a half-dozen men from other companies whom I knew only by sight. They were mostly New Yorkers, a cohesive clique of cultural snobs, who for the most part ignored me while they talked of music and ballet and opera and used strange words such as sostenuto and toccata as commonly as the rest of us used four letter profanity. So began my music education in the midst, and in spite, of hostile company.

After the war I had seen a distorted map of the United States illustrating the New Yorkers' view of themselves in which Manhattan constitutes perhaps ninety percent of the area, and the rest of the country is a mere appendage. New Yorkers are quite unable to adapt; Americans in extremis, they bring Manhattan with them wherever they go, even to the primeval forests of New Guinea.

Soon Fortune fell into a long sleep lasting through a night and a day and another night. Upon awakening he was not only coherent for the first time but startlingly alert despite his spindly appearance. When I stopped by late in the morning after KP, his eyes brightened at seeing me. Still too weak to rise, he asked, "How long have I been out?"

"A hell of a long time," I said, surprised at his awareness of what had happened to him. The morning was clear and the air uncommonly cool.

"Sooner or later it was bound to happen," he said. I looked puzzled. "The malaria attack," he explained.

"The doctor said it was dengue."

"Shit, some doctor! How long did you say I was out?"

"Too long for dengue, I suppose," I said annoyed at the thought of the doctor's adamant refusal to reconsider his diagnosis. I was also annoyed at Fortune for having let himself fall victim to an attack. Malaria was not a problem with us and for good reason: We were on atabrine, a preventive pill that we took daily for protection. None of us were spared the frequent plunge of the parasite-laden proboscis of an anopheles mosquito into our bloodstream, guaranteeing infection. But the disease remained dormant within our systems as long as we took medication.

(Indeed much to my mother's consternation when I returned home after the war and discontinued atabrine, I came down several times with all the usual symptoms, chills and fever, of a malaria attack, which after a few months in a temperate climate decreased in severity and eventually disappeared for good.)

Our complexions, a burnished yellow, offered the telltale clue that we had atabrine coursing through our veins. Not so Fortune's whose skin was pallid. Obviously, he had made no effort to protect himself. What drove this man to such foolish daring? Did he thrive on a constant contest with death? Was the pain and suffering he had just endured worth the victory? Was it sweeter that way?

"I don't understand you," I said, vexed. "You could have prevented this from happening. You had malaria before, and you volunteered for the tropics knowing the risk you were taking, yet you avoided the atabrine."

He was too weary to argue, and he waved his hand as if to say he was bored. But after a few moments of thoughtful silence he added: "Don't I always come through?"

"You live on the edge, Barry," I said, "and I'll never understand."

He smiled faintly, a passing glint of resignation in his eyes. "Neither do I, so let's forget it. Okay, good buddy, okay?"

After KP each day, I brought him his three squares and gradually he began to fill out and regain strength. Often I delayed having dinner at the chow hall so we could dine together in the tent. I enjoyed sitting with him at dusk when my day was done. We would chat about any subject under the sun, especially about Lucia, who had written to him of her considerable concern over our recent rift. "Will you tell her we're friends again?" he implored. I assured him unhesitatingly that I would. Along with his strength and alertness, his old impatience and irascibility returned. I knew that he was on the verge of normalcy when he began ordering me about again, demanding this and that.

"We'll be leaving Finschafen pretty soon," he said. From past experience I had no reason to doubt this pronouncement. "Care to know where we're going?"

"I suppose while you were delirious you figured out the code," I said sarcastically, knowing damn well that he knew and was determined to flaunt it.

74

"Well, if you're not interested..." He pushed his almost full tray of food to the foot of his cot. "This is rat food. Can't you bring me something besides bully beef?"

"We've run out of fresh food," I replied. "Until the next supply ship comes in, we're serving only canned."

"Hell, they're saving the good stuff for the big push," he complained. "It's a brilliant strategy; we're going to bypass the Japs at Wewak, cutting off their supply line, and starve them to death. And it won't cost us a life." Becoming animated, he raised himself on his elbow. "And there we'll be in Hollandia, north of them, mopping up. Good chance I'll be able to get a few Japs, eh?"

As he talked his eyes became watery with eagerness. He closed them to better savor his mental picture, then he lay back on his cot weary from the strain. "Y'know I could use you up there," he sighed. "We'll be starting from scratch building a whole communications network." He grasped my wrist and pulled me towards him. "You'll be important. Nobody can climb poles and string lines like you. How about it?" He held onto me and waited.

The offer was tempting. Although the intelligentsia made KP bearable, the activist in me was frustrated. Unlike Billiard Ball and his hero of *The Magic Mountain*, I yearned to be involved. It was a marvelous uplifting feeling to be part of an organized major effort. And no doubt this time Fortune would be too busy for his usual wheeling and dealing. Yet, I held back, fearing that to re-enter his fold meant being obligated and subject to his arbitrary wishes. "I'll think about it," I said, "and let you know."

During those evenings, after the usual dinner with Fortune, I would stop in the music tent for an hour or so on the way back to my tent. Although I was virtually blackballed by the New York sophisticates, being a hick from New England, I found the music too enrapturing to pass up. The record library, consisting of old 78s, was small, so the same pieces were played over and over, but they were solid and varied. While serving the chow line, soon I was humming the "Ode to Joy" of Beethoven's Ninth Symphony, and reliving in my mind's ear the thrill of the cataclysmic conclusion of Stravinsky's "Firebird."

With a new art thus revealed to me, I wanted to share it. I tried Billiard Ball. "How would you like to listen to some music after KP?" I asked.

"No, I don't think so," he replied.

"A bunch of us listens every night," I said. "Mostly New Yorkers."

"Yes, I know who they are." He returned to his reading with finality.

Disappointed, I was baffled by his refusal. How could a man as erudite as Billiard Ball be so deaf to music? Perhaps he himself had explained it once when he said, "By nature all human beings are narrow specialists. It's a rare person that's good at more than one thing." But I had expected more of him.

While I pondered Fortune's offer of joining the communications crew, Lucia Fox's reply to my painful latest letter arrived. She made an irresistible appeal; her very salutation, "My dearest Hal," softened my doubts. "How sad it makes me to see you and Barry drifting apart. He has written, too — miracle of miracles — telling me how much you have come to mean to him. You can't imagine how highly he values your friendship. Please understand how much we both need you. I beg you to never tell him what I am about to say: He confessed he wept after you left his crew. He did, Hal. He simply couldn't believe you'd actually leave him. He grieves from the loss of your comradeship."

Her words surpassed belief. Was Fortune actually capable of such emotionalism? Either he was laying it on or she was following his instructions. No, she was sincere; that's how she was. Nor could I be sure he hadn't revealed a hidden side of himself. Finally, her closing words drew me in. "He depends on you like a true brother." That was a strong statement to a young man who had pined for just such a relationship. "And you have a special place in my heart, too, so please, Hal dearest, make up your differences with him and be his friend again. And please, I beg you, keep writing; I treasure your letters." For the first time she ended with the word "Love."

I was fervently moved, and ready at that instant to rush back to Fortune and commit myself to him anew. How sweet is making up between friends and lovers. Unable to sever the bond between us, I realized that nursing Fortune back to health told all. The decision made, I took off to see Lucia's beloved renegade to give him the good news. Upon entering his tent, however, I was astonished to find his cot empty, the sheets cold. The cover of his footlocker was left open, suggesting that he had departed in haste, and his pistol was missing from its usual place. But wasn't he too weak to leave his tent? Hadn't he insisted upon my waiting on him precisely because he was still incapable of visiting the chow hall? Puzzled, worried, I roamed the camp searching until I found Chief Bull Dunham at the transportation shed.

"Sure I seen him. He checked out in his jeep couple of hours ago—said he was goin' to a movie."

"He doesn't go to movies," I said.

"Listen, the man's got trouble. I wouldn't try to second-guess him. Remember, he's brought it all on himself."

Brought what on himself? I wondered. But I was too distraught and angry to mull over Bull's cryptic words, being concerned only that Fortune had conned me, taken advantage of my loyalty. I had been his friend, his nurse, his manservant, and now his fool. A deadly anger welled up, directed partly inward for allowing myself to be taken in. Returning to my tent, I ignored Billiard Ball's hale greeting and lay on my cot trying to cope with my rage and indignation. I stared into space until dawn, rehearsing in my mind the next confrontation with Fortune.

After KP I paid him my regular visit. When he saw me enter the tent, he lay back on his cot moaning. "I had a fever last night," he said.

"Is that so?" I said.

"Goddamn, y'know this thing is lasting too long, but I'm getting better. My appetite's improved which is an encouraging sign. Say, where's my breakfast?"

"Up at the chow hall, but it's too late for breakfast now." Blinking, he sensed my strangeness. "Tell me, Barry, how was the movie last night?"

He giggled like a mischievous child caught red-handed. But I was incapable of summoning up feelings of anger. Having resolved to give up on him, my anger had been spent during the night. Yes, his chronic manipulating was tiresome, and any hope of reform futile. "What will you do after you've used everyone and there's no one else left?" I said in measured words. "Barry, you're very sad. I have only pity for you." At that I turned and quickly left the tent, refusing to give him a chance to respond. From then on, Fortune never mattered to me in the same way again.

But Lucia, the faithful innocent, certainly did. I realized with full force what she was letting herself in for. It was important that I protect her somehow from Fortune's callousness and manipulation. Such a delicate matter would require a guarded approach because nothing on earth is more idealized than lovers' feelings for each other. I must never condemn Fortune to her, or hint at my low estimation of his character. As much as she seemed to want my letters, so did I hers. I found her warmth refreshing, her trust uplifting, her sense of joy a balm to my pessimistic nature. Thus irrespective of Fortune, I dealt with her not as Fortune's girl but as my friend, developing a relationship of our own.

There was a postscript in Lucia's previous letter: "Would you send a photo of yourself? Barry has only given me a sketchy description of what you look like. It would be so nice to be able to match your gentle words with the real person." Flattered by her curiosity, I was certain she would be disappointed. My most recent photo, taken while on liberty in New Orleans, showed a tall, bow-legged male biped in navy whites. A shock of unruly black hair hung out from a white sailor's cap perched on a small pointed head. The face was too long, the chin too small, and the eyes, well, while large, friendly and honest, were the sole redeeming feature. Nevertheless I sent the photo, expecting it to burst her bubble. It's about time she saw me as I truly was.

As expected, Fortune's prediction of our imminent move was accurate in every detail. Our destination was to be

Hollandia, a small seacoast village up north in Dutch New Guinea. Before we landed, the army would have the place secured, leaving perhaps a few missionaries in the neighborhood—that's all.

By the time the commander had us assembled, his ostensibly momentous announcement was old hat. We gasped anyway, and were attentive to his warning of certain dangers. Watch out for ticks in the tall grass; they transmit typhus, a fatal disease without a cure. Don't drink water from the local streams or springs; it abounds with dangerous microbes. Stick to the lister bags with their treated water. Avoid the flies whose bite could cause elephantiasis, a horrible disease characterized by enlarged, ulcerated genitals. "Hell, no wonder the Japs are surrendering Hollandia," said Billiard Ball. "They're probably all diseased and dying anyway." Whereas before the commander spoke we were like racehorses champing at the gate, afterward we resembled frightened mares reluctant to leave our stalls, although no one was ready to admit it.

We went about our business of preparing for the move with mock enthusiasm. Things became more ominous when we were issued live ammunition, a first for us. Probably won't need it, said our lieutenant, but we'll have it just in case. A rusty Liberty ship, a wartime cargo vessel swiftly constructed on a production line, arrived at the dock. Such ships were known to break in half in rough seas. It took a week around the clock to load her, starting with the heavy equipment—the bulldozers, cranes and ten-wheelers—and ending with our tents, until only we remained ashore. We gathered on the wharf once again in loose formation under a blistering sun.

Standing on the ship's deck above us, Gluck spoke through a bullhorn. "Attention, men, attention. The commander has something to say."

"I'll be brief," the commander began. "The opportunity we've all expected has come. Our big mission, the one we've been trained for from the very first day our battalion was formed only nine months ago is at hand." The heavy air seemed to increase the weight of the bulging packs on our backs. We peered up at the commander from beneath our wobbly green steel helmets like shy turtles. Sweat trickled down from our temples along the sides of our cheeks. We were surely ill-trained to handle this anxious moment. "When we get to Hollandia, we will have thirty-five thousand of the enemy bottled up behind us. But you can be sure the army will see to them. Our job is to build, not destroy. We've been trained by the marines; we're combat ready and if need be we'll fight. Right, men? We're a can-do outfit. Remember our motto. Say it, men, say it. Our voices thundered in unison, resounding throughout the harbor. "Can-do, can-do, can-do." The commander grinned and raised his clasped hands over his head. "God bless every one of you." He turned and walked up the gangway to the ship's bridge, Gluck following.

I found some comfort in the commander's short speech. For one thing he stressed the building aspect of our function; for another he implied that the army would have everything secured. Although I was hardly thrilled by his hint at the possibility of combat, most of us were thirsting for action. We laughed and jostled each other, jubilant at the prospect.

Billiard Ball, however, from his peculiarly cynical perspective, interpreted the commander's speech differently. "So it's come to this: First we'll have a doubtful voyage on a hulk that may never make it beyond the three-mile limit, then if it does, we'll land in a disease-infested prehistoric jungle. If by God's grace our balls haven't swelled up to the size of cantaloupes, we'll survive only long enough to be a practice target for some invisible Jap sniper-marksman. For just such a bloody dismal end, I have dedicated my entire life to learning."

"Oh, c'mon," I said. "You heard the commander."

He saw that his cynicism was unnerving me. "Ah, ignore me," he urged, playfully nudging my helmet askew with his rifle butt. "It's just the incongruity of it all that gets me. Remember what I said: We're survivors, you and I."

I took his cue. "Don't worry, when your time comes, you'll go down in style."

"You mean the Japs reserve silver bullets for Ph.D.s, eh?" he said, and both of us laughed.

To some degree, all of us shared Billiard Ball's momentary lapse into despair. Being mostly ignorant of what was happening in the rest of the world, we only suspected that the war was progressing in our favor, albeit at a snail's pace and more than likely continuing on for a generation. At that stage of the war, its end was beyond imagining. In my deepest conviction I was reconciled to never having a chance to live out my potential. As with Billiard Ball, I too thought it was a rotten shame.

Standing, waiting on the wharf, I gazed at the palm forest, which miraculously showed no sign of our recent habitation. The pythons could now take over Finschafen in peace. Strangely I felt a twinge of sorrow at leaving the fetid place. I had become unwittingly attached to it. As I turned my back on it forever, I spied Fortune working his way toward me through the crowd of platoons. Having avoided him since walking out several weeks before, I was alarmed at the sight of his still sickly, chalky pallor. His gait was ponderous and he was laboring unduly from the heft of his backpack. As he drew near I saw that he was breathing hard and drenched in sweat as if his fever persisted.

He reached for my hand, grasping it tightly as in a death grip. "I want us to be friends again, Hal. Can't we be friends?" he implored. "Let's shake hands. What d'you say?" my hand remained passive, limp. He had changed; the old swagger was gone, and his once confident, calm eyes were now darting and wild. "Before I die I want us to be friends."

I winced at his absurd sentimentality. "Don't be ridiculous," I said.

"Yes, I know how it must sound but I truly mean it, Hal."

"You're afraid to die after all. What a hero," I said scornfully.

"I'm not afraid to die so long as I die in class."

"You look awful."

"I'm getting better."

I recalled Lucia's letter describing Fortune's grief over my break with him. His contrition seemed out of character, but so did his general behaviour. He had stood on this very wharf almost three months earlier unable to contain his elation at the prospect of adventure. And now, expecting the same response to the upcoming challenge at Hollandia, I was

81

puzzled to find him so subdued. His preoccupation with death was startling.

"I appreciate what you've done for me, Hal, I really do, and I place great stock in our friendship. I'll do whatever is necessary to earn your loyalty again," he said, "and I'm sorry if I've hurt you in any way."

"How can I trust you?" I replied.

"Try me," he said, extending his hand again.

What did I have to lose? I had missed our friendship. Despite everything I never stopped liking him. I took his hand and grasped it in both of mine. He smiled in gratitude. "Let's stick together once we're up there," he said. "And cover me. Know what I mean? Stay behind and cover me."

"Jeez, Barry, the commander says the place will be secured. There's nothing to worry about."

He drew close to my ear and whispered, "Now we've got ammunition. I don't want to get it in the back. That would be a helluva way to die."

Over the ship's PA system, Gluck's raucous voice blared instructions to commence boarding, starting with Headquarters Company, of which I was a member. Reaching for my duffel bag on the dock beside me, I said, "I think you're crazy."

He shook his head. "You're the only one I trust, Hal. Remember that."

Surely the man was paranoid. Though it was true many in the outfit resented his special privileges, and even more the hold he had over them. Indeed, I had learned much later from Bull Dunham that Fortune, having been threatened that night I found his tent empty, had fled for his own safety. Still, I considered his fears unfounded and exaggerated. But it remained that I may well have been the only person in the battalion he could trust. Once again, I was sucked in, no longer keenly anticipating our future together as in the past. Instead he compounded my trepidation. Yet I knew I'd cover him until death. I saw no other choice.

VIII
Hollandia

The Landing and Soon After

As the Liberty ship lumbered north, I was thankful that the ocean was calm, knowing that rough seas were hard on such vessels. I had read about the North Atlantic Liberty ship disasters in the compressed overseas edition of *Time* magazine.

Again we followed the coast, which consisted of a steaming, forested plain extending for miles inland to a distant blue mountain range. "I'll bet dinosaurs are still roaming those forests," said Billiard Ball. "Whatever made them extinct in the rest of the world had to have missed this godforsaken spot." But I would have wagered that the thousands of bypassed Japanese bottled up on the plain, abandoned by their troubled forces elsewhere, were far more dangerous than any real or imagined creatures. Months later we heard stories of their hell, of their brutal internecine struggle, and of their acts of desperation, including cannibalism.

Upon reaching Humboldt Bay on a clear, breezy morning, we steamed into one of the small inlets making up the harbor at Hollandia. Fortune and I stood at the ship's bow gazing at the town situated on the level floor of a narrow valley hemmed in on three sides by steep, thickly forested hills. The town possessed a certain quaintness, a benignity that reminded me of the small mountain villages of New Hampshire. A stream traveled the length of the valley floor and emptied into the harbor at one end of a short white sandy beach. This was no setting for violence and the spilling of blood. "Hell it wasn't," said Fortune, staring through his precision binoculars, another of his prized possessions. He handed me the glasses with a nervous and trembling hand.

Upon studying the scene in close up, I discovered that the town was actually a shattered ruin. The standing structures were nothing more than white stucco walls and corrugated metal roofs splattered with gaping holes. Only the spire of the small white church remained miraculously intact.

"It's history now," Fortune shouted. He was relieved and elated. "The taking of the town has already been done for us." Not that he was a coward—least of all that.

Commander Rutledge was true to his promise; unquestionably, Hollandia was secure before we arrived. We debarked calmly and without incident, unloading onto barges that carried us the quarter mile to the beach, where our supplies were piled up and equipment was scattered awaiting disposition to a permanent location on the site of the former town. But the going was hard as we browsed through the ruins to find viable places for our encampment. Bomb craters made the few streets impassable. The detritus of former battle—shell casings, broken bayonets, Japanese sabers, and smashed American water canisters—were strewn about haphazardly. The bodies of the fallen had fortunately been removed, although evidence of the killing was clearly visible in splotches of dried blood on the grass and white stucco walls.

How relieved we were to find the battle over, to land in peace, and to get on with our intended purpose—the business of construction. Knowing how often other battalions had been wiped out due to mix ups in landing schedules and unforeseen reversals, we had good reason to doubt the commander's assurances. Indeed it was not unusual that a battalion of Seabees, having secured the military objective, would greet a contingent of astonished marines primed for battle coming in for a landing. At other times a battalion would join the marines or the army infantry in the fight and turn the tide. Our battalion was spared such a test, although many, hungry for combat, were disappointed. Fortune quickly saw that he had nothing to fear, certainly not a shot in his back, simply because we "took" Hollandia without a shot being fired.

Given no choice, my agility at pole climbing in demand, I was ordered to report to Fortune's group. I did so with enthusiasm, flattered by the recognition and pleased that I could do something better than anyone else in the battalion.

"When do we start?" I asked Fortune.

"Not until the battalion splits up for projects at different spots. But I have a few ideas for how to kill some time, if you want to come along." I noticed the familiar glint of eagerness in his eyes and the suppressed excitement in his voice, the telltale signals of a man ripe for action. All at once he seemed to have been restored to health, his color good, his gait firm again. Sure enough, he had recovered his old self-confidence and no doubt forgot the reason he had ever lost it.

What an exuberant group of men we were during those first days. Everyone pitched in, completing one task, then going on to another with direction practically unnecessary, working around the clock until utterly exhausted. Our tents were erected on the old stone slab foundations of former houses. Stretching a canvas roof above the floor of the church, we installed a mess hall with full kitchen and dining room, its entrance beneath the sturdy spire. At the edge of the jungle in the rear of the valley, the medical tent was set up. In no more than a day and a half we had created another town, population 1,080 men, self-sufficient, vital, ostensibly secure. This would serve as our temporary base from which to explore the wild country surrounding us.

"You're good men," the commander said, nodding his head, smiling, as he made his rounds inspecting our works, accompanied by a silently critical Gluck. "Every goddamned one of you."

But this narrow valley was too confining to be a permanent site and not sufficiently central to the locations to which our various companies would be assigned. Rutledge sent out the engineers to survey the countryside and draw contour maps to guide him where best to build roads and construct docks and lay down airstrips, and then locate our permanent home. How different this was from the struggle I had envisioned. If this was war, then we were experiencing its best side. Wasn't it really more like pioneering, the opening up of a new, pristine land, but using twentieth-century labor-saving technology? But I crowed too soon. It was war indeed and I knew it on the third night.

Resting briefly and settling in to enjoy a job well done, we heard the uneven drone of bombers in the black sky. Thinking they were ours we ignored them. Then came the bombs, raining down on us in a deafening fury. "Just remember, we're survivors," Billiard Ball exhorted. I was too frightened to respond, to share his faith. Frantically we dug shallow foxholes with our mess kits, helmets, and bare hands and lay in them shivering and clinging to the dirt like lizards. Not until dawn did we rise up ever cautiously, only to find the canvas town in tatters from shrapnel and cratered here and there. Miraculously there were no major casualties, only a few injuries. Clearly the Japanese bombardiers over Hollandia lacked the proficiency of the ones over Pearl Harbor.

But now we knew they knew we were there, and the necessary preventive steps would be immediately taken. With all the meticulous advance preparation to protect us from danger, with all the warnings given of what we might face, none had taken into account the obvious fact that we were within range of Japanese bombers. "The goddamned Command," cursed Gluck. "They never even mentioned the air."

"The trouble is," said the commander, "we're beginning to underestimate the enemy now that we're winning. That's dangerous, very dangerous."

Concentrated on the floor of the valley, we were especially vulnerable, so the commander ordered that we disperse through the nearby forest where the leaf canopy would protect us. Between the trees we randomly strung up hammocks especially designed for jungle use. They were equipped with mosquito netting which could be neatly zipped closed once the occupant was inside. As standard procedure, guards were posted. Because of the air attack they looked skyward for the enemy rather than into the gloomy, mysterious night forest. So they missed the infiltrating agile Japs who thrived at night in the jungle like cats on a hunt.

Unheard, unseen, they slithered through our perimeter. They pounced on the hammocks and plunged their long knives up through the sagging bottoms into helpless slumbering bodies. The darkness filled with agonizing screams as the victims writhed in their tiny mosquito-net prisons. The entire camp erupted into panic; no one knew where or what to strike. I lay in my hammock trembling, paralyzed with terror as I felt warm urine flow down my crotch and settle under my buttocks. Five men died, seventeen were wounded, of whom none were the enemy. The unscathed didn't sleep soundly until war's end, and some perhaps never would again. The memory of that night still haunts me. As I tell of it, I tremble.

Gluck frothed with anger. Commander Rutledge was outraged; he called a meeting of his officers. "I had every assurance the area was secure, absolutely clean," he explained in a tone partly apologetic, partly revealing pain at the casualties and the suffering, and partly exhibiting hurt at being betrayed.

"If we had only known the Japs were around..." Gluck interrupted, unable to suppress himself.

Rutledge waved him quiet and continued: "First we must set up a dense watch along our perimeter. Arm the guards with the few BARs [Browning automatic rifles] we have and the rest with carbines. No aught-threes [single-shot rifles, vintage 1903], understand? And make sure no one sleeps in zipped-up netting." The officers were all with Rutledge now, looking to him to relieve them of their burden of pain and to direct them toward action, any action.

But Fortune found the commander's defensive steps much too tame and ill-fitting the crime. He thought vengeful retaliation was needed. "Those Jap bastards. Do they think they can get away with this? They'll pay for every drop of American blood they spilled." One would think the night attack had been directed at Fortune personally, that he had been privately humiliated.

"What can you do?" I asked.

"Just watch me," he replied resolutely.

While the commander met with his staff and laid out a considered and measured strategy, Fortune met with his crew and whipped them into a vindictive frenzy. "Let's not wait meekly for the bastards to come to us and stick us with their long knives. Let's go after 'em and give it to 'em—give it to 'em good."

Without authorization or the knowledge of the battalion staff, Fortune led his crew into the jungle on a Jap hunt. I refused to join him. "I'll bag one for you and bring back his head," he promised.

They came out of the jungle two days and one night later—tired, proud, and unscathed, their faces caked with mud and their clothes torn. On one shoulder each man had his carbine slung, its ammunition depleted; on the other he carried a long pole at the end of which was a human skull. Their entrance was dramatic, fit for a movie. At first the sight of the skulls shocked us, thinking they were Japanese, until, noting they were bleached white, we realized they were of humans long dead. Nevertheless the men listened to stories of triumphant firefights with an elusive enemy uncannily camouflaged with natural foliage. "They were fuckin' invisible; they'd strap themselves high up in the trunks of the trees with leafy branches attached to 'em and fire at us. But they were lousy shots and every time they'd make a stir in their perches we'd see 'em, then pow, we'd knock 'em off as easy as they did us in our hammocks." It was heartily satisfying to hear of their kills, of which each man claimed at least one. I was surprised at my own cold need for retribution, even though I could kill only to defend myself, and even that would come hard.

The story of Fortune's crew's adventure spread through the camp. With the near universal need for vengeance running strong, volunteers flocked to join him for another foray. It was carried on in a revolving sequence in which a small group of a half dozen would disappear for two or three days and return weary but exuberant, only to be replaced by another. They always brought back souvenir skulls and reports of their successes. Although the officers knew what was happening, they looked the other way, for they were sympathetic to Fortune's aims. But eventually the size of the raiding party grew to several dozen, causing consternation among the company commanders and their platoon chiefs, whose units were constantly shorthanded.

Indeed, due to the understaffing of crews, the battalion's work was falling seriously behind schedule. Commander

Rutledge, usually the last to know about any nonconforming activity, demanded that Gluck find a reason.

"Jerry, I'll have your answer before day's out," Gluck promised. Gluck too was kept uninformed by the lower echelons. For once, no one wished to provoke his well-known resentment toward Fortune.

We had begun construction of our camp at a permanent site about three miles south of Hollandia. There the hills rose less sharply from the sea and it was dry. Through the trees one could catch enticing glimpses of the blue bay below. Beyond the site and behind the narrow shore, an enormous sago swamp stretched for several miles. It was malarial and forbidding, there to be tamed, even obliterated.

Good timber was available right where we needed it, the stream in Hollandia was still near enough to be our water supply, the limestone cliffs jutting out of the hills here and there were ideal for making cement, and the site was midway between two planned major projects. But before tackling these we had to settle ourselves decently, beginning with the construction of "officer's country." At the urging of his fellow officers Lieutenant Commander Gluck gave the order that officers' country be given precedence over all else—before the stringing of lines of communication, before carving a road into the hillside, before constructing our showers. Overnight Gluck, the loner, became popular with the officers, and because of his newly acquired acceptance, his junior officers were unreservedly willing to answer his question: "Why'n hell we fallin' behind?" By nightfall Gluck reported back to Commander Rutledge.

"It's Fortune," he said. "Y'know what that sonofabitch is doin'? He's dispatchin' armed teams into the jungle huntin' Japs. He thinks he's some kind of general or somethin'."

The commander's neck grew taut. "By whose authority..."

"He's doin' it on his own, Jerry, s'help me. We don't know how many men are involved, but he's sure as hell takin' away enough to slow us down. I unnerstand he rotates the teams. Y'know what they call themselves? Soldiers of Fortune. Can you beat it?"

The commander slapped the top of his desk and sat back in his chair. Gluck erroneously prepared himself for a blast of temper. "I see," the commander said at last, calmly.

Gluck was confused by Rutledge's soft reaction. "Jerry, do you realize how much this man has fouled up our schedule?"

"Certainly, and I realize we haven't been attacked once since that awful night. I can't tolerate Fortune's unsponsored, freewheeling flights of daring, yet wouldn't we have fallen further behind had we been harassed and more men murdered? But yes, we've got to stop it," the commander concluded with little enthusiasm. Perhaps Fortune's action was a measure he too should have taken.

"It won't be hard to find Fortune's boys," enthused Gluck. "They got skulls stuck on poles standin' next to their hammocks."

"What! Are they Jap skulls?"

Gluck shrugged. "I s'pose so. Who knows?"

"Get that goddamned Fortune in here," Rutledge seethed. "Of all the inhuman, grisly acts...You hear me, Gluck? Get him in here. I'll not permit the deliberate, cruel desecration of a human body, enemy or not. Never!" Gluck departed immediately on a search for Fortune, whose whereabouts were particularly elusive these days.

Rutledge had jumped to the wrong conclusion. Although the skulls were not Japanese, Fortune and his followers seemed to take pleasure in showing off the death symbols. It bound them together somehow in a cultish way. And Fortune, like Gluck, was now a favored son. I would say, in fact, he was revered. All the mounting resentment against Fortune since those Finschafen days had vanished. He had become the quintessential free-spirited "soldier of fortune" so many of us wished to emulate.

Although I had turned down Fortune's offer to be one of his "soldiers" and seek out the enemy, I had involuntarily become one. The enemy had found me, usually while I was on the job stringing temporary telephone lines along the densely forested hillsides. Often I was part of Fortune's four- or five-man crew, which more than coincidentally always seemed to work in hot spots. There, *zing*, a sniper's bullet would whistle by. Then, bang, a scream, a sudden rustle in a tree's high foliage, and a sniper clothed in leaves would fall limp, hanging head first from a branch to which he had tied himself. "First skull today," Fortune would mutter.

Fortune was, to be sure, a crack shot, but that was not always enough. First we had to identify the location of the bullet's source, more often than not an impossible task. Most of us, reluctant to wait around for a second bullet to find us, hightailed it to a safer spot, except for Fortune, who hung back as if he had been personally challenged. Frequently someone would follow his example and remain behind with him to fight, motivated by the urge for adventure or to counteract their cowardly inclination. They too wanted skulls to show off.

Late one afternoon on our way back to camp, Fortune took a detour that brought us to a height overlooking Hollandia and its wedge-shaped harbor. "There's the burial cave," said Fortune, as if he were a proud tour guide. "Probably hundreds of years old. More skulls here than you can count."

Then I saw the enormous crevice in the hillside, a gaping chalk-white limestone opening perhaps twenty feet high, leading into a dark cavern. As impressive as this was in its sudden contrast with the verdant sameness of the surroundings, I was more startled by its contents: a profusion of bleached human skulls and skeletal limbs and rib cages piled several feet deep, white on white, at the entrance and along the cavern floor disappearing into the darkness. Many of the skeletons were intact, wrapped in strips of canvas and tied down to individual sledlike platforms, as if they had been readied for a journey through eternity.

Fortune picked up a skull and slipped it under his arm like a football. This man was no Hamlet speculating on the vibrant life it once contained. "This is wrong," I said. "We're invading a sacred place. We should leave the skulls alone." Fortune laughed and ignored me.

Each skull mounted on a pole represented a kill, and where there were several, they were arranged in a line before the victor's tent. It was similar to the air force custom wherein the pilots marked the fuselage of their planes with silhouettes of the enemy aircraft they downed. I was convinced that Fortune was somehow hooked on death and sought to control it much as a snake charmer manipulates his cobra.

While waiting for Fortune to be found and delivered, Commander Rutledge began to stew over the man's infractions. In a few days his impatience reached a boil. What audacity Fortune had, acting independently of his command. His earlier tolerance and even admiration gave way to outrage. It was compounded by what I call the "episode of the excess jeeps" which finished off any hope of Fortune receiving clemency once he did appear.

An MP captain and his sergeant landed in Hollandia harbor aboard a supply ship and requested permission to see the commander, to whom they presented a list of serial numbers. "These identify the jeeps missing at Finschafen," the captain said.

"Certainly, none of them are here," the commander replied. Gluck remained uncharacteristically silent and simply stared at the dirt floor of the temporary office tent. Having heard back at Finschafen that the army had begun a campaign to track down its missing mobile hardware, he never imagined that they would pursue the effort all the way to Hollandia.

Bull Dunham was called to appear with the battalion inventory list of jeep serial numbers. Upon comparing lists, thirteen jeeps were found to belong to the army. "Goddamnit, Dunham," Gluck erupted, "you shouldn't have allowed it." Dunham, knowing that Gluck was well aware of the situation, couldn't tell whether Gluck was truly angry or just performing for the benefit of the MP.

"Yes, sir," he replied, "but there's no way I could stop Fortune."

"Well, by heaven, I'll stop him," thundered the commander as he slammed his desk with the palm of his hand.

"Y'know, sir," interjected the MP captain, "if I might comment, I think you Seabees are the worst bunch of thieving bastards in the Pacific theater. MacArthur is going to hit the roof when he hears about this." As he saluted and turned brusquely on his heel to leave the tent, I was passing by on foot. Sure enough, I recognized him as none other than the officer who had nabbed Fortune and me for speeding on the Finschafen coastal highway. He stared at me momentarily, a puzzled look of recognition crossing his face, but he was distracted by the aide who captured his attention with the comment: "Worst goddamn outfit yet." As they walked away down the dusty street to the harbor, I heard the captain reply, "Hang onto your wristwatch. Not a fuckin' thing's safe here."

The commander would deal with Fortune on several counts now: the jeep stealing, the jungle escapades, and the "desecration of a hallowed burial ground," as he put it. He would cut him down to size and see to it that he would never have to contend with him again. Quite simply he ordered Gluck to commit Fortune, once found, to the brig. There he would await a court-martial, to be held at the commander's convenience.

Only minutes after Fortune emerged exhilarated and weary from a Jap-hunting excursion, I got word of his arrival and rushed to greet him. So did Gluck; with an entourage of SPs, he pounced. "You're goin' to the brig. All your stuff, your footlocker, everything's been taken from your tent," he said with delight. "You've gone too goddamned far, Fortune."

"For killing Japs?" Fortune protested.

"For everythin', for every lousy fuckin' thing," said Gluck. "I warned ya back in 'Hafen, didn't I?"

The SPs took an indignant Fortune by each arm and led him off.

What about him? Was he finished for good? I'd watch for sure, prepared to bet he'd rise again. Too often I had witnessed the improbable happen.

IX
Hollandia

Problems at the Top and Bottom

Commander Rutledge had many troublesome matters on his mind during those early weeks of getting the battalion settled and ready for its first projects. Indeed, they were the commencement of his eventual demise that Fortune had predicted long ago aboard ship.

Having disposed of Fortune, Rutledge was next forced to deal with the navy's traditional caste system. The high Command, which consisted principally of officers of the regular navy, mostly Annapolis graduates, ignored his suggestions to change a particular plan or try an idea that made good sense in view of unforseen conditions. Often the Command made decisions based on imprecise prior information.

One such case concerned the construction of a storage and staging area at a location that was occupied by a five-hundred-foot-high steep rise dubbed Pancake Hill.

"Less than a quarter mile south is a flat beach that would serve the purpose," Commander Rutledge suggested. The Command was adamant; the original plan would prevail. "But the project is unnecessary. It will slow down our other projects. Be flexible," he protested. "You may know the sea, but you don't know the land," he said angrily.

The Command felt that the naval reservists were still wet behind the ears, and the worst of them were the civil engineers who didn't know port from starboard. "We know war and you don't," was the acid reply.

Rutledge, an experienced earth-moving engineer who had worked on the Hoover Dam and a string of earthworks for the TVA, was the ideal man to eliminate the "mountain." It consisted of leveling the hill and pushing it into the impenetrable sago swamp along the bay shore, thereby creating about 100 acres of flatland. Rutledge proposed bringing in a dredge to assist by sucking up the sand from the shallow bay bottom and transporting it by pipeline to the swamp. The Command laughed at the idea. They imposed a virtually impossible completion deadline and to meet it, the battalion had to work around the clock. Nevertheless, we fell behind. Eventually Rutledge got his way. A decrepit, old-fashioned steam-driven Australian dredge joined us. By the time the job was done, not a piece of earth-moving equipment was operable for lack of replacement parts. But more about this project later.

As he came to understand the true nature and magnitude of the Hollandia assignment, Commander Rutledge became disenchanted. It consisted of a road five or six miles long, a fleet post office, a small hospital, one dock, the leveling of Pancake Hill, and to his disgust, the construction of a vacation home for MacArthur a few miles inland on top of a hill overlooking Lake Sentani.

Compared with the grandiose construction projects Rutledge had planned and supervised in civilian life, these projects were tame and failed to challenge him. Many would be useless even before they were completed. The war was moving fast, especially the sea war as we racked up victory after victory, rendering much of the Humboldt Bay complex obsolete within weeks after our arrival. Rutledge nagged the Command for another assignment, one that would take us to a forward area. He received no replies.

The commander had an ongoing problem with his officers. As Gluck's reputation improved among them, the commander's had deteriorated to a new low due to having countermanded Gluck's order to construct officers' country first. "Damnit, Gluck, don't you realize our enlisted men are the core of this outfit? Their needs must come first."

"Sure, sure, Jerry, I couldn't agree with you more. 'Course our officers' morale will take a dive if we deny them their accustomed privileges."

Officers' country was planned to resemble a posh tropical resort with private conical tents located on a palm-fringed beach of yellow sand in a secluded cove. The tents were to have hardwood floors. A long tent with a mahogany bar and a veranda with bamboo chairs overlooking the water's edge was to have been built. Also planned were private showers with water fed from a gigantic metal cauldron filled from a diverted spring. To heat the water, a black man was to tend a wood fire beneath the cauldron. (Black men in the World War II navy did only menial tasks.) The project was to be the realization of Gluck's and his cohorts' long held dream.

Construction had only begun when the commander discovered what his officers were up to. He announced: "Not until every enlisted man has a tent-roof over his head, a plywood floor beneath his feet, a freshwater shower to refresh himself and a decent head to shit in, will I allow the officers' club to proceed." As a result the officers continued sleeping on the ground in pup tents or in hammocks like the rest of us. As our tents were built they moved in with us, used our showers and sat beside us in the enlisted men's heads. Moody and resentful, they felt humiliated, and despised Commander Rutledge.

During the early construction phase, before showers were feasible, all water was hauled to our camp by tank truck from the stream in Hollandia village. It was chemically treated, stored in lister bags, and used only for drinking and cooking. While stringing a telephone line through the jungle, I happened on a freshwater spring. I used it in the same way I used Fortune's secret cabin aboard ship. Each evening before chowtime I went to the spring, filled my steel helmet with water and took a "whore's bath." Rinsing my sweaty clothes, I hung them on branches to dry and be retrieved the next evening. After performing this ritual for a week, I felt guilty over not sharing my water wealth; recalling how Fortune had restrained me on the ship, I invited Billiard Ball to join me.

Billiard Ball referred to our ablution at the spring as "the miracle of healing water." "I haven't felt this close to nature since being caught in a thundershower on Fifth Avenue," he joked. Sharing our secret spring seemed to seal our friendship and he opened up to me. "I've never loved," he said. "I often wonder whether I can. Trouble is I don't trust; I raise a barrier whenever someone reaches out to me. But here, in this place, I'm beginning to trust." He doused me with a helmet full of water and I returned the action, as we cavorted like children.

We were the cleanest Seabees in Hollandia for several weeks until one evening three of our shipmates discovered the spring. Within hours the word spread and the demand was more than the spring could meet. Eventually the officers claimed it for diversion to their cauldron. No matter, our loss was soon moot as the showers the commander promised began operating.

Although a portion of the commander's power derived from his rank, his true power came from the adoration he received from the enlisted men. We knew he was our only and true champion. And chances are, were it not for us, his officers would have mutinied. Of course, without us, the officers were helpless. Even Fortune, languishing in "prison", virtually forgotten, expressed admiration for the commander. "But the officers will get him sooner or later," he said. "Watch."

X
Hollandia

Changing Careers

Dearest Hal,
It has been more weeks than I can
remember since your last letter. I can't
help worrying. I imagine terrible things
happening to you and Barry. Or have you
stopped writing as you warned me you
would? My entreaties have been futile. No,
you have too much heart. Something has
happened to prevent you. Oh, Hal, how I
treasure your letters. I read them over and
over. They are an absolute pleasure, so
spirited and interesting. Please, my
dearest friend, let me hear from you.

Affectionately,
Lucia

In fact, shortly after our landing I had responded
favorably to Lucia's highly emotional appeal to continue our
correspondence for Fortune's sake. Apparently the mail
service from Hollandia, where few ships visited, was slower
than Finschafen's.

However, my motive was now chiefly personal and
unrelated to Fortune's need for a trusted friend. After
Finschafen Fortune seemed less superhuman, a considerably
shrunken personality. As my awe and dependency decreased
so did our closeness. Although I remained within his orbit
during the working day, I avoided him the rest of the time.

Lucia had not foreseen this turn, nor had I, and I wasn't
about to reveal the truth. Suddenly, my freedom from

Fortune and my new emotional independence made me too eager to receive her letters to risk their termination. I found her responsiveness, her high good nature, and her warmth soothing to my loneliness. I knew that she belonged to Fortune, and that she could never be mine. I was torn, wanting to keep on with her, yet knowing how futile it was and how increasingly painful it would become.

Three more letters, one containing her photo, followed, ignoring my silence until in the fourth letter she joyfully mentioned receiving my correspondence. The photo was as I had pictured her: delicate figure; wavy dark hair cut short; large, wide, trusting eyes; thin, high-boned features. Her appearance aptly fitted the letters. A sentence from her third letter affected me like a caress: "Still I haven't heard from you, but I keep writing just the same, knowing that you are too considerate to forsake my deep fondness for you."

In another letter she rhapsodized about the outdoors while off on a skiing trip to Big Pine in the San Bernardino Mountains with some girlfriends. "It's so heavenly here in Southern California; the air was so crystal clear while driving through the valley that I felt I could reach out and touch the mountains." She wrote of another weekend in which she and her friends "took a trip through the San Fernando Valley to Santa Barbara, where we visited their marvelous gem of an art museum. As far as we could see, all the way to the mountains on both sides were orange groves laid out in straight rows. Have you seen them? The air was so fragrant. Although I have never been to New England, I'm sure it is beautiful, but could it ever surpass Southern California? Hal, have you ever considered making this place your home?"

One letter ended on an uncharacteristically impatient note: "We may have won the war in Europe, but the horrible war you're fighting in the Pacific seems endless. I worry that we'll become middle-aged before it's over. How cruel it is knowing that we are wasting our most precious years."

I was still too young to worry seriously about aging. Becoming conscious suddenly that she was ten years older than I, I understood but failed to share her concern. After all, it was her self-confidence and purposefulness wrought by her very maturity that attracted me. That she confided her honest fears to me drew us still closer. I could have sung when she wrote: "I treasure your letters. Each word you write matters to me, even those the censors blank out. I try to imagine what they say."

I no longer mentioned Lucia's letters to Fortune, who was virtually forgotten by all but myself after only a few weeks of his confinement. Nor for that matter did he ever ask me whether I received letters from Lucia. He was too preoccupied with his frustration at being immobilized. Despite this his spirits remained high; he was convinced he could beat the rap. To hear him talk, he was simply a misunderstood hero. "The Old Man can't publicly admit it, but he knows in his heart I did the right thing. Hell, the men flocked to volunteer. As for the jeeps, he sanctioned them. Okay, the skulls may have offended him, but cripes, that's no big deal. I offered to put them back."

"You're missing the point," I said. "You usurped his authority. That's why he's sore."

"I saved lives," Fortune insisted. "I'm not worried. The Old Man can't bring himself to punish me."

After we finished installing the essential communications lines, I was used wherever young, strong, adaptable hands were needed. Thus I began a series of apprenticeships with an assortment of teachers whose idiosyncracies ranged from heroic to insane. Having learned the joy of self-discovery, that I could often do more than I knew, I found this perhaps the most instructive and satisfying phase of my Seabee career.

Take Big Red Redfield for example, who habitually held two six-penny nails, drooling with his saliva, in a wide slot between his lower teeth. I helped him build tent platforms using two-by-fours and plywood. He taught me how to hold a hammer—always at the end of the handle—for maximum efficiency. In one stroke he could drive home a spike which for lesser men would have required three or four swings. At his constant encouragement and with daily practice, I got to do it with three strokes and eventually two, then I was made an electrician's helper.

First Class Petty Officer Blackie "Hot Wires" Blackburn was in charge of installing electricity which emanated from a constantly clamoring diesel generator behind the chow hall. Until our tents were hooked up, I visited the diesel every morning to shave, plugging my electric razor directly into an outlet in its body. The vibration lasted a good five minutes after I stepped onto firm, quiet earth. Blackie was enamored of the diesel; its motion soothed him. He would take his weekly ration of beer and drink it alone on the diesel platform.

More than the generator itself, he worshipped the electrical current it produced. Unlike most men, he found unsurpassed delight in working with hot wires — wires "coursing with juice," to use his phrase — wires that threw off sparks every now and then, wires that would sizzle ordinary creatures of the world. He was a jocular, heavy-set, apish fellow with one cast eye, its pupil like a coal. The black hair that covered his torso would literally spring erect as the "juice" flowed through him.

In constant dread of electrocution, I pleaded with Blackie to turn off the power while we worked with the wires. Not a chance; indeed, my fear amused him. "It's good for your system," he said as he struck two wires together to make a shower of sparks. "Ever see anything prettier?"

After a few weeks I had had enough and went to Chief Winter, whom I had heard needed a rodman for his surveying party. The chief, fortyish, light-haired, wispy looking, agreed to take me on, provided I was prepared to rough it away from camp for a couple of weeks. "I need someone to help me map the peninsula across the bay," he said, speaking in his unassuming, soft way. "We know nothing about the place, what the natives are like, whether there are still Japs around. I suspect that no white man has ever set foot there." None of his regular crew was anxious to join him, and only as a last resort would he order someone to go against his will. As for my situation, nothing could be more life threatening than my job with "Hot Wires" Blackburn. I figured there was a better chance to survive on an unexplored peninsula.

After dumping us on a shimmering thin white strand of sand, the small landing craft slowly disappeared. A sago swamp bordered the beach and encroached on it in places. We set up our pup tents in the shade of a stand of tall palms, and worked only during the cool of the early morning and evening. We relaxed on the hot afternoons, stripped naked in the ocean breeze under the palms writing letters or reading or swimming in the dazzling aquamarine sea among the lushly multicolored coral formations.

Late afternoons we returned to work, often remaining naked and barefoot, lugging instruments on our shoulders. No natives or Japs ever appeared, but we found well-worn footpaths along the forest high ground. The chief speculated that we were being watched. "These paths are probably thousands of years old," he said. "So long as we don't disturb anything, I don't expect trouble." He was a committed conservationist long before the idea was popular. "We must preserve all naturally living things and respect their right to a place on earth."

It was customary that I would take the lead along a path, hacking away low fronds and branches with a machete. At certain points the chief would stop and send me into the undergrowth with my rod so he could take a reading. On one such occasion, he hollered at me to freeze. Instantly I became a statue; I heard a shot ring out; the ground near my feet quivered. Slipping past me as I stayed frozen, the chief bent down at my feet and retrieved two sections of a snake no more than a foot in length.

"It's a Coral snake, I believe," he said quietly, examining it in detail. "Yep, that's what it is. In three seconds, maybe only two, you'd have been gone. It doesn't look vicious—actually it's kinda beautiful—but this here's the deadliest reptile in these parts. You all right? It's okay to move now. Close calls make you appreciate life more. Let's go, son; let's get on with the job."

Those two weeks with Chief Winter were among my happiest and most peaceful overseas. I was without a care and I felt secure, as a child would with a father. The chief, always patient and gentle in both action and word, seemed to promulgate appreciation for the world. He was a man to emulate. My heart was sad when the launch arrived to carry us back to duty and other responsibilities.

Whenever I have felt overwhelmed with problems, I have retrieved that brief interval on the peninsula like a happy dream. Although I saw the chief only casually and rarely after that, when we passed each other, our eyes met sparkling with understanding, and we nodded meaningfully without a word. It was all beyond words: He saved my life.

As soon as I got back to camp, I visited the brig, where I found Fortune in his cot gravely ill again. His face was flushed and glossy with sweat and he was delirious. A corpsman was in attendance but did nothing. I left and returned immediately with a bucket of water and a towel, which I dampened and pressed against his burning brow. After several applications he responded and grasped my hand weakly. With his eyes closed he smiled wanly. "This time I'm dying," he said.

"So why are you smiling?" I asked.

He opened his eyes which looked like watery, red-streaked slits.

"Because you're here. It's good to see you before I die."

"Don't be so dramatic, Barry. You can't die. How'll we win the war?"

"Listen," he whispered, motioning me to draw nearer. "I'm leaving everything to you." He pointed to the footlocker behind his cot. "Take the Forty-Five from in there, it's yours." I knew then he was dead serious. He withdrew a worn folded paper from beneath his pillow and pressed it into my hand. "This is my will. See to the Fox, Hal. Take care of her. You'll be a rich man."

"Christ, you're not dying," I said as much to myself as to him.

He closed his eyes, then he began to shiver. The heat pressed down on us from the tent roof. His hand fell twitching to the dirt floor. As I watched him sink, my eyes welled with tears. I cared about him more than I realized. I prayed that he not die. But I wouldn't find out for sure whether he did or not until months later.

On my next job I committed murder every day; I slew trees, great mahoganies, majestic teaks. I was a pipsqueak David, felling enormous, helpless Goliaths with giant two-man saws and long-handled axes. Screaming "timber" as the awesome things toppled off their fractured bases and crashed to the ground with a bounce that made the earth tremble, I grew hoarse by day's end. After a few weeks, despite my naturally stringy physique, I noticed a change in my muscular development. My biceps and pectorals had expanded, my thighs had thickened, and my overlong neck was fatter and seemed shorter as a result. Of course, I was hardly a match for "Pee Wee Pappy" Polakowski, the squat chief in charge of our detail, who although in his forties, was still a powerhouse with muscles that rippled and surged like a stormy sea. Pee Wee Pappy hailed from Chicago. "The West Side, just off Skid Row. Everything I know, I learned from the stew-bums on Madison Street," he explained as proudly as if this were equivalent to a Ph.D.

"But you certainly didn't learn lumberjacking there," I commented.

"Hell, I was a fuckin' building wrecker. I can swing a ball like no one you ever saw. So if I could do buildings, which there ain't any to wreck over here, I told 'em I could do trees and they went for it." To Pee Wee Pappy the logic was unequivocal.

Destruction was Pee Wee Pappy's game; I could see from the glint in his eyes as each tree crashed down how much joy it gave him. But I found it anathema to my formative conservationist principles. Chief Winter's quiet but persistent influence during our stay on the peninsula endured. How could we blithely annihilate a beautiful natural object that had been alive for centuries, and as a final insult destroy it, to lay bare its two hundred or three hundred rings, in no more than an hour and a half? At each felling, I felt that I was betraying myself and maybe God, the one I didn't believe in.

To sublimate my troubled conscience, I exhausted myself from the sheer physical labor and lost my voice eventually from the screaming, until in a few weeks after denuding a hillside, the cutting was halted. We had accumulated enough timber for the time being; there remained the task of cutting the logs into usable boards, my next assignment, which I found much more redeeming.

The sawmill was located near the foot of Pancake Hill at the edge of a saltwater lagoon. It was a sensible place to have it, for the mahogany and teak logs could be dragged down to the bay shore nearest the cutting site and floated easily to the lagoon. The freighters from stateside also found it a convenient place to discharge by allowing them to dump their loads of pine timber directly into the bay from an offshore mooring.

The logs were corralled inside a large floating perimeter of beams tied end to end in a vast circle. This is where I worked, balancing on the tightly packed bobbing logs. I would grab one with a long-handled spike, lead it to a wooden ramp, hook a motorized cable around one end, and ride it up the ramp to a platform, where I'd unhook it and roll it off the ramp into the path of the whirling saw. I found the job enticingly rife with risk and challenge. Each night at eight I began work anxious to perform my balancing act, eager for danger, for the pleasure of skillfully beating the odds.

There was a circus quality, an abandon, to the atmosphere of the place. We worked at night under brilliant floodlights that illuminated the entire ramshackle mill and a portion of the corral nearest the shore. Spirits were high; laughter commonplace, although most of the time it was drowned out by the deafening screech of the saw. I welcomed the lights when they were behind me as I searched the corral for my next log, but they blinded me when I turned to the shore, forcing me to look downward to see my way. At first I fell often, trying to walk the rolling, dancing logs in my attempt to line them up for their trip to the ramp. I always seemed to find a black hole of water to fall into; after a while, as I became more surefooted, the dunkings became rare.

"Whitey" Whitehead, so named for the shock of blond hair that fell down his forehead in front of his eyes, poodle style, operated the winch that controlled the cable. By manipulating a lever he regulated the cable speed and its starting and stopping. He would speed up then stop suddenly to see whether I could hold my footing as I rode the log up the ramp.

The sawmill gang, admirers of my agility, unknown to me took bets on my falls during the evening. Would I fall? Where would I land—on my head, my feet, or my ass? And how many times would I fall during a shift? The game went on for weeks. Whitey, half crocked on 3.2 beer, cackled gleefully while I performed my balancing act. At first I cooperated innocently, enjoying the opportunity to test my skill, but after awhile the game became tiring, then annoying. Finally one of my mates, seeing my irritation and the increasing danger, told me about the betting. "You sonofabitch, Whitey," I blew. "You're all sonofabitches."

"Hell, it was just a little fun," Whitey said.

"The least you could have done was let me in on the betting," I said.

"Mebbe you're right," Whitey said sheepishly. "But I'll tell you one thing, son, the odds always favored you stayin' on and landin' feet first. So you oughta feel good about that." I did; I was mollified.

It felt good to be part of a high-spirited, finely-tuned unit. For four or five hours at a clip we worked in silence or singing without being heard against the redoubtable din of the screeching saw. How easy it was to become lost in yourself, hemmed in by the soft, black night, feeling removed from the rest of humanity, imagining that the war was unreal and that the mahogany boards we were making would end up in shiny pianos and hand-carved chests in a calm, fresh world.

When the saw was stopped for sharpening, and the air became startlingly quiet, we gathered in a circle swapping nostalgic stories of our lives stateside. Inevitably a craps game was formed, even though it was prohibited. At two o'clock one morning the commander showed up, but before making an appearance he sent his driver ahead to warn us. We instantly broke up the game and were innocent when the commander arrived. "You're doing a fine job, men. I'm proud of you," he said, nodding and smiling beneath his visor decorated with "scrambled eggs." Who knows when he slept? He visited every shift. "We're the best damn Seabee battalion there is," he said as he departed. And we believed him.

When the shift was over at three, a truck delivered us the five miles back to camp. Weary, dirty, and sweaty, I restored myself with a cool shower and clean shirt and jeans and went eagerly to the movies, which ended just before dawn. It was the commander's policy that the night shift and day shift should have equal pleasures and privileges. Who could deny we had one hell of a commander?

After the movie I returned to my tent and lay on my cot as my mind drifted to Lucia. I had delayed writing her about Fortune until I knew his fate. I was coming to admit the possibility that this time he might not make it. How many attacks of malaria could a person take?

One night, preoccupied with Fortune's condition, I walked the logs and rode them up the ramp like a robot. Were Fortune to die, how would I break the news to Lucia? What would I do with the inheritance, the millions? Would I survive the war to enjoy such riches? Certainly at the moment I stood little chance of survival, unless I concentrated on my work.

There was no moon; it was a cavernous night. Whitey attempted to test my footing but I screamed at him, angrily warning him of my ill mood. I bounded into the corral to escape and fell in.

Whitey saw me go down, saw my head glance a log, saw me fall into a black hole of water, and waited for me to come up. He waited in vain. In panic he rushed to the water's edge, scanning the surface. The saw was stopped and the entire crew joined him. He waded out to his armpits calling and searching. Finding a small log, he floated himself in the midst of the jouncing hulks and saw me, one arm flung around a log, groggy, blood pouring down my face. He dragged my log ashore, picked me up, and hauled me in a run to a weapons carrier. He placed me gently into the truck section and without permission rushed me off to sick bay at camp.

The wound with its profusion of blood was not as serious as it appeared. The same corpsman who had been attending Fortune treated me, wrapped a bandage around my head, then led me to the now empty cot that Fortune had been lying on earlier. "Lie down here until the doctor sees you," he said, "in case you've got a concussion."

I refused. "Where's Fortune," I demanded. "Where did they take his body?"

"You'd better lie down. I think you've got a concussion," the corpsman said in response to my raving. "Fortune's been transferred to the army hospital near Pancake Hill. Better lie down now."

"Do you think he'll make it? I mean he was pretty damn sick."

"Yeah, the army's got top doctors." I closed my eyes and realized how relieved I was that I wouldn't have to contend with Fortune's millions. Falling into an untroubled sleep, I began to heal both within and without. Fortune would make it now, eh?

XI
Hollandia

Folly and Error

Infamous Pancake Hill. The leveling of the hill was a supreme endeavor emblazoned forever in the memory of each and every man of our battalion. Nothing we ever did before or after compared with it in magnitude of sheer effort. Nothing ever measured up to it in expenditure of human agony, of lives, and of machines—not the great teak and mahogany docks, not the clearing of an airstrip in the recalcitrant jungle, not the miles of road carved through limestone along the steep, forested hillsides, and not the Fleet Post Office complex. Nor had we ever done anything before or since that was more challenging to the imagination, more dramatic in execution—more futile and useless.

Although chosen against the commander's advice, the project was without doubt his greatest opus. Once committed to the task, he dedicated himself without reservation. Here was an opportunity to bring into play all his previous engineering experience. Yes, he would flatten the hill in record time despite the Command's constraints caused by the siphoning off of vital equipment and men for spurious schemes—MacArthur's house for one.

In its pristine form, the hill was a five-hundred-foot high wooded elevation about a mile in circumference at the base. The southern perimeter plunged into the bay, leaving a narrow sandy beach on which the base sawmill was located. To the north an impenetrable swamp stretched near the shore for three or so miles, separated from the bay by a strip of orange sand. The swamp was an evil place, reputedly the home of hordes of poisonous snakes and swarms of plasmodium parasite (malarial) infected female anopheles mosquitoes. It abounded with deceptive mud holes of quicksand that sucked down its victims so quickly as to defy their rescue.

There was little flatland to be found around Hollandia. Nestled on a tiny valley floor, the port itself was one of the few natural level places available, but it was too restrictive. The other nearby level spot lay to the west of Pancake Hill, a valley about a quarter mile wide, bordered by another rise. But beyond that the land leveled off for ten miles all the way to Lake Sentani. Yes, Rutledge had recommended ignoring the hill and placing the arsenal and the heavy equipment storage dump in the small valley below it, and the warehouses and hospital behind the hill on more distant but spacious land. The topography easily permitted a connector road to be built from there to the bay. And the Command's insistence on hugging the shore and concentrating its installations in one spot for the sake of convenience, would prove unfortunate. Our ultimate purpose was to provide the staging area for the coming advance into the Philippines.

When Rutledge and his staff studied the topographical maps and visited Pancake Hill, he said nothing of his preference, made no reference to his altercation with the Command. Once an order was given, whether Rutledge believed in it or not, he faithfully carried it out. "There's our flatland," he said, pointing to the hill, a forested truncated protrusion between the expanse of the sea and the level swamp. The entourage stared at the hill, then at each other and rolled their eyes.

"Excuse me, Jerry," said Gluck, acting the courageous spokesman. "Where I come from, heh, heh, they call that a hill."

"Well, so it is, Gluck, so it is, but not for long. We're gonna move a mountain, Gluck, we're going to move it right into that vile swamp over there—kill two birds with one stone, make us some flatland and eradicate the mosquitoes."

"Jesus, Jerry, that's a tall order. There's plenty of level land inland a short ways. Shouldn't we consider—"

"Bear in mind, Gluck, that speed and efficiency will be important when the fleet arrives for the push. It makes more sense to concentrate our installations in one spot near the bay. The decision is made, Gluck. The subject's closed." Rutledge's tone silenced Gluck with its ring of finality and impatience.

The leveling of Pancake Hill was coincident with the construction of officers' country, which suffered delay after frustrating delay as a consequence. Our entire complement of bulldozers was commandeered, diverted from "lesser" tasks. They swarmed over the hill seemingly in all directions, tearing at it hungrily. But actually there was a system. The D-4s and D-6s (small and medium-sized bulldozers) ripped down the trees; the D-8s scoured out paths taken by the earth movers, which gulped up the soft red dirt to run it over the edge of the swamp. After they dropped their fill, other dozers pushed it into the thick stagnant water. They were assisted by payloaders and the giant-wheeled dump trucks, which transported more earth.

Every day in my spare time I visited the site, fascinated by the plodding daily progress. It was barely perceptible, but with the passing of each week the change became obvious, as more trees disappeared from the hillsides and the gentle cone grew steadily broader and flatter. Whether directly connected with the undertaking or not, each man among us was concious of the project. It had become our raison d'etre, as if the hill were an enemy and the leveling a battle.

When at last the rise was defeated — reduced to boring, treeless flatland — and the swamp eradicated, the victory was hollow. By the time the job was done, the war had moved so quickly that the new land arrived too late to be of use.

Billiard Ball offered his usual comment on the project: "The leveling of Pancake Hill symbolizes the modern American ethic. We don't accept the world as it's given to us; we don't try to adjust to it. Instead we automatically rush in to make a new world, only to discover that it's a mistake or useless after all."

"Maybe someday we'll strike a balance," I said, "between the best of what's here and what we can bring to it."

"Good luck, my friend," he replied bitterly.

The saga of Pancake Hill was not over at its demise. (We continued to call it a hill long after it ceased to be one.) Very quickly it became a hellhole for everyone who worked and dwelled there. As planned, our many installations and those of several neighboring outfits were crammed together onto the former swamp, rather than well spaced. There were a hospital, warehouses, equipment and transportation storage dumps, a post office, electrical generator sheds, and a tent village for the personnel who manned the nearby facilities. There was a section devoted to ammunition storage. From the air, the hill appeared as a smooth dark brown slash between the blue sea and the lush greenery. It served as a convenient landmark for aircraft on their approach to the airstrip farther inland. And so it was for the Japanese reconnaissance planes, who could spot it easily by day, and for their bombers at night when they dropped incendiary flares.

As we had learned early on during that fateful night after landing at Hollandia, the engines of Japanese planes had a characteristic uneven drone. When they were overhead we would think they were having engine trouble and were about to conk out. One brilliant afternoon we heard a rattletrap chorus overhead and spotted their planes, gray spots in the blue, passing over, but they disappeared too quickly for our fighters to scramble and confront them. That night while watching a movie we heard them again, heard the now familiar rumble as they approached, heard their sputtering as they drew close. But this time we heard something new: the whistle of their bombs dropping, the boom of nearby explosions, and the thuds of those more distant.

The target: Pancake Hill, more precisely, the ammo dump. They found it, hitting it dead on. Although we were back at camp, a good five miles away, the land beneath us trembled, the tents shook, and the air vibrated. The sky surged brightly like an aurora borealis. Departing our tents, we gathered en masse at the open air-theater, where we had an unobstructed view of the glowing horizon. The show continued for hours, well into dawn, as the ammo dump expended itself. We spoke in subdued tones, as if in the presence of some awesome cosmic force.

"I pity those poor bastards on the hill," Billiard Ball said. "They gotta be diggin' foxholes with their bare hands."

"The shrapnel must be flyin' around like a blizzard," said Whitey.

I was worried about Fortune who was on the hill in the field hospital. "He's too sick to dig a foxhole," I said.

"All you can do is hope," said Billiard Ball.

"He's gotta be gone because the hospital's next to the ammo dump," said Whitey.

"My God," I said grief stricken. "My God."

After it was all over, after the explosions stopped around midmorning, those of us not on duty climbed aboard the throng of vehicles—jeeps, trucks, weapons carriers, even bulldozers—and headed for the hill. We found the land cratered and pocked like a moonscape, the buildings ripped apart to jagged shreds. The field hospital was no more, nor was there a sign of it ever having been—only empty, steaming craters where it had stood. An organized crew was scouring every inch of the place, lifting every fragment, looking for survivors or corpses. As we limped through the ruins, and the immensity of the destruction came home to us, our anger grew. We cursed the Japs, "Godamn them, goddamn them." Seventy-eight men died, twenty-seven from our battalion; five were missing and never found. Billiard Ball erupted bitterly, "How stupid can we be? We created a perfect target, then gave them a bonus—a real live ammo dump, Christ."

Was it stupidity, or innocence owing to inexperience, or arrogance? Whatever the category, we felt the need to lay it on ourselves. Certainly Jerry Rutledge did. Despite having warned the Command of the danger, he bore the brunt of the blame and the pain. We underestimated or ignored our vulnerability, but berating ourselves wouldn't undo the tragedy or, for me, bring back Fortune.

I believed in the necessity of the war. No question our cause was justified. As good news of American successes accumulated, I came to believe that our ultimate invincibility was assured. I had faith in our commander and the implacable power of our machinery. But why did we not take precautions; why did we place an ammo dump near a field hospital; what goddamned fool was ultimately responsible?

When Fortune's body didn't turn up, he was classified among the missing. Although technically neither dead nor alive, his status was a matter of faith. What could I tell Lucia? Billiard Ball shrugged. "I wouldn't hope too much. Prepare yourself for the worst." I visited Gluck's office seeking an answer.

"We'll let you know if we find anything," Gluck said gently. Even he, shaken by the event, had forsaken his usual bluster.

> Dearest Lucia,
>
> Barry is ill, a bout of malaria again. I'm afraid he keeps forgetting to take his yellow pills. But the worst is over and he's on the mend. A few days ago they transferred him from sick bay to the field hospital, where he'll get more professional care. I understand they have quinine there, which works better than atabrine, as you no doubt know.
>
> It will be awhile before he's up and around. Unfortunately, I'm unable to see him as often as I'd like, for the hospital is some distance from the camp. Usually, in cases like this, once he's able to travel, they'll send him to Port Moresby or Brisbane for recuperation. Some guys have all the luck.

This little fictional scenario, interspersed with a grain of truth, I thought had to be convincing. It revealed enough to prepare her for a reversal, yet offered her hope that things would turn out all right. She would also understand the absence of references to Fortune in my future letters. If I rarely saw Fortune or, better still, if he were transferred out of the area, she would not expect otherwise.

My letter continued:

> I have been working in a sawmill with a wonderful bunch of guys at a job I enjoy. Our comaraderie is warm and marvelous,

and recently when I had a small accident
(I'm okay now, none the worse for it),
they stopped everything and came to my
rescue.

Having delayed addressing Lucia's invitation to make
southern California my home, I evaded it again: It was more
than I could handle. This was not the right time, not while
Fortune's fate was unsettled, to take her seriously. I stuck to
innocuous subjects instead.

Actually, when I wrote of my work at the mill, my career
there had already ended. Where were the limits to my
capacity for coloring the truth? After the frightening fall, I
became extra cautious. What if Whitey hadn't found me? I'd
have slipped under and drowned. My old confidence was
gone, and with it my surefootedness. Although I tried to hide
the fear, expecting that it would pass, I couldn't deny its
disturbing effects. The saw seemed voracious, always needing
more logs than I could arrange to line up at the ramp. My
performance worsened, and each failing night fed the cycle
until I gave up, like a burned-out fighter pilot. "I can't do it
anymore. Don't ask me to walk the logs. I can't do it," I
confessed to the chief.

I was told to sit tight while awaiting reassignment. For
several days I lay on my cot in a depressed limbo, feeling
humiliated and a failure. I had become a has-been at the
tender age of twenty. Was there any doubt about where I'd
end up before long? They'd send me to KP, dreaded KP, with
all the other misfits.

I was in a chronic state of panic for the next three
months. Nothing was going right: the tragic disaster of
Pancake Hill, Fortune's disappearance, my loss of nerve, a
hated job. My reading at the time, Dostoyevski's *Crime and
Punishment*, was hardly remedial, antidepressant literature.
My attitude reflected the general mood of the battalion. The
shock of Pancake Hill was at the root of our outrage over
MacArthur's "mansion."

Our wrath, especially the commander's, had some
intrinsic justification. The "mansion" project drained us of

our most skilled craftsmen just when we desperately needed them to rebuild the hill. Complaints to Fleet headquarters were unavailing. Gluck was indignant. "I'll bet the general rammed this one down the Command's throat."

But Rutledge decided not to press too hard. "As they say, Gluck, nobody listens to God, only the Democrats listen to Roosevelt, but everybody listens to MacArthur."

The site for the house was dreamily situated at the summit of a hill cleared of trees, affording a panoramic view of blue Lake Sentani and the endless forest beyond. At the end of each day when the men of the detachment assigned to constructing the house arrived back at camp, they described in detail its luxurious appointments, its multitude of flush toilets, walls of glass (an innovative architectural concept then), and marble-floored entry. Although they marveled at these features, and so did we upon hearing of them, they could not hide the underlying feeling of shame and resentment. "Big Red" Redfield, the carpenter was typical: "I hope his majesty the sonofabitch likes the job we're doin'." "What an imperial bastard," exclaimed Billiard Ball.

During the next weeks, as the progress on the hill became stymied for lack of enough jouneymen, we began to steam and finally explode into rebellion. Virtually to a man, as if in unspoken conspiracy, we lined up at the bursar's office and canceled the automatic monthly withdrawals from our paychecks for purchase of war bonds. Gluck was hysterical over our action. What kind of impression would this make on the Command? How would it reflect on the battalion's officer corps? Walking up and down the line, nabbing several of the more influential enlisted men, Gluck attempted to dissuade them from their action. "What you're doin' is an act of mutiny. Where in hell's your sense of patriotism?" But the men were adamant. None would risk his standing among his mates.

The war moved north too swiftly to allow MacArthur to make use of the house. That, apparently, combined with our mass action, had a salutary effect on his public relations policy. The mansion was quickly converted to an escape cottage. A contingent of Wacs and nurses had arrived nearby.

This led to romantic entanglements and some marriages. As a wedding gift, each couple was granted a week of bliss on top of the world in MacArthur's "Honeymoon Haven." Soon everyone, forgetting MacArthur's original intent, reinstated his bond purchase plan.

"Why don't they send Barry home?" Lucia implored in her next letter. "Don't they realize he will mend faster here? Why doesn't he write? I know how much he dreads writing, but under the circumstances I should think he would try. If only he would send me a postcard." Her words showed desperation, and also impatience, perhaps annoyance. How long, I wondered, could I stall her with my fictitious scenario? Were she to grow deeply angry at Fortune, I would have to tell her the truth, and then wouldn't I, despite my best intentions, become the butt of her anger?

"You know how Barry is," I replied immediately. "He thinks he's a superman, that nothing serious can ever happen to him, but he always pulls through, so of course he doesn't realize how worried you are." I surmised that she was as familiar with his sense of indestructibility as I was. Hadn't she once nursed him back to health from near death? She must have seen how death tantalized him. But he was concerned only with how he would die, not with death itself. A bullet in the back, especially an American bullet—what could be more contemptible? A Jap bullet straight through the forehead—that would be more like it. Or would death by shrapnel from an American shell while he was lying helpless on a cot in a field hospital qualify as proper? If he never turned up, Lucia was bound to understand why I lied. Because how could I ever be sure he wouldn't?

Customarily when my spirits were down, I sought solace in music and fiction. During free daytime hours I read Dostoevski; at night after chow hall cleanup I visited the music tent, which was still monopolized by the New York gang. The outstanding soloists were Huberman, Cortot, Myra Hess, Menuhin, and Paderewski; the records were 78s made of brittle shellac; the fidelity, by today's standards, was very poor. Yet, here on records in the midst of the raw, usurping jungle, I heard the impeccable, incredible performances of the best artists of the day. The playing was so stirring one moment, so delicate and sweet the next, so superbly civilized. The contrast between the high art and the primitive surroundings somehow made the music more vital, more intense. It has never been so to me since.

I felt sad that I had no friend with whom to share my feelings for music. What a shame Billiard Ball was such a musical moron. I begged him to visit the music tent with me. "Forget the music. Take a book along," I said. He categorically refused. For a moment there was a spark of warmth in one of the New York gang's coldness towards me. We had just listened to Schubert's Quintet. "Terrific, don't you think?" he commented. "Just terrific." But it didn't go any farther.

I drew closer to Billiard Ball during my unhappiness, abetted by the fact that we worked side by side in KP and had similar hours. On days off we hitchhiked around the countryside together, exploring the army encampments in the hinterland and visiting the air force installations. For hours at a time we sat in the shade under the wing of a parked plane observing the airstrip—a loud, tumultuous, exciting place with its sleek fighters and bulbous bombers constantly taking off on missions and returning in various states of dismemberment. No jets in those days, only propeller planes. "The pilots are only kids," Billiard Ball remarked, "no older than you." As they ambled by on their way to their planes, they waved and smiled. But those returning from a flight were visibly weary and ignored us.

One of the very young pilots, a compact fellow with a crew cut and mischievous, amused eyes, passed our spot on his way to a revetment where his plane was parked. He motioned us to follow. We hesitated. He half turned and said over his shoulder, "Don't you want to go up? It's a routine mission, a little reconnaissance, about a half hour, that's all."

"Your destination?" Billiard Ball asked as we caught up with him and walked by his side to his plane.

"Other side of the bay, just to keep an eye on the Japs over there, maybe stir them up a bit. By the way, name's Diver."

118

An A20 attack bomber, distinguished by two large pods housing the engines, one under each wing, stood in its revetment. A machine gun jutted from its nose like a shortened sword. In the underbelly of its fuselage was a dark gaping hole about six feet long and three feet wide – the bomb bay. Reaching up into the bomb bay, Diver retrieved two parachutes.

"Put these on," he ordered.

"Where's yours," I inquired.

Shrugging, he grinned. "My number doesn't come up today."

"Mine doesn't either," I rejoined.

"If you don't mind," said Billiard Ball. "I'll wear one."

"Okay," said Diver, "hop in there."

"Into the bomb bay?" Billiard Ball and I asked in unison.

"Room for only two in the cockpit," Diver explained. "If one of you prefers..."

"No, no, we'll use the bomb bay," we said and followed him into the opening.

"See that canvas strap up in there? Kneel on the edge and just hang onto that. Make sure you don't let go, okay?"

The strap straddled the width of the fuselage about a quarter of the way out into the bay opening. Were we to release our grip, there was no way to avoid hurtling into the void. Tempted though I was to request a parachute, my pride wouldn't allow it. Furthermore I believed I'd survive. Had I caught a case of Fortune's fatalism after all?

We crouched along the edge of the bomb bay, grasping the strap so tightly that our knuckles were white, and remained silent. Billiard Ball's complexion had taken on a greenish cast. As the pilot revved the shrill engines making ready for takeoff, the plane shimmied and shivered. During our roll down the runway, at first we stared at the tiny patch of ground beneath us, which quickly became a blur. But as we lifted, a clear, widening expanse evolved. Mesmerized, I gazed down on the largest world I had ever seen. This was my first air flight. The color was dazzling: an aquamarine Humboldt Bay, a purple Lake Sentani, an unbroken lush green forest extending to the azure mountains on the far horizon. Here was Fortune's rich and magnificent tropical land.

Only one landmark was familiar—the disfiguring brown slash that was Pancake Hill. Lake Sentani reminded me of home, of New England's freshwater lakes, of Sebago Lake in Maine, where I had spent many summers. "Let's go for a swim in the lake after we get down," I shouted to Billiard Ball. But the sound of my words was lost in the whistle of the wind and the clatter of the engines. So I mouthed the word "swim" and pointed to the lake, and he mouthed the word "crocodile" and snapped his teeth shut. But I saw him also say "beautiful, beautiful," and I watched his eyes gleaming and watery with excitement, as mine must also have been.

Then in an instant we were engulfed in terror. The plane veered into a sharp, sudden dive. We heard the rat-a-tat of a machine gun. Was it ours, were we being pursued? What in hell was going on? While clutching the strap, our fingernails tore into our flesh, but we drew no blood for our hands were bloodless. When, after seemingly endless moments, the plane reached the bottom of its dive, we experienced an excruciating sensation caused by the tremendous compression. Then up again we went, then another dive, and another, as the world turned to chaos. Finally, organization returned and we resumed horizontal flight and headed for the airstrip.

After we were parked and the engines were shut down, we remained in our crouch at the edge of the opening. Diver, puzzled by our delay, came around to investigate. "Liked it so much, you don't want to leave, huh?" he said.

"Bullshit," Billiard Ball muttered. When at last we attempted to rise from our position it was extremely painful. Our joints were locked into position. Diver had to help us uncoil as if we were arthritic old men. As I tried to walk, I had the sensation of being short legged.

"What was going on?" I demanded, only partly suppressing my anger.

"Didn't you see the Japs?" he asked. "There were swarms of them. The bastards fired at us, so I gave it to 'em." But Diver gave only half a mind to us for he was observing a fighter plane coming in for a landing.

"But you said no combat," Billiard Ball reminded him. Then Billiard Ball pointed to another plane, a fighter, behind the one Diver had been watching. "Isn't that one coming in awfully fast?" Billiard Ball asked.

Gaining swiftly on the first fighter, the following plane was soon directly above it. The three of us fell silent while we watched and cringed, suddenly understanding the inevitability of what would happen during the next few seconds.

As the bottom plane touched the ground, the one above, oblivious to anything wrong, slipped onto the one beneath, briefly settling on it like a hen on an egg. Seeming to become aware of his error, the pilot of the plane on top tried to rise, but it was too late. His landing gear was already entangled in the plane below. The two planes, firmly joined, began to weave down the airstrip, then to tumble together in a confused frenzy in which neither alone was distinguishable. The mass careened off the runway into the jungle and burst into a fireball. Then it blew into smithereens.

From the moment the planes merged, Diver began to moan, "Oh no, oh no, oh no," and when they exploded he screamed and smashed the air with his fists and fell to uncontrollable sobbing. Reaching for him, Billiard Ball embraced him like a father and tried to soothe him, saying, "I know, I know. It's a terrible thing." And I, too, wept as the two men stood locked together. I wept for poor Diver, and for the boy in both of us that we were losing.

XII
Hollandia

A Rebel in Our Midst

I stood at attention before Gluck's disheveled, paper laden desk in his oven of a tent-office, sweat rivulets trickling into my stinging eyes. I blinked, partly for relief, mostly in surprise at Gluck's question: "When did you last hear from Fortune?" Gluck lay back in his chair waiting for my answer, a round face and a big round belly: two circles — one small, one large. The small circle spoke again: "Y'unnerstand what I said, sailor?"

"No, sir," I answered. "I mean, yes, sir...I mean...I thought he was dead, sir."

"Fortune dead? Hah, Fortune'll never die, not that sonofabitch." My pulse quickened; it was hard not to show my elation. "I take it then he ain't been in touch with you."

"That's right, sir. But where is he, sir?"

"Who's askin' the questions, you or me?"

"You, of course, sir."

"Wal, know your rank, sailor. Where in hell has he disappeared to? We'd like to know."

"Are you...are we sure he's alive, sir?"

Gluck sat upright, silent for a moment while fastening his eyes on mine, judging my sincerity. "Y'mean you didn't know he was in Brisbane?"

Less than an hour before I had read Lucia's latest letter, one of a weekly series in which she bemoaned my silence and Fortune's. But the tone in this one differed from the others. "I've given up on Barry. I know better than to expect him to write. But knowing your loyalty and how considerate you are, I can't help worrying that not hearing from you means something terrible has happened."

122

Since her speculations were drawing closer to the truth, how much longer should I keep her in the dark? Hadn't the agony of my silence finally exceeded the agony of her possibly knowing? I had made up my mind to tell her, as deftly as I could, all I knew about Fortune's unknown fate, hoping that the substance of my account would pass the censor undistorted. In fact I had already started framing my masterpiece in euphemism when I received the summons from Gluck.

Brisbane, how in hell did Fortune end up there? "No, sir," I said, still standing at rigid attention. "I had no idea that he was in..."

"You didn't know he's AWOL, either? You're absolutely positive you ain't heard from him?"

"That's right, sir." I began to bristle at his insinuation that I was covering up. But actually wouldn't I have protected Fortune had I known his whereabouts?

"Wal, if you hear from him, we want to know, see?"

"Yes, sir."

"Y'unnerstand, he's a deserter."

"Yes, sir."

"Friend or not, y'owe it to the battalion."

"Yes, sir."

"You're a fuckin' liar, Arnold."

"Yes, sir."

After Gluck dismissed me, I reported to KP to join in the preparation of the noonday meal. Immediately, unable to withhold my excitement, I confided to Billiard Ball what I had learned about Fortune.

"They'll catch up with him, and when they do, they'll throw the book at him. I urge you not to protect him, or you'll be considered an accessory," Billiard Ball advised.

"But I haven't heard from him."

"Don't worry, you will. You can bet on it."

The chow line had begun to form outside the large screened-in, low-roofed, two-by-four post-and-beam structure. I assisted loading the steaming trays of food—bully beef, ersatz potatoes, canned creamed corn—our typical roster of Seabee-issue delicacies, on the serving counter. "Y'lucky they ain't C rations like the army has," Gluck reminded us with monotonous regularity, like a nagging mother. The undiscriminating among us were always the first in line, as if each meal would be our very last. By the time we were ready inside, the queue extended the length of the building and out into the dusty street. At last the door opened. As the men filed past each of us at the serving counter, there were the usual gibes: "Hey, I ain't seen anythin' so good since I ate in that flophouse on Skid Row," or "Even when my wife's mad at me she treats me better than this," or "Y'know I was noticin' this stuff looks better after it comes out of me than before it goes in."

The chow line was an institution. It was there that the various battalion companies intermingled and everyone got to know everyone else and friendships were made and we sensed ourselves as being a complete, integrated, smoothly tuned unit. A stranger in our midst stood out like a flashing beacon.

That lunch hour, such a stranger appeared. He was dressed exactly as we were, white skivvy shirt, olive drab shorts, GI cap shielding his eyes. However he was notably distinctive, slighter than the norm, quieter and more withdrawn—not our typical mate in the chow line. But the mates on both sides of him were too busy gabbing among themselves to notice.

After passing unobstrusively through the doorway, he took a tray from the stack and reached the first food station, where I stood with full scoop raised ready to fling its contents of whipped ersatz potatoes. I knew immediately that he wasn't one of our boys. As our eyes met, his seemed to plead. A swarthy Asian, younger than I, and spindly, he waited while the spoon remained suspended. I recognized him; he knew I had. He was the enemy, now starving and harmless, desperate, willing to take an outrageous gamble. I flung the creamy ersatz on his tray and smiled and he moved on. Had I committed a traitorous act? I felt confused. Instinctively I wanted him to make it, but I knew that he had little chance of getting through the rest of the serving line.

The moment of discovery came only two stations down from me. There was a wild commotion and everyone put down his tray, forgetting the food, and pressing around him, grabbing at him. They hustled him outside to the street and began to pound him, knocking him down, cursing him, kicking him, picking him up so that another would have his turn. Someone drove up with a weapons carrier. They tied his hands behind his back and, attaching a tight noose around his neck, they tethered him to the rear of the vehicle. It started slowly; he ran behind, blood streaking down his temples, trying to keep up to prevent being strangled by the noose.

A few hundred feet down the dusty street the weapons carrier turned and headed back at increased speed. While choking in the dust billow he ran as fast as he could to remain erect. Our boys had now formed lines on both sides of the road, shouting and cheering, as the weapons carrier and its helpless victim swept past. After three passes, too exhausted to keep up, he stumbled. The vehicle dragged him along the road, his head bouncing against stones protruding from the road surface. By the last pass he was hardly more than an amorphous white lump of matter blotched and streaked red.

After the weapons carrier stopped, the men crowded around the lifeless mass and stared quietly at it. Some nudged it with their shoes, as if to verify its finality. Slowly, noiselessly, one by one they headed back to the chow line, picked up their trays, the food now cold, and resumed where they had left off.

Horror stricken, I watched the episode, which lasted no more than twenty minutes, from my station behind the counter. There were other passive watchers, among them Gluck, whom I spied standing alone at the far end of the chow hall. Having made no attempt to interfere, he disappeared after it was over. Billiard Ball was with me only at the beginning and quickly retreated to the kitchen, refusing to watch.

The line of men moved on in front of me, trays extended. I dished out the potatoes like an automaton, unable to rid my mind of the cruel recurring montage of what I had just witnessed. It was impossible to go on. I flung my spoon deep

125

into the mound of ersatz potatoes and ran off blindly into the glare of the tropical day—damn the consequences. Indignation, anger, disillusionment, shame—the same feelings I had experienced in the elegant lounge aboard ship—now consumed me helter-skelter, cutting off reason and reality. For the moment, I flailed at the world. In time I would be more specific.

Over the next few days I showed up at morning muster but failed to report for duty. Billiard Ball covered for me at KP. "I can't keep it up much longer," he warned. "Tomorrow the KPs are having short-arm inspection. You'd better be there."

"What do you mean, short-arm inspection? How in hell can we contract the 'clap' out here? The WACs and nurses are—well, they gotta be okay and no one in his right mind would consort with the natives."

He slapped me hard on the back. "Why, by jerking off, you dummy."

I burst into laughter for the first time in weeks. No matter, I wouldn't soften. "Let 'em come after me," I said.

Following Fortune's technique, I procured some plywood, screening, two-by-fours, and nails. From my former boss, Red Redfield, I borrowed a hammer and saw and commenced constructing a private apartment beneath one of the tents situated along a steep slope. It was a symbolic act. In effect I renounced having any association with my mates. It turned out that I had set a precedent for other loners in the battalion to follow. Claiming the "below deck" portion of the remaining tents built on the hillside, they too set up similar housekeeping units. Their motives probably differed from mine though; unlike myself, none were in passive and uncompromising rebellion.

Beyond the satisfaction of renunciation, I found living in the apartment a welcome relief in other ways. The privacy was luxurious: I wrote and read at will without distraction. In one prolonged creative binge I sent letters to every relative I could think of, to every high school friend and acquaintance, to all my former teachers and even to the principal. To Lucia I wrote what I had learned about Fortune — that he was safe, well, and in Australia. (She replied weeks later, "—then why hasn't he written? Hal, he's too cruel.")

But soon I received unwelcome visitors: first my squad leader, who advised me to report to duty, followed by my platoon chief, who warned me of the risk I was running by not doing so, followed by the young lieutenant who spelled out the consequences — a court-martial and the brig. To each of them I said, "I really don't care. Do whatever you want to me."

Then they changed tactics and sent Chief Winters. Could they have known how much I admired him? Of course not. It's just that Chief Winters was the right sort of man to deal with problem situations like mine. He spoke gently as we sat side by side on my cot. "I understand that many others have tried to persuade you to cooperate. Please believe me, Hal, when I say I don't intend to do any such thing." He cleared his throat, searching for his next words. "No one who has talked to you seems to understand why you're doing this."

"I'm not sure myself," I replied. "I don't seem to care about anything — about what happens in the war, about what happens to me. I always feel like I'm about to weep; I have to hold myself back."

"When did you start feeling this way?"

"Chief, the feeling sort of crept up on me."

"Commander Gluck is running out of patience. You know a court-martial would be a serious blight on your record." Chief Winters sighed as if to emphasize the sad prospect. "They say you blew up at everybody in the chow hall that day."

"That's not true. I just left; I gave up."

"It's an awful waste of a fine man — what you're doing."

My eyes filled with emotion. "Thanks, Chief. Coming from you — I appreciate what you're saying."

He reached his arm across my shoulders and pressed me to him. "Whatever is troubling you, I'm sure you have good reason. But don't be sore at the whole world. Choose what good you can find, no matter how small, and focus on it." He walked the two steps to my doorway, then turned. "We can thank God the coral snakes in the world will never take over, can't we?" He knew my trouble; he knew it before I did.

Billiard Ball made no attempt to talk me out of my rebellion. If anything, he goaded me on — thought my apartment was "incredibly innovative," thought my refusal to report to KP "a courageous act," considered my fearlessness in the face of threats of punishment proof of a strong character. "With all the skills you've learned, you're justified in refusing to do any more KP. Just because you're a kid, they're pushing you around. I'd call it age discrimination."

Although I still simmered with resentment against having to do KP, my major complaint was vaguer and deeper. "It's not the KP so much that bothers me," I said. Billiard Ball raised one of his eyebrows. "I'm just fed up with everything. I don't care what they do to me. I'll go to the brig. Somehow, I'd feel relieved if they'd punish me."

And then quickly our situations were reversed. Billiard Ball revealed his foolhardy decision: "Incidentally, I've volunteered for Biak." Biak was a small unsecured island off the north coast of New Guinea. The Command had requested that a contingent from our battalion accompany an invasion force to build an airstrip presumably while under fire. "Incidentally, you say! Just incidentally! You're nuts," I shouted. "You're looking to get killed."

"I'm no less rational than you. Look at what you're doing," he shot back.

"But what's your reason?" I demanded.

"Just plain boredom, and I'm tired of KP. I want to participate, to contribute. I think you can understand that."

"Sure I can," I said, "and I also remember how you abhor killing."

"I'm not volunteering to kill; I'm volunteering to build."

"You may have to kill or be killed. We've got enough killers, murderers, in the outfit already," I said bitterly. "You're absolutely the wrong man to go."

It came out just like that, so spontaneously that I startled myself. Billiard Ball caught it. "War does vile things to us," he

128

said. "It legitimizes our darker instincts, removes the shallow veneer. We're still the same primitive souls underneath no matter where we are, what the circumstances."

"I always imagined that Americans were somehow superior in their humanity," I said.

"Well, we have high ideals, that's true, and we have a sense of mission about them, but we're not superior. When our boys killed that Jap, we were helpless victims of ourselves." Billard Ball stood, his head barely clearing the ceiling. "You're quite right, Hal, I'm not much good for Biak. My instinct for cruelty and violence is far too repressed. Nevertheless, I'm going because I have to."

In wartime Hollandia in November 1944 at the gentle age of twenty, I could find no space in my heart to forgive my mates for our "crime." Yes, "our" crime. When we, Americans, won in the 1936 Olympics I felt proud; I shared in our victory. When we committed a dastardly deed, when we murdered, I felt guilty. I shared the shame, and perhaps I carried more than my share. Commander Rutledge, at the mature age of fifty-one, suffered from the wanton act of his beloved men, all good men for the battalion. Billiard Ball philosophized it all away; he had no need to reckon with ideals that he never had in the first place. But for Rutledge and me, there was no way out.

More than a week passed from the time I stormed out of the chow hall until I was told to report to captain's mast, the customary ritual for dealing with misconduct. Besides Commander Rutledge, Gluck was there silently judgmental while seated facing me next to the commander's desk. Rutledge sifted through some papers before him, then he looked up, squinting at me as I stood at stiff attention. "You have a clean record, son, yes, I'd even say an exemplary one. You've been a consistently good man for the battalion. Why do you want to spoil it?"

"I don't, sir."

"Then I fail to understand your refusal to work."

"I like to work, sir. I've learned to do a lot of things in the battalion, and I've always tried to do them well."

The commander rifled through the papers again. "Yes, I see from these reports here, from Redfield and Blackburn and

Pappy and from Chief Winters that you're a hard worker and a swift learner."

"Thank-you, sir."

"Don't thank me, son, thank yourself. It's your ability. No one can take that from you, so for God's sake, let's put it to use."

"Yes, sir."

"Then you'll return to work?"

"No, sir."

The commander's face reddened: "You're goddamned defiant, sailor."

"Sir, I've served on KP most of the time I've been with the battalion, more than most of my mates. It's not very satisfying." Taking a cue from Billiard Ball's argument, I added, "If only I could do something that makes a significant contribution."

"KP's a goddamned significant contribution," Gluck piped up. "Somebody's got to do it." Rutledge winced.

"Sir, may I request a transfer?"

"That's not necessary, son," said the commander, seeming wounded. "I'm sure we can work this out. If you'll report back to KP, we'll soon find you a job more to your liking."

Standing at unrelieved attention, I shifted lightly from one foot to the next. "Uh, when would that be, sir?"

"You've got gall, sailor," Gluck interjected.

The commander turned to me and spoke with candor in his voice. "I can only promise that it will happen. It depends on when something suitable turns up."

"Thank-you, sir. I think I'd rather go to the brig."

"What!" Gluck thundered. "You sonofabitch."

"Please, Gluck," the commander interrupted, "let me handle this." Testily he went on: "What in hell's eating you, sailor?"

"I want out, sir. I really want a transfer."

"Don't you realize we're a fine outfit, one of the best?"

"I don't think so, sir."

"You don't?" he bent over his desk toward me. "Why not?"

"I'm ashamed of us, sir."

130

At this the commander rose from his desk, strode to the doorway of his tent, and peered outside. "Gluck," he said, "would you look up Chief Warrant Officer Smithson and have him report to me? I'll deal with this sailor myself." Reluctantly and puzzled, Gluck departed.

Commander Rutledge returned to his desk, sat down, and closed the dossier before him. He raised his strangely tired and saddened eyes, confronting mine. "What are you ashamed of?"

"Of what we did."

"I take it you're referring to the incident of the Jap prisoner?" I nodded. "And you were involved?"

"No, sir."

He leaned back in his chair, grasping his hands butterfly fashion behind his head. "Ah, so that's it." Then he bent forward and almost whispered, "Between you and me, son, I'm ashamed, too. It's a burden I carry, that I'll always carry because in the end I'm responsible."

"I don't see how you can blame yourself, sir."

"Yes, well, we have no choice, you and I, don't we? Maybe you should try to follow your own advice."

Stunned for a moment at this revelation of my hypocrisy, I stammered, "I...I can't help it."

"Neither can I," he said. For several moments we were silent, yet in touch with each other. "Listen, son, I'm rejecting your request for a transfer. Go back to your tent. You needn't return to KP. Is that clear? Wait there until I have something for you. Be patient. It will take a while."

I would have gladly waited a lifetime had he asked.

Instead I waited three weeks — three long, boring weeks, during which I foolishly anticipated replies to the dozens of letters I had written earlier to everyone I was related to or knew in the world of my past. Upon Billiard Ball's recommendation long ago, I had asked my parents to send me *The Magic Mountain*. At last it arrived, and I began reading. In a sense, the hero on his mountaintop, and I in the commander's protective limbo, were in similar circumstances. I too was now in an unreal, safe, remote world, the kind that Billiard Ball had yearned for, a yearning he had suddenly forsaken.

131

At night, by the light of a kerosene lamp (only the regular quarters were electrified), I wrote more letters. No doubt my prolificacy exhausted the censors, those detested snoopers. Good, I'd drown them in my flood. One night I tried my hand at a story, my first, about the effect on its master of a dog dying after being struck by a car. I sent it to Lucia, who read it and said she wept, but since she had to be biased, I was unconvinced of its worth. I told Lucia that I was awaiting a new assignment, that I too had heard nothing from Fortune, and that should she or should I hear, each should let the other know. Without Fortune to dwell on, it was a tranquil phase in our correspondence. Billiard Ball was also gone, and without distractions to occupy me I worried about him as well.

When the contingent returned from Biak, rather what was left of it, Billiard Ball was one of them. He was still in shock, lying on his cot in the field hospital, eyes open, staring off into space, unable to talk, making no sign of recognition as I sat beside him. For days he was little more than an unresponsive robot. His left hand with two fingers missing was bandaged.

Gradually his awareness returned and soon we talked of small matters, of my unique situation but never of his, never of what happened to him. His old self, his flippant, sarcastic, arrogant, witty, bittersweet self, was now gone. Taking its place was a weighty solemnity, a sad humility, an almost sentimental warmth. His self-enclosure had thinned. "Thanks for spending so much time with me. Thanks for your concern. Thanks for your friendship. Thanks." A tear streaked down from the corner of his eye. Had the horror of his experience shattered the barrier he had mentioned during our early Hollandia days at the spring, the barrier that prevented him from expressing deep affection?

What had happened at Biak was the result of a calamitous mix-up in scheduling. Our boys found themselves going in first—the lead group of the assault wave, the ones to bear the brunt of the enemy's untrammeled firepower. They never got to build their airstrip, never got farther than the beach, where, decimated, they were retrieved, brought back to an LST offshore, and returned at a listless pace to Hollandia. Billiard Ball had to be told what had happened. He had no memory, only the fear.

Life in Hollandia was now assuming the quality and style of life in Finschafen. The Command was concentrating on actions almost two thousand miles to our north and west, pointing to the Philippines. A sense of winding down prevailed, a slowing of pace. Every project, necessary and otherwise, had been completed. Nothing urgent happened anymore. Alone at dusk one evening, I walked up the beaten path to the native burial cave, and sat gazing down at Hollandia harbor appearing as a vast horseshoe of glittering lights. We had created a near metropolis. I thought it a remarkable achievement, typically American, an assertion of our domination over the world around us. How uncomplicated and confident we were. Abundance was everywhere; solutions had only to be implemented. Our mission was clean and clear.

Chief Warrant Officer Smithson, thin, long-legged, graying, sporting a meticulous black-dyed mustache, sat where Gluck had sat three weeks earlier beside Commander Rutledge's desk. I stood at attention before them, my eyes shifting from one to the other. The commander smiled broadly. "Mr. Smithson has an opening aboard his vessel, which in my opinion presents a golden opportunity for you. Ask your questions, Smitty."

"Yes, yes." After clearing his throat at some length, he inquired, "Would you consider yourself mechanically inclined?"

"I'm not sure, sir. It depends on how complicated..."

"How about your father?" Rutledge interrupted. "Would you say he had ability along those lines?"

"Oh, well he was quite good with his hands. When I was a boy he'd tinker with his Model T just about every weekend."

"Good! Like father, like son," the commander said proudly. "Go on, Smitty."

"Yes, yes, have you had any experience with steam engines?"

"Steam engines?"

"Let's put it this way, son," the commander interjected. "In your physics course in high school, did you learn about steam engines, their principle, that sort of thing?"

"Yes, sir."

"There you are, Smitty. He knows what they're about."

"Yes, yes, and are you prepared at all times to take on the responsibility of keeping the Mudhog on an even keel?"

"What he means, son," said the commander, "is that if you don't do your job right, the vessel will flip over. But I'm willing to vouch for his dependability, Smitty."

"Yes, yes, then you understand what you'll be doing?"

"I think so, sir," I replied, giving no hint of my confusion.

"Good," said the commander, rubbing his hands together in satisfaction. "We'll take the necessary steps to transfer you to the harbor dredge immediately."

"You mean, sir, I'm leaving the battalion?"

"That's right. You'll become a member of the 1186th Detachment. Isn't that what you wanted, a transfer?"

"Yes, sir, but I thought..."

"Of course, the dredge operates under our wing, so you'll always be close by. Do you have some complaint, son?"

Among the thoughts rushing through my mind, most prominent was the happy realization that my KP days would be over, and that I would learn a new and permanent skill and become an expert. "No, sir, I appreciate your kindness."

The commander turned solemn. "I regret losing you. You've been a good man for the battalion, but I think you'll be better for it." His voice became thick and wistful. "Sometimes a change is necessary." Was he prescribing that for himself as well? Had he at last arrived at some inkling of his inevitable demise? He stood up, and grinning, shook my hand. Then to Smithson, he said, "Take him, Smitty, he's all yours, one of our best."

XIII
Hollandia

A Truly Memorable Evening

Thousands of GI's from units large and small scattered throughout the greater Hollandia area, converged on our camp. The migration actually began in the morning, evidenced at breakfast by our abnormally lengthy chow line. By lunch the number of diners had doubled, and during supper we were so overflowing that the kitchen ran out of food and had to send out to a nearby airforce supply depot for C rations. Bob Hope, Jerry Colonna, and singer Frances Langford, an illustrious trio of entertainers for sure, along with a bevy of female dancers, were to perform at our amphitheater.

As overseer of the social scene at the officers' club, arranging for Bob Hope and company's performance would be the crowning achievement of Smithson's career. He was responsible for scheduling all entertainment, arranging for nurses' and Wac's visits, and providing the appropriate hospitality for visiting VIPs, in short, performing a social director's role. The commander chose Smithson for the job partly because he was interested in club matters but mainly because running the Mudhog was an easy task and he seemed bored. Furthermore, by assigning him the job, the commander augmented his control over the dredge, which technically was still directly responsible to the Command.

During the performance, no audience could have been more responsive, more respectful, more tuned to every nuance of every word, of every expression, of every movement. Nothing the entertainers did could possibly be wrong. They symbolized Home, America, All That We Were Fighting For. It was like a glorious revival meeting during

135

which each of us was electrified and transported back to paradise and the sentimental past.

Backstage after the show a crowd, joined by the commander and Smithson, gathered around the performers. Always winning and charismatic, the commander invited Mr. Hope and his company to attend a brief get-together before they took off. "For a short while, I suppose," Mr. Hope responded, winking. "Y'know, Commander, they don't pay me much for doing this." Smithson, standing at the commander's elbow, offered to lead the way to officers' country.

"Just a minute, Smitty, aren't you going in the wrong direction?" said the commander.

"I don't think so, I've already made arrangements at the BOQ." (Bachelor Officers' Quarters)

"Well, that's too bad. I expect that Mr. Hope and his friends would rather go to the enlisted men's club."

"I see, yes, yes. I had assumed Jerry, er Commander...that is the officers expected that Mr. Hope..."

"I don't give a shit what they expected, Mr. Smithson."

Bob Hope suddenly quipped, "Say fellas, which one of you is on our side?"

The surrounding crowd snickered, but Commander Rutledge, in no mood for glibness, glowered at Smithson who turned sullen. "Tell the officers if they want to meet Mr. Hope, they'll be welcome at the enlisted men's club." Smithson left the scene in pique and immediately removed his belongings from officers' country where he resided, to the Mudhog.

The enlisted men's club, a long tent with a veranda attached situated on a palm fringed beach, was built shortly after the nurses and Wacs landed. "The men should have a place to entertain the women and recreate," the commander had said. ("I wonder how literally we should take that," Billiard Ball remarked.) A raised section of the floor, shaped like a ship's prow, was used as a stage and dance floor. Simulated port holes appeared on the curtain backdrop, and the prow's curve was painted blue with white waves furling upward. The bar, made of bamboo and plywood, served beer

136

and soft drinks. The enlisted men were proud of the club, and so was the commander who boasted that there was nothing like it in the Pacific theater.

As we ambled down the dark path to the club, Bob Hope said, "I hear your boys hired Dottie Lamour to be hostess of the enlisted men's club." At those words, we whooped and hollered as if it were true.

Reaching the club, which was jammed from end to end, Hope and the commander invaded the crowd. "Is it true what they say about the Seabees, Commander?" Hope asked.

"What's that, Mr. Hope?" The commander was smiling wide.

"Oh, call me Bob, please. Everyone does except Bing who's afraid it will go to my head. Well, they say you're giving night courses in souvenir making to the natives."

The crowd rollicked and the commander cackled, "Not a bad idea, Bob, not bad at all."

"So it's true. Every Seabee is becoming a millionaire selling to the navy boys from the ships in the bay." More whoops, whistles and joy.

"That's a trade secret, Bob."

"Sounds like a good investment opportunity. Can you use another good man?"

"Sure can. You'd make..." As the commander spoke, hundreds of voices joined him in unison, "a good man for the battalion."

The girls from the troupe arrived and mingled and everyone fell in love. Save for the commander, not an officer showed up. It was a truly memorable evening.

XIV
Hollandia

Reunion and Departure

We called her Mudhog, and some referred to her as "the dredge out there," but she had no name, only a number, 1052, painted in bold white on both sides of her pea green bow. She was surprisingly self-sufficient, providing her crew with all essentials and even some amenities not available ashore (which was about five hundred feet distant and connected by a pipeline about four feet in diameter). In her hold she possessed a store of onions, a delicacy because of their scarcity overseas. No one ever had trouble indentifying members of her reeking crew, who were dubbed "onion heads" by the "land sailors," the battalion boys.

That first morning the sea was brisk; whitecaps flecked the blue bay, and the pipeline, which also served as the path to the dredge, bobbed like a chorus line. Thanks to my prior log balancing experience, I managed to trip along the bucking tube as professionally as the regular crew. Upon clambering over the rail, I followed the sound of a lone hammer chipping paint on the opposite side of the superstructure. "Where could I find Mr. Smithson?" I asked the bare-backed mate at the end of the hammer.

He snorted, "Not here, I can tell you."

At this time Smithson resided ashore in officer's country, preferring its free-flowing liquor and handsome, resort-style living. I was to learn that only on important occasions, such as an inspection by the Command, did he come aboard. "Well, I was supposed to report to him..."

"Oh, so you're the new engineer," the paint chipper interrupted, a whiff of onion on his breath.

"Engineer? Not me," I objected.

"Says you. Oblong's your boss; you'll find him below."

Oblong was a bare-bodied, barrel-bellied, grease-annointed, rough-cut chief engineer who spent most of his days and nights in the sweltering engine room. "Yup, that's me, Henry O. Oblong, chief engineer of this bucket of slop."

"Well, I'm Hal Arnold, your new..."

"My new assistant, and after you've learned somethin', I'll promote you to assistant engineer."

"I thought I was supposed to be the water tender," I said.

"That, too. Assistant engineer and chief water tender. See this steam engine?" He pointed a greasy black finger toward a drastically disassembled machine. "You're gonna learn how to take her apart and put her back together blindfolded. And when you learn how to operate her, you're gonna know how she's doin' by her sounds. When she purrs like a fuckin' smooth kitten, it's okay, but when she starts laborin' and rattlin', she's unhappy, see?"

My training began immediately. "See this gismo?" instructed Oblong, lovingly selecting a part from the disorganized array. "It fits with that one."

Just like Hot Wires Blackburn and his friend the generator, Chief Engineer Oblong worshiped his steam engine and tried to make sure I did too.

Late in the evening after the Bob Hope performance, Smithson mysteriously appeared aboard and claimed his cabin. He spent the night and the following morning, during which he sent down to the galley for breakfast, then remained in his quarters incommunicado for the better part of the next few weeks before our departure from Hollandia. Occasionally he emerged only to mount the gangway to the bridge, where he stood hour after hour gazing out at the bay and observing the coming and going of the cruisers, battleships, and destroyers that were gathering for imminent action in the Philippines.

Smithson's surprise appearance puzzled the crew and was the dominant topic of conversation among us. Why did he give up the cushy job in officers' country? What led him to isolate himself so immutably? Although I attributed his actions to the humiliating episode after the show, I made no mention of this to my shipmates.

139

Throughout these weeks he paid no attention to our activities aboard the Mudhog; he hadn't the slightest idea of the condition of our unreliable engine, of the condition or morale of the crew, or of how well or poorly the Mudhog was fulfilling its assignment. Perhaps he had risen above it all, and viewed our business from a larger perspective. It really made no difference whether we operated or not. The Mudhog had served admirably in filling the interminable swamp during the leveling of Pancake Hill, but now we had more flatland than we could use. No matter, "the dredge out there" continued, when operable, to chew away the bay bottom with its rotating snaillike snout, sucking up the mud with a quantity of seawater and transporting it through its lurching tube to the rotting sagos, making land we didn't need.

The Mudhog hardly fit the definition of a ship, although her crew insisted on calling her so because she floated in water and loosely resembled one. Indeed she had no capability of locomotion except for two vertical columns near her stern that rested on the sea bottom and jutted one hundred feet into the air. They acted as stilts, allowing her to move forward slowly and awkwardly in giant steps. Most of the crew lived aboard, sleeping below deck in bunks in the fantail. Only two of the crew slept ashore—I, because no one ordered me to move and, until recently, Mr. Smithson.

In less than a month I became an accomplished steam engine operator, familiar with the interpretation of mechanical sounds and rhythms, and a fairly decent mechanic, having had two opportunities to take apart the engine and put it back together under Chief Engineer Oblong's guidance. Most of the time, however, the engine remained disassembled, waiting for parts to be delivered from Australia, where the vessel originated. Had Australia been Japan's ally instead of ours, the Mudhog would have been a contemporary Trojan horse.

When I mentioned the Mudhog's superfluousness to Billiard Ball, he issued his usual tutorial big picture comment: "War, by its very nature, is a futile, wasteful human endeavor. Yet some expound the theory that it has a cleansing effect, and sets a stagnating humanity on a new, more progressive course, until that too becomes obsolete. Take the Mudhog and multiply it by a million other stupidities like it all over the world's battlefields, and you can begin to understand what war means in the sweep of history: the eradication of the old order followed by renewal."

"You lost me," I said. I preferred to dwell on simpler and more practical concerns, such as helping Oblong keep our hopeless steam engine operating at least ten percent of the time.

In the beginning I was enchanted with Oblong's generosity of spirit. He held nothing back, and when I showed lack of confidence, he urged me on: "If you're gonna learn, you gotta bite the bullet." But after I mastered the job I discovered his true motive: to catch a nap during watch as I operated the engine or, in the morning, to sit in his oil-sodden desk chair drinking beer as I performed the necessary engine repairs. By lunch he would withdraw to his bunk to sleep off his drunk. During periods of steady operation, which rarely lasted more than two or three days, he would stay sober and attentive, relieving me for half of the twenty-four-hour day. Under these stressful conditions, aided by the Mudhog's natural state of decrepitude, I prayed constantly for engine failure, with considerable success.

One clear afternoon, while Smithson basked in the hot breeze blowing across the Mudhog's bow, a crusier dropped anchor in deep water a few hundred yards off our port side. Smithson was both fascinated and baffled, for the ship had positioned itself a considerable distance from the rest of the gathering armada. Never before had a vessel of such magnitude and regality approached us so closely. Smithson could even hear the announcements from its public address system roll distinctly across the water to his ears. Studying its flags closely, he exclaimed, "By God, it's the flagship of the fleet."

Soon Smithson spied a launch being lowered along the cruiser's side. Raising his binoculars, which constantly draped from his neck, even at night, he observed three sailors aboard her, two wearing white caps and blue chambray shirts and a third dressed in whites. Often while the ships awaited provisioning as they lay at anchor farther out in the bay, their crews were allowed to come ashore for the day to explore. And there we were, Seabee hucksters salivating over the innocents, selling at ridiculous prices our own handiwork of cat's-eyes bracelets and carved idols, which we represented as rare native works of art.

But these three were not the usual overflowing and bustling landing party coming ashore to prowl. The launch took off handily, furrowing through the waves and trailing a white wake that pointed in our direction. Surveying the shore, the sailor in white stood in the center like Washington crossing the Delaware. Expecting that the launch would eventually change course (who on a cruiser could possibly have business with anyone on the dredge?), Smithson was startled when in short order the launch was upon us, standing by, off our lee side.

"Permission to come aboard, sir," the sailor at the helm shouted to Smithson. "Would you drop a ladder, sir?"

A ladder. Was there ever a ladder on board the Mudhog? "Yes, yes, wait a minute," Smithson shouted back as he rushed to the bridge and phoned down to the engine room: "Do we have a ladder someplace, Oblong?"

"Not on this bucket, sir," Oblong answered.

"Well someone wants to come aboard from a launch. Oblong, there has to be a ladder somewhere. Every ship has a ladder. I'm sure we have one." As Smithson's agitation increased, his voice rose in pitch. But the fact was, the Mudhog wasn't a ship, nor did it ever have a ladder, for its natural mode was to be tethered to the land.

"We'll use the winch, sir," Oblong suggested. Leaving the engine room, whose grease-slicked deck was strewn with pistons and a wide assortment of the steam engine's vital parts, I followed Oblong to the main deck, where by then our entire crew of ten, having been alerted, was bending over the rail shouting ribald remarks at the prim members of the launch. Looking down from the Mudhog's height, I could catch only a glimpse of the sailors' faces. The sailor in white was strangely familiar. Perching on the hook at the end of the cable, he clung to the strand as the winch hoisted him up and lowered him to our deck.

"Permission to come aboard, sir," he said, smartly saluting a dumbfounded Smithson. It was none other than Barry Fortune himself, fresh, immaculate except for a grease mark on his shirt from the cable, his face filled out and full of color as I had never seen him before.

"Do you have a Hal Arnold, Seaman First Class, aboard, sir?" he asked. He explained to Smithson that on the order of the fleet admiral (a distinct fabrication), he had some business to take up with me.

Standing among the crew listening in, hardly able to control my joy at seeing him, I came forward. As our eyes met, mine turned misty. Smithson, disappointed yet obviously fascinated that the admiral had a message for a lowly seaman first, retired to his cabin, apparently to speculate on the matter.

After reaching the privacy of the engine room, we allowed unembarrassed tears to fill our eyes and embraced. Until then I had no idea how much I had missed him, how unexciting my days had become without him.

"Barry, you're a miracle," I said.

"I'm just a boy from Detroit," he chuckled.

How did he survive Pancake Hill? Too sick for treatment in the local field facility, he was already winging his way to a hospital in Brisbane by the time the bombs fell. Had he actually gone AWOL? Hell no! While he was recuperating, he took off and traveled around the country, which was teeming with Americans on leave. Suspecting that he may have returned to duty, the hospital contacted the battalion headquarters to confirm, and it was then that Gluck had called me in for the third degree.

Fortune raved over the Australians. To them practically every GI was a hero. The Aussie women gave our boys anything they wanted, even themselves, especially themselves. They had a sense of gratitude. Many left their own men for ours. "If there's a heaven for GIs," he said, "Australia's the place."

"And Lucia?" I asked. "Have you contacted her?"

He shifted uncomfortably from one foot to the other, avoiding my eyes as he looked down at the deck. "I placed a call from Brisbane but couldn't get through." My response was a heavy disapproving silence. "I tried, Hal, believe me." I offered no reprieve. "Do me a favor, friend; write her, tell her I'm back and everything's okay."

After reporting in at battalion headquarters, he was again incarcerated, this time under guard, confined to the very tent he had occupied several months earlier. The matter of his court-martial was still pending. As before, I visited him regularly, and on the first visit I returned the wrinkled paper on which he had written his will, bequeathing me his fortune. "For a while, I suppose, I learned what it feels like to be a millionaire," I said.

"How did you like being rich?"

"The truth is somehow it made me feel sad. I just prefer to make it on my own, Barry, and all I ask is to be free to have the opportunity. Understand?"

"Bullshit," he replied. "I believe a man should take whatever comes his way. The way you think, you'll work your balls off and starve. Luck's a big thing in life. It gets less credit than it deserves."

I thought of Billiard Ball's comment that we were truly victims of ourselves, that we're programmed by a combination of inheritance and experience. "You'll never understand me, Barry," I said in resignation.

I also returned his .45 pistol, wrapped in a white skivvy shirt. Why had I kept it and not turned it in? Of what use could it possibly have been to me? Now I knew. Along with Gluck, I never stopped believing that Fortune would make it. But to return in such style—on a cruiser, on the admiral's flagship! "How in God's name did you work that?"

"Well, I called Secretary Knox, the secretary of the navy, and I told him I needed transportation to get back to my outfit. That's how you get results—always go to the top."

"Then why not the White House, Barry?"

"It crossed my mind. Roosevelt's not well. 'Course it's only a rumor."

Given a distinguished visitor's treatment, Fortune's two week sojourn aboard the cruiser was luxurious.

"But why did you come back when you knew they'd slap you in the brig?" I asked as he unwrapped the pistol and examined it with loving tenderness.

"It's unfinished business; it's got to be settled. I believe I'll be exonerated. And I like this battalion. Commander Rutledge is tops in my book." He pulled the trigger of his pistol in several successive clicks. "Y'know, I never expected to hold this piece in my hand again. And it won't be long before I'll have a chance to use it."

"Not here," I said acidly. "We killed the last Jap months ago. I saw it with my own eyes."

"That's right, not here," he said. "Up north, Mindoro."

"How in hell..." I exclaimed, then caught myself short. He knew; of course he knew, he always knew.

So I, Fortune's dutiful friend, wrote Lucia of the good news, of the happy reunion, of his good health, of his failed attempts to phone her from Brisbane, of his fabulous voyage aboard the cruiser. Would she really buy all that? Putting myself in her place, I had to ask: How hard had he tried to reach her? For the first time it occurred to me that she no longer mattered to him. Indeed my letters were probably what kept their relationship from foundering long before. I was too efficient, too conscientious a surrogate. So few of our best intentions stay on course. It was all a mystery, all those conflicting feelings and loyalties, all those hidden motives. I hadn't learned yet that sooner or later conflicts resolve and motives surface in the form of future deeds.

A week later we were dismantling our camp, following the early procedure with which we became familiar almost a year earlier at Finschafen. This time, however, like a procession of squealing creatures heading for the ark, most of the equipment moved under its own power to the red sandy beach beside Pancake Hill. There, one by one, each machine inched its way through the gentle surf up the ramps and into the cavernous holds of five waiting LSTs (Landing Ship

145

Transport). Why LSTs? Our destination, Mindoro, an island in the central Philippines along its western fringe, had no docks, thus requiring beach unloading. And what was our assignment? To build an airstrip, then to sit and wait for a bigger project somewhere on Luzon, the most important island in the chain. Although we were issued the usual precautionary live ammunition, Mindoro was safe, no ifs, ands, or buts. In fact the Japs never really had secured it for themselves because of the presence of primitive hostile native tribes who came down at night from the island's central mountains, armed with poison arrows, to kill off the intruders.

Weren't we intruders? "Nope," said Gluck during a pep talk, "they love us. Everybody loves us."

"I can't imagine why," whispered Billiard Ball. "If we don't give them VD, we screw up their culture with cigarettes and beer and treat them like second-class citizens in their own country."

"That's why they love us," I said. "It's more fun being corrupted and going to the dogs."

"Well, what have we here," commented an amused Billiard Ball, "an idealist gone cynical?"

Slowly the laden LSTs, low in the water, plodded out of Humboldt Bay one after the other. Following up the rear, a seagoing tug dragged the helpless Mudhog, with only Oblong and Smithson aboard, like a reluctant dog on a leash. It was a hot, overcast morning, depressing to the spirit. Sitting on the deck of the LST, gazing back at the widening green shoreline now scarred with a ribbon of road visible here and there, I was overcome with sadness. Here I had spent almost a year of my life; here I had made myself comfortable and found a home such as it was. And wasn't I among the lucky ones, departing alive and still well? The nostalgia, the good memories, had already begun. Would I ever forget the secluded coral beaches, the cool, secret spring in the jungle, the wild lemon trees in an ancient clearing, the silent, timeless burial cave? Soon, as the distance grew, our handiwork disappeared. The docks, the roads, the buildings—all melded into the dark green luxuriant hills

146

appearing exactly as they had the day we steamed in. For a moment, suspending memory, it was as if we had never been there.

But then I turned away and looked out to the wind-whipped sea, eager for the future. Adventure awaited us, and God knows what danger, what misery. It didn't matter. Toward the end at Hollandia we felt useless, neglected, superfluous. The exhilaration and excitement of our first weeks ashore had faded quickly. Yearning for the tang of another beginning, we were ready to move on. Would I return someday? Would I live to have the chance to do so?

XV
Mindoro

The Making of a Hero

Save for the dull thumping of engines, our caravan of LSTs moved noiselessly through a maze of blue-green islands across the waist of the archipelago. Only the quiet waves spreading out from the bow rippled the glassy dark green sea. We felt the gentlest breeze as we passed through the still air. There was an eerie hush, giving a dreamlike quality to our passage. Was the war no less a dream? Or was this a threatening calm replete with foreboding? The trance snapped when we broke out into the busy open blue water of the South China Sea.

Heading north, we watched Mindoro's faint silhouette in the haze to our right. After a few hours we turned toward the palm-lined beach. For most on board, our interest lay in the unfamiliar shore ahead, but others were distracted by an object astern, low in the cottony sky, coming upon us quickly.

At first we were innocent of its meaning; as it drew closer we heard the uneven rattle of an engine, could make out the symbol of the rising sun. It kept coming, its features growing more and more distinct: ailerons down, rudder straight. I could see the rivets in its skin. Then shrieking directly overhead, it dove into the LST a few hundred yards ahead of us.

The shock wave of the ensuing explosion slammed me against the turret of an unmanned antiaircraft gun, pounding the air from my lungs and leaving me gasping. Others were blown across the deck and into the sea. A torrent of deadly debris—crackling, hot, searing—poured down. Most of us, unable to shield ourselves, were struck, and writhed in agony. The LST ahead went down. The sea around us swarmed with

148

our mates, some panicky, some dazed, some torn, floating among their own fragments.

We had heard of the kamikaze — the divine wind. We had heard that the Japanese were now so desperate they had to make every attack count — that they chose expendability for accuracy, for results. We had heard that their fighters had become little more than one-way manned motorized bombs, that their pilots were conditioned, like ancient Shinto warriors, to seek nobility and a glorious afterlife in self-sacrificial death. We had heard and disbelieved. It simply defied our own intense mindset on the value of life. Was not self-preservation an ingrained characteristic of human nature, an absolute compulsion? We were impotent against such dread behavior, such irrational efficiency. And now we were its victims, caught in a chilling madness.

Another speck, black against gray, appeared aft from nowhere and grew progressively larger, its features now defined, its rasp deepening, its trajectory clear, its target indeterminate. Yes, it was us; no mistaking that it was us. Fascinated, motionless, as if hypnotized, we watched, awaiting the inevitable. Except Barry Fortune, man of action, challenger of fate, foiler of death. He leapt into the turret of the stern machine gun and blasted at the oncoming Zero, never stopping, never knowing whether it counted. It was his contest. Survival didn't matter; duty, accolades didn't matter; only winning. He was no less driven than the Japanese kamikaze; whoever would die would do so nobly in his own eyes. As he blasted away, I saw him screaming, exultant.

Then without warning, the Zero blew up over the water aft of our fantail. So Fortune was victor, but with a price. Chief Bull Dunham of the motor pool, anticipating Fortune's need for more ammo, and racing toward the turret with a fresh supply, was too late to make it inside when the kamikaze exploded. He fell to the steel deck, less than a yard from Fortune, with a metal shard as large as a bread knife protruding from his forehead. "Had his goddamn name on it," said Fortune with a shrug.

A week later when the commander had Fortune brought before him for commendation as prelude to receiving the

Silver Star, and incidentally to inform him that reference to his prior infractions would be expunged from the record and thus eliminate any possibility of court-martial, my hero-friend listened politely. When asked to say something, he had no comment.

"I admire your modesty," said the commander. "To have nothing to say after saving the lives of an entire company of men, and its irreplaceable equipment—that is the epitome of humility, don't you agree, Gluck?"

"Wal, I can't get over it. Got to hand it to ya, Fortune. You're a mighty good man." Beaming, Fortune thanked Gluck.

"A mighty good man for the battalion," boomed the commander.

The Japanese attack was small scale—only two kamikazes, no more. After rescuing the survivors from the chaos, we got to the beach and found ourselves in the midst of a Marine battalion handily mopping up the remnants of an enemy garrison. Presumably the principal invasion took place only a few hours before our arrival. Hundreds of Jap prisoners were huddled together under guard just above the tide line. "For once we aren't the first ones in," commented a testy Billiard Ball, his memory of the debacle on the beach at Biak still fresh. "How come they made such a mistake?" It was good to see him manage himself so soundly through our crisis, good to see his former asperity restored.

Actually the Marine losses during the Mindoro landing were minimal, far less than ours. Who said not being first guaranteed a safer landing? In ordinary times the progress of one's life evolves gradually, usually allowing enough time to find a coherent thread of cause and effect. But in war it occurs in a series of random bursts too radical and swift to absorb. Billiard Ball had preached that we are all victims of an inherited past, predestined to be what we are. Then there's Fortune's theory, which he constantly tested, that absurd luck is the controlling agent. Neither idea precludes the other. Without a God, I was trying to understand my life, to find some meaning in what was happening. Still, how could I possibly have learned so soon that there's no meaning out there. Most need a lifetime, if at all, to discover the answer: The meaning is within us.

Two days after our misbegotten landing, the Mudhog, atilt and low in the water, straggled in, having fallen behind soon after we left the gentle waters of Humboldt Bay. How fortunate that her sea tug couldn't keep up, thus avoiding our disaster, but she had problems enough to contend with while en route. The pair ran into a severe storm, which at one point caused the towing cable to break, leaving the dredge helpless and close to foundering. The storm being of short duration, she rode it out, although taking on substantial water, which made her list badly to one side.

Owing to the height of her superstructure, those gigantic cylindrical steel columns projecting into the air, she was extremely vulnerable to capsizing. No one was more aware than Smithson that once her angle of list exceeded a certain point, she was bound to go bottom up. Throughout the storm, too seasick to feel panic, he was only thinly concerned with the increasing angle of the Mudhog's deck. But after the storm quieted and her true condition came home to him, he plummeted down the gangway to the engine room to alert his right-hand man, Oblong. Sleeping off his drunk, Chief Engineer Oblong was too vague-minded to remember what to do to right the vessel. For the next night and half a day, Smithson strapped himself to his tilting bunk, weighing his alternatives. The sea was too rough to transfer to the tug, and Oblong would have been in no condition to do so even in a calm. Their two lifeboats were useless: The one on the port side would be swamped during the earliest stage of a capsize, and the starboard one was already at too high an angle to fall freely into the water. "So I prayed," said Smithson solemnly, a not usually devout man but a believer, "and God answered in the affirmative, as you can see."

Smithson lacked Rutledge's charisma and charm, indeed had none of the self-confidence and decisiveness and commitment that attract loyal followers. After Rutledge, I was incapable of transferring my loyalty to Smithson. He impressed me as a petty, small-minded, ridiculous man. But he was more. It didn't escape me that had he tried hard enough, he could have saved himself from danger by deserting the besotted Oblong. From then on I began to feel proud of being part of the Mudhog detachment.

Until the dredge resumed its normal vertical state, it was impossible for the crew to come aboard. And only Chief Engineer Oblong and I knew how to bring her back. Alarm over the severe list prompted a launch to be rushed out to greet the dredge. Smithson, refusing to leave her, requested that I be found and delivered to duty immediately.

"Get down to the engine room and help Oblong straighten us out," he shouted to me as the launch approached the Mudhog. Smithson had to hang onto a rail to prevent himself from sliding down the slanted deck. I shinnied up a rope that lay on the vessel's side and partly exposed rusty bottom.

Keeping his ship level is the water tender's main responsibility, which is done quite simply by pumping water from one ballast tank to another. The tanks occupy strategic locations fore, aft, and amidships to provide balance. Thus it is critical to know which water lines lead to which tanks and which pumps to use to make a required water transfer. It's a delicate, slow-motion balancing act.

Slipping down to the engine room, I found our chief engineer, beer in hand, singing merrily above the din of the clanking pumps, all six of them operating, some moving water, others sucking dry, none of them performing with any rhyme or reason.

"Hey there, Hal, fella," he bubbled, "just in time to relieve me. Gawd, what a rough trip it's been. Take over, fella. Remember what I taught ya. Jus' like a woman, touch her in the right spots, and she'll come." He leaned his greasy old desk chair against the oblique bulkhead, spilled himself into it, and instantly fell asleep. In three hours our decks were horizontal again, and I was, by acclamation of the crew and Smithson, hero of the day.

Our stay on Mindoro was brief, hardly more than a fortnight, during which we completed the construction of an airstrip. It was a simple job, requiring mostly bulldozers and graders, on a site that was a loamy, flat, rice field farmed by peasants. I asked Gluck, most meekly, whether the owners of the land were compensated or whether we simply took over, giving no heed to civilian considerations. He glared at me as if I had just committed treason. "They're goddamned lucky we're here at all," he said and walked off.

Most of the rest of us had little to do except mark time for the next major project farther north on Luzon. We roamed about the rich green coastal land observing the water buffalo immersing themselves in the lazy muddy streams to keep cool during hot afternoons. We met the Filipinos for the first time, mostly small-boned, swarthy farmers who spoke clear accented English. For their watermelon and mangoes and papayas we traded cigarettes and beer and candy—the seductive junk of GI opulence. As Gluck said, they loved us. Occasionally we'd see a Mungyan who wandered down from the distant mountains. Always silent, slender, and sleek, they wore only a loincloth and carried a spear reputedly tipped with poison that killed instantly. Watching us from a distance as we constructed the airstrip, they seemed fascinated with our frenetic activity and our startling machinery. The fascination went both ways.

The tragedy and violence of our arrival seemingly forgotten, we were like sight-seeing tourists on a holiday. How quickly we adjust to contrasting events. Billiard Ball explained: "It's impossible to conceptualize pain. We involuntarily blank out bad experiences so that we can live with ourselves. When you come down to it, all of us are hopeless romantics, even the bitterest." Was he unwittingly showing me his hand? I wondered.

With the procedure at Hollandia still fresh, we reloaded the LSTs quite proficiently. Some, in fact, were never unloaded at all and sat offshore waiting for our early departure. For where? For Luzon, we knew. For Subic Bay, predicted Fortune, as Mindoro faded on the horizon. More specifically to a barren slope across the water from Bataan.

Again the dredge trailed our flotilla, with Smithson and Oblong still aboard. Smithson considered the risk small, for the voyage would be brief and in protected waters between the islands.

"That's one hell of a thing you're assigned to," Fortune remarked as he looked back at Mudhog's superstructure looming high behind us. "Y'know I can get you off her whenever you want."

"Who said I wanted to get off her?"

"Hell, you can't convince me you like doing duty on that tub of crap. Someday when your kids ask what you did during the war, what are you going to tell them? That you served aboard some scow that moved on stilts? C'mon, Hal, I can get you back with me in communications. It would be like the old days in 'Hafen."

"Sorry, friend, I like it where I am," I insisted.

"Still stubborn as ever, I see." He shook his head in resignation. "A stubborn ass."

Fortune couldn't even tempt me. Long before, I resolved to avoid being placed in a dependent position, one that might require me to compromise my values and become a victim of his warped system. Furthermore, I was extremely satisfied with duty aboard the Mudhog. While on Mindoro, shortly after my gallant rescue (during which the dredge could have gone over, with me in the engine room without a chance of surviving), Smithson advanced me to petty officer, machinists mate third class. "Yes, yes, you're a good man for the 1052," he said. I took pride in my rating, a lowly one to be sure, but one that denoted a skill at some specialty, and best of all, granted in the field for special performance.

I liked the work. I liked listening to the subtle sounds of the engine and analyzing what they meant. I liked turning the correct bolt, or adjusting this valve or that to keep everything in balance and running smoothly. I liked being water tender and the tremendous responsibility that went with it. No job demanded more vigilance, more expertise in the intimate workings of the vessel. I liked counting for something, being needed, becoming a man at last.

I could not expect Fortune to understand. Our outlooks were at such variance, I wondered how we could be such close friends for so long. What was the source of our mutual fascination? Was it the attraction of opposites, the seeking of qualities in others that one really admires but cannot possess? Did this principle also apply to Billiard Ball, intellectually snobbish, unflappable, always rising above the trivia of life? Here, too, my personal style hardly resembled his. And how different my two friends were from each other. I marveled at this, unable to plumb the wellspring of our need for each other. Their friendships imparted joy and warmth, playing like a quiet background melody whenever we were together. I would never have such friends again, at least not among men.

One relationship that seemed to be going poorly was Fortune and Lucia's. I hadn't heard a word since informing her of Forune's return, nor had Fortune. Tempted though I was to write and discover whether there was a problem, I held back. If there was one, it couldn't be me, and if I mattered to her, apart from Fortune, she would come through. Slowly I was arriving at a clearer picture of my position in the triangle. It hinged upon Lucia's perception of where Fortune stood. In my opinion, he had forsaken her somewhere in Australia. Proof came a couple of months later at Subic Bay, a place that changed our lives beyond dreaming.

XVI
Subic Bay

Living the Good Life

Subic Bay is a place where history was shaped. The peninsula on its eastern shore, Bataan, was our earliest battleground, the scene of our first defeat on land, of a cruel, humiliating forced march and of unremitting guerrilla warfare before MacArthur returned. Our battalion encamped on a low barren hill on the western shore in the province of Zambales. From that shore the low mountains of Bataan were always visible in the humid, hazy, mysterious distance, a reminder of that earlier agonizing drama.

There was no opposition. The Filipino guerrillas had driven the enemy into the faraway mountains before we landed. Unlike Hollandia this location had neither an overwhelming brash lushness nor steep slopes to contend with. We created, unhampered, round the clock, the infrastructure of a Seabee camp in hardly more than two weeks. Our principle purpose was to build a submarine base, and simultaneously to construct docks and warehouses to service the fleet which used the bay as a protected anchorage and staging area for future campaigns: Okinawa, then Japan itself.

In the beginning, the Filipino people who lived there were deliriously happy with us, and understandably so. We had liberated them from an extremely oppressive conqueror who, while suffering defeat after defeat at our hands on the islands to the east and south, took out their frustration on them. They told us stories of Japanese brutality in retaliation for guerrilla harassment, stories that are typical of an occupier's wartime behaviour toward subjugated people. Perhaps harshest of all was the near starvation of the population as the Japanese stripped the fields of rice to supplement their own dwindling supply, cut off from its source by our navy's interception. No heed was paid to future needs, to the necessity of nurturing seedlings for subsequent plantings.

We found a people beaten down, robbed of their material goods, accustomed to enduring physical hardship as a way of life, yet believing almost mystically that MacArthur would return, as he said he would. Through a certain resignation they managed to retain their dignity, finding succor in each other as the key to survival. Highly heterogeneous, belonging to perhaps hundreds of tribes and speaking scores of different local languages, they were never more united.

Billiard Ball knew nothing of the Filipinos, of their history or their customs, although he spoke Spanish, the language of the older generation, the Filipino grandparents. But he was familiar with their conquerors. He was, among other things, a student of Japan and he could speak and read Japanese fluently. What he learned of the Japanese shocked him at first.

"The Japanese are a cultivated people," he said, "with a body of customs and a view of life that teaches a high respect for each other. And maybe better than any people in the world, they have learned how to live together in close quarters and work toward a common goal. But their culture is only a veneer. Why should I be so surprised at what they've done to the Filipinos?"

Gradually his cynicism was swaying me. The evidence was before us. Neither of us had yet heard of a cruelty on an even larger scale by another civilized people that had established concentration camps in Europe.

Most of the local folk were destitute and lived in two towns, Olongopo and Subic, several miles apart near each corner of the head of the bay. Watching us arrive and build our camp a few miles south of the towns, they kept their distance until we were settled, then gradually, crossing the water in dugout canoes, they commenced infiltrating us. The women offered to launder our clothes, make up our bunks, keep our tents clean and maintain the heads (latrines). The

157

men proposed selling our cigarettes on the black market at thirty-five precious American dollars per carton. It was so easy and natural for us to be masters and rich entrepreneurs, and them to be servants and hustlers. So we began living the good life.

Thus began their corruption. They had come to us innocently with an air of humility, with wonder at our wealth, and a wish to express their gratitude for our rescuing them. Every American was a little god. We never noticed, never listened. Instead we were bent on using them for our own purposes, and they readily submitted, unaware of the consequences. Over time their men became pimps and thieves, their women prostitutes, "businesswomen" they were called, or live-in girlfriends in return for food and a semblance of security. They were vulnerable; they had nothing, only services, only themselves to offer in order to survive.

Billiard Ball observed this state of affairs: "Under the Japs, at least their culture held together. It was a source of strength. It was all they had. But under us, it's falling apart at the seams. Damnit, if they'd only stop worshiping us and see us for ourselves. They mistake our so-called wealth for greatness."

Coming to our defense, I argued, "But we are great. We're saving the world. We're generous, well meaning, noble. Our flag has the world's respect."

Billiard Ball sighed. "Don't confuse what we say and believe with what we actually do. They don't coincide. Look around you and watch what happens after we've been here a while."

Had I asked Billiard Ball for his forecast of our status in the world twenty years later, would he have had the foresight to predict that our banner would be fouled in the dirt, our youth would flee north of the border to avoid fighting for our country, our politicians, like Don Quixote, would summon us to fight imaginary demons, and our people collectively would feel ashamed of our cruelty, of what we had done to the Vietnamese? No, that would have been beyond even his imagining.

Fortune had quite a different view. "I can smell opportunity in the air," he said. "The resources here are enormous, untapped, waiting for the taking. Look out there. The mountains are covered with mahogany and teak. Thousands of hungry Filipinos will work for a song. It's an ideal combination." He was a lion stalking prey, waiting for the kill. "This is the place for me after the war," he said. I could tell that he was more than just talking, that he had set his course.

Our new camp, in keeping with the American custom of constantly improving our lot, was more elaborate than the one at Hollandia. The tents were essentially the same, but our plumbing network had expanded, permitting the installation of numerous showers at convenient locations instead of at one central area. The mess hall was more spacious and the serving counter was clad with stainless steel sheets. The sick bay and battalion offices were no longer mere tents, but solid structures with metal roofs and screened walls. The roadways were covered with a layer of small stones, which reduced the dust and the mire, so annoying at Hollandia. There was a quality of permanence about the place, as if we expected to be there a long time. It hadn't occurred to me that others might use it after us.

The Mudhog sat motionless out in the bay with nothing to do, yet connected to the shore by its large tube, which served no purpose other than as a convenient means of foot access to land. The bay was already naturally deep enough to allow the largest ships to nestle up to the docks we built. The Mudhog's crew was on a perennial vacation, growing heavy and lazy with hardly more to do than eat and drink beer. All day long they sat by the gunwhales watching the ongoing construction on the shore like sidewalk superintendents. By evening, weary from the day's boredom they lounged around. After a month of such living, the entire crew bore a common profile. They resembled fat turkeys, including Smithson, who practiced his idleness in the privacy of his stateroom or on the bridge surveying the scene day after day.

I shared in none of this lifestyle. Choosing to dwell ashore, I remained a member of the battalion in form if not officially and preferred my old friends. During duty hours I reported to the dredge; off duty I returned to my tent without tarrying. The Mudhog crew accepted me on such terms, accepted the cordial distance I kept between us, mainly, I believe, because of my crucial role. As water tender I was somewhat revered for my expertise. Everyone remembered the near disaster on Mindoro.

Duty aboard the Mudhog was easy and essentially dull. Having no need to operate the engine any longer, only water tending was required. With the engine down, the vessel's bilges accumulated water at a slower pace, making water transfers necessary only at infrequent intervals. Thus I could miss a duty assignment or two without anyone being concerned. Oblong was always aboard anyway, never interested in time off, since his favorite recreation was a bottle in hand. He was always happy to fill in if I asked, in return for which I would give him my weekly beer ration—an entire case.

My life therefore was centered on land and, during the first month specifically, with my bunk-mates at camp. Again Billiard Ball was one of them. Recognized at last for his knowledge of Japanese and Spanish, he was consulted often by the Command to translate documents. His need to feel useful now fulfilled, he tended to moderate his acid attitude toward everything. He began to laugh more often and enjoy rather than analyze events, and we grew closer.

Blackie "Hot Wires" Blackburn, for whom I worked under painful duress during our first weeks at Hollandia, was also a member of our "family." However, he was a substantially subdued version of his old, lunatic self because of a back problem that confined him to his bunk for days at a time. "I'd give anything to have just two minutes with my chiropractor back home," he'd moan. Fortune also shared our tent at my invitation, at least temporarily. Billiard Ball mildly objected: "Our tent will become a black market headquarters if he comes in." But it turned out that Fortune had little contact with the rest of us and was rarely there, even at night to sleep.

The fifth bunk-mate was my loyal life-saving friend, Whitey Whitehead, who under my very eyes began undergoing a slow process of disintegration by alcohol. How sad to see this good man gradually lose touch with the rest of us. His sole interest was moonshine made in his homemade still somewhere in the wild bush beyond our camp. His decline gave me much personal pain. Being extremely fond of him, and failing to comprehend what drove him to such self-destruction, I was concerned and felt helpless. "Why?" I lamented to Billiard Ball, seeking his greater wisdom for an answer.

"I think the soft life is doing him in," he offered. "To be happy and feel secure he needs structure, discipline. His life as a construction worker was hard. Things have gotten too easy and freewheeling for him."

Whether Billiard Ball's analysis of cause and effect was correct or not, it was certainly true that our style of life was decidely soft, not to the extent of the deplorable sloth aboard the Mudhog but perhaps substantially more carefree than anything we had known since childhood. All our basic needs were met with no required effort on our part. Morning musters were dropped, accountability beyond duty hours was nonexistent, and overnight and weekend liberties to Subic or Olongopo and even Manila some eighty miles away were granted with abandon.

Thus Whitey frequently awoke from a drunken sleep about eleven in the morning and got away with it. Falteringly he oriented himself, then finding his empty five-gallon gasoline can, he headed into the bush. Early evening he returned all smiles, brimming with amiability, swinging his gasoline can and listening with pleasure to the sound of moonshine sloshing within. "Shhh, don't breathe a word about this to anybody," he cackled, believing that no one knew when in fact the entire battalion did. After all, he had banged away for everyone to hear fashioning his still from a fifty-five gallon drum. We kidded him, asking him whether it was a secret weapon. He replied that it was a new invention to make medicine that would cure clap in less than three hours.

Through Fortune he procured a supply of canned pineapple juice from our warehouse. "Where in hell did it all go?" Gluck demanded, with no one offering an answer.

Being a generous man, Whitey always asked if we'd like a swig from the can. Everyone refused except Blackie who tried it once, and only once, thinking that it would give him relief from his pain. "Whitey, y'oughta patent it for cleaning plumbing," was his comment. Each morning for three weeks, Whitey lay in his bunk and, raising the five-gallon can to his lips, took drafts of his brew until he lapsed into a stupor and passed out.

One morning returning to the tent less than an hour after his departure, Whitey was singing, generally boisterous, and, we assumed, undoubtedly already drunk. No sloshing sound came from the five-gallon can, not this time, suggesting that he had imbibed it all. But he was genuinely elated and quite sober. "Can ya beat it?" he howled. "They found my goddamn still, they found it and stole it."

"Who," I asked.

"I dunno who, and I don't care," he said joyously.

"Then what are you so happy about?" asked Blackie.

"Hell, couldn't you see the kickapoo juice was killing me?" From that morning on, Whitey was a normal man, and I stopped worrying about his welfare.

April was soon upon us, another spring without spring, sorely missed, and especially sad: We heard of Roosevelt's death. He was our father, our great leader, in a class with Lincoln and Washington. Though we were clearly winning the war, we felt lost without him. Some of us cried. Would we lose now; would the war go on for a generation now? Many of us, myself especially, never knew any other president. In my mind he was more like a benevolent monarch, and perhaps had he not died he may well have had license to become one. Part of my adulation for him was inherited from my Roosevelt-worshiping father, who lost everything, his business and property, under Hoover. Like Hitler with his economically suffering people, Roosevelt gave my father's generation hope of quick relief and a golden future. Could there ever again in our time be a president as great? Certainly not Truman, that haberdasher, that small-time city politician. God help us all.

Roosevelt's death deeply affected our outlook on many things, most notably our relationship with home. Billiard Ball revealed that the censors, having to work into the early morning hours during this period, had never been so busy with outgoing mail. And a few weeks later mail flooded in from the States.

In the outpouring was a letter from Lucia to Fortune, but not one to me. He read it quietly while sitting beside me on my bunk during one of the few evenings he spent in the tent with the rest of us. "Here," he said, handing it to me, "it's nothing personal."

Quite the contrary, it read in part: "My dearest, of course I forgive you for your long silence. You can't imagine what your birthday card did for me. Where did you find such a lovely thing? It's a true work of art. I had the poem inside translated from the Spanish, and it was so beautiful that tears came to my eyes. I love you, my loved one, and I count the days, the hours, knowing that each brings the moment of our reunion that much nearer."

Of course I knew immediately why he had me read the letter. Besides telling me that he was now in her good graces, it indicated that he had taken some initiative, albeit a simple card, and had stopped ignoring her after all. But I was less impressed by those revelations than saddened by her obsequiousness, her grasping at the smallest crumb of his attention to renew her hope.

In any case, seeing that the two were "together" again, I decided to resume my correspondence with her. I wrote her of Fortune's heroism at Mindoro, of his eligibility for the Silver Star, that we were now sharing the same tent, and that he was extremely busy and consistently in high spirits.

I didn't tell Lucia that we saw less of each other than before. Since Fortune no longer took me into his confidence as a consequence of my having rejected his overtures, his activities were really a mystery to me. I suspected that he was intensely involved in the black market. Not until years later, long after the war was over, did I discover that Fortune was, during this period, making the appropriate contacts and laying the foundation for his future business empire in the islands. Hadn't he once talked to me of lumbering, of becoming a virtually monopolistic supplier of raw material to the furniture makers of the world? But at the time his words had passed over me.

As Fortune and I drifted apart physically if not in spirit, Billiard Ball and I drew closer to each other. The ambience of the islands affected us similarly; we were entranced with the basic simplicity of the people and lured, once the ice was broken, by their open hospitality. However, making contact with those who were unsullied by our influence was difficult, for such people went out of their way to avoid Americanos. The opportunity to meet had to be fortuitous; for us, it almost had grave consequences.

The sunlit afternoon was dreamlike in its stillness as Billiard Ball and I walked through the fields and bush exploring the land behind the camp. From our low hill we gazed upon a long valley that extended to a mountain range, with peak rising behind peak seemingly into the cosmos itself. Near one of the summits, when the sun struck at a certain angle, a streak flashed down the mountainside. Fascinated by such a strange sight, I had a brief sense of déjà vu, then in astonishment I remembered. Hadn't I seen the mountain before, the waterfall before, from our ship at sea during the crossing? Then it was a mirage, an illusion. Now it was real yet mysterious. Could the source of such a waterfall so close to the peak be a lake? This simple waterfall, this silver tinsel down a blue mountainside, had consumed my imagination and flitted through my mind like a recurrent musical theme. I had asked many Filipinos about it. None knew, or cared to know. Were I granted the answer to one of the many unsolved questions in my life, I would inquire about the origin of the waterfall.

So sacred was my fascination that I didn't confide to Billiard Ball during our meander that day, my secret wish to find the stream and follow it back to its source. After reaching the luxuriant floor of the valley we heard the sound of rushing water and soon discovered the stream running full, clear, and strong. Stripping to our skin, we dove into it with sublime joy; I was convinced that those cool waters originated from the lake in the sky.

We played in the current, letting it sweep us downstream for a short distance, then swam back against it close to shore where it was weakest. What a glorious sense of freedom! We cavorted like children, splashing each other, giggling at the other's antics, revealing an aspect of Billiard Ball that I had seen briefly only once before at the spring in Hollandia. Soon we stretched out our clothes on the beaten grass beneath a palm tree and lay in the buff in the sun listening to the gurgling turbulence and the breeze passing through the fronds.

Suddenly on the light air we heard voices drawing near, girls' voices, then we heard the slaps and thuds of paddles beating. "Laundry girls," said Billiard Ball without opening his eyes.

"I hope they don't find us, not like this," I said nervously, sitting up.

Of the desperate Filipino women (and very few weren't), some chose prostitution, which was lucrative, and some did laundry, which was arduous work and earned them little. Regularly they visited our tents and took our soiled clothes, then returned them the next day clean and neatly folded in large woven baskets that they balanced on their heads like jeweled crowns. Their walk was a marvelous smooth glide; their posture unsurpassed, of a grandeur befitting a fashion model.

The washing process consisted of beating the clothes against a rock beside a stream, and laying them out on the grass to dry in the always hot sun. Most of the laundry women were in their teens, and they usually traveled in pairs, often coming from distant villages. Among themselves they spoke Tagalog, the national language, a blend of native tongues and Spanish. To us they spoke in halting English. They, not the prostitutes, were our genuine link with the undefiled Filipino culture that too many of us chose to ignore.

Billiard Ball and I lay silent, basking in reverie with eyes closed, until a series of high-pitched shrieks jolted us. They came from the direction of the laundry women not far downstream. We bolted up from our reclining positions, bounded through the low shrubs, and raced toward the panic. Quickly we came upon two Filipino girls, one kneeling in the shallows of the stream, arms wrapped around her bare bosom, her white dress hanging from her waist in shreds. She was silent, cowering, as an Americano, one of our boys, hovered over her. The other girl lay screaming on the ground in the grass, her skirt thrown up over her face, while another Americano was kneeling on her, loosening the belt to his blue jeans. We could hear the whimpering of other women peering out from behind the surrounding low shrubbery.

Spontaneously Billiard Ball and I went for each man, I taking the man in the stream. Catching him by surprise from the rear, I flung my arm around his neck, pulled him down beneath the surface of the water, and with all my might held him there as he struggled and gasped. So enraged was I that my strength seemed superhuman, and I trembled from fear of such overwhelming anger, from the horror of my urge to kill. I released him. He surfaced dazed, and weakly crawled to the bank and vomited.

Billiard Ball, a massive man and former champion college wrestler, had his man in a stranglehold. He spoke with controlled calmness, belying his outrage. "Apologize to this woman, or so help me, I'll break your back." The man muttered that he was sorry. "Not good enough," said Billiard Ball. "Say ma'am."

"I'm sorry, ma'am."

"Louder," insisted Billiard Ball.

"I'M SORRY, MA'AM."

"Now get the hell out of here, you cocksuckers."

The two ran off terrified, as if fearing for their lives. Rarely had I heard Billiard Ball use profanity, and I began laughing, partly at how odd it sounded in his distinctly enunciated speech, partly at his word choice in view of the near rapes, and partly from relief at defeating my frightening and enigmatic impulse to murder.

As I turned to the girl in the water, she slipped deeper into the stream, staring into my eyes, obviously still frightened. Her almond-shaped eyes were large, exotic, expressive, her features smooth, coffee colored, delicate. How extraordinarily lovely she is, I thought. "You needn't be afraid anymore," I said. She smiled weakly, dropping her eyes to the rest of me. At that instant I understood. "My God, Billiard Ball," I shouted, "we're as bareass as new born babes!"

"Christ, so we are," he boomed. "Let's get the hell out of here." Dashing into the shrubs, we whooped as we ran, jubilant from our triumph over evil. The sound of screaming followed us, this time not of fear but of women laughing. "We gave them a great show, eh, Hal?" Billiard Ball shouted.

"I'd say we just saved America's reputation here at Subic Bay," I shouted back.

Neither of us knew then that our cause was already lost.

XVII
Subic Bay

Fires of Love and Death

Our least satisfied human need overseas was love. A smouldering fire burned within us. Indeed, early upon our arrival at Subic Bay many were tormented by the sight of the lithe, beskirted Filipino laundry women who called on us.

The Command, aware of the power of our frustrated sex drive, warned us of the danger of seeking satisfaction indiscriminately. Lectures were given and movies shown demonstrating in frighteningly graphic terms the consequences of gonorrhea and syphilis. But their persuasion lasted no longer than our next liberty to Subic. The married men especially demanded relief from sexual tension exacerbated to the limit by an abundance of ready and able women. In some instances we sought love, even loyalty and tentative commitment, a genuine caring and being cared for, and received it. Thus within a few months, our new improved sick bay was overflowing with VD casualties; the greater enemy was not the Japs but ourselves.

We bought our love in Subic. The town, a seamy, ramshackle collection of bamboo and thatched huts built on stilts, was a parody of an American slum. Pigs and dogs and chickens, looking to pounce on the garbage the inhabitants routinely threw out the glassless windows, roamed beneath the huts. The narrow dirt streets, dotted with putrid puddles and mounds of stinking animal waste, were lined with souvenir shops offering cheap and tasteless native wares. There were so-called nightclubs with mediocre orchestras, and bars that served American beer and liquor—our own rations making the circuit back to us via the black market. Here the "businesswomen" came in droves from all over Zambales and Pampanga and the outlying provinces to set up shop.

Being inexperienced and fearful of the risk of disease, I steered clear of Subic except as a debarkation point on my way to Olongopo some ten miles farther along the bay, or to other villages in the hinterland and to Manila. My main interest was the people. Although they were easy to approach, they were difficult to get to know. Always polite, accommodating, obedient, willing to do business, they nevertheless maintained a cool distance from the Americanos. At first they were in awe of us, of our so-called wealth, and they felt inferior to us; then, as they saw our ways, particularly in places such as Subic, they avoided us.

Billiard Ball, who in a few short weeks had mastered a newly acquired handbook in conversational Tagalog, suggested that through language I could win them over. "Don't speak English when you address them. Here, study this book; learn some common Tagalog expressions."

"Would you help me, especially the pronunciation?" I asked.

"M'lad, I thought you'd never ask," he replied, barely containing his enthusiasm. Missing the teacher-student relationship of our Finschafen days, he was starving for the opportunity to teach again.

In a week, I learned enough of the language to test it in the field. If I met a Filipino while walking along a road or standing at the pier awaiting the launch, I'd greet him in Tagalog and he'd smile and reply in his jargon. Of course I'd understand only a fraction of what he said. I'd nod my head as if hanging on every word, then I'd slip into English.

So it happened at the dock with Rosalio, a small, neatly attired, handsome young man perhaps a year or two older than myself. "You speak Tagalog?" he asked. "Where did you learn it? Were you here before the war? Were you with MacArthur on Corregidor?"

"No, no, I'm too young for that," I said, catching his distinction between the earlier Americanos of the protectorate and the present ones of the liberation. "I'm learning Tagalog only now."

"Ah, you speak it well. I am Rosalio," he said extending his hand. "I was with the guerrillas on Bataan."

169

We talked more about ourselves, striking up an excellent rapport. He asked me to visit him at his house and meet his wife and son, and I said I'd be very happy to.

"Once I knew many Americanos," he said with severe seriousness. "They were in the march from Bataan. Now they are all dead."

Steadily, as the lessons progressed and I used Tagalog more, my facility improved so that eventually I could hold a sustained conversation with the laundry girls who visited our tent. It was an occasion for fun and laughter, always drawing a small crowd from the neighboring tents as I showed off my linguistic ability. Strangely, Billiard Ball, seeming bored by my display, rarely spoke with the girls. A few of my mates, sick of the whores, tired of the filth and frightened of the danger, wished to meet women who chose not to compromise themselves, women with whom they could form a more rounded relationship.

No longer would my mates let me go on liberty alone. They drafted me as their bird dog to scout up girls. I cooperated because, who knows, I might find someone right for myself. Warming up quickly to my Tagalog, the girls usually assumed that my silent mates, pretending to understand, were equally proficient. The men soon won over the girls with their famous easygoing American charm. Many of the relationships I instigated blossomed beyond expectations. As for myself, I found no one. There was Lucia, of course, and, still haunting me, the memory of that strikingly beautiful laundry girl in the stream, her wide brown eyes pleading for mercy.

After my mates found girlfriends, I resumed solitary sojourns in the vicinity of the bay, usually for a day at a time. Visiting Rosalio in Olongopo, meeting his modest, pretty wife, sitting with them on the floor in their thatched hut by the river and eating their scarce rice, watching their infant play with my fingers. I felt the warmth of family again, a feeling I hadn't known since leaving my own home two years earlier. The couple had a quiet, comfortable love. Their son bound them in common cause as only a child can. "Stay for the weekend if you don't have to return to camp," Rosalio urged. "We will go fishing in my *banca*. Do you enjoy fishing?"

"Oh, yes. As a boy I used to go fishing in a lake in New Hampshire," I said, forgetting that he would be unfamiliar with such a place.

"Fishing with dynamite?" he asked.

"With dynamite?" I repeated in puzzlement.

"I'll show you," he said, "if you stay over."

That night for the first time I slept on a mat on the smooth wood floor in the same room, the only room, with Rosalio and his wife and child. To my surprise I slept peacefully through the night. When I awoke in the morning, the last to do so, I was well rested, and eager for the breakfast of eggs fried in a small hearth on the floor, and rice and goat's milk, all scarce items that Rosalio's wife served.

Rosalio loaded the *banca*, an outrigger canoe carved from a log, that rested on the riverbank below the hut. Our equipment consisted of a bundle of netting and a half-dozen fist-sized packets of dynamite. Gently we paddled through the confusing maze of a brackish estuary as I sat on the bottom of the boat near the bow. After we made a few turns, I lost my bearings and was completely in Rosalio's hands. The water was like a brown mirror reflecting white cloud puffs and thick shore vegetation; it rippled silently behind us as we glided on.

Rosalio pointed into the depths. "There they are," he whispered. He took a packet, lit a wick protruding from its tied opening, held it suspended in his hand as it burned down, then tossed it into the dark mirror. It sank immediately and, after a short delay, exploded. A shower of fish and water erupted from the surface. "The fish are only stunned. We must collect them quickly." Hundreds of them, white and silver flakes the length of my hand, floated on the surface. Deploying his net, Rosalio paddled through the school of unconscious fish, scooping them up as the net trailed behind. "Now you have fished with TNT," he said. He explained that you cannot throw the dynamite too soon or the water would put out the burning wick. And it must not sink too deep.

"Have there been accidents?" I asked.

"I have friends who now have only one hand. They were inexperienced, but they were hungry," he said with a shrug. "*Sawi*. Hopeless. Sometimes it is hopeless."

171

Two days later I too said *sawi* as I lay moaning on a cot
in sick bay wishing only to die. For the next week, ill with
chronic nausea, diarrhea, and fever, I had lost all appetite for
food. Normally thin and gangly, I now looked deathly gaunt.
The outline of my bones poked through my yellow skin,
fluorescent from jaundice. There was no known cure, no
medicinal treatment, no hope for early relief. The disease
would have to take its natural course toward either recovery
or death. "What're my chances, sir?" I beseeched cold,
brusque Doctor Cunningham.

"You're young, sailor. I wouldn't be surprised if you
make it."

I was so miserable I wasn't sure I wanted to make it. But
after a week I passed a crisis and began to want to live. Both
Billiard Ball and Fortune looked in on me. Whitey dropped by
and was movingly sympathetic. And Blackie, though racked
with pain, crawled the few hundred feet from our tent to my
bedside to wish me well. Gaining strength each day, I reached
out to the world again and learned that others not so young
and resilient had died. "When will you sailors stop eating
unsanitary food off base?" Doctor Cunningham reprimanded.
Was this a consequence of Rosalio's hospitality? I wondered.

"Rat shit," said Billiard Ball. "Jaundice comes from rat
feces in our flour."

Most of the sick bay population was disabled from
gonorrhea — the clap. During the final days of my
hospitalization, Whitey appeared among them. It was his
third go-round, he boasted, as if this somehow confirmed his
manhood. Twice before he had been an outpatient, but now,
hardly able to walk, his confinement was essential. Lieutenant
Commander Gluck, on a hot campaign to stamp out the
source of the disease, began an investigation, which
amounted to little more than an inquisition of the infected.
Whitey headed his list. "Who was she, sailor? What's her
name, huh?" Gluck demanded.

"Sorry, sir, I don't know, sir."

"Whadya mean you don't know? You telling me you
fucked her, and you don't even know her name?"

172

"Trouble is, there were so many, sir, I just can't remember." He threw up his hands and shrugged his shoulders.

"Wal," Gluck said in exasperation, "how many you talking about, three, four? Just give me all their names."

"Oh, that'd be at least twenty, sir, maybe more."

"Twenty!" exclaimed an incredulous Gluck. "Christ, you're a fuckin' machine."

"Yes, sir," Whitey replied, unable to supress a proud chuckle.

At an impasse, Gluck moved on to the next patient.

Motioning me to his cotside, Whitey confided, "That sonofabitch, he'll never get her name outa me, you betcha."

"You know which one it was, Whitey?" I asked.

"'Course I know. I got only one girl. I like her, see, and she treats me like a king."

"But, Whitey, she keeps making you sick."

"Look, if I tell 'em, they'll send her away. I'm not takin' the chance of losin' her. I'll never tell 'em. They can court-martial me first."

I realized that Whitey was bent on a course of self-destruction. A generous, constant friend, having once saved my life from drowning in the log corral at Hollandia, he was impossible and unforgettable. When I awoke the next morning his cot was empty; he had disappeared without explanation, presumably banished, at Gluck's order, for a cure someplace far away from women. Unwittingly, by exaggerating his prowess, he undid himself. The fact was, my friend Whitey was no longer a good man for the battalion.

Gluck attacked the problem of our high VD casualties from a rather self-righteous and moral point of view. To him, promiscuity and, heaven forbid, miscegenation were anathema. "It's fuckin' unAmerican," he proclaimed.

But Commander Rutledge was primarily concerned with VD's debilitating effect on the minds and bodies of his men. "These dastardly diseases are making our boys old before their time," he grieved.

He was also troubled by our increasing tardiness in meeting the Command's schedule for completing assignments.

173

"You have a habit of being chronically out of sync with the rest of us, Rutledge," the Command complained. "In war, for your information, it's better never than late. Either you get things done on time or we'll have to make some fundamental changes."

At its peak, a good twenty-five percent of our battalion was laid up. The remainder of us, the healthy ones, in order to make up for the reduced complement, had to work extended hours. Twenty-hour days were increasingly routine. Many held two jobs; Billiard Ball, in addition to his regular censor's and translating duties, helped as a day laborer in dock construction. Once recovered sufficiently from the jaundice, I, too, although not officially a member of the battalion, volunteered to pitch in during off-duty hours from water tending. Often I worked with the pile drivers doing manual chores under spotlights at night, and from time to time operated a gigantic D8 bulldozer, a deeply satisfying assignment that, I suspect, fulfilled my repressed need for power. Despite such efforts, however, we continued to lag behind schedule.

As the Command's pressure, now emanating from Manila headquarters, became increasingly relentless, our weariness grew and began taking its toll in the form of more accidents. A devastating one at the waterfront involved two flat pontoon barges that were tied up to each other. One of them — the work barge — provided a compact area for rigging tasks and the storage of various tools used in dock construction. Six men, including Billiard Ball, were on the work barge performing assembly chores. The other barge, used for gasoline and diesel oil storage, had just been loaded and was filled to capacity with hardly any freeboard, so that occasionally a wave would lap over its rusty steel deck.

One of the men on the work barge was welding, creating a brilliant shower of sparks. Suddenly there was a blinding orange streak; an envelope of fire permeated the air above the barges. The welder himself and two others were instantly reduced to charred lumps. The other men, their clothes aflame, became live screaming torches. Plunging into the crystalline green water, they swam in panic in several

174

directions. Fearing an eventual explosion, two of the survivors struggled to make distance by heading away from land; the third, Billiard Ball, swam at a strong pace towards shore.

From the deck of the Mudhog barely a hundred yards away, I saw the barges suddenly explode into the air in countless fragments. Covered with a fuel slick, the surface of the water burst into fiery brilliance. Even from where I stood, the searing heat of the flames lightly scorched my face and penetrated my clothes. I leapt from the dredge to escape, then raced along the tube to shore, mindless of any risk of falling into the water. There on the beach hundreds of my mates, attracted by the sound of the explosion and the raging inferno, had gathered, stringing themselves along the water's edge watching helplessly, anxious to know who had died, who would survive.

Billiard Ball, an accomplished swimmer, managed to stay ahead of the burning slick and was first to approach the shore. I waded out to meet him, then supported him as we plodded through the shallow water while he caught his breath. "I'm sure I broke an Olympic record," he wheezed between gasps, turning to look back on the terrifying scene behind him. Beyond the patch of flames, we could make out an upraised arm grasping at air. We could hear faint cries of "help" above the crackle and whisper of the fire. At this, Billiard Ball plunged back into the water and swam out through the flames. He grabbed his drowning mate from behind the chin and slowly, with one arm splashing a free path through the fire, he made his way to the beach.

It was an incredible rescue, the more so because Billiard Ball was already exhausted. "How did you do it?" I marveled.

His singed face was a grim mask. "It was simply mind over matter," he replied stoically.

He had unhesitatingly performed a selfless act by risking his own welfare for someone else's. Behind the cynical facade lay the true Billiard Ball.

This disastrous episode was hardly on the order of the night murders at Hollandia town or of the folly at Pancake Hill, or of the mix-up in scheduling on the beach at Biak or of our unexpected vulnerability during the Mindoro landing.

Nevertheless, it was somehow less sufferable because, due to its miniature scale, it was easier to absorb.

Everyone knew the basic cause of the disaster. In our hurry to get things done, we had grown careless. The commander exploded: "Who in hell was stupid enough to permit welding on a fuel barge?" Although the welding actually occurred on another barge tied up to the fuel barge, no one was about to correct him. He wanted retribution, but we could see that no amount of it, no imputation of fault, no punishment of the officer directly responsible, could assuage the commander's own sense of personal blame. Over the next few weeks he stopped smiling, withdrew into a depression, and isolated himself.

The fire and explosion were the culmination of the larger problem, that of our reduced complement because of illness. Prior to the blaze the commander and Gluck held long discussions exploring ways to stem the revolving flow of casualties and the spread of VD. "We can't keep this pace much longer," said the commander. "It's not enough to get our infected boys back to work. They've got to stay healthy and on the job." The commander considered doing away with liberties, in effect quarantining us, but he realized that would be too harsh. Having been overseas for eighteen months, we needed an occasional change of scene to maintain our morale. He also thought of controlling the prostitutes by legitimizing them.

"The Command would never go for it," countered Gluck. "It ain't wholesome. It's against every American principle."

"I think in some ways the Japs are smarter than us," said Rutledge. "They bring women along for their boys."

"Hell, if we did that, our boys would never get anything done," Gluck snorted. "I've got the answer, Jerry." A leer crept across his face as he prepared to explain. "I know how ya feel about the natives, but all I ask is that you hear me out. I say burn Subic. Burn the whole fuckin' place down to the ground. It's the only way to get rid of garbage."

A wave of revulsion at the thought of such a despicable measure surged through the commander. "The Filipinos aren't the enemy, Gluck. Part of our job here is to maintain goodwill."

"Yeah, but that doesn't mean we gotta sleep with the goddamned gooks."

With Commander Rutledge in seclusion—desperate but immobilized by conscience—Commander Gluck jumped into the void and took charge. "I'm gonna do it, Jerry. I'm takin' it on myself to burn Subic." The commander heard him and made no response; silence, in Gluck's view, signified consent.

Blackie was chosen to join the contingent of two platoons assigned to the "Clout Clap Campaign," as Gluck dubbed it. Equipped with rag torches and a barrel of kerosene, the detail met at 5:00 A.M. at the camp dock and boarded a landing craft.

Blackie described what happened upon his return. "You'd think we were going into combat. Gluck had his steel helmet on and his pet pistol at his hip and a carbine hanging from his shoulder. He gave us a pep talk about the Clout Clap Campaign bein' for our own good but everybody was snickering 'cause he was stumblin' over the three C's.

"The first thing we did after we landed was to get the girls out of the huts before settin' the place on fire. Well, they thought we were coming in on some special liberty to fuck. Goddamn were they surprised. Sayin' 'I was good to you. Remember how you say you love me? Remember?' They don't make it easy for us. We keep apologizin', tellin' them it's the brass and not us that's kickin' 'em out. They fought us and screamed and booted us in the balls, which they said we wouldn't need anymore as far as they were concerned.

"Gluck was pacin' up and down the main street through the stinkin' puddles wavin' his pistol and hollerin' orders: 'Tell the fuckin' whores we'll torch 'em in their huts if they don't get out pronto. Tell 'em we mean business, men.' And he started singing,

> 'We're the Seabees of the navy,
> We can build and we can fight,
> We'll pave the way to victory
> Over clap with all our might.'

"Some of us were cleaning out the whores and some of us were runnin' from one hut to another pourin' kerosene and, just behind, some of us were racin' around with torches setting the huts on fire. Whoosh, they went up quick like tinder.

"And then it happened; it was awful. Two kids. They must have been hidin' in one of the huts and got doused with kerosene. I saw them runnin' down the middle of the street all afire, bloody screamin', runnin' toward Gluck, and he was yellin', 'Save those kids, save those kids, men,' but no one could help. When the kids reached him he wrapped himself around one of them, then the other, and caught fire himself, and he ripped off his clothes. The kids were still in flames writhing on the ground. He dragged them into a puddle but they stopped movin', and he sat in the muddy water with the burned bodies and said over and over, 'Oh, my God, oh my God, my God'; it was awful seein' him like that."

My recuperation from the jaundice was excruciatingly long and slow. Even after being dismissed from sick bay and returned to duty, I wearied easily and spent my personal time lying on my cot sleeping or reading. Billiard Ball, despiser of fiction, handed me a book "to give me some insight into the Far Eastern mind." It was Forster's *A Passage to India*. Immersing myself in it, I was able to remain oblivious to Blackie's moans of pain in the neighboring cot. I concluded that the irrationality of the Indian people was beyond my understanding. Yet I had no difficulty relating to Rosalio and his family. They seemed hardly different from people I knew back home, save for the trappings. Or had I misunderstood what made them tick? Six weeks had passed since my visit to Olongopo. As soon as I felt strong enough I would see them on my first liberty.

Approaching Rosalio's raised thatched hut, I had a sense that things were not right. His *banca*, beached in the grass along the river's edge, was filled with rainwater. The customary animals, the hens and pigs that scavenged the garbage beneath the hut, were missing. The bamboo shutters had been lowered over the window openings. Peering into the shadows within, made darker still by contrast to the brilliant afternoon sun, I knocked on the bamboo wall next to the doorless entrance. I heard a grunt and a baby cry but could see nothing. "Rosalio? Is it you? This is Hal, your long-lost American buddy."

"Go away," Rosalio's voice said from the darkness.

I entered and, after my eyes adjusted, found Rosalio seated on the floor huddled against a wall, a somnolent infant son in his arms. "What's happened, Rosalio?" I crouched down before him. "Why are you this way? Where's your wife?"

"Subic," he said.

"That's not a place for her," I said. The rebuilding of Subic had begun a few weeks after the fire and some of the girls had set up shop again mainly to service the line navy sailors.

"She's a 'businesswoman' now."

"What?" I cried in disbelief. I reached my arm across his shoulder to offer comfort. Ignoring my gesture, he rested his sleeping child on a floormat and stood up.

"I wish you to leave, Hal," he said.

"Tell me what happened, Rosalio. I can't believe your lovely wife has done this to you."

"She has done nothing. She is a 'businesswoman' with my blessing," and with these words, he broke into deep sobbing. His arms hung unresponsively by his sides as I embraced him and when he pulled away I was shocked to discover the cause of his anguish; his right arm terminated at the wrist in a stump of grafted skin. The dynamite—a split second of bad timing. He could no longer fish and support his family. His loving, sweet-tempered wife was now the breadwinner. "*Sawi, sawi,*" he murmured. Hopeless, hopeless.

I returned to camp distraught over Rosalio's tragedy and exhausted from my lingering weakness. After Chief Dunham who died at Mindoro, then Whitey who was exiled, Rosalio was another friend that I had made and lost during my sojourn overseas. I was still too sad to rise from my cot as I lay naked late into the following hot morning. Blackie was there in undershorts, his face grizzly, his balding head resting on a soiled, sweat-soaked pillow. Someone was knocking timidly on a two-by-four that framed our tent entrance. Raising myself onto an elbow, I saw an apparition in a white dress, the comely girl from the stream, and behind her the other girl whom Billiard Ball had rescued. With them was a

179

distinguished-looking silver-haired man dressed in a loose-fitting sport shirt that hung below the waist of his neatly creased trousers. "May I come in, please, sir?" asked the apparition. Hastening to cover myself with a sheet, I sat erect on the cot, futilely searching for words and finally only nodding. The other girl spoke: "This is my father and my cousin, and we have come to thank you for helping us." Staring at the white sheet, the apparition smiled.

"I'm really not a nudist," I said embarrassed, recalling our last meeting. "I do wear clothes most of the time."

"You saved my daughter and niece from a terrible humiliation," the silver-haired man said in precise, refined English with barely an accent. "Please accept my heartfelt gratitude."

"I'm happy that my friend and I could be of service." I said. "How did you find us?"

Amused by my question, the three babbled in dialect (not Tagalog) among themselves, then the cousin said, "It has taken us many weeks. Only after my uncle met with your commander and described you were we certain." Of course we were unmistakable. What other pair, a naked giraffe and a bald giant, would fit our description?

Names were exchanged. He was Lucio Quiboloy, mayor of the village of Lugao in the central province of Pampanga. His daughter, the apparition, was Anita, and her cousin was Dolores. I introduced them to Blackie, who, uninterested and lost in his misery, remained motionless except for waving his hand in recognition. "He's got a serious back problem," I explained.

"Ah, is that so?" said Mr. Quiboloy, gazing upon Blackie with surprising interest.

Dolores spoke again: "We wish to invite you to Lugao to stay with us as our guests. And, of course, we include your friend, Billiard Ball. May we expect you this weekend?" Anita nodded, her eyes assenting to everything her cousin said, but she remained silent.

"I'll speak to Billiard Ball, and if we can get liberty we'll be there."

"Good," said Mr. Quiboloy. "The people of my barrio are very anxious to meet you." As my eyes met Anita's, I felt myself blushing. I was helplessly attracted to her.

Mr. Quiboloy peremptorily turned his attention to Blackie. "Show me where the pain is, sir," he said with authority. Momentarily astonished, Blackie, always ready for sympathy, turned on his stomach and pointed awkwardly to a spot near his lower spine. Quickly, before Blackie had a chance to realize what was being done to him, Mr. Quiboloy grasped his shoulders firmly from behind and manipulated his torso until he heard bones snap. As Blackie, now bellowing in pain, fell back on the cot, Mr. Quiboloy reached for my hand in parting. "In a short while, your friend will be relieved," he said as he and his alluring charmers departed.

I watched Anita walking down the path from our tent and observed her poised gait and proud posture. I studied her graceful figure under the cool white dress made from a GI mattress cover. Until she disappeared from sight I could feel my heart pounding uncontrollably.

Within a half hour, an incredulous Blackie was up and about, a reincarnation of his old "Hot Wires" self, but better. He said that it would no longer be sufficient for him to work on wires flowing with a mere one-hundred-ten volts. He was going for two-twenty, and once inured to that, onward to four-forty. "Who knows, someday I might even tackle an electric chair," he dreamed out loud.

The letter from Lucia was short, just a card with a winter scene sent in an elegant perfumed envelope.

> Dearest Hal,
> Why have you stopped writing again? Have you been so busy winning the war, or has some beautiful native girl stolen your heart, leaving you no time for me? I understand. But don't drift too far away.

Both Barry and I want you to be best man
at our wedding.

Affectionately,
Lucia.

XVIII
Subic Bay

Hospitality GI Style

I suppose Gluck could be accused of possessing a special arrogance for believing that he could eradicate prostitution. After all, having survived the rise and fall of civilizations, it's not called the oldest profession in the world for nothing. Being essentially a service that fulfills a common biological need rooted deep in our hypothalamus, it comes with the territory—no question about it. To his shock and chagrin, Gluck's Clout Clap Campaign backfired on a scale that he couldn't have imagined.

After Subic burned, some of the girls returned to their hometowns and villages to bide their time. It was especially hard on them, for usually they were the sole support of their unemployed parents, children, grandparents, and yes, husbands. To be called a "businesswoman" was denigrating but also apt. Other girls, endowed with true entrepreneurial spirit, managed to stay in business by relocating to new premises. Quite simply they entered into joint ventures with us and moved into our camp. They shared our tents, our slender cots, our community showers, our food, even our heads.

Within hours of the razing of Subic, the migration began. But the love style would change: Unlike the practice at Subic, there was minimal promiscuity. Pairing was the norm. The logistics were awkward but workable. One cot now served two. Since we had several showering sites, one was selected for girls only; a similar setup was arranged with our heads, except for certain hours. However, it wasn't unusual for a girl in need of relief from nature's call during prohibited hours to join us in the "reading room." In the chow hall at mealtime, each man having a woman at his tent went back for seconds, and brought a meal to her while it was still hot. As Gluck was quick to observe: "They never had it so good."

He was outraged. "This is one lousy fuckin' way to run a battalion," he complained. "Jerry, how long we gonna let this go on?"

Rutledge remained passive, but not from depression. The new situation was surely superior to the Japanese method of service prostitution, which he had praised. He now saw a solution to the VD problem, of getting us back to work and keeping us there, and of meeting the Command's deadlines again. "Let what go on?" Rutledge said.

"The whores, Jerry."

"Whores, Gluck? You mean the laundry women? Would you have our boys go back to their own washing again?"

The scene so lifted the commander's morale that he began to mingle with us on the job and smile again. As expected, absenteeism dropped in proportion to the declining incidence of VD, but Rutledge made one stipulation, formally posted, that everyone immediately understood and approved. "Henceforth, every laundry woman visiting the battalion areas, entering the tents, or in any way having contact with battalion personnel in the conduct of their business must be certified by the medical staff. This measure is necessary to prevent unsanitary practices and for the protection of our health and safety." The words were purposely ambiguous. There was no suggestion that cohabitation was going on, no mention of venereal disease. Yet by innuendo his notice made it clear to everyone that he must be in control in exchange for his sanction.

For me, as for Gluck, the presence of women on the premises was troublesome, although for somewhat different reasons. From a practical point of view, we were of one mind: I considered the girls a distraction that was bound to make us less efficient. I lived by a body of absolute values, among them belief in the inherent goodness of Americans (a creed under mounting attack), the necessity of loyalty in friendship, and the control of one's libido. On all three counts we were failing.

Our actions were not kind and good; we were cruel and selfish. The women swarmed to us like moths to flames, mesmerized by our relatively opulent GI standard of living (every GI seemed to have his own jeep), our irresistible informality, our free-flowing generosity, and our power. We were not serious, but they were, referring to us, their lovers, as "husbands," insisting that they were really married. It was purely a figment of their imagination, a symptom of their idolatry. "What will happen to you after the war when your 'husband' returns home?" I'd ask them. The reply was always the same, without hesitation: "He will come back and take me with him to America." Didn't MacArthur return? They were a veritable chorus of Madame Butterflies.

On the matter of loyalty we were detestable. The married ones with wives back home were adulterers almost to a man, intentionally misleading their lovers into believing that they were single and available. Finding this especially hard to accept, I terminated even casual friendships with my married mates. As for our blatant sexuality, I found its openness intolerable. The sights and sounds of intercourse filled the night. Since there was no privacy, there was little respect for the feelings of those who chose to remain alone, particularly of the inexperienced and shy like myself.

My tent-mates, however, appeared to be celibate. Blackie, whose back had reverted to its painful condition again, was too preoccupied with himself to be interested in women. Indeed, I doubt whether he could partake of sexual relations without causing himself excruciating pain. "All I ask is to see that Quiboloy guy again," he begged. I promised that I would go to Lugao on the weekend and arrange for Anita's father to return to our camp to administer a treatment.

Billiard Ball exhibited no interest whatever in women; rather he adopted an attitude of lofty amusement. "Boys will be boys; let them play," he said. Fortune was certainly too occupied with business matters to be distracted. Often he wouldn't show up at the tent for three or four nights at a time. Moreover he was committed to Lucia. Hadn't they made marriage plans?

Having finished Forster's *A Passage to India*, I then took up Proust's *Remembrance of Things Past*, much to Billiard Ball's displeasure. "The existing English translation is a travesty," he declared. "If you can't read it in the original French, you shouldn't read it at all."

"That's a ridiculous thing to say," I responded. "I'm not going to learn a language just to read Proust. Since you're so damn unhappy with the present translation, it seems to me that might be a worthwhile project for you to tackle."

For once he offered no reply. Instead he fell momentarily into deep, silent thought, then, raising his eyebrows, he said: "Y'know, that's a helluva good idea."

While reading fully clothed on my cot one evening I fell asleep. Waking in the middle of the night, although fractionally conscious, I was vaguely aware of the sound of rhythmic creaking and weak cries. They came from within the tent but I was too sleepy to bother investigating.

I rose early the next morning before the others. My eyes strayed across the tent to Fortune's cot, where I could make out indistinctly through the mosquito netting two nude sleeping figures entwined. As I studied the pair more closely, I thought I saw a patch of golden hair. Fortune had succumbed. I felt anger, as if I, as well as Lucia, had been betrayed.

After I returned to the tent from my morning ablutions, Fortune and the girl were up and dressed while Blackie and Billiard Ball still slept. Fortune whispered in order not to wake them: "This is Nina, Hal." Giving him a hostile stare, I ignored his introduction. "Hal is my best, my most trusted friend."

"Like shit," I muttered without his hearing me.

Nina reached out her hand and smiled, showing perfect teeth, unusual for Filipinos because of malnourishment and lack of dental care during the occupation. But everything about her was unusual: I had never been so near such a striking beauty. Her dress, stylish, as if out of an American magazine, white with red flowers, clung to her like a caress. Apart from her golden hair, which draped over her shoulders, she was tall, almost as tall as Fortune himself. And her bearing was confident and dignified, denoting good breeding. Her skin color was Caucasian, smooth, glowing, and pink. But her eyes were Asian, iridescent blue, hypnotic. I had heard of

186

certain exceptionally handsome people in the islands; of mixed Spanish and native blood, they were called mestizos.

Softened by her smile, and realizing that it was unfair to be resentful, I took her hand. "Welcome aboard," I said. By then both Billiard Ball and Blackie had awakened. Fortune made introductions through their netting. Blackie sat up, ignoring the pain, and exposed his hairy torso, making me feel strangely embarrassed. "Where are you from?" I asked in Tagalog.

Nina turned to me and laughed gaily like high-pitched piano keys. "How did you learn Tagalog?" I reached into my footlocker and showed her my Tagalog-English dictionary and the grammar book Billiard Ball had given me. "I think it's wonderful that you've taken the trouble to learn our national language," she said in colloquial American English.

"Thanks," I said. "I've found that speaking Tagalog is the best way to win over your hearts."

"Oh, yes, that's so true," she said, and in Tagalog added: "I'm from near Guagua in Pampanga."

"Tell me, Nina," interjected Billiard Ball, whose cobwebs had now dissipated, "do you speak other languages besides Tagalog and English?"

"Actually, as a child I spoke Spanish, and I learned enough Italian, German, and French to get by when I lived in Europe."

"But you can't be that old," said an impressed Billiard Ball. "You look hardly twenty."

"Now, Mr. Billiard Ball, do you think it wise for a girl to tell her age?" she jested. "But to explain, I matriculated at several schools in those countries and graduated from the Sorbonne just before France fell."

Dazzled to our core, we were reduced to mush in her hands. Where did Fortune find this jewel? Yet how could I possibly be her friend?

To avoid further awkward morning confrontations, awkward to me that is, I moved out of the tent to the Mudhog, with the excuse that its crew was shorthanded and might need my expertise on a moment's notice.

"Expertise!" Blackie snorted. "For what? Peeling onions? Goddamn Onion Heads! Biggest screw-offs in the Pacific. You oughta be ashamed of associating with that crew."

I could see that Blackie was having a painful day. His objection notwithstanding — in a way I was pleased that he tried to keep me aboard — I left, taking over an empty bunk below deck in the Mudhog's fantail, and using the vessel's ample creature comforts at will.

> Dear Lucia,
> Forgive me for neglecting you. Yes, I have been extremely busy fighting the war, such as reading Forster and Proust and listening to Beethoven. Seriously, I had a bout with jaundice that laid me low for more than a month and I lost all desire to live. Now I'm well again and ready to pick up where I left off.
>
> Unfortunately, I see very little of Barry, who is always busy with projects of his own. But I know he is well, and quite fascinated with the islands. I wouldn't be surprised if he retained some interest here after the war. I, too, enjoy the islands, especially the people whom I'm getting to know intimately.

I went on to tell her of Rosalio's plight, but I made no mention of Anita, of the incident in the stream, and certainly no mention of Nina. Reading between my lines, she might have found a possible clue to Fortune's future direction. More telling, however, is what I didn't say: I made no reference to her mention of marriage, or to my being best man. In closing I wrote:

> I promise to write regularly from now on. You may depend on it; and you can count

on me no matter what the future brings.
Your loyal friend and admirer,

Hal.

Had I gone too far? Would such a cryptic comment make
her worry? Still, how else could I let her know that she had
my support in the event that Fortune should hurt her? I was
convinced that sooner or later he would.

At dawn on a pink Saturday morning, with small duffel
bags slung over our shoulders, Billiard Ball and I caught the
first launch of the day to Olongopo. We stood at the bow to
let the salt spray graze our cheeks and wake us up. Looking
off to the west toward the Zambales range, I stared at the
brilliant red streak plunging down the mountainside,
resembling a raw, bloody wound in the dawn's light. "You
won't be satisfied until you have the answer, will you?" asked
Billiard Ball.

"What answer?" I said, and I saw that he was following
my gaze to the streak that was gradually changing to tinsel.

"You know," he replied, "I'm much in favor of scientific
inquiry, but I hope that some things will always remain a
mystery. You always want answers. Sometimes faith is
enough."

"I do have faith," I protested. "Unlike you, I still believe
in man."

We were on our way to Lugao, to the country of
conscience and painful regret, to an experience that would
remain locked in my soul until now.

XIX
Lugao

Hospitality Filipino Style

The ten-wheel army truck jostled us like empty kegs as it roared along the rough, winding dirt road through the mountains from Olongopo to the central plain of Pampanga province. Unable to talk because of the clatter of the diesel, Billiard Ball and I sat in the back, silent, lost in thought, studying the sheer cut through an ugly wasteland of shattered stumps of the once forested mountainside as it swept behind us. It had been the target of an awful naval barrage. When we reached the divide, the driver motioned from his open cab, pointing to the panorama of the green expanse below extending northward to the horizon and westward to faraway blue mountains.

Heading down the mountainside at breakneck speed, we rocked from side to side as if in a bobsled race; Billiard Ball prayed. Soon after reaching the broad valley floor, our road intersected with a concrete-paved two-lane highway, the first I had seen since leaving the States. "I'm heading south to Bataan," said the driver. "Lugao is the other way."

We clambered from the truck platform, waving thanks as he roared off, leaving us in the silence of a tranquil, empty, treeless land. We gazed down the road, too hot to touch, shimmering in the distance. "My friend Rosalio spoke about this highway," I said. "A terrible thing happened along here. They call it the Death March, the march of the American prisoners from Bataan. Can you imagine what it must have been like in this heat, day after day without cover, without water?"

We spied a vehicle, its dust cloud showing up now and then in the distance along the open sections of the mountain highway. Upon reaching us, the driver, an army sergeant in

190

green fatigues, inquired of our destination, then invited us to climb aboard. I sat next to him behind the lowered windshield, while Billiard Ball sprawled in the rear seat. As we sped along, the driver commented, "Lugao, huh. Nothin' much goin' on there. Y'oughta go to Manila. That's where the real action is. Hell, Lugao is all Methodists. They've got no use for GI's. I pick up a lot of gooks along this road. But the ones from Lugao, they just shake their heads and make a sign they'd rather walk."

"Isn't it rather unusual to find Methodists in the islands?" asked Billiard Ball. "After all this is essentially a Catholic country."

"I s'pose so. All I know is their women won't fuck. They won't even dance; it's against their religion," responded the sergeant.

Disgusted with our stubbornness, the GI had little else to say and we settled into silence. There was only the drone of the jeep motor, the hot wind against our faces, the blistering white strip of concrete beneath the wheels, the empty, flat, green vista. The earth was ravaged and wasted with stubble and green weeds. Before the occupation, at this time of year the fields would have been filled with tall rice grass, ripe for harvest, bending in the breeze sweeping down from the blue mountains.

Soon we passed a solitary thatched hut, set back from the road beside a sluggish, turbid stream in which oxenlike work animals called *caribao*, were immersed up to their heavy necks, lowing and trying to keep cool. Later we saw a great white stucco mansion set in the center of a rice field. Two giant shade trees overspreading a well-tended plot of lawn stood on each side of the house. The scene was out of character with the bareness and poverty of the countryside. "That's a hacienda house," said the sergeant, "where the big shot lives who owns all this land."

Despite its splendor, the mansion was oddly stark. The huge front door was wide open, as were its windows with their gauzy curtains whipping in the hot wind. Through the entrance I saw a barren hallway with a milk-white marble floor. The place appeared abandoned save for the neatness of the lawn.

Barely a mile beyond the great house, the sergeant dropped us off beside the path to Lugao. "You're almost halfway to Manila," he said. "Sure you haven't changed your mind?"

"Yeah, I'm sure, Sarge. These are our kind of gooks. Thanks for the ride," I said bitingly.

The path was hardly wide enough for an automobile or a donkey cart. As we negotiated the puddles and *carabao* droppings, the path curved and burrowed into a shady thicket of tropical vegetation before giving way to a bright clearing of neat thatched huts on stilts surrounded by bamboo fences. In the center of the compound was a white stucco church whose walls were splattered with the marks of machine gun bullets. The corrugated metal roof was rent with large gaping holes. Shades of Hollandia, I thought.

Appearing from nowhere, a swarm of naked boys and girls encircled us. They pranced about, dashing like innocent uninhibited puppies, some shouting in dialect, others in Tagalog, but too fast for me to catch. "Americano, Americano," a nude girl child squealed, announcing our arrival. "Obviously, we are an event," Billiard Ball observed.

Walking deeper into the barrio comprising two dozen or so houses, we saw a group of adults gathered before the church waiting to greet us. I recognized Anita and her father, Mr. Quiboloy, and about a dozen younger men and women, all surprisingly well attired in colorful summery shirts and slacks and dresses. "I have a feeling they've put on their Sunday finest for us," I remarked.

"I'm afraid so," said Billiard Ball. "I wish to hell they weren't making such a fuss."

My heartbeat quickened at the prospect of seeing Anita again. But my attention was also drawn to a small, distinguished-looking, white-haired man standing next to Mayor Quiboloy. As we drew nearer I noticed that his features were singularly sharp, lean, and craggy but, despite his age, his brown eyes were markedly clear. They were the eyes of a younger person, but soft, suggesting a man at peace with himself.

Mr. Quiboloy extended his hand. "We are most happy to see you again, Hal. This, I presume, is Billiard Ball. How do you do, sir. May I thank you on behalf of the people of our humble village and personally for my wife and myself as well. We are forever in your debt for your courageous rescue of my daughter and niece." Shaking hands with the mayor, Billiard Ball, obviously taken with the greeting, glanced at me quickly, happily surprised. For the first time since I could remember, he seemed at a loss to respond and simply nodded in acknowledgement.

"May I introduce Reverend Mr. Corum, our minister," continued the mayor, at which point the white-haired man, reaching to shake our hands, spoke.

"Ah, you are both welcome to our village. We hope you will feel at home with us during your stay. But I know that our ways and customs are different from yours, so please, I beg you, let us know your wishes if by chance we displease you." Like the mayor's, Mr. Corum's English was measured and flawless. He spoke in a sonorous voice with hardly a trace of accent.

"While we are your guests," replied Billiard Ball, "your ways will be our ways. Of course, we must be ourselves and we hope you will do the same."

"Spoken well," said the reverend. "By all means, we must be ourselves." I saw pleasure at Billiard Ball's words in his eyes. "Not all Americans are as wise as you. But then our honorable mayor has informed us that you are not the same as the others."

"We have all kinds," replied Billiard Ball.

"Yes, so do we," said the reverend. "Now you must be hungry and thirsty from your journey, so let us have a repast together at my house."

The barrio exhibited a quality that I had not found in Olongopo, certainly not in Subic. The thatched houses weren't unusual, except for being neater and in excellent repair. The streets were worn dirt, but there were no puddles. The banana trees between the houses were the same as elsewhere, only they were trimmed of dead branches and replete with fruit to be harvested. The pigs and chickens looked fatter and roamed about less feverishly. The general impression was of order and stability. Could Lugao, being a hidden backwater, have escaped the terror of occupation? I sensed a peculiar certitude in the people, unlike their countrymen who were conscious of past defeat. On the contrary, the folk of Lugao behaved as if they had been victors. Still there was the pocked and crumbling church, providing silent testimony that the barrio had not been spared at all.

Although lunch was served in Reverend Mr. Corum's house, Anita joined the reverend's wife as principal hostess. She hovered over us, keeping our water glasses filled, catering to our smallest need. It was generally understood that we were her special guests. As we sat with legs crossed in a circle on the bamboo floor, she proudly placed plates of American C rations before us. "I hope this will make you feel at home," she said.

"Oh, it will, Anita. Thank-you, you're very thoughtful," I said, hiding my disappointment and catching Billiard Ball's knowing smile of amusement.

After lunch we were ushered into the reverend's small all-bamboo living room, a cheerful, cool place with a cushioned bamboo settee and several similar bamboo chairs. A small, plain red jute rug covered the center of the floor. After the bare Filipino houses I had seen in Olongopo, after Rosalio's house, this one appeared opulent by comparison.

As if by a prearranged signal, people began to fill the room, soon spilling over into the kitchen where we had eaten. The reverend made a point to introduce each one who entered, giving not only names but occupations. Despite the difficulty in absorbing the flood of detail, I remembered a teacher, an agricultural expert, a chief of police, a college student from the university in Manila, a nurse, and many rice farmers.

The teacher, young, sleek, dark and alert—introduced as Alejandro—seemed intrigued with Billiard Ball's credentials. "Is it true, sir, that you are a professor of languages at the great Columbia University in New York?"

"Former professor of Romance languages, mainly French," chuckled Billiard Ball. "I'm strictly a Seabee now."

"Of course, I understand. But my, my, French. If only I could be so fortunate to read Flaubert in his native language."

194

The dialogue progressed as if they were alone, but no one interrupted; everyone listened closely.

"English has its greats, too," said Billiard Ball impatiently, anxious to get on to a more mundane subject that would appeal to all.

"Of course, who could be finer than Shakespeare? And the moderns—I enjoy Auden, and I presume you've read "The Lovesong of J. Alfred Prufrock." What a marvelous poem of our time!"

Billiard Ball was amused. Was this man showing off? Yet he seemed to speak knowledgeably; on the surface his references were accurate.

"But I must not monopolize you. Forgive me," said Alejandro.

"I think we've exhausted the subject," said Billiard Ball coldly, then, regretting his harshness, added, "Maybe we could talk another time."

"Ask for Hando, the teacher, whenever you are ready."

"Perhaps you can teach me your dialect," said Billiard Ball.

"That would be my pleasure." Tears of joy welled up in Hando's eyes.

"Will you tell us about America? What is it truly like to live in America?" requested the reverend. He was holding a copy of *Life* magazine in his lap. Both Billiard Ball and I laughed at so large a question: We hardly knew where to begin. "Is it true that everyone is rich in America?" one of the peasant farmers asked.

"Most are better off than the people of Lugao," said Billiard Ball, "but our large cities have enormous slums full of poor people, and many farmers in our southern sections are destitute."

"But all Americans have jeeps," someone offered.

"Most families have a passenger automobile," I explained. A murmur of wonder rippled through the audience.

America, America, the land of everyone's dreams, the closest place to heaven on Earth. What other nation could compare? So the world viewed us, and we could not agree more. But it was a romantic image, an exaggeration. We were superior only in comparison to the world's corrupt and villainous nations. In a real, an absolute sense, we had far to travel toward becoming what the rest of the world and we ourselves thought we were.

Twenty years later we came face to face with our reality, saw what cruelty we were capable of. It showed us that we were less different from the rest of humanity than we thought. Would Billiard Ball, a clear-sighted man, have imagined that a Vietnam was possible? Would I? Yes, I think we knew it was. The seeds of that tragedy were planted in the soil of this war right before our eyes. We Americans, feeling we were right and invincible, took on a mission to proselytize the rest of the world.

"So then in America most people are prosperous if they can afford automobiles?" asked Mayor Quiboloy.

"Today, yes," replied Billiard Ball, "as a result of the war. Until recently we experienced the worst economic depression in our history, in which many Americans could find no jobs, and some went hungry like yourselves under the Japs. The depression lasted almost a decade." There was a gasp of surprise.

"But look at you now," the mayor said, "so very powerful, every American GI rich, your wealth abounds everywhere."

"I suppose it seems that way," Billiard Ball said evenly, "except that our wealth is borrowed—borrowed from the generations that will follow us. The future will pay for this war. Our government simply goes into debt."

"What an excellent idea," said the mayor.

"No," said the reverend, "it's wrong to have one's children pay."

"They won't really have to," Billiard Ball explained, "because each generation will pass it on to the next." But Billiard Ball had failed to foresee that during the postwar years monetary inflation would reduce the burden by cheapening it. That way everyone paid without knowing. "We are sorry," said Billiard Ball, rising from his chair, "but we must leave now." There was a spontaneous chorus of regret. "Our liberty pass is good only until midnight and we have to hitchhike to get back."

"Ah, but you must return. Isn't it an American custom?" the reverend chortled, and everyone laughed at his implied reference to the general. "Come back soon, very soon."

"Yes, soon," we replied without a second thought.

Throughout the session in Reverend Mr. Corum's living room, Anita stood opposite me along the wall listening. From time to time when our eyes met, I smiled and so did she in her demure way. How I longed to be alone with her to talk and learn what she was like. It wasn't possible, not this time. As we said good-bye on the path to the highway, I pulled two white mattress covers from my duffel bag and presented them to her and her cousin.

"When will you return?" she asked.

"Next weekend," I said.

"Will you stay longer next time? Until Sunday?"

"Yes."

"I shall make a dress from your mattress cover this week, and wear it when I see you."

The crowd had suddenly become excited. Having retrieved a carton of cigarettes from his duffel bag, Billiard Ball had handed it to Mayor Quiboloy. "This is for all the people of the village in return for your wonderful Filipino hospitality."

"It is too much, Billiard Ball, too much," the mayor said.

Billiard Ball tugged me by the arm, urging me to break away. "C'mon, Hal, all good things must come to an end." We raced down the path not daring to look back.

Soon after we reached the Bataan highway, a passing ten-wheel army truck picked us up and took us to Olongopo, where we would catch the navy launch. Billiard Ball and I hardly talked on the three-hour trip in the truck; we were deeply engrossed in our private memories of the day's events. After leaving Lugao, I felt oddly incomplete, as if I had just experienced a mere chapter in a long and fascinating story. "They're such a marvelously warm people," Billiard Ball said at last. "Take that Hando, for instance. I think he's genuine; a bright, delicate type, yearning for a kindred soul. I really would like to see them again. How about you?"

"Wild horses couldn't keep me away."

"Do you realize we told them a hell of a lot about ourselves?" commented Billiard Ball.

"Well, yes, they're curious. Everybody's curious. You'd think we were little gods," I replied.

"But we didn't learn a bloody thing about them. Next time, let's do the asking and the listening," he said resolutely. I grinned, exhilarated at the prospect.

The truck dropped us off in Olongopo at dusk a good hour before the navy launch was due. After telling Billiard Ball Rosalio's story, I suggested that we pay my old Filipino friend a visit while we were waiting. I wondered how he and his wife were faring.

The *banca* was gone from beneath the house, and when we knocked on the doorpost a stranger, a withered old man, appeared. "Where's Rosalio?" I demanded. He replied in a dialect I couldn't understand. "Rosalio, Rosalio," I repeated, losing patience.

"Just a minute, Hal," interrupted Billiard Ball, who then spoke in Spanish to the old man. He replied animatedly, flailing his arms, and I caught references to "Manila, Manila." "He tells me he is Rosalio's grandfather. He says Rosalio and his wife and child have moved to Manila," Billiard Ball explained. "It seems there's more opportunity for 'businesswomen' there."

Waiting for the launch, we could hear the hiss of gentle waves breaking on the shore. The air was filled with the smell of wood smoke issuing from the cooking fires within the clustered nearby nipa huts. Billiard Ball and I sat on the pier eating the fruit that the people of Lugao had heaped upon us. It was the most peaceful time of day as we looked out on the darkening bay. The fishermen were slowly paddling in from the estuary toward the beach, their *bancas* laden with the day's catch. They stuck bamboo poles into the sand and hung their nets on them, to dry in the next morning's sun. Then they lugged their heavy woven baskets full of fish from the *bancas*, and stacked them neatly on the beach. It was not a bad life, being a fisherman on the beautiful estuary. This is what Rosalio used to do. I would miss my friend.

Exactly at midnight I reported to the Mudhog for a six-hour stint of duty. Oblong, confident that I would show, had turned in before my arrival. Weary though I was from the long and exciting day, I welcomed the chance to be busy, for I was too restless to sleep. Checking the angle of the vessel's list, I started a couple of pumps to slowly redistribute the ballast water over the next few hours. There was only silence and the sound of water slapping the Mudhog's sides as I climbed the ladder to the bridge. I was overwhelmed with a compulsion to write about the day's experience, about Lugao.

"Dear Lucia, I've just had a wonderful day," I began, but I couldn't tell her everything. I couldn't write about Anita. What could I write? I could tell her how Billiard Ball and I were made to feel welcome. "Somehow I was one of them. It was like home away from home." I could tell her how they hung on our words as if we were high priests on a visit from paradise. "They believe everything we say without question. What a frightening responsibility! We have to be sure to tell the truth, and that's not easy to do." I could tell her how Billiard Ball shone with his erudition and savoir faire, how he met Hando, a surprisingly well-educated young male schoolteacher who loved poetry and read literature, how the two hit it off stupendously right away. I could tell her how Reverend Mr. Corum sounded when he spoke rather like I imagine Lincoln should have when he gave the Gettysburg address. But I couldn't tell her that I feared she had lost Fortune.

Oh, poor dearest Lucia. What was she to me? A girl I had never spoken to, never touched, one who loved another. What was it between us? Was she only a phantom of my heart filling an aching void? I wanted more, much more, yet I was unable to pull away.

XX
Subic Bay

Can't Anything Go Right?

Practically the entire sleeping crew of Onion Heads spilled out of their bunks to the deck all at once, miraculously escaping injury. When they tried to stand, they fell again. Too sleepy at first to understand what was happening, they eventually realized that the deck was so sloped that it was futile to try to stand upright.

One by one they managed to climb up to the main deck, and saw the angle of the superstructure in relation to the rest of the world. "We're gonna flip over. Sonofabitch, where in hell's the fuckin' water tender?"

After sealing my letter to Lucia, I lay on the hard deck of the bridge to relax and day dream. But apparently my weariness was too great and I sank into deep slumber. Habitually a profound sleeper, I was not awakened easily. After all, hadn't I once slept through a bombing at Hollandia? It was four in the morning; the pumps had been operating untended for three hours transferring more water than necessary to one side of the vessel and bringing her close to the point of no return.

Only after a bucket of water was splashed over my head did I become conscious. In an instant, after trying to stand, I understood the impending danger. I sprang into motion, my heart pounding with fear as the Onion Heads cursed me for my negligence. I crawled like a frightened mouse along the slanted deck to the ladder leading to the engine room and slid down as if on a chute, skinning my shins. The pumps were still operating, performing mindlessly. Trembling, I accelerated their motion, *thumpa, thumpa, thumpa,* switched the proper valves, and stemmed the flow of ballast water just short of the vessel's critical angle. Imperceptibly the list began reversing. In the privacy of the engine room I began sobbing quietly from relief, and from shame at my unforgivable carelessness.

Had Chief Warrant Officer Smithson been on board, no doubt I would have been immediately confined to the brig. What I had done — falling asleep on duty — called for severe punishment, most likely a court-martial and reduction in rank. Fortunately I had a brief reprieve before he would learn of my infraction, for, unknown to all of us, Smithson was in Manila visiting headquarters to discuss the permanent disposition of the Mudhog. After unsuccessfully searching the theater for dredging opportunities, the Command had concluded that the Mudhog was no longer needed.

As soon as the vessel regained her horizontal orientation, a blasé Oblong took over, and I visited my old tent to seek Billiard Ball's commiseration. But Billiard Ball was sleeping, tired still from the strain of our trip the previous day. Blackie was quite awake, complaining more than ever of his back pain. "Did you speak to the gook?" he demanded.

"Yes," I replied. "He'll come, in a week or so."

"In a week!" Blackie exclaimed. "Can't you see what's happening to me, Hal? I'm wasting away from the pain. I haven't slept more than ten minutes each night for months."

"I know, Blackie, but he has matters in his village to tend to first. After all, he is the mayor."

Blackie's feeling of desperation was not without cause. Weeks before, upon learning that a navy hospital ship had cruised into the bay for a short stay, his hope brightened. After pleading with Dr. Cunningham, he was granted an appointment with an orthopedic surgeon, who immediately took a battery of X-rays and recommended a disc operation. "The sonofabitch wouldn't guarantee a thing; he says the chance of success would be no better than fifty-fifty," whined Blackie. "That's not good enough for me, and when I pushed him, he admitted I might be worse off than before. When I told him my chiropractor back home could fix me up in two minutes, why, you'd think I'd insulted him personally. 'We don't recognize chiropractic as a procedure in this navy, sailor,' " he said. "It's like a swear word, s'help me. So I asked him, what use am I to the navy the way I am? If he'd recommend some leave for me, I could go back to the States for five minutes, get fixed, then scoot right back here and become a useful Seabee again. You know what? He practically threw me outa his office. I wouldn't let that fuckin' butcher cut my hair."

So except for the brief interlude following Mr. Quiboloy's manipulation, Blackie was consigned to immobility and pain by a stubborn, narrow-minded naval medical corps. A stalemate prevailed. Even if Mr. Quiboloy came again, his continuing availability was undependable. Only a quick end to the war would save Blackie from seemingly interminable suffering.

Glancing over at Fortune's cot, I saw that it was empty and stripped of sheets. His personal belongings, his shoes usually lined up on the deck, his footlocker and books, were gone. I hadn't seen him since meeting Nina that morning a couple of weeks earlier. Finding him in the communications tent, I got caught up on his latest activities. "Yeah, I moved out of the tent four or five days ago," he explained. "It was an awkward situation, especially for Nina. That was no place for her."

"But where have you gone?"

"I had a shack built down by the stream. Sort of like a honeymoon cottage. Nina calls it Dream River. Neat name, eh?"

I was in no mood to respond to such trivia. The affair was going too far, perhaps irreversibly so. Ignoring my disapproving silence, Fortune went on: "She's an unusual girl, Hal. Couldn't you tell when you met her? She says she wants to marry me."

"So what! Don't they all? Hell, we're the living end, aren't we?" Despite my sarcasm, and the fact that I was blatantly arrogant, he took no offense. How blind I was not to have been flattered, not to have seen how he valued my goodwill. But how intolerant and judgemental are those who haven't lived long enough to see their own foibles unfold.

"And I want to marry her," he said with disarming directness, forgiving my interruption. "I've met her family, and they approve."

"But what about Lucia?" I blurted. His eyelids fluttered for a moment; he remained silent. "What about Lucia?" I pressed. His eyes glazed over as he seemed to withdraw into himself, then after a few moments he rose from his swivel chair, and without a word left the tent, left me sitting there alone to come up with my own answer.

The announcement came over the PA system the next morning at reveille. I could hear it all the way out on the Mudhog. "Hear this, hear this. All hands report to the movie theater at 0800 after breakfast. Work details will commence at 0830. Hear this, hear this. All hands..."

At the chow hall speculation was rife. Were we going to move out, maybe to participate in the invasion of Japan? Or had our time come to go home? "How about it, Fortune?" I asked. "You know everything. What's going to happen?"

"It's not what you think," he said, "but I won't tell you, not this time."

"Then you know?"

"Yes, I know."

"Then why the secret?"

"I can tell you it's bad news, but it has to come from the Old Man; you'll understand later."

Was this a new Fortune? He always loved to shine, to be one up on everyone and let them know it. Did this signal a change in his ways or was it simply an isolated aberration? I thought I had detected a new seriousness in his demeanor. It seemed to coincide with his involvement with Nina.

The entire officer corps of the battalion was seated in a row across the wide stage. Dressed in freshly pressed tans, they sported their appropriate marks of rank, and some wore battle ribbons to honor the impending mystery event. In the lineup I spotted Smithson, who must have just returned from Manila. In the center, just behind a slender lectern of two-by-fours and plywood, sat Commander Rutledge, silvery,

203

handsome, trim, and splendid in full beige regalia with epaulets. Despite the heat he wore his formal visored hat, the one bedecked with gold scrambled eggs. Gluck sat next to him, rotund and perspiring and similarly dressed, gazing out at us with an odd imperiousness. Rising, the commander took a few steps to the lectern and studied us in silence while waiting patiently for us to quiet. Then he spoke.

"I won't keep you long, men. I know you're all anxious to get back on the job." There was laughter, and he delayed speaking again until it abated. "We've come a long way together, haven't we, men?" A murmur of assent rumbled through the assembly. "When I think back to our beginning in boot camp at Camp Peary, when I think back to the bunch of green men we all were, and when I look at you now and think of all you have done, of all the hell you've gone through, my heart swells with pride. It has been an honor, my good men, to have been associated with you. It has been an honor to have been your leader. Thank-you all, every man of you, for your loyalty and untiring support. Thank-you all."

He spoke with a new tone, something we hadn't heard before; there was a sadness, as if he were mourning the past. By then we knew what he would say next. "Yes, the time has come for me to say good-bye. I have been given a new assignment, and in my place..." Before he could complete the sentence a spontaneous chant arose: "You're a good man for the battalion, you're a good man for the battalion." His eyes became watery, and after we quieted, he was momentarily too choked up to speak.

At last he said, "And so are you, every damn man of you. And I know you'll keep on doing your best for your new commander. He's someone you all know and respect." He turned to Gluck seated behind him. "I'm leaving you in the good hands of Lieutenant Commander Gluck." He waited for our reaction, but there was none. "Remember, men, your job isn't done. I ask you to help Commander Gluck make our battalion better than ever. Make him as proud of you as I have been. And never forget what you are, men: Americans with a glorious heritage. Never forget you're the light and hope of all mankind. Be an example for our Filipino hosts and all the world to follow, good-bye, my friends, good-bye and God bless you all." We leapt to our feet cheering and clapping and whistling. Grinning and waving, he strode from the stage to a waiting jeep. It drove off in the direction of the dock, where a launch took him away from us forever.

"Now that, I'd say, is a grand exit," commented Billiard Ball. "It will be a hard act to follow, for sure. He's a true blue patriot if there ever was one. He believes with all his heart that America has a great mission, the poor fool."

"What's wrong with that?" I asked. "I think it's admirable."

Billiard Ball watched Gluck rise and walk to the lectern. "What's wrong? We're not qualified, that's what's wrong."

Apprehensively we sat down again on the benches. The morning heat began to press down on us. Gluck had removed his dress jacket, already soaked through from perspiration, revealing the sidearm at his hip. "Maybe you realize it and maybe not, but there goes a man who never did a thing he didn't believe in. I want you to know, I operate the same way. I intend to carry on the same policies he started. 'Course, every man has his own way of doin' things, but that's all you'll find different. Everyone knows some things in this outfit need changin'. F'r instance the cohabitation in the tents goin' on around here. It ain't regulation, it ain't good for nobody's morale, and it's gotta stop. So I'm issuin' an order right here and now: All whores gotta be outa here in twenty-four hours. That's number one."

Immediately a clamor of disapproval arose and we began stomping our feet in the dirt, raising a cloud of dust. As Gluck tried to speak again, our din drowned him out. We could only see his mouth make words, and his face grow red with anger. Pulling the pistol from his hip, he fired two shots into the air. They sounded like a thunderclap renting the air, and the uproar stopped as if by a switch. "Who do you think you are?" Gluck shouted, his chest heaving with indignation. "This is the navy an' we're fightin' a war. You keep this up, an' I warn ya, you'll have no liberty for the next six months. Now I ain't standin' here to hear myself talk. The whores are goin', every goddamn sonofabitch of 'em. And number two: I don't want

205

to see anymore clap cases." Staring at us in challenge, he paused to let us absorb the meaning of his edict. " 'Cause we ain't treatin' you anymore. Anyone gettin' the clap from now on, I'll slap him in the brig. Unnerstand? That's all I gotta say for now, so let's get back to work and win this war."

"We're in for dark times," commented Billiard Ball.

"Hell, I just hope he keeps that pistol pointing up," I said.

Commander Rutledge's departure was a stunning loss to all but the officers of the battalion, and possibly a secret loss to a few of them too as they discovered his humanity, his concern for every individual, and his tolerant, democratic spirit. I knew how terribly much I would miss him, how much I believed in his innate wisdom. If circumstances had allowed, I would have embraced him to let him know of my high regard. He had revealed a part of his soul to me once, and it mirrored mine. What kind of man was this who would concern himself with every personal, petty problem brought before him while he had larger matters to deal with? I was only one beneficiary of his spiritual generosity; there were hundreds more. Yet many were critical of his style, Gluck among them; they judged that he ran too loose a ship. It was a far cry from regular navy, that's for sure.

The question nagging us all was why the transfer. Why now, before our job was done, before the war was over? Wouldn't it be more appropriate, since we had been together so long, that he remain with us to the end?

Fortune who had often predicted his demise, wasn't the least surprised. "It's been in the works for months, ever since we left Hollandia," Fortune explained. "The navy regs drove him wild. They don't call him 'Riled Up Rutledge' in Manila for nothing. He was constantly raising hell at the Command, pestering them for more equipment or a bigger project. Back at Hollandia, when he heard about the invasion plans for the Philippines, he demanded that we be chosen for the first wave at Leyte. When they said no, he still wouldn't give up. So they gave him Mindoro, a comparatively minor action. 'Course no one figured on the kamikaze, and he received praise for our valiant defense under fire, as you know."

"Thanks to you," I said. "But I don't understand. He was courageous and daring and willing and he was doing the job; he got things done. I don't see how anyone else could have performed better. What did they expect?"

"Beside the point," said Fortune. "It was his abrasiveness, his seeming contempt for the system. In the end, his officers did him in. Everyone knows how they hated him, especially since the early weeks at Hollandia when he insisted that our tents be built before theirs. We always came first and they resented it right up to the end. So when they got a chance, they went for his jugular. Someone snitched to the Command about how the women moved in with us."

"But things improved after that: The incidence of clap dropped, we were back on schedule again," I said.

"Yeah, he argued with the Command, pointing out that the Japanese brought their own whores along with them and how he thought it was a good idea. Control would be more effective than prohibition, he claimed. Well, the navy wouldn't buy that. It was immoral, unAmerican, that kind of shit. When he got back to camp he stalled, and when the brass heard from their sources that the whores were still on board, they gave him an ultimatum. But he moved too slow for them." Fortune sighed. "It was inevitable: they relieved Rutledge of his command as a disciplinary action. What a goddamn fool."

"I always thought you admired him," I said.

"Sure, like I admire a saint."

"Who did him in, Barry?"

"I told you, the officers."

"It was Gluck, wasn't it?" Already the women were leaving. We could see them skittering down our hill toward the river like rabbits in panic.

"Another thing about Rutledge, he was too goddamn trusting," said Fortune.

For the next few days, after surreptitiously removing some essential belongings from the dredge, I slept in the old cot at the tent. Since my water tending duty began at midnight and ended at six, after Smithson retired and before he awoke, I successfully avoided him. It had been a miserable week; starting with the near capsize nothing had gone right. Blackie was showing signs of desperation; Fortune was deserting Lucia; Rutledge was gone; Gluck, mad with power, had taken over; and I was bound to be court-martialed.

Entropy, Billiard Ball called it. When things go wrong, they go wrong in bunches. And when things go right? Same thing, he said, but nothing stays the way it is. Was there possibly some comfort to be found in entropy? What goes wrong will eventually go right. It was the week of the Hiroshima bombing — man-made disorder on an unprecedented scale, suffering at a new intensity. The superbomb had been only a rumor, perhaps too fantastic to be reliable. An entire Japanese city had been destroyed by an incredible explosive device using a principle called atomic energy. Few of us had taken the rumor seriously. None of us could conceive of such a powerful weapon, let alone its immediate terrifying consequences to the Japanese people, and certainly not its long-range effect on all humanity. But that a superbomb fell on Japan was confirmed later. How could one ever find solace in it? It would end the war, thereby saving many more lives; thus went the rationale. Entropy perhaps? But then nothing stays the way it is.

XXI
Lugao

Anita's Story: A Weekend of Discovery

One would think we were a couple of returning heroes. "Americanos, Americanos," the naked children shouted, zigzagging like circus clowns in mad circles around us as Billiard Ball and I ambled abreast down the beaten path through the shade of the green canopy. Heavy duffel bags hanging from our shoulders were laden with gifts: bottles of beer, cartons of cigarettes, cans of fruit juice. Repeatedly sweeping past us like zephyrs, each child snatched a bar of sweet chocolate from our extended hands. We were no less boisterous than they, shouting along with them, asking their names, having a good time ourselves, caught up in the infectious joy of their freewheeling abandon. Such was the character of our entry into Lugao time after time.

As we walked down the village street, people waved from their houses repeating our names, people we didn't recognize from our earlier visit. "Hullo Beelyard Ball and 'Al. Hullo. *Comusta*."

Anita emerged from one of the houses to greet us. "You must both stay with my family," she said. Then Alehandro appeared and said to Billiard Ball, "I have been waiting all week. Please, if you wouldn't mind some metaphysical discussion I would be honored to have you as my guest."

"How can I resist metaphysical discussion?" said Billiard Ball with a smile. As the two walked off, I heard Alehandro say, "And I imagine you have read *Man's Fate* in the original French? How lucky! Malraux is right. For our time the answer lies in courageous action." Had Billiard Ball found himself a revolutionary?

I followed Anita up the ladder to her family's one-room house, similar in its simplicity to Rosalio's but larger. Both

had the same style cooking hearth near one wall, the split
bamboo floor, the same immaculateness. Squatting before the
hearth, Anita's mother, looking in her fifties (but only in her
thirties, I learned later), was preparing the noon meal. She
acknowledged our entrance with a nod and a warm smile.
Sitting cross-legged on a floor mat in a corner, Anita's wispy
maternal grandmother, her skin wrinkled like an elephant's,
grinned, showing toothless black gums. She mumbled
something incomprehensible to me in Spanish. Shortly Mr.
Quiboloy, wearing a wide-brimmed hat woven of jute, came
in from the hot fields. We shook hands warmly. "Thank-you
for having me, Mr. Quiboloy," I said.

"You may call me Lucio, now that we are old friends," he
responded. We all sat on the floor in a circle and ate brown
rice and chicken from clay bowls while Mr. Quiboloy spoke of
their lot in Lugao.

"I am only a small tenant farmer," he said — to clarify his
role, not to complain. "The family in the hacienda on the
Bataan highway owns the land."

"The fancy place we passed on the way?"

"Yes, the fancy place," he said, and everyone laughed at
my odd description. "I keep fifty percent for myself and fifty
percent is for the landowner. The incentive is small, but what
choice do we have?"

"The Hukbalahaps think we have one, Father," said
Anita.

"How dare you speak of them in our house," Mr.
Quiboloy said in a flash of anger. Turning to me, he
explained. "The Huks are radicals, Communists; they know
only one way: violence." Then, addressing Anita, he said,
"Where do you get such foolish thoughts? Is that what you are
learning in school? Is that what Alehandro teaches?"

"Where are the Huks from?" I asked.

"From everywhere," Lucio replied. "Some dwell within
our own barrio, but since I am not a sympathizer, I cannot be
sure which ones they are. You see, I believe in Philippine
democracy. I believe we should be like America, where
everyone has an opportunity to succeed and live well."

"But that's not always true. You remember our
discussion last weekend?" I said.

"Oh, yes, I have not forgotten. Still, you have not had to live through our poverty and pain. You have never had that in America."

How could I argue? I knew of no pain firsthand. I never saw anyone starving. Through the desperate thirties there was always food on our table and ample clothes to wear and a snug apartment to sleep in. Although my father had lost the wealth gained during his most vigorous years, and he had lost his daring and capacity to dream for the rest of his life, he never lost his belief in America. In its worst times the nation somehow provided opportunity for survival.

When the meal was over, Anita handed me a sleeping mat, which I unrolled on the floor beside those of my hosts. It was too hot to be out in the high sun of the early afternoon. What could be more sensible than to have a cool siesta? In two hours Anita awakened me from a soft sleep. Lucio had returned to the field, her mother was elsewhere, and her grandmother squatted quietly in a corner weaving a mat. "My father has asked me to show you the mango tree," she said. "Will you come with me, please?"

We walked down the path to the highway, at first side by side, but soon she fell behind. "Am I going too fast for you?"

"No, no," she said, urging me to keep on ahead. She continued to linger behind.

"Are you tired?"

"No, no," and she giggled in amusement. "It's the custom in Lugao that I walk behind."

Since the concrete highway was blistering, we walked along the narrow dirt shoulder, which was less hot but still burned through the soles of my GI boots. Anita, barefoot as usual, didn't seem to mind. Nor, in her white dress and wide-brimmed woven hat, did she seem bothered by the afternoon sun beating down on us, while I perspired heavily and had to stop to rest now and then under a tree. Although several passing ten-wheel army trucks offered us a lift, she refused them. Grudgingly I submitted to her wish. "We have only a few miles," she said, a promise of small comfort. Soon we passed by the grand white stucco hacienda, a stark contrast to Anita's house.

"So this is where the rich landowners live," I said.

211

"Oh, but they are no longer rich, Hal. They have the land, but that is all. The Japanese took all the crops. The land is of little use without seed. And the Japanese removed all their possessions, leaving the house bare. They are mestizos and very proud, but the Japanese took that away too. A commander occupied the hacienda and humiliated the family, making them his servants. He hoped that by doing this, the rest of us would be pleased and that we would cooperate with him."

"And weren't the people happy to see the selfish landowner get what he deserved?"

"Oh, no, the Santos's are good people; they are always very kind. When we have malaria, they bring us quinine. When a typhoon ruins our crops, they give us rice to eat and new seed for the next planting. The Japanese commander had mistaken how we would feel. We knew he was cruel."

At last we reached our destination, the small solitary thatched house on stilts beside the sluggish stream that I had observed on our first trip along the highway. We climbed the ladder to the house and entered its cool, dim interior, where I saw a mostly naked old man seated on the floor. "This is my grandfather," said Anita as she uncovered a basket of fruit, vegetables, and rice that she had brought for him.

He reached for my outstretched right hand with his left; his other arm hung limp by his side. "*Comusta ka,*" he said in a clear, high voice.

"*Comusta,*" I said, returning the greeting. He then spoke to Anita in dialect, pointing to a small woven box beside his hearth, which she retrieved for him. From it he removed a GI dog tag, which he held suspended for me to see.

"It is an American soldier's necklace," said Anita.

"May I look at it closely?" I asked, astonished that he would have such a thing.

The dog tag bore the name Roger B. Anderson and his serial number and blood type. "Where did your grandfather get this, Anita?"

"From Lieutenant Anderson," she replied plainly.

"I don't understand. GIs don't give away their dog tags."

"Let us sit and I shall tell you about Lieutenant Anderson." She peeled a banana for her grandfather, and

handed me one with a dark green skin. "It is quite ripe even
though it is green," she said. It was, and tasted sweeter than
any I had ever eaten. "He is there under my grandfather's
mango tree." I followed her gaze through the doorway.
Symmetrical and spreading, a low tree stood between the
house and the stream, creating a cool, grassy oasis beneath its
graceful branches.

Baffled by her indirection, I tried to deduce her meaning.
"Buried? In a grave? Under the tree?"

Anita's grandfather, having sensed my sudden
comprehension, broke into excited dialect, and struggled to
rise. "My grandfather says that you may keep the necklace,"
said Anita. She addressed him sternly and he sat down again.
"My grandfather's bones give him much pain. They never
healed correctly after the Japanese broke them. He should
stay with us in the barrio, but he refuses. My grandfather is a
stubborn man."

Later I learned that Anita made the trip to her
grandfather's house several days a week to bring him food
and often to stay and cook for him. I could sense an
unspoken bond between them, a mutual appreciation. Anita
once confessed that she felt much closer to her grandfather
than to her own father. The old and young are on common
ground: Both are concerned only with the fresh simplicities
of life, the very business of being alive.

Anita began her story: "The Japanese marched thousands
of American prisoners through Pampanga from Bataan, giving
them no food or water, and whipping them when they fell
behind. They made them walk on the hot concrete so that
they left bloody footprints from their scorched and wounded
feet." I winced, recalling my recent distress walking under the
sun, even along the cooler shoulder of the highway. Anita
spoke with a chilling earnestness, as if she were describing a
scene in progress, making no comment, stating only facts.
"Some were already weakened from wounds in the battle on
Bataan and could not keep up. Lieutenant Anderson was one
of these. When the men fell and did not rise after being
kicked and beaten, they were shot, and their bodies were
collected on wagons pulled by *caribao* that followed the

marchers. Lieutenant Anderson was shot there at the edge of the road." She stared out at the glaring white concrete. "But my grandfather and grandmother saw him move; he was still alive. So before the wagon passed they dragged him from the road and hid him under the trees by the stream in the field behind the house. They nursed his wounds for many weeks." She interrupted her account to consult with her grandfather in dialect. "Yes, my grandfather says it was almost a month before the American opened his eyes and spoke."

"Did you meet him?" I asked.

"Much later in the barrio," she said, "but I was only a child." I had failed to realize immediately that she had become a woman in the intervening four years.

"It was very dangerous for my grandparents. The Japanese often warned us not to help the Americanos or we would be shot. When the monsoon came and the land was covered with water, Lieutenant Anderson was moved to Reverend Mr. Corum's house in Lugao. But soon the Japanese returned to search for the Americano, saying they had heard we were hiding one of the marchers. Someone, maybe from the barrio — we shall never know — had betrayed us. They entered my grandparents' house and asked my grandfather to give them the Americano, but he would admit nothing. They broke his limbs and he passed out from the pain." Tears welled up in her eyes at the thought of his suffering. "Then they took him and my grandmother to the barrio where all the people were gathered and they showed what they did to my grandfather and they threatened to kill us one by one until we gave them the Americano. My father and Reverend Mr. Corum replied to the Japanese commander that killing us would be useless." She faltered; the words came hard. "The commander ordered a soldier to stand my Nanai by the wall of the church." With tear-streaked cheeks, she went on. "And he shot her. Oh, I loved my Nanai so very much." She had to stop, and her grandfather reached for her with his one good arm and took her into it and comforted her with the soft words of his dialect as he, too, cried.

Her story was too appalling. I was speechless. I wanted to take on her pain, to share the suffering of her memory. But regaining her composure, she resumed. "After the commander killed my Nanai, the Americano, Lieutenant Anderson, appeared from Reverend Mr. Corum's house. He had witnessed the commander's cruelty and understood that others would also die unless he was found. The soldiers took him and flung him to the ground and beat him with their rifles. And then the commander ordered his soldiers to stand him by the wall of the church where my Nanai had stood. Blood was pouring from his head and they shot him. Then they left us."

"What happened to the bodies of your Nanai and Lieutenant Anderson?"

"We took them and prepared them and, after a deep mourning, buried them side by side under the mango tree, as my grandfather wished."

The sun appeared like an enormous orange balloon balanced at the apex of a faraway mountaintop. The heat of its slanting rays was now comfortably diminished in the late afternoon. "We must return to Lugao," said Anita. Embracing her grandfather, she bid him good-bye and I shook his hand again. "Let me show you the graves." Together we stood beside them, each marked by a simple boulder, nothing more. "The rounder rock is my Nanai's grave." The next few moments we shared in silence. Soon she raised her eyes and asked, "Do you like mangoes?" Taking one from the tree, she gave it to me. It was sweet and moist.

"Absolutely delicious," I said.

"It is by far my favorite fruit," she replied. "And don't you think it is a beautiful tree? See how it spreads its branches like the arms of dancers; see how it shades the earth and makes it green."

It was in the flash of that instant, transcending all feelings of desire, that I understood I had fallen in love with Anita. It was then I knew I had found someone who surpassed all I could ever hope to be. "Yes, it's a beautiful and rare tree," I answered.

During our walk back to Lugao we hardly spoke, save for one short exchange. "I have never been alone with a man, never with an Americano," she said. "But my father said I could be with you, for he trusts you. At first I was very frightened, but now I am happy that we have spent this time together."

"What are you afraid of? That I would bite you?"

She laughed. "No, no, of course not that."

"What then?"

Delaying her reply, she slipped farther behind me as she pondered how best to express her thoughts. I stopped, waiting. "That I am not worthy," she said. "That you would be ashamed of me. That we are like monkeys."

"Oh, my God, Anita. Don't you realize how beautiful you are?"

"Americanos are beautiful. Mestizos are beautiful."

"No, you are." I gently enclosed her hand in mine. It was the first time we touched.

"I hope you will come back often," she said, hesitatingly withdrawing her hand.

"Nothing can stop me," I promised.

That evening Billiard Ball and I had supper at the reverend's. Anita, like soft music, was ever-present in the background, assisting Mrs. Corum. Afterwards we retired to the cozy living room, joined by Lucio, Anita's father, and Hando. The gathering, being more intimate, dealt with both controversial and heartfelt matters, ranging from Shakespearean drama and symphonic music (Bartok no less), extolled by the uncommonly erudite Hando, to local politics and agrarian reform. Lucio, farmer and mayor, was a graduate of an agricultural college, a respected expert. "We must not be impatient and greedy," he said, referring to a program he was promoting among his fellow farmers. "Rather than harvest all our rice for today's consumption, we must set aside a portion for seed even if it means we will be hungry a while longer." But few were paying heed to his recommendation. "It is not easy to believe in the future when the present is still so hard," he sighed.

"Yes," Hando agreed, "we must take the necessary steps now to become masters of the future. And we must be concerned with more than rice seedlings. Reform, dividing the haciendas and distributing the land, is essential."

"Isn't that what the Huks are striving to do?" I asked.

216

"But they are trying to do it by violent means," said Lucio. "That is wrong."

"Our people have been exploited for more than three hundred years," said Hando with vehemence, his smooth, feminine amber skin taut and glistening. "The hacienda system is too firmly implanted. It will never submit to being destroyed peacefully."

"But violence never knows where to stop. The innocent end up being victims," Lucio countered with equal insistence. "If we expect to be independent, we must also have stability."

"Perhaps America should be our model," said the reverend, addressing Billiard Ball. "Unlike us, you do not kill your politicians over elections. You do not have our corruption. Sadly, we have few patriots and everyone is for himself."

"But Roxas will unite us," said Lucio, referring to the new presidential candidate in the elections to take place less than a year hence.

"Roxas was a collaborator; he betrayed us," Hando said dourly.

Finding their intensity contagious, I listened, unable to decide who was right. With independence near at hand, at a crossroad in their history, they were contemplating the formation of the new nation and how best to correct ancient, firmly established inequities and injustice. Would their hopes and arguments ultimately be meaningless?

Would Billiard Ball and I care to attend church in the morning, asked Reverend Mr. Corum. We politely begged off, and he took no offense. "I have never met a Jew before," he said. "But your religion and the history of your people are a part of my education as a clergyman. Do you attend your church?"

"Well, the truth is I don't practice a religion," I said sheepishly. "But I was born a Jew and I insist on belonging. The Jews have been a scapegoat ever since their exile from Babylonia over two thousand years ago. I can't escape the past and I feel a duty to accept its consequences."

"That's very noble of you."

"I don't see it as noble. It is necessary for my self-respect."

217

"But as a Jew you have nothing to fear in America," said Hando, who was listening intently.

"Probably not. Tolerance is part of the American tradition," I replied, "but I sometimes worry when I'm singled out and despised by prejudiced Gentiles. When I was a child I was often victimized by my schoolmates."

"I see," said Hando, "then you are a Jew first?"

"Hando, you are being discourteous to our guest," said Reverend Mr. Corum.

"Please forgive him," said Lucio. "He often oversteps decent bounds."

"Really, I'd like to answer the question," I said. Having ignored the reverend's rebuke and Lucio's apology, Hando kept his clear, penetrating, catlike eyes fastened on mine. "No, Hando, I am first an American."

"Ah, what a lucky man you are. If only I could first be a Filipino."

"And you, Billiard Ball, do you have a faith?" asked the reverend.

"I suppose I'm an atheist," he replied, "but I don't disapprove of religion, although it's the major cause of war and misery throughout the history of civilized man."

"Not religion itself, if you will forgive me for contradicting you," said the reverend, holding up his finger tutorially, "but man, in the name of religion."

"Yes, Reverend," said Billiard Ball, nodding vigorously. "I stand corrected."

Such were our conversations. They were of a depth and seriousness and range I had never experienced before. We discussed political systems, communism versus democracy, psychology, man's startling discoveries of his hidden self, his search for meaning in life (There is none according to Billiard Ball), the crisis in physics, the pessimism of contemporary philosophers, the shocking renunciation of tradition in modern art and music, the truth of literature, and on and on. Billiard Ball and I found, in this comparatively primitive village, a gold mine of astounding sophistication. And who was the principal force behind all this magnificent cerebration? Reverend Mr. Corum, of course, supported by two lesser and opposing forces: Lucio and Hando.

The reverend was on an endless voyage in search of life's truth. In an unobtrusive, self-effacing manner, he subtly enticed us to follow him, to think aloud without fear of criticism or reproof. But attacks on those personalities present or close to us were forbidden. Despite his extraordinary sophistication, there was a deceptive simplicity, a childlike quality, an innocence about him. His gentleness was saintly. I was always eager to be in his presence, to hear his views on any subject, to hear his questions. His quiet power was the source of the barrio's pride in itself. It was he who made the barrio an enclave against alien influences. Admiring America, he distrusted Americans and their careless style. Loving God, he rarely invoked His name. And not once in conversation during the time I knew him, an all too brief five months, did he mention Lieutenant Anderson's name, or speak of the cruel Japanese commander or refer to Nanai's untimely death.

On a subsequent visit I vividly recall a discussion on the nobility of sacrificing oneself for another. "It is natural to the human spirit," the reverend stated. "Don't we place our children and all those we deeply love before ourselves? Hadn't we practiced this spirit toward the prisoners of the Death March? And didn't we bear witness to the highest form of sacrifice by the Americano? Yes, I believe that in the end our goodness will prevail, for it is the most universal human trait."

"All of history disputes your thesis," Billiard Ball retorted.

"May I say, if you wish to call up history, then we shall find support for any view of man's nature," replied the reverend.

"Checkmate," I whispered to Billiard Ball.

That night Billiard Ball slept at Hando's house, and I at Anita's with three generations in a single room. Being a product of a comfortable urban middle-class environment, certain practical questions came to mind. How did one have sex, unless perhaps very quietly; where did one find privacy, and where was the bathroom? I never found the answer to the first; wherever one could, and rarely, was the answer to the second, and to the third the answer was a question: What is a bathroom? One bathed in the local stream and went out in the field to defecate. I found this hard to cope with, but in the nick of time I learned that there was an outhouse behind Reverend Mr. Corum's.

In the morning Anita served me the traditional rice, from America, she said, and eggs and some goat's milk, a menu similar to that at Rosalio's. On a like occasion during a later visit, to my awkward chagrin, she served me a bottle of Budweiser. Since beer was available only on the black market, it must have cost Lucio a large sum. Thinking back to our prior group discussion comparing the Filipino and American diets, I recalled mentioning that America's favorite drinks were Coke and beer. But I did not explain that I cared for neither, particularly beer. The magnanimity of these people was unbounded. I could not fail to come to love them.

After church, which Billiard Ball and I did not attend, a volleyball net was set up across the width of the dirt street. One side of the street was bordered by banana trees and the other by the white stucco wall of the church, which still bore the chips and holes of spent bullets when Nanai and Lieutenant Anderson were murdered. The volleyball game, in which Hando, Billiard Ball, and I and other new friends participated, was an exciting, happy event, full of joking and laughter, and watched by everyone in the barrio. The prize for the winning team was a carton of Camels, donated by Billiard Ball. At one crucial stage I accidentally hit the net, costing our side the loss of the ball and, quickly, the game. My mortification at being responsible for the loss was so evident that the winners insisted upon splitting the carton of cigarettes equally with the opposing team. Their sensitivity to the feelings of others was beyond me.

Again, as on the previous weekend but more so, we departed that Sunday afternoon with unbearable sadness. But our hearts were also full of fresh pleasurable memories, and the prospect of more such visits. Tears filled Anita's eyes as we said good-bye, and Hando embraced Billiard Ball. Reverend Mr. Corum held my hand in both of his, reluctant to let it go.

On the ride to Olongopo in the back of an army truck, I told Billiard Ball Anita's story of Lieutenant Anderson. "Poor devil, Anderson," said Billiard Ball. "It was a heroic act, and it shouldn't go unacknowledged. As soon as we get back to the base, I'll report our discovery."

"No, don't," I said belligerently. "Don't you see he's a symbol to the barrio people? They took an enormous risk in saving his life and keeping him. Christ, it cost them Anita's grandmother's life, and they were ready for anything rather than give him up. I'd hate to think what could have happened if Anderson hadn't surrendered himself. He represents a victory to them. He gave them cause for self-respect while being humiliated by a cruel enemy. Look how Anita's grandfather watches over and cares for the grave."

Billiard Ball weighed my argument for several minutes. "I understand what you're saying, Hal. You look upon these people as being like your own, don't you?"

"It's true, I've never felt so at home, so much a part of them, as if I belonged."

"I can see that, but that isn't what I mean." Puzzled, I waited for him to continue. "They are like the Jews against the world. You, your people, and they have suffered and still suffer and refuse to submit. It is, I think, what attracts you to each other; it's what you have in common."

Confused, surprised, I stammered, "Maybe you're right. I'm not sure. I have to think."

"Getting back to Anderson, consider this, Hal," said Billiard Ball. "Don't you think Anderson's family would like to have his remains? Shouldn't they also know about his meritorious act of heroism, what a special individual he was? Maybe he left a wife or son or daughter behind to feel proud of him for the rest of their lives were they to know. And wouldn't we also deprive our country of a chance to honor its best?" I stared at Billiard Ball in silence. By the time we reached the dock at Olongopo, we were no nearer to a resolution. "Okay, Hal," he said, "I'm going to follow my own conscience. Like you, I think Anderson was first an American, and should go home. I'm going to report Anita's story." He did, and I didn't hold it against him.

XXII
Subic Bay

Nina's Story

"Git up to Mr. Smithson right away, sailor," said Oblong when I reported to the engine room to relieve him.

"At this hour?" I said. It was midnight.

"Hell, he's tear ass; he's been layin' for ya all weekend. If he sends ya to the brig, I dunno what I'm gonna do. He oughta know I can't handle this shitbox by m'self."

Smithson was in the bridge reading a *Time* magazine, sitting with his feet crossed and resting on the very desk on which I had written Lucia, and beside which I had fallen asleep on that nearly fateful night. I stood before him at ramrod attention. "Yes, yes, Arnold," he said, clearing his throat and remaining in a semi-inclined position. "It has been reported to me that as a result of your negligence we came within a hair's breadth of a capsize."

"Yes, sir. I fell asleep without meaning to, sir."

"And are you aware of the seriousness of the consequences? Not only would my ship have gone down, our boys could have drowned."

"Sir, I deserve to be punished. I'll never forgive myself for what I did. But as I say, sir, I didn't intend to fall asleep. I was resting on the deck, thinking of what happened on liberty that day, expecting to go to the engine room any minute, and that's the last thing I knew."

"Yes, yes, well, that's all beside the point. Certainly a proper penalty for your infraction is confinement to the brig, demotion to seaman second class, and a court-martial."

"Yes, sir," I said, my voice cracking with fear at his extreme suggestion.

"But I am of course aware of your relationship with the admiral."

"The admiral, sir?"

"Yes, yes, the admiral. What's his name? Yes, yes Kincaid, the one who sent you the message from the cruiser at Hollandia." The memory of Fortune being lifted by a cable in dress whites up the side of the Mudhog flashed clear and bright. "Of course, I realize there are only two of you trained to man the pumps to keep this ship afloat, until...you see, we must also take a certain eventuality into account. Did you know that the Command is trying to dispose of my ship?"

"Actually, sir, I have heard a rumor..."

"My Mudhog, my remarkable, dependable, loyal workhorse, is going to be retired. I suppose one can understand. There's quite nothing for her to do, for the moment. The order is to take her out and scuttle her. It's asking too much of any captain, the final insult, wouldn't you say, Arnold? And worst of all, right off these islands is the deepest ocean in the world. Something over five miles. Were you aware of that?"

"No, sir, I wasn't."

"Yes, yes, the indignity of it all."

Smithson lapsed into sad, quiet contemplation, trying, I suspect, to prepare himself for the outrageous and painful destruction he must perform, while I remained standing at bone-aching attention. "Arnold, I've decided not to throw the book at you, after all. Instead I'm confining you to the base."

"Oh, thank-you, sir, but for how long if I may ask?"

He looked beyond me into the night. "Until the deed is done. And that will be when I'm ready, Arnold, when I'm ready." Breaking through scudding clouds, a full bronze moon played hide and seek over the bay. A destroyer at anchor nearby appeared and disappeared alternately like a ghost ship. "There's a damned lucky captain," he said. "At least he'll take his ship home."

Although my punishment was neither severe nor permanent, it was nonetheless hard to take. I was constantly eager for my weekend sojourns at Lugao. The time in between at the base was merely filling in. Nothing was more important than being with Anita, being with her people. I wanted to become one of them, an impossibility of course, but I didn't understand that at the beginning. Thus, deprived of the opportunity, I pined for "my" barrio and was miserable.

With more time on my hands than I wished, I wandered alone on long hikes into the bush following the stream deep into the wild hinterland toward the high mountain waterfall. Always it remained too far away; always before reaching the base of the mountain I had to turn back to camp as darkness fell. What was its lure?

I resumed writing letters again to everyone in my address book. On rainy afternoons, while the New York music clique was at work, I listened over and over again to every record, exhausting the classical library and discovering Schubert. His exquisite chamber music melodies filled my brooding heart with wonder at his art and delight in being human. I took up Proust once more, having earlier put him aside in favor of dreaming of Anita.

Then one afternoon we heard the news over the PA: "The Japs are crying uncle. The war is over."

So sudden was peace that everyone was caught off balance. Rumor of the superbomb was confirmed. Only months later did we learn that more than three hundred thousand lives were lost at Hiroshima and Nagasaki.

To this day I regret my innocence. I regret that I celebrated our victory rather than mourned. The price our enemy paid gives me pain. Yet, it would be foolish to resent the bomb; its time had come, whether created by a defending, mission-bent America or a zealous, ambition-driven Axis. I was proud and thankful that the United States solved the nuclear riddle first, for I believed in America and in our good intentions. Yet I feared for all humanity. What is more dangerous than a well-meaning, self-righteous people bent on a mission?

At Subic Bay in August 1945 we saw ourselves, the possessors of unlimited power, as the guarantors of peace forever. But we quickly lost our monopoly and as a consequence wars on a world scale will never again be won.

Lucia's newly arrived letter, although written before peace was declared, sensed that the war was shortly coming to an end. The people back home apparently could more accurately assess its progress than we. "Everyone says the bomb will soon bring the Japanese to their knees," she wrote. "I pray that it will be so. In any event it's only a matter of time. Now that the war is over in Europe, we see thousands of boys passing through on their way to the Pacific. Have you heard of the discovery in Germany of awful death camps in which the Germans murdered hundreds of thousands of Jews? It is so hard to grasp. How can a people be so inhuman? I am so grateful that you and Barry are alive and American."

This was the only time she even hinted at my Jewish background. I responded with numbness. Only much later did I feel guilt at not also being a victim. Wasn't sharing an unjust death part of the Jewish experience, and necessary to every Jew's pride in himself? The luck of being an American is my burden and with it the shame, as the truth has been revealed, that my nation did so little to rescue whomever it could. How can I trust "civilized" humanity, which countenanced the decimation of a people and did not recognize its responsibility to prevent it, and did not see the Nazi act as a reflection upon itself? How can I have faith that we will not yet destroy ourselves with our new unlimited power?

Lucia's letter continued: "Call it woman's intuition, I just know that you and Barry will come home to me unscathed, and Barry and I will be married quickly, and you will be our best man. I lie awake nights dreaming of that marvelous day to come. Please watch over him. Knowing how headstrong he can be, I worry. See that he does nothing foolish or daring at the last minute. With deepest affection, Lucia."

Her letter was dated only a week before it arrived. Obviously she had not heard from Fortune. His double dealing and insensitivity angered me. How much longer did he intend to evade the issue? Why did he keep her on the string? I couldn't contain my disgust. I would show him Lucia's letter for a reaction; maybe it would shame him into telling her the truth. But before doing so I felt compelled to write her for my own sake, confiding my future plans, and declaring my loyalty regardless of her unsuspected doomed relationship with Fortune.

> Dear Lucia,
> Just as your woman's intuition told you, the war is suddenly over. I can hardly wait to go home to see my parents again. And just think, at last we'll meet. I'm bruised all over from pinching myself in disbelief. All the while I've been overseas I never thought I'd actually return. I was reconciled to dying here. Not until I met the people in Lugao did I believe otherwise. Somehow they restored my faith in the future. They lifted me from despair and made me want to survive.
>
> It will still be some time, I fear, before I ship back. A point system determines the order in which we are selected to return. Since I'm the youngest, still single and without any children that I know of, I have the fewest points and am least eligible. If you are planning an early wedding I'm afraid I'll not make it. Thank-you for the honor. That you want me as best man is enough.
>
> Anxious though I am to go home, my friends here in Lugao make my stay here bearable. But more important, I can be patient after hearing of the marvelous opportunities awaiting veterans: a so-called GI Bill of Rights, which will enable everyone to go to college at government expense. That would really be something to look forward to. My parents can't afford to send me, nor was I a good enough

student in high school to qualify for a scholarship. Now what should I be? What should I do with my life? I like literature; I'd like to write or teach. Are writers and teachers made or born? I'll have to consult Billiard Ball. Choices! Choices! It's all so exciting.

I gather you haven't heard from Barry recently. He and I see little of each other these days since I moved to the dredge. But I can assure you he is well, still talks of having a business in the islands, and still tries to persuade me to stay here with him. I know whatever he does will be successful and he'd probably make me rich. I love the islands, but I yearn to go to college in the States. I want to learn everything that I possibly can.

I often wonder whether you will like it out here. Life is so different from what you are used to in LA. It will take some adjustment. No doubt Barry will be in touch with you soon.

Your caring friend,
Hal

Placing Lucia's neatly folded letter in the hip pocket of my shorts, I went looking for Fortune. Not finding him in the communications tent, I headed for his and Nina's hut by the mouth of the stream. Dozens of rickety, single-room shacks made of plywood and thatch dotted the slope near the stream, and many more were under construction. A sign nailed to a scrub tree at the entrance to a worn footpath proclaimed the community—Dream River—named after Fortune's shack.

All this had sprouted as a result of Gluck's anti-cohabitation policy and grew over the next weeks into a

veritable village. Gluck should have foreseen it. Who in the
world was more resourceful than Seabees abetted by that
superprofessional goods procurer, Barry Fortune? Now the
girls were better off than they had been since the war began.
Each had her own cozy hut, a clear stream nearby in which to
wash clothes and refresh herself, a steady supply of food,
including hot bread in the morning, hot dogs at least once a
week, and a devoted lover called a "husband" who swore he
would someday return to bring her back with him to the
glamourous States.

The project was accomplished in such secrecy that a
month passed before Gluck realized that our camp virtually
evacuated each night to Dream River. "Sons o' bitches, I hope
they fuck themselves to death," he stormed before devising a
countermove. Ever since peace was announced, his ardor for
change and achievement had waned, but with his discovery of
Dream River it was restored. He thrived on opposition. In
marked contrast to Commander Rutledge's consensual style
of winning our hearts, Gluck ruled in an adversarial manner.

Not so with his corps of officers, however, with whom he
was inordinately permissive. He reinstated the standard naval
officers' lifestyle: all the liquor one wanted, women galore,
and being waited upon by our demeaned black boys in white
jackets reminiscent of pre-Civil War plantation life. Nor were
the women Filipino — absolutely not. They were pure
American, "white and clean," nurses from the hospital ships
that tarried in the bay for a few days before moving on, or
Waves and Wacs on liberty imported from their Manila bases.
The BOQ was dubbed Fucking Heaven. It was the true model
for Dream River.

Our readiness was deteriorating, discipline growing lax,
the pace of things winding down. Idleness was pervasive as
projects were halted. But Gluck, bored and demoralized,
suddenly found purpose and challenge in the "Dream River
Campaign." He called a series of staff meetings to plan a
strategy for "The Eradication of Immoral Activities," or as he
put it "getting rid of the fucking lovenests." "It ain't nothin'
more than another Subic," he said.

In fairness to his cause, Dream River weakened his
control and hindered his ability to track us down, especially

as we became eligible to return home. For many, life in Dream River was far better than the one they expected to resume back in the States. As a result they overstayed their term for weeks, as, lost in their private paradise, they weren't interested in going home.

When I knocked, Nina was alone seated on a cot sewing a dress by hand. It was late afternoon. The air was sultry and still and smelled of smoke from cooking fires. Women's voices and laughter drifted from neighboring huts. Fortune, she explained, had gone to the mess hall to bring dinner. "If you'd like to join us, why don't you find him? It would please me," she said smiling warmly. "Barry speaks of you so often. And I hardly know you. We must become better acquainted."

"Thank-you, but I can't," I said, disarmed by her cordiality. "I'll have supper on the dredge before duty begins at six o'clock."

"But sit down for a while," she said, pointing to another cot against an opposite wall lined with colorful drapes. "Barry will soon be here." Save for the two cots, the only furniture was a wooden table against the back wall on which several books were strewn, one of which I observed was entitled *History of Art*. Above the table hung a frameless Van Gogh print of golden fields. And above the cot on which she sat were posted several enlarged photos of her and Fortune standing cheek to cheek before a great hacienda mansion in the background. Despite its sparse and commonplace furnishings the room was singularly homey and intimate.

How striking she was. I was distracted by her blue Asian eyes, her sharp Caucasian features, her long draping hair as golden as the Van Gogh wheatfield. "Please, sit down, if only for a short while," she insisted as I hung back. "Tell me about Barry. I know so little of his life in the States. He makes light of it, you know, saying it's unimportant; he says he's starting on a new phase. Now tell me, does he have something to hide?" She laughed and said coyly, "Was he an American gangster, perhaps?"

229

"Maybe, for all I know," I said, accepting her invitation to sit, playing along with her carefree mood, "but you can bet he was good at it."

"I know he is very rich," she said. "All the rich young men I know are spoiled and aimless and without courage. Barry is quite different," she said defensively. Her words rang with a strange bitterness, as if she were renouncing some part of her own past.

Then she asked point-blank yet plaintively, "Is he married?"

"Have you asked him?"

"Yes." She hesitated. "Of course he says he isn't."

"As far as I know that's true," I said, finding myself sympathetic to her not-unfounded apprehension. Unlike the other women in Dream River, she refused to delude herself that her American lover wasn't capable of deceiving her. How sad it was, the uncertainty. How admirable of her to admit it.

After some pensive moments she said, "I can't imagine there not being a woman in his life, someone back home, but he insists not, so I accept what he says at face value." Watching my reaction, she got only silence and a frozen stare.

"They say it won't be long before you'll be going home," she continued. "I imagine you can hardly wait to be with your family. Do you have a girl waiting for you?"

I watched, impressed as she sewed a seam, her hands plying the needle with machine-like dexterity. "No."

"No girl back home, a fine boy like you? Do you have one here?"

"In a way. There's one, a Filipina from Lugao, near Guagua."

She shrieked with surprise. "Really! What a coincidence! But our hacienda is near Lugao. You must pass it on the Bataan highway on your way to the barrio."

I raised my eyes to the photo on the wall above her head. "Is your family name Santos?" I asked.

"Yes. What is your friend's name?"

"Anita, Anita Quiboloy."

"Oh, yes, one of our tenants. From a fine hardworking family. She's only a child; oh, but of course she must be a

230

woman now. I've forgotten time. I know her father, the mayor of the barrio, an educated man." She went on with mounting enthusiasm. "My father often called on him for advice. Anita must be an excellent girl. I just know it.

"But our hacienda, it's falling apart now. Before the war it was truly a splendid place. While I lived in Europe, I always kept a picture of our lovely hacienda on the wall over my bed to ease my homesickness. I loved it then, but later, later..." Her hands began to tremble. She pricked a finger with her needle and sucked the blood from it until the bleeding stopped.

Nina was not what I expected, not what I wanted to find. I had resolved to keep a distance from her, be unresponsive to her beauty and charm, resist her friendly overtures. But I was lost at the outset; she was utterly genuine, modest, intelligent, direct, seemingly without vanity. What was her crime? Indeed she was not unlike Lucia, warm and captivating. I had to hear more; I had to get to know her better. And I savored her remarkable beauty, studying her as I would a Rembrandt, her eyebrows, lips, earlobes, the curve of her delicate chin. And as with Lucia, my heart reached out, for clearly she was innocently in love with Fortune. But the real question was, in the minds of both of us, was he with her?

"I'm puzzled," I said. "How can you live like this, in this place, under such primitive conditions, after the hacienda?"

She laughed. "Do you think surroundings matter to a woman in love? I would go anywhere and live under any conditions to be with my darling Barry. Do you love your Anita?"

"Yes, I do; I love her," I replied, astonished by my own words.

"And would you complain if you were to live with her in a small hut?"

"No, but sooner or later..."

"Yes, sooner or later you would want something better, but it isn't necessary at the beginning, is it? Not when your love is freshly in bloom." Her eyes sparkled with conviction and she paused, searching it seemed for more answers. "Even

231

so, I can't go back to the hacienda to live; the memories there are too painful."

"You mean from the occupation?" I asked.

"Yes, they soiled my girlhood."

"Anita told me," I said, "about the Death March, and Lieutenant Anderson and the cruel Japanese commander."

"The commander and his staff lived at the hacienda with my family."

"Then you knew him?"

"Yes, I knew him." Her tone was strangely tense, curt. "He was a petty man who used his power to support a false sense of importance. He stripped our home and left us with only sleeping mats. He made my parents wait on him like servants. We did his bidding for fear of our lives—not our own but of someone we loved. That's how he worked." Her story seemed to gather upon itself; the words pouring from her relentlessly. "I had just returned from school in Europe as it fell into darkness. My life here was happy and held such promise. I would read books to my heart's content and I would go to parties, to receptions at the Malacanang Palace, the presidential residence in Manila, and concerts at the university, and to the mountain hotel resort in Baguio. And then I fell in love with a young man, Ramon Reyes, from another hacienda. He was very ambitious and dreamed of someday managing our combined lands, which together would become the largest hacienda in the province, maybe in the entire islands. I had reached that special time in a girl's life when she flowers into a woman, and she feels that the whole world welcomes her entrance.

"Then the Japanese came and MacArthur fled Corregidor and we were helpless and the commander appeared at our door. He made a point of humiliating my parents in little ways, such as having my father polish his boots, and my mother follow him about to clean up the cigarette ashes he would purposely flick on the floor. And he took our entire rice crop, leaving no seed for the next planting. But the hacienda of Ramon's family was untouched; it went on as before, yielding rice each season, never occupied by the Japanese. Ramon stopped visiting me, and when I tried to visit him I was told he wasn't there. They were of course collaborators.

"The commander soon learned of Lieutenant Anderson. After his terrible deed that day in Lugao he was extremely agitated and that night called me before him. I would be his concubine, he said." She tried to cover her weeping with her hands, while the tears rolled down her arms in thin streaks. "After that it was night after awful night after awful night."

I rose and sat beside her and handed her my handkerchief and held her hand as her sobbing quieted. "After the commander fled, the Huks killed many of the collaborators, including Ramon and his family. They say that Alehandro, the teacher from Lugao, led them. The hacienda was then relet free to the former tenants, but much of the land is of little use to them until they have seed."

"Does Fortune know about this?" I asked.

"Of course. I had to tell him."

"He knows about your relationship with the..."

"He knows everything. I couldn't possibly hold anything back. And for the same reason I've told you, his best friend."

"Nina, I..., I..., thank-you for being so open," I said, remorseful for prejudging her. "But I have to go. Duty calls."

"To your strange ship with the long snout?" she said.

"You won't see it around much longer," I said.

At those words Fortune entered carrying two trays of food wrapped in newspaper. "Hal and I have just had a long talk," said Nina as Fortune handed her one of the trays. "I like your friend." She eyed me playfully as she went on. "Don't you think you should ask him now?"

"Ask him what?" said Fortune unwrapping his dinner.

"Oh, how could you, Barry? Excuse me, Hal," and she whispered into Fortune's ear.

He nodded and facing me, placed his arm on my shoulder. "I'd...we'd be honored to have you as best man at our wedding, Hal."

"Sure, Barry, I'd be pleased," I said unhesitatingly. "But it depends on when. They might ship me back before...what date did you have in mind?" I watched Nina, her eyes wide with expectancy.

"Before you have to go home, definitely before that," he said. "We shouldn't keep the man waiting, should we, Nina? He insists on going home. When would you say?"

"Today, tonight, this minute," she replied.

"I have duty tonight, Nina," I said.

"Then the end of September," she said, gazing at Fortune adoringly.

"The end of September, in a month, it will be," he said and they kissed.

"Thank-you from my heart," said Nina, as she came to me and hugged me to her and kissed my cheek. What was this penchant I had for Fortune's women? If it were my choice I'd have made her mine in two seconds flat.

Fortune walked me out of the hut. "In a few weeks I'll be discharged in Manila," he said.

"Then you're not going home?"

"This is home now," he said. "Stay here, Hal. We'll be partners and I'll make you rich." I pretended I hadn't heard his invitation.

"Who will tell Lucia?" I asked, and he left me to walk on alone as if he hadn't heard my question.

Sauntering along the path on the way to the Mudhog, I berated myself for my cowardice. Why hadn't I handed him Lucia's letter? As she had so often done before, she would look to me for the truth. Damn right she would. Fortune's courage extended only to hunting Japs and downing kamikazes. I'd have bet my right arm I would be the one to give her the heartbreaking news. But not by letter. I'd tell her when I visited her in LA. It was the least I could do.

XXIII
Subic Bay

Love and Friendship

Knowing that my forced absence would be of great concern to friends in Lugao, especially to Anita, I asked Billiard Ball to carry a message of explanation. I visited him at my old tent (which he still shared with Blackie) just before he took off for a weekend at the barrio, his first since we were last there together. "Tell them I'm sick, a malaria attack or something, but that I'm recovering," I instructed him.

"That'll do for a while," said Billiard Ball, "but what's your excuse if Smithson drags this thing out? I think you ought to tell them the truth."

"I can't. What will they think of me?"

"Christ, Hal, you didn't commit a crime."

"It was almost as bad," I said contritely.

Saddened over what I was missing by not accompanying Billiard Ball as he waved good-bye, I lingered in the tent at Blackie's request. He was in an extraordinarily happy frame of mind, that is for Blackie, because he had just received his orders to ship back home. "As soon as I get there, who in hell do you think I'm gonna see first? Not my wife, not my girlfriend, but my chiropractor. I'm gonna kiss him." For Blackie his discharge and his civilian future signified the end of constant physical pain and frustration with the navy medical corps. Anita's father, whose first treatment gave him relief, had never made it to our camp again as planned.

"They're flying me back because of my disability," he said. "I'm puttin' in a claim. The navy's gonna pay for this the rest of my life. But I'll need witnesses. You, for instance."

"Blackie, I'm sorry. I can't lie for you. You told me you had the problem before you enlisted."

"I thought you were a friend," he said heatedly.

"I am, Blackie."

"Hell you are. A friend would lie for a friend."

"I don't think a friend would ask a friend to do something against his principles."

"You're a sonofabitch," he said. They were the last words we ever spoke to each other. All friendships are conditional within limits, but rarely tested.

Upon returning from Lugao, Billiard Ball informed me of our friends' worry over my health. Anita, not surprisingly, wanted to return to Subic bay with him. But Billiard Ball, expanding on my fabrication, explained that I was being well cared for and given the most advanced medicine. "I hate lying to these people. They are so damned sincere and well meaning," he said. "When they start asking questions, one lie leads to another. I felt like a huckster."

"You're a true friend," I said facetiously.

"Bullshit," he muttered.

Obviously I couldn't depend on Billiard Ball to keep my phony excuse alive for long. Every day I asked Smithson, "Are they going to take her out to sea today, sir?"

"When I'm ready, sailor, when I'm ready, and not until," he replied. The Mudhog was nothing less than an extension of his being. It seemed more important to him than even going home. He would hang on until the Command lost patience. The rest of the crew had shipped back except for Oblong and me whose services were still essential to keeping the Mudhog upright.

Three weekends passed. I was beside myself, spending the days sitting in the bridge reading Proust, staring by the hour toward the sea, daydreaming of seeing Anita again.

As if my wish had come true, I heard her soft melodious voice calling my name. I raced down the gangway to the deck following what I thought might be my imagination. It was a brilliant tropical afternoon with soft breezes creating gentle wavelets on the bay, perfect for a crossing by *banca* from Subic. She and Hando were paddling around the Mudhog, calling, "Is Hal Arnold there?"

"Yes, he's here, he's here," I screamed back. "Hi, Anita, hi, Hando."

"Oh, Hal, I'm so happy to see you," she yelled as she spied me leaning over the gunwhale. "Are you well?"

"Yes, I'm fine. I'll explain." My heart pounded with excitement. I hadn't realized how lonely I had been without her.

"Where's Billiard Ball?" Hando inquired.

After I joined them in the *banca*, we paddled ashore where Hando left us to search for his friend while Anita and I sat on the sand. Taking Billiard Ball's advice, I told her of my punishment, of why I was unable to visit her in Lugao, that I was never really ill. "Please forgive me," I begged.

"I'm only happy that you are well," she said. We walked toward the stream, past Dream River, along the paths we both knew well. We reached the place where we had first met when I had rescued her from her attacker. "I could never return here again until now, with you," she said. Then we walked on to the secluded copse by the shore of the stream where Billiard Ball and I used to have our siesta in the shade. The current was gurgling and running strong.

"Let's have a swim," I said.

"But I can't," she said shyly.

"I saw you swim before," I countered.

"It's not that."

"Well, I'm going to," I said, stripping quickly and diving in. She stood by the shore laughing, watching me perform the foolish aquatic antics I had learned as a boy. "Come in. It'll make you feel like a million," I urged. At last she did, removing her clothes and jumping in up to her neck. We frolicked, and raced each other against the current, letting it sweep us downstream together while locked in an embrace.

Having her naked body wound around mine was beyond my imagining. She was a part of me, more than I thought possible. We climbed from the water and let the soft air dry us as we lay side by side on my shirt spread out on a cushion of grass. I turned toward her and caressed her breasts and kissed them and moved my hand along the length of her body and stimulated her clitoris as her vagina softened and became full and wet. I devoured her mouth. As she pulled me closer, tighter to her, the tension within me was overpowering, and I plunged myself into her and ejaculated uncontrollably.

"I love you, I love you," she said plaintively.

"I'm sorry, I wanted it to last longer; I wanted the pleasure and joy to go on forever. But I'm awkward, like a giraffe." I felt her tears and kissed them. "Why are you crying? Have I hurt you?"

"No, my love, you could not hurt me. I feel happy and sad, both. It is my first time."

"Same with me, Anita."

"With you, too? I thought all Americanos were experienced lovers."

I smiled and tenderly kissed her forehead. "But why are you sad?" I asked.

"I had wished to save myself for my husband," she said, averting her eyes, "but I have made love with a man I love and I'm not less for that, am I?"

"I love you all the more for it," I said. We embraced and kissed again, enthralled with discovering each other, and ourselves as well.

The afternoon was passing swiftly, and Anita was to meet Hando at the *banca* in time to cross the bay and travel home before dark. Walking back along the path toward Dream River, we could hear the sound of diesel engines up ahead. Soon a band of women ran past us, terror in their faces, screaming in dialect. "What are they saying, Anita?"

" 'Run, run. The machines are attacking us,' they are saying."

As we drew nearer to the enclave, we saw two D10 bulldozers criss crossing the slope, sweeping aside and crushing beneath their squealing treads everything in their path: trees, huts, clotheslines. It was an orgy of calculated destruction. More women, standing by the bay shore, were weeping in the arms of their lovers, who were vainly trying to comfort them. It was Gluck's swan song for all to remember. "You bastard, Gluck," I yelled into the empty air while Anita, watching the devastation and deafened by the roar of the engines, clung to me in total bewilderment.

Billiard Ball and Hando were already waiting for us at the *banca* by the Mudhog's pipeline. Hando was impatient to leave because of the late hour. Heavy storm clouds were forming over the mountains and heading toward the bay. The early stirring of the monsoon had begun. While waving good-bye to our friends, I saw that a tugboat had tied up to the dredge in my short absence. The scuttling would not be far off. "I'll see you in Lugao soon," I shouted to Anita.

"I love..." she yelled back, as her last words, muffled in the breeze, trailed off. Did she say I love you? Or I'd love it? Or just I love? Anita was embodied love; it was her dominant emotion. The last words didn't matter. Billiard Ball waved to Hando, his creased and sculptured face radiant, calm, content. "Bye, good friend," he shouted with an odd softness, not unlike Anita's, not caring whether Hando heard or not, but for his own sake.

"Gluck's finished off Dream River," I said. "What gets me is how he relishes and abuses power. And he's so damn crude about it."

"Not hard to understand," Billiard Ball said. "The burning of Subic, now Dream River, they're his affirmation against the universe."

"Damnit, Billiard Ball, come down to earth."

"I'm right here, never more so. The man's afraid...of his mortality, of everything in his uncontrollable, absurd life. He's trying to take charge, but he sees he can't really, so he's in constant panic. If he weren't so dangerous, I could sympathize with him. We could all love him, even you and me. The least we can do is pity him."

Smithson, too, was losing control. His safe little world had only hours to go. He would have to start all over again, to find some other corner to dominate and fend off the universe. The tug wouldn't linger. By tomorrow at this time the Mudhog would be in a deep grave. "You know, tomorrow I'm replicating evolution," I said to Billiard Ball, thinking that he would appreciate the sheer size of my metaphorical concept. "I'm leaving the sea to come live on land."

"Then, my friendly fish, be my guest. Blackie's gone. We'll have the tent all to ourselves."

239

After spending the next morning struggling with rusty bolts to disconnect the pipeline from the Mudhog, Oblong and I tossed a thick hemp line from the forward capstan to the tug. Once free, the pipeline writhed and bounced in the waves like a dying dragon. A launch pulled alongside to remove us and our personal gear. "You can go ashore now," said Smithson.

"Aren't you coming with us, sir?" I asked.

"No, I'll stay with her."

"We're willing to join you, sir," I said, looking to Oblong for agreement.

"Sure we are, sir," said Oblong.

"Thank-you, men. But I'd rather do this alone." The tug steamed off with the Mudhog trailing behind, a small funeral procession. Smithson, the grieving master, stood stalwartly in the fantail. It was the last time I saw him.

"It's an awful shame what the navy's doin'," said Oblong. "My engine was never in better shape. It's like somethin' in me's goin' down with her."

Officially Billiard Ball and I shared a tent at camp. Actually we slept there only one night a week, on Sunday's, for the purpose of picking up our mail on Monday morning and checking the list of the homebound. The rest of the time we lived in Lugao. Both of us being single, with hundreds of married men yet to ship out, we knew we wouldn't be leaving for a long while. There was the purely logistical problem of insufficient ships to carry all the personnel home in a short time. After all, it took years to bring us out there.

Lucia's letters were always waiting on Mondays without surcease, pleading letters, worried letters, distressful letters. "Tell Barry just to send me a postcard with the word 'love' on it. Is that too much to ask?" she wrote. "I'm sorry, Lucia. I haven't see Barry in weeks," I wrote back. And I hadn't, not since the leveling of his shack in Dream River. I couldn't help her, console her. She had to come to her own conclusion. My letters too had changed; they were shorter, and more factual, their earlier verve missing.

Lucia must have noticed. She had lost. She had lost Fortune to someone who was perhaps her emotional double.

She had lost me, what little I mattered. How could her delicate words compare with Anita's molten touch? She was alone. She had only to learn it was so.

And I too was alone. I had only to learn it was so.

XXIV
Lugao

Drinking from a Small Cup

Billiard Ball and I took to barrio life with surprising ease. Each of us, however, pursued different interests. Billiard Ball spent most of his time with Hando, so much so that I saw him less while he lived in the barrio than I did at camp. But while traveling together on our Sunday afternoon trips back to Subic Bay, we swapped stories on how we spent the previous week.

"Have you any idea how excellent a teacher Hando is?" Billiard Ball asked, sitting beside me on the floor of a truck rattling across the Pampangan plain. "I've attended some of his classes. He has a way of making things interesting for his young students; you can tell they want to learn from him. A fine teacher, Hando."

"From what I hear, he's a Communist," I said.

"I couldn't tell one way or the other," he replied. "We never discuss politics. But what does it matter?"

"You know that the Huks resort to all kinds of violence; they even kill," I said.

"I can't imagine Hando doing such things. He's too gentle and sensitive."

Our ten-wheeler was passing Nina's stately, lonely, barren hacienda. Anita told me that Nina was living there now with her parents and an Americano guest. I was pleased; to live there meant that she was mending herself. And the Americano must be Fortune.

"They say Hando once led a raid on a nearby hacienda and murdered the family," I continued. "I wouldn't expect him to tell you about that."

242

"If it were true, yes, that would be a problem for me," said Billiard Ball, clearly perturbed, "but what you tell me is based on rumor, I gather."

"I don't actually know. How well do you really know him?" I asked.

"We are a well without a bottom, my friend," he replied. "And the cup we drink from is very small."

On Saturdays, when there was no school, Hando and Billiard Ball often took off for Manila, where Hando introduced his brilliant Americano friend to his former teachers at the university. They also spent time with many of Hando's erstwhile colleagues, several of whom had become professors at Santo Thomas University. Billiard Ball was gloriously back in his element, the cloistered academic atmosphere from which he was wrenched the day he was drafted into the Seabees and for which he had been pining ever since. Now he was living in two distinct worlds, perhaps three: that of the sophisticated intellectual, that of a low-ranked Seabee, whose duties were trivial and whose social contacts were anti-intellectual; and that of the warm, family-oriented society of Lugao, which he embraced with less enthusiasm than I. After a while his interest in Lugao seemed to center principally on Hando, although he never deliberately kept himself aloof from the barrio folk. He always joined in Reverend Mr. Corum's evening discussions, and in the volleyball games, both with Hando of course.

But Billiard Ball took no part in the daily life of the people. He had no desire to be incorporated into the fabric of their community; to work in their flooded, muddy fields; to stoop beside the others, even beside Grandmother, planting rice seedlings — from America — from the red light of dawn at the cock's crow to the red light of sunset; to wear a coolie hat and trousers cut off to the crotch; to turn bronze, hardly distinguishable from the local folk; to become one of them, as I did. I yearned to belong; I came to belong. I ate the rice and vegetables and defecated in the fields. I squatted when resting, as was the custom, rather than sit western fashion. Every night I slept on my own floor mat in the same room with the rest of Anita's family. Soon I was speaking Tagalog

243

more often than English. Soon I realized that I was happier than I had ever been.

Monsoon season arrived in full and inundated the land. The American ten-wheelers had to crawl through muddy sheets of water that rushed across the invisible highway. Nina's hacienda mansion, set on slightly elevated ground, became a virtual island. Water overflowed the banks of the usually sluggish stream bordering the barrio, flooding the streets and paths and the space beneath the thatched houses. Anita said that it was a time of cleansing the land of all the year's accumulated evil, that every monsoon was a new beginning. I too felt cleansed and reborn.

Although my skin was now indistinguishable in color from my hosts', my eyes were a giveaway. "Hey, Sky Eyes," my peasant friends shouted in Pampangan as they waved to me in the fields. "Time to head home." Trudging back together we joked. "After you've eaten enough brown rice, your eyes will turn as brown as ours," they said.

"Your eyes are beautiful against your dark skin, Hal, truly the color of the sky. I would love to have a baby with such eyes," Anita said.

The early afternoon was the hottest time of day, too hot for work, time for a lunch of brown rice and goat's milk and roast chicken and mangoes, and, after that, time for a siesta until the day began to cool. Then we went back again to the fields and toiled for a few more hours. Before dinner the men and women took turns bathing in the muddy river, using the precious bars of soap from my goodwill package. "You make us feel rich," my friends said. They were referring also to the cigarettes, the chocolate bars, the beer, and the mattress covers. These, remarkably, made the difference, from their point of view, between living a life of subsistence and living the good life. I could see the change in the appearance of the people gathered at Reverend Mr. Corum's in the evening. Now that their bodies were clean, the men wore comfortable creased slacks and ironed sport shirts of many hues and the women always had on softly textured fresh dresses. I could feel their new sense of well-being.

After the monsoon subsided and the planting was over, our work in the fields was less arduous. With more free time we could socialize again, and we had more energy to play volleyball before dark. Anita and I took long walks beside the stream, sluggish again and within its banks, and we stopped at secluded places to talk. She wanted to learn everything about me. What was my life like back home; what was school like, my parents, my town, the countryside? I spoke of my desire to go to college.

"I too want to go," she said, "but I think my parents cannot afford it."

"I'll send you the money," I said, rashly.

Instead of being pleased, as I expected, she was dejected. "Thank-you. I would not take it," she said finally.

I was blind to my own inference that we would not be together, that she didn't figure in my future plans. And I was blind to the main reason for her curiosity: She wanted to learn about my world, assuming that it would become hers as well. But she withheld expressing her thoughts, her hopes. We lay under a tree on the edge of the field in silence as dusk fell, she dreaming of spending her life with me, I of going home and preparing for a career. And we made love.

Our lovemaking caused her much anguish. She, like the rest of the people of her barrio, wished to live by the strictures of her religion. Sensual pleasure, or any activity suggesting it — even the innocent act of dancing — was prohibited. Were she to have a child, she would bring shame on her family and suffer brutal ostracism. But her desire was overwhelming. She submitted, wanting me as much as I wanted her. Each time we made love, we gave ourselves to each other more freely and passionately. Each time we were more eager than the time before, each time more comfortable with our intimacy. "But I love you" was her only answer to pangs of conscience and fear of dangerous consequences.

And what of my pangs of conscience? Were we no different from the deluded lovers in Dream River? I wanted her; I loved her. I knew also of her inner torment and the risk she was taking. I knew we needed each other more and more deeply as the weeks passed. She was giving herself without reservation. But I evaded the main issue between us: our future. I hadn't, I wouldn't, make the slightest commitment to her. She hadn't openly asked for one, but my inner voice was doing it for her. Not yet, I couldn't yet bring myself to a decision. So I delayed until the day vaguely in the future when I would have no choice.

Sunday afternoons and the time to trek back to base came too rapidly. Billiard Ball and I always parted from our friends reluctantly, knowing that we would return in a few days, but fearing that each return would be to say our last good-bye. I was surprised to learn that Billiard Ball's feelings were as ambivalent as mine.

"I'm just amazed at how well you've taken to barrio life," I said on our trip back to camp.

"Do you think for a minute I'm impressed with creature comforts, the mere trappings of civilization?" he snorted. "There's more intellectual vitality out here than in most places back home. I can't remember when I've been happier, more at peace with myself."

We had arrived at our Magic Mountain, only to have to come down from it to go home and become involved in the chaos of the universe. The agony of Lugao was in the past. Now all was peaceful and sweet and fulfilling.

Of all my friends in the battalion, Billiard Ball was the one who changed the most. His transformation from a cold, distant, bitter man to one who found peace and good feeling within himself was indeed marvelous. But even from the beginning I recognized his humanity beneath the callous shell. To see him flowering now was a joy.

Plummeting down the highway in the rear of a weapons carrier, we passed the mango tree beside Anita's grandfather's house. The grass beneath the tree was now tall and growing wild except for a small section over Nanai's grave. At last Anderson had gone home.

"I feel pretty much the same as you," I said to Billiard Ball. "I can't remember being more content, having such a sense of belonging. I've never felt more accepted."

"You've been yearning to belong for a long time, haven't you?" he said. I didn't reply and he went on, "You're a Jew in name only."

"I hadn't thought of it that way," I said, startled at his bluntness.

"You're not even sure whether you're happy being an American."

"How can you say that?" I protested.

"A lot of things say it: your rebellion in Hollandia, your resentment against the system of inequality on board the ship. You've told me how angry and ashamed you were at our treatment of the Filipinos. And now you've taken to them as if you've got to make up for our abuses. My good friend, I've watched you struggle with yourself. You're no longer proud to be an American."

I had no idea he had perceived my doubts. Hadn't I even concealed them from myself? It felt good to hear them spoken out loud. "I'm not sure I'd be willing to go to war again," I confessed.

"Neither am I," he said.

We had never talked so frankly before. What had happened that demanded we be so painfully honest? I think it was Lugao. The place tore away all pretense. "What keeps you coming back, Billiard Ball. I have Anita. Have you found someone too, someone you haven't told me about?" I asked brazenly.

He glanced at me cautiously. "Yes, I have a lover, too," he said in his old, protective, clipped manner.

"For God's sake, why didn't you tell me before? Who is she?"

"I'm not sure you'd approve," he said tensely.

"Certainly, I'd approve," I said perplexed. "Why shouldn't I. It wouldn't matter to me who she was as long as you were happy."

"Because, Hal, good friend, she's not a she."

"What?" I shouted.

Bewildered I remained silent. Billiard Ball, expecting shock, continued. "It's Hando. We're entirely compatible. Please understand, Hal."

"I'm trying, I truly am," I said. I knew nothing of homosexuality. It wasn't accepted as a sexual option by our society, and rarely was it discussed.

247

"Back home my life was a torment of frustration," he explained. "For the first time I feel absolutely free. Can you understand that?"

"I'm just...I would never expect..."

"Well, you have the common view, and it's wrong. I have a good relationship with Hando. He's true to me, whereas back in the States every damn affair ended in disaster. It just works out better here."

"What can I say? I'm...I'm happy for you."

"Thank-you, Hal. I hope you'll try to get used to the idea." I nodded that I would. "And you should know that I loved you," he added cautiously, "but I knew you would have different feelings. I knew long before Anita came into the picture that you were heterosexual."

"You bet I am," I said, "but how were you so sure?"

"Your letters to Lucia," he said. "I was a censor, Hal, remember."

"Christ, they were none of your damn business, Billiard Ball."

"Hey, I didn't deliberately read them for their content, but I couldn't help but learn how you felt about her. You love her, you know."

"C'mon, don't be ridiculous. I've never even met her," I said in vehement protest.

The vehicle dropped us off in Olongopo just in time to catch the last launch. We crossed the bay in silence. Evidently Billiard Ball had decided he'd said enough, perhaps too much, or realized that I needed time to absorb it all. Was it possible that I could love two women at the same time—one real, responsive, adoring; the other a trusting, loyal spirit full of beauty?

Walking up the hill to our tent, I said, "I think I've gotten myself into a real mess."

"Welcome to the human throng," Billiard Ball rejoined.

On Monday morning Roger Billiard's name appeared on the list of returnees. After reporting to muster, we headed right back to Lugao. "I've prayed and waited almost two years

248

for this moment and now, suddenly, I'm not ready for it," Billiard Ball lamented.

"Maybe someday you'll come back," I suggested.

"No, Hal. Once I'm home, I'll settle in for good. I do miss teaching. My professorship is waiting. That's what I really am, a teacher, and nothing else. Hando will understand. He knew it would happen."

Billiard Ball said good-bye to Hando privately, and to the rest of the barrio, to Lucio and Reverend Mr. Corum, gathered beside the church at the entrance to the path to the highway. "Thank-you for the pleasure of your wit," said Reverend Mr. Corum in his stentorian voice, "and thank-you for the kindness of your heart."

Despite the formality of his words, for this was the reverend's way, Billiard Ball looked genuinely moved. Everyone shook his hand and begged him to write and to return. He and I embraced, our eyes growing moist. "Look me up at Columbia when you're in New York," he said with forced brightness. In his hand he carried a sheaf of papers tied with hemp. "Proust," he said. "My translation, the beginning," and he turned and departed alone.

While I had labored in the fields and thought that he was idle and dallying in Lugao, he had been hard at work after all.

Billiard Ball and I corresponded intermittently over the years and five years later I called him on the phone from Chicago while still a student. His Proust translation had just been published and received glowing reviews in both *The New York Times* and *The Saturday Review*. "Congratulations," I said. "Billiard Ball, I'm absolutely proud of you." He erupted into laughter. "What's the joke?" I asked.

"Why, I haven't been called by that name since, well, since Lugao, I suppose. By the way, I've sent you a copy. You might take note of the dedication."

While waiting for it to arrive I speculated that Hando's name would appear on the page. But no, it read: "To Hal Arnold, whose idea this was, and whose cool well had slaked my thirst for companionship and refreshment when I was most parched."

We continued to correspond, especially after I, too, became a teacher and we had a common interest. It has now been five years since I last heard from him. Having remained at Columbia for his entire career, he finally retired. My letters were returned marked, "Forwarding Address Unknown." He would be in his middle seventies now. I fear he may be dead.

XXV
Lugao

The Last Good-bye

A joyous time had come to Lugao. A wedding. Fortune's and Nina's wedding. Since Fortune was Jewish and Nina Catholic, but neither of them practiced the religion of their birth, Nina chose Reverend Mr. Corum to marry them in his modest church. She knew of the reverend's courage during the occupation, of how he held his people together through the worst cruelties and the hardest times. He had also visited the hacienda before the occupation to thank her parents for their generosity to the barrio farmers in times of bad harvests. And she knew of the reverend's frequent defiance of the Japanese commander's wishes. She knew more than most. Frequently at night the commander lay beside her seething with outrage at the reverend's behavior. Reverend Mr. Corum, without his knowing, was thus her secret ally.

The wedding was small and simple, with only Nina's aged parents, an aunt and uncle from Manila, and a girlfriend from Dream River (whose "husband" had left for the States) who was staying at the hacienda. A businessman friend of Fortune's, and his wife, also attended; reputedly he had the highest political connections both with the American Command and Malacanang Palace. I was best man.

For the wedding Anita pressed my dress white uniform and stitched the third class machinist mate symbol on its upper sleeve. Not since stateside on liberty had I worn my formal whites. After trying them on, I found them too snug. Despite the hard work and the spare diet, my lean frame had filled out. "In your uniform you are the handsomest Americano I have ever seen," said Anita, stepping back as if

251

she were ready to take a picture. "But I think I should let out some seams."

Fortune wore a custom-fit white business suit. He was a civilian now, having been discharged in Manila only the week before. Nina was dressed in a traditional long white gown, glowing like a radiant star, dazzling everyone with her perfection. "God has outdone Himself," I heard someone whisper as she walked down the worn aisle of the battered church.

The wedding reception was held at the hacienda to which the reverend and his wife and Anita's father and mother were invited. So was Anita, but she refused to attend. "I do not have a proper dress," she said. "Anyway, I would not feel comfortable there. I would not know what to say."

"But you would be with me," I explained, to no avail.

In fact the reception was very plain, like the wedding, and small, with simple food, not unlike what I had been eating at Anita's house. The Santos, having lost their once large liquid wealth, could afford nothing more. Nor would they allow Fortune to have his way; he had offered to pay for a grander affair, perhaps grander than anything the islands had seen since the liberation. Nevertheless it was a happy occasion, with a small guitar orchestra for dancing, and French champagne, which Fortune contributed without consulting Nina's parents. For me the wedding was unforgettable, and sad only because Anita was not at my side to enjoy it. I had put Lucia out of my mind.

The following morning, a Sunday, as Anita and I walked, I described the entire event — the ceremony, the reception — and answered her questions on specific details. "And what were her shoes like?" she asked.

"Shoes? She wore a gown, Anita. How could I see her shoes?"

"I would have noticed her shoes," she said scornfully. I realized that my description was upsetting her. Then she asked: "Will you also be staying in the Philippines like Barry Fortune?" She was opening up the unspoken issue between us for the first time.

"No, Anita, I plan to go home."

"I can understand. You must miss your family," she said calmly. "Will it be soon?"

"I think so," I replied. Since Billiard Ball (with only a few more points than I) had gone, I didn't expect to wait much longer.

Anita sat for a long while studying our reflections in the murky stream. Her lips trembled as she tried to form her next question. "Will you return?" she asked, looking into my eyes.

With dry lips, my heart throbbing like the Mudhog's pistons, I hesitated, then said, "I hope so." It was noncommittal, an evasion. Yet her face lit as she tried to wring the faintest hope from my words.

"Oh, if only you would, Hal. If only I may count on it. Will you promise?"

My heart was shredded into conflicting emotions. I loved her and needed her—but not enough. How could I be honest and not hurt her? "I don't think I could ever be happy in the islands, Anita. I've thought about it. Fortune even asked me to join him, but I had to turn him down."

"You are not now happy in Lugao?"

"Of course I am."

"Then, why..."

"Lugao isn't real, Anita. It's not the way the world is. It's a dream. I can't live in a dream for the rest of my life."

"I...I am sorry, Hal, I do not understand what you say."

"If I say I want more from life than Lugao has to offer, would you understand?"

"Yes, I think I understand. Then I would go with you...to America, to anywhere in the wide world." I knew she was afraid of America, just as she was afraid to attend the wedding reception. When, from time to time, in answer to her questions, I described life back home, she would say, "It is so big," or "I would not know what to do." Yet she would uproot herself if necessary, for my sake.

Viewing my life as beginning over again, cleansed like the land after the monsoon, of all past mistakes, I wanted to leave my Magic Mountain. I would go to college under the GI bill; I would become a teacher; I would travel about the world and absorb its variety and experience its unlimited opportunities.

I must be free, unfettered by obligations. To have a wife at this stage was out of the question. And to have a Filipino wife in America in 1946 would be an insurmountable handicap. As a Jew, even in America, there was enough prejudice to contend with. Why compound my disadvantage? And the prejudice would work in two directions: My parents would be a certain obstacle to our marriage. And to a brown Filipino shiksa yet? The victims of prejudice are no less guilty of having their own. What a coward I was. Why not rebel? I had already felt alienated from my origins. My love for Anita acknowledged none of these constraints. Yet I was as afraid of bringing her to my world as she was of entering it.

Hurting too from the pain I was inflicting on her, I could find no relief. My self-reproach at playing safe exacerbated the hurt still more. "We are no different than the lovers of Dream River after all," she said. "You are like the other Americanos."

"No, no, Anita," I insisted, repelled by the comparison, "I never tried to deceive you. I never made false promises." But had I been truly honest with her, with myself? Hadn't I deceived us both? Wouldn't I have preferred a more sophisticated woman, someone well-educated with cultivated tastes, a lover of art and music and literature, someone like Nina perhaps, or better, someone American—Lucia? Wasn't Anita's sweet simplicity her most serious detraction? "I'm sorry, I'm sorry, I'm sorry," I repeated, breaking both our hearts.

She flung herself at me, sobbing, crushing me in a desperate embrace. "I love you so very much, I love you, I love you," she cried.

"And I love you," I said tearfully, and we stood locked together for a long time, knowing that it would be our last embrace.

Alone in the rear of a ten-wheeler, my mind gushed with plans and prospects. The break with Anita had to be complete. There was no point in prolonging our suffering. I would no longer see her, at least not alone. I was eager to go home, to be with my doting parents, to be back in New England. It would be especially beautiful there, mid-autumn when the maple leaves were brilliant orange and red and yellow and the evening air was tangy with a hint of winter. A life was waiting in which wars would never be fought, in which wars could never be won. There was talk of forming an organization of the world's major powers, to be called the United Nations. It would replace the battlefield, serving as a forum for settling national differences. Springtime had come to civilization. Everything was fresh and clean once again. We were burying the rubble of folly, the human skeletons and shattered cities. A new life was awaiting. I was in a big hurry to begin.

In place of the usual list of eligible returnees posted on the battalion bulletin board, an announcement signed by Gluck appeared, stating that Monday of the following week all personnel, regardless of number of qualifying points, would be embarking for home. The remainder of the battalion, some three hundred of us, was shipping out en masse. Furthermore all battalion personnel were prohibited from leaving the base. Gluck would thus prevent all planned partings between lovers. But, being a member of a defunct unit and not officially a member of the battalion, I ignored the order and headed back to Lugao for my last good-bye.

The truck driver dropped me off at the Santos's hacienda so that I could say good-bye to Fortune and Nina before going on to Lugao. Although I had planned a brief visit, Nina wouldn't hear of it. "You say your unit doesn't leave until next week? Then why not stay with us in the meantime? What will you do with yourself in that awful camp?"

Fortune was just as insistent. "We've been out of touch too long," he said. "And I have a favor to ask. Maybe you could do a few things for me when you get back to the States. You know, help me clean up some old business matters." He was referring to the dissolution of his electronics business partnership in LA.

I was easily persuaded, for I had no wish to linger at camp, nor could I stay any longer in Lugao near Anita. Always fascinated with Nina, I welcomed this opportunity to become better acquainted with her. And I had been intrigued with the hacienda mansion itself from the first time I had seen it.

That evening we had dinner in a grandiose teak-paneled dining room containing the only original furniture—a large mahogany table and Queen Anne chairs—left from before the occupation. The Japanese commander had used the room for his staff meetings. Nina's aging parents also joined us. Speaking English clearly, her father boasted of his frequent pre-war visits to America. "An immense country. Americanos are a great people," he said, but then his thoughts drifted off, and his proud bearing suddenly collapsed into melancholy. The mother sat silent, ignoring her husband's words, her eyes riveted to the plate placed before her. There were two servants, a husband and wife team whom Nina hired at Fortune's urging when she moved back to the hacienda.

Not until dinner was over and Nina offered to give me a tour of the house did her mother speak. "Forgive our forlorn and barren house," she said weakly.

"The war is over, Mother," said Nina. "We'll have beautiful things again. You'll see." The mother shrugged. Signs of opulence were already returning: ironed white linen napkins, crystal glasses filled with Bordeaux wine, a dish of vanilla ice cream, and of course the servants always at your elbow. After my lifestyle of the past two years, I savored each touch of elegance. For Nina's mother, however, the old happy times were gone forever. The war's damage to their pride, to her husband's sanity, to her own sensibility was irreversible. She lived in tragic emptiness, in both her house and her soul.

As Nina led me on a tour of the house, she enthused over plans to decorate this room a certain way, that room another way. She would find old furniture as close as possible to the original. "We had a beautiful mirror there," she said, "and what a marvelous portrait of my father used to hang here." Only the dim outlines of their frames remained. Despite the bareness, the house had a grandeur owing to its vaulted frescoed ceilings and marble floors, its tall, wide windows with blowing curtains, and its thick, stucco sturdiness.

The parents retired. We returned to the dining room for want of another furnished room to sit in and talk, and we drank liqueur. Unaccustomed to imbibing, having had wine through dinner and again after dinner, I indiscreetly unraveled my long-standing resentment against Fortune.

"What's this thing you want me to do for you back in the States?" I demanded.

"Nothing difficult. I'll give you power of attorney to sign some papers on my behalf," he said; observing my near inebriated condition, he added, "I'll provide the details later."

"Why'n hell can't you do it yourself?" I asked. "You've got other unfinished business back there, too." There was a tense silence. I was bent on pursuing a searing confrontation. Nina rose nervously and placed the flask of liqueur in a cabinet by the wall. "I'm goddamn tired of doing your dirty work, Fortune. You know who I'm referring to."

"She's none of your concern," he said. "I'll deal with her in my own way. So let's drop the subject."

Nina walked behind his chair and, after bending down to kiss him on the temple, she wrapped her arms around his neck. "Barry has told me about her, Hal," she said. Then she sat beside Fortune, and faced him directly. "I feel badly for her too."

"I promised you I'd take care of the matter, and I will," Fortune said.

"But you haven't, Barry. I must make a confession: I sent her a copy of the wedding announcement from the newspaper in Manila. She most surely knows by now."

God bless Nina. I knew then why I hadn't heard from Lucia in weeks. "Nina," I said, "I love you, I love you," and she came to me and kissed me on the cheek. What I meant to say, had I been drunker still, was, "I love you, I love you, Lucia."

Nina led me to a small upstairs bedroom that overlooked the fresh green fields visible under a full moon. There was no chair, no rug, no chest—only a bed. "I can vouch for the bed," she said, patting the innerspring mattress. "This was my room when I was a girl."

After she said goodnight, I fell on the bed fully clothed and slept. When I awoke, it was still night, the room filled with moonlight. A breeze rippled the thin curtains, wafting in the sour fragrance of the damp fields and the din of crickets. How I had grown to love this land. But I knew that the beautiful past was over for good. I lay on the floor, placing the pillow from the bed beneath my head. The mattress was too soft for me now. I missed hearing the rhythmic breathing of Anita's family. I missed knowing that she was across the room.

"Barry has gone to Manila on business," Nina explained after I came down for breakfast at the luxurious hour of eight, "but I'll join you for coffee." I was happy that the two of us could talk alone, as we had months before at the shack in Dream River.

"Your hacienda is more than I expected," I said. "I'm glad to see that you can be happy here."

"Barry makes the difference," she said. "He's made everything possible again. Of course, he has little interest in the land. The last thing he wants is to become a farmer, and he abhors the tenant system. But he knows that I love the hacienda despite everything that's happened, and we'll live here most of the time. There's more than twenty-five thousand acres, much more than we need, so Barry has suggested selling ninety percent of the land to the tenants at low prices and on easy terms. Don't you think it's a splendid idea?"

"Excellent," I said. "I've become attached to this land. I don't know when or how, but someday I'll come back."

"We'll always have a room waiting," she said and sipped some coffee as she prepared her next thought. "I've been wondering—forgive me, Hal, tell me if I'm being too forward—but you've said nothing of Anita. Are you..."

"It's over," I said. "I can't bring myself...it's that we'd be miserable in the States. I had to end it, Nina. I hate myself for it, but there's no other way." I saw a clutch of peasants working the field. "I think I know them. Aren't they from Lugao? If you don't mind, I'd like to work beside them for a while."

"Not at all," she said, surprised.

"Do you have a coolie hat I can wear?" I asked.

For the next four days, Nina and her servants catered to my smallest needs. Every moment was filled with simple pleasures. Mornings I worked in the fields with the peasants, returning to the house for lunch and a siesta. I read my long-neglected Proust in the late afternoon, and dined with Nina and Fortune for evenings of talk and sometimes chess with Nina.

We talked mostly about Fortune's plans, which were already well launched, and mine, which were still only dreams. He was accumulating land, buying mountainsides of teak and mahogany, and acquiring options all over the islands. "The archipelago has more than seventy-one hundred islands, with more timber than we'll need for the next century. I'll be the world's major supplier. Think of it, Hal. You could be a part of it, if only you'd come down from the clouds. Each location will have a sawmill near the sea to facilitate shipping, similar to our Seabee operation in Hollandia. With your sawmill experience, it's right up your alley, Hal. You'd be perfect to set them up." He had covered every detail, anticipated every eventuality, thought through every consequence. "And we'd bring prosperity back to the islands. The operation's labor intensive. We'd put people back to work."

"Yes," said Nina only partly in jest, "I agreed to marry Barry on the condition he improve the lot of our people."

"Seriously," Fortune continued, "profit and the general welfare need not be mutually exclusive. By now you know I don't do things just for the money."

His argument was exciting but, for me, not persuasive. "You just won't give up, will you, Barry?" I said, despite not wishing to seem ungrateful.

"I believe it's an opportunity of a lifetime, Hal, and I never needed someone like you, someone I can trust, more than now."

"Don't you long to go home, Barry?"

"No, not really. I'm home right here."

How could he so easily renounce what he was? But I should have understood. He had never thought of himself as an American or a Jew or anything but an individual of the world, dedicated only to his own goals. "But I can't wait," I said. "I long for my country. I want to spend the rest of my life there. Maybe we're not as great as I used to think. I still think there's no better place to live." The very throb of America was pulsating within me, its lure irresistibly ingrained.

"What do you plan to do with your life?" Nina asked.

"Go to college first, maybe teach," I replied.

"Teachers make peanuts," Fortune said. "When will you learn to be practical?"

The tenant farmers with whom I worked informed my friends in Lugao that on Sunday morning I would pay them a farewell visit. As usual, the children raced boisterously about me as I walked into the barrio. Reverend Mr. Corum's Sunday service was in progress. I entered the church, taking a seat on a bench at the rear, but not without the reverend noticing. He began his sermon, speaking at first in Tagalog, then in English "in consideration of our American visitor." He spoke of the history of his people, of their eternal domination by foreign powers, of the benign democratic influence of America, and of the recent clash of American ways with theirs. He spoke of the forthcoming independence that would bring about a restoration of their dignity as well as their lands. He spoke of the importance of retaining their national purity, their identity as Filipinos. "Let not the materialism of America be our model," he said. "We must instead embrace its democratic ideals and generous spirit. And do not judge all Americans by the thoughtless GIs who have liberated us. Remember the courageous Lieutenant Anderson, another kind of American. And we have seated among us at this moment an American who works by our side and thinks of us as his equal. For this we shall always be grateful. We shall always remember him." His comments were political until the end, when he said: "Life is a great sine wave traveling through the ocean of time. When we are in its trough, as we have been for so long, through our faith in God we can endure and await the next crest. My people, I can feel the rise, I can see a new crest approaching. May God be with you."

During the closing hymns a plate was passed from hand to hand. When it reached me I added an American half dollar to its pitiful collection of centavos. As the plate continued on its way, the congregation, never having seen such a coin, was awed. "How much is it worth, Hal?" asked the reverend, holding it up for all to see.

"One peso," I said. A murmur arose.

"Indeed, you are more than generous," said the reverend.

"But I have more," I said, holding a carton of cigarettes above my head. It was worth seventy pesos on the black market. There was such pandemonium that the reverend had to demand quiet. As he strode past me to the door of the church, he took the carton, opened it, and passed out two cigarettes to each poor parishioner on his way out. There was no doubt that my name would now figure in the history of Lugao for all time.

As it was with Billiard Ball's departure, I embraced Lucio and Hando and Reverend Mr. Corum. I shook hands with others and thanked them over and over for their kindness. Anita watched from afar and our eyes met and hers were brimming with tears. I blew her a kiss as I promptly left. I knew that if I lingered I would fall apart.

Later there was a tender good-bye with Nina. She saw me off with Fortune, who had offered, had insisted, on driving me to Subic in his jeep (genuinely his, not government issue) and staying overnight at camp to watch me embark on Monday. "It's enough just taking me to Subic," I said. No, he had to spend the night with me. It was a gesture more expressive than words. Leaving the jeep in the seaside village, we hired a fisherman to take us across the bay in his *banca*, for the launch no longer ran. A giant aircraft carrier loomed beside the battalion's dock.

We hardly slept that night because of our nonstop reminiscing. We lay in our underwear on our cots in the dark. "I'll never forget that look of ecstasy on your face when you took your first hot shower in the stateroom," he said.

"And I'll never forget your astonishment in the middle of that movie at Finschafen when you wanted to leave and I said 'Fuck you'," I recalled. We laughed together, then with seriousness I said, "And I'll never forget how you saved us all from the kamikaze, Barry."

When the first glow of morning arrived we were still awake. Fortune asked, "One more thing, will you be seeing Lucia when you're in LA?"

"Certainly. I have every intention of it."

"Will you tell her what happened, how sorry I am?"

"What did happen, Barry?" There was no reply. But I knew the answer just the same.

When the truck came by to pick up our belongings, Fortune helped me load my footlocker aboard, and he stood by as I fell into the mustering lineup. He followed us as the last remnant of our battalion marched down to the dock and boarded the aircraft carrier Hornet. The camp was left intact, our flag still flying. I stood waving to Fortune in the throng, high on the flight deck, and heard him shout above the commotion, "Everything I have is yours, but don't expect me to write."

"I'll be back," I hollered. That was my last sight of him until that fateful afternoon on television forty years later.

EPILOGUE

The End Is the Beginning

Fortune is dead. Billiard Ball is probably dead. And Lucia, my own Lucia is dead.

Billiard Ball knew I was in love with Lucia long before we met. Not surprisingly, I was the last to know. But it was no surprise to Lucia. She was more beautiful than her photo, more alive than her letters, more than I had imagined. She was Nina's American counterpart. On the surface, at least, she seemed to have reconciled herself to Fortune's rejection by the time I met her in LA. Two weeks later I asked her to marry me while I awaited discharge from the naval base at San Diego. Her reply was instantaneous. Perhaps, as they say, I got her on the rebound — but one that lasted forty years.

Now there is only Nina. "Won't you stay with me a while at the hacienda before you return?" she asked as we drove from the cemetery in the limousine to her Manila apartment. "Of all the friends we have, none knew Barry like you." In her bereavement she needed me. We are always alone, but never more so than when we are finally alone.

"Of course, Nina," I said, "I'm on sabbatical. I'll stay as long as you want. Your wish is mine."

How unbelievably nostalgic it was to see the Santos's hacienda again. Through layers of remembering, I had romanticized the place. Never speaking of it to Lucia, I stashed it away in my mind's eye like a great work of art in a museum's inventory. But the reality, shining white and clean and surrounded by a parade of tropical flowers, surpassed my secret image. "Nina, you've created a vision, a beautiful dream."

"Would you like your old room?" she asked as if it had been preserved, unused as I had left it forty years before. She led me through old familiar rooms, now hardly recognizable, with Oriental rugs here and there, softening the cold nakedness of the white marble floor. The once barren great room was furnished with deep, soft, comfortable sofas and chairs arranged among antique tables and chests from dynastic China. A portrait of an aged Fortune hung over the fireplace where her father's portrait had once been. I walked among the wondrous treasures touching everything.

In the evening we dined at the same table, sat on the same chairs as we had during my last sojourn when we were both young. Had time magically ceased in that exalted room? Nina, sitting across from me, was now wrinkled and white-haired. But her eyes still sparkled, her voice was spirited, and remnants of her youthful beauty persisted like a glowing sunset. "How good to be here after the city, how peaceful it is," she said after the servants cleared the table and we sat sipping tea.

"Yes," I said. "I spent one of the happiest weeks of my life here, and now...nothing changes."

"And everything changes," she said.

My "old" room had the same bed, but now there was a thick Chinese carpet, an antique chest of drawers, and a fine mahogany desk. I began writing, continuing almost to dawn until, from weariness, I lay on the hard floor beside the soft carpet and fell asleep. I had begun my story, Fortune's story, this story.

Most mornings I arose late and walked around the grounds among the flowers, and along the paths through the paddies, and sometimes down the highway where I used to walk with Anita. I walked to Lugao. The path was the same, the thatch houses the same, but the church was no longer damaged. I didn't recognize a soul. I was a stranger, a curiosity to the barrio people.

Nina and I usually had lunch together. "And how did you sleep last night?" she asked one day.

"I didn't," I said and explained that I had spent the night writing about Fortune and what it was like as a young man in the war.

"What a wonderful idea," she exclaimed. "May I read it?"

"If you wish, but only up to the point at which you appear," I said facetiously.

"Then I must write the second volume," she said laughing for the first time since the funeral. "Because only I know Barry's life since the war." Her eyes grew distant. "It was never dull, never for a moment, and often I confess it was exhausting. His energy was boundless."

"I remember," I chortled. "He was a master juggler."

"Yes," she said, "he always had to have countless deals going at the same time. I've always regretted that you didn't accept his offer. Do you know he never found anyone to replace you? No one would ever tell him what he didn't want to hear. No one was honest like you. Why wouldn't you join him, Hal?"

"For one thing, I wanted to get an education. For another, I was homesick for my country," I explained. "But frankly, Nina, I didn't approve of what he was doing, the cutting down of precious virgin rain forests. I couldn't bear doing it when I was in the Seabees. And then, of course, there was Lucia."

"But she most certainly loved you," she said.

"How could I be sure, nor was I about to take a chance then. I suppose I hadn't felt secure with her for some time. My parents wouldn't accept her because she was ten years older than I was. But we had a wonderful honeymoon driving across the country to my native New England."

I became silent and lost myself in remembering. Our honeymoon was also a celebration of my homecoming. Our trip encompassed the grandeur of America. Following no special route, we made friends with strangers everywhere, with restaurant waitresses, with hitchhikers along the highway, with motel clerks, and gas station attendants. Everywhere we heard the same catchy songs, the same radio advertisements. We saw the same Sears Roebuck and Western Auto and Socony gas station in every town. Everywhere we were one culture, one united people, full of goodwill toward each other and enthusiasm for the future. My beloved America.

"I suppose one could say that Barry and I spent our honeymoon in the shack in Dream River before we were married," Nina said. "But, you know, Hal, we were never happier than then. Our illicit love. I had him all to myself, without distractions, without business deals interfering. It was bliss." She was suddenly radiant, as I used to know her, and then just as suddenly she lapsed into a deep sadness and began to sob. I sat beside her and reached my arm over her heaving shoulders. She buried her face on my chest and the tears of her release soaked through my shirt to my skin.

"I've been to Lugao," I said when she finally composed herself. "I saw no one I knew. What has happened to my old friends, Nina? Where have they all gone?"

"Reverend Mr. Corum died, many, many years ago, Hal. He was old when you knew him."

"Of course. And Hando?"

"He was a Communist, you know—the government soldiers killed him a long time ago in an anti-Communist drive."

"And Anita's father, Lucio?" I asked, leading up to my most important question.

"He too died perhaps ten years ago, but her mother may still survive."

"Possibly then I didn't recognize Anita yesterday nor she me," I said. "Did she marry?"

"I have no idea. You see she left the barrio to live in Manila very soon after you returned to the States."

"Left Lugao? But why, Nina? She never wanted to leave the barrio."

"I am not sure, but some say she had to leave because she was with child. Her mother went with her."

"No, no, that can't be true," I said.

"Yes, it may have been only talk."

"I'm sure she would have told me."

"It would have been yours?" she asked. I nodded imperceptibly.

That night unable to either write or sleep, I lay on the floor turning over in my mind again and again what I had learned of Anita. At sunrise, I dressed and walked along the quiet level highway to find the mango tree and Anita's Nanai's grave, but the tree was gone and the stone marker was gone and there was no sign of Lieutenant Anderson's empty grave.

Only the barest signs of the shack were visible, a few stilts jutting from the earth.

Then I walked down a path where we used to walk together when we were young, and by the sluggish stream where Anita and I made love in the cool, tall grass. I knew this was business I had yet to finish.

In the weeks that followed, all my inquiries on trips to Manila led to dead ends.

I had come to the hacienda for renewal. Hadn't I found it here once? But it was so elusive. Hadn't I learned long ago that no experience is repeatable in its essence? Why does my illusion persist? Why my hunger for reliving those months of my youth spent here? To escape what? What is wrong with my beloved America?

After I received my masters degree, we left Chicago for Lucia's hypnotic Southern California. But the enchantment soon waned as the hills and canyons were sliced into subdivisions and the air became fouled. Each summer the four of us, I with Lucia and our two sons, toured the nation to find the natural beauty we missed. Instead we found more denuded hillsides, vast abandoned pits, nondescript buildings, and cities with miles of poverty. How I deplored the desecration around us. The scale of the universities, the corporations, the government, the cities, had become so immense that I felt smaller and smaller. I yearned for more manageable, more intimate proportions.

"I insist on going with you," Nina said after I asked to use the car to go to Subic.

"But I'm only going to take a look at the place and turn right around," I said.

"Nonsense, we can reminisce together."

The road through the Zambales range, the former dusty, rutted road I had traveled so often in the rear of a ten-wheeler, was now paved. At Subic I tried to hire a fisherman to take us across the bay. "Not allowed," he said. "Big American naval base."

"Take us anyway," I said. I wanted to see my mountain, my waterfall.

"You're a ridiculous romantic," Nina said with a twinkle.

Silently we sat in a *banca* bobbing in the bay gazing upon the slope now covered with permanent structures where our tent camp once stood. I gazed at the dark, distant mountain, fascinated as much as ever by the thread of silver plunging down its side. "Once I'd have probably risked my life to find the source of the waterfall. Now I'm too old to find out. And just as well. Remember Billiard Ball? He used to say that some things are best unanswered. He was right, you know. I have already found too many answers."

Each night I wrote, each day I walked, and each evening Nina and I talked or played cards or listened to Bach and Bartok or read. Never having taken time to read Billiard Ball's translation of Proust, I began. We spent the weeks of the monsoon in Baguio at Nina's isolated mountain retreat. But the hacienda soon beckoned. An old song, old when we sang it together in the fields forty years ago, fluttered strangely across my mind:

> Planting rice is never fun;
> Bent from morn till set of sun;
> Cannot stand and cannot sit;
> Cannot rest for a little bit.

I tried again to help the field workers (no longer tenant farmers) plant seedlings in the flooded rice paddies. But it was too painful in my joints, and I lay down before dinnertime on the Oriental carpet in my room to soothe the ache. Nina sat astride my buttocks and massaged my weary, wasting muscles. We were like a married couple except at night, and I have grown to love her warmly, as I loved Anita and my Lucia.

I have been writing this story for almost a year of nights. Now it is done save for these few remaining lines, and I must go home. "Please stay," Nina begged.

"I miss my sons," I said.

"But they no longer need you." I understand that she is telling me that she does. She came to my room that night and lay on the floor beside me and we fell asleep together entwined. Oh, it was so satisfying to be close to her.

In the morning she asked again. "You could help me manage the hacienda and the businesses."

268

"I need my sons," I explained. "Come with me to the States."

"Then will we come back here?" she inquired.

"No, Nina."

"But you love the hacienda so much," she protested, sitting up, yet holding onto my hand.

"I do. But I can't live in this country, not the way it is. Nothing has changed, no one is better off than they were forty years ago. Corruption and cronyism are the system. It's suffocating, don't you see? I miss the freedom, its very atmosphere. I hadn't realized how much. There's a vibrancy at home. It's part of me. So come home with me."

"At my age, leave the hacienda?" she said, waving her hand. "I would never adjust to a strange place. I couldn't die anywhere else."

"I understand," I said.

"When will you let me read your story?" she asked the night before I departed.

"I'll leave it with you and you can send it to me."

"Do you think it will be published?"

"Does it matter?" I asked. "I wanted only to write it, nothing more."

Tomorrow Nina will drive me to Manila. Tomorrow I shall go home for the second time, feeling no less anxious than the first, when Fortune drove me to Subic Bay and saw me off on the aircraft carrier bound home for America. Tomorrow will be our second good-bye, and our last. Tomorrow.

ABOUT THE AUTHOR

In July 1943 at the age of 18, the author was drafted into the Naval Construction Battalions in which he served for two years and nine months. During the war and for fifty years since he has been writing constantly: letters, plays, movie reviews, essays, short stories and novels. Eighteen of his articles on business management have appeared in *The Wall Street Journal*. In addition to a book of essays on business, he has published a business novel, his second, under a pseudonym. A collection of short stories, a travel journal, and his war letters are currently being readied for publication.

After the war he graduated from the College of The University of Chicago, which he attended under the GI Bill. For twenty years he was CEO of his own plastics materials company, selling it in 1985 to write full time. For two years, from seven to nine each evening, he wrote this book, his first novel, while still a CEO.

Currently he resides by the sea in mid-coast Maine with his artist wife.